THE TWIN PARADOX

by

CHARLES WACHTER

Publisher, Copyright, and Additional Information

The Twin Paradox by Charles Wachter published by Trevaney Bay. 5777 W Century Blvd Ste 1110-114 Los Angeles, CA 90045-5600

ISBN- 978-1-7353612-2-2

Third printing, April 2021

Editors: Michael Rowley, Jonathan Oliver, Will Tyler
Cover design and interior design by Rafael Andres

For my family

THE TOOTH

Middlesex, England
April 1, 1727

Isaac Newton, the first one, died yesterday.

He had a bladder stone infection and refused last rites, a bastard to the end. On the way to London for burial, the mud froze, making it tough for the old university horses. At one stop, the cabman let people peek into the casket for the price of a shilling. Their breath steamed into the space, unable to defrost the stiffening god. The coffin smelled of urine and lilacs. A jeweler offered two pounds for Isaac's molar.

They pried it from his face with a horseshoe pick.

***

Moscow, USSR
248 years later
1975

It took until Christmas for the little girl to talk about the man at the park. Arkady sunk in his chair by the fire as she talked. He thought back to their trip to New Jersey. Outside, the Russian winter pressed like a grindstone on his house, crushing in through tight window frames.

"No reason," Arkady said to one of his daughter's more pointed questions. Alcohol played slyly on his lips. He twirled a small, antique ring between his fingers slowly. There was a very old human molar mounted on the ring.

Arkady dropped it in his bourbon, watching it sink. He downed the drink, catching the tooth in his lips as he finished and cleaned it with his shirt. He put the ring on his daughter's slender finger.

"It's a tooth!" she squealed. "Will the tooth fairy come for it?" Catherine asked seriously, borrowing from the tradition she picked up when they were in America.

"Yes, he will." He swooped her up, carrying her past a broken radiator to her bed, and then watched her fall asleep, thinking of the vast sums of money he had been loaned to acquire the tooth. He put two extra blankets on her bed to keep her warm.

He had been forced to organize a purchase to buy Isaac's tooth when he realized he couldn't steal it from the Embassy where it was kept. After its unceremonious removal centuries ago, the tooth had bounced around England until a pastor eventually sold the blasphemous relic to an aristocrat. The lord promptly set the enamel root into a new gold ring to show off at the House of Commons; however, like all valuable things, it was soon hidden and then forgotten about over the generations. Almost two hundred years later, Arkady had it. *Arkady!*

Catherine was asleep now. He took the ring and popped the tooth out of the setting. He went to his study, limping as he went. His spine was twisted from scoliosis, making it seem like he was always distracted, turning to hear something.

The house was also a butcher shop, the front serving as a portal for Russian peasants looking to eat dead animals. Tucked in behind the meat lockers and racks of knives—now dark—Arkady lived with Catherine.

In the study, old papers and abandoned carpentry projects were strewn about. Oversized books sat on tilted homemade bookcases, and tools for butchery lay scattered everywhere. He put the molar in one of many empty vials strewn around his cramped space and sealed it with a rubber stopper, putting a butcher's label on it. He wrote "Isaac Newton" in grease pencil.

Arkady transferred the vial down to the shelves. They were covered with more vials—a forest of them, their labels turned out for inspection in the candlelight. In some vials, there were tissue specimens floating in formaldehyde. In others, pieces of tendons, toes, fingers, or bone could be seen. There were a lot of jars with just clumps of hair inside. Each vial had a different name on it, and most of the labels read like a grade school summary of history's most important people.

Leonardo Da Vinci was a cored piece of pelvis in a vial. Max Planck—scalp and hair. Edison, Freud, Bohr, they were all there too; Beethoven and Marie Curie were represented by fingers. For Marie Curie, it was her middle finger above the knuckle, somewhat appropriately. Galileo, Darwin, Heisenberg, Euler, Gauss, Boltzmann, Kekulé, and *others*.

Arkady spent a lot of time labeling and relabeling the specimens, using his grease pencil carefully, like they were for sale in his shop window. *He had the time.*

He had been waiting days for his contact to show himself, but the phone never rang. Holed up with a six-year-old's infinite enthusiasm for talking—his daughter's impossible, unstoppable energy that seemed to draw from the ether itself—he used the vials as a chance to teach Catherine some history.

He organized them by importance, history, and region. He thought it would be more effective to learn about them that way. Of course, Catherine was more interested in putting all the toes together and then the fingers, hair, etc., grouping them visually. He acquiesced, pulling vials thematically, hunting for the glass bottles like a cook looking for spices.

He started with the Americas, spinning a vast yarn about the dawn of the industrial age and a man named Ben Franklin. Henry Ford was there too, as well as Tesla, whose toe still had the skin on it because he was embalmed. There were less famous Americans as well, but no less towering in their intellect. Steven and Wallace, architects of the Panama Canal, and their counterpart, the infamous Frenchman de Lesseps—all engineers known not only for their genius but also their great spirit, work ethic, and ability to get things done.

Tesla's wrinkly toe led Arkady and Catherine into a discussion about death and what happens to the body underground. It had come up often on their grave robbing trips around the world. Catherine always came back to the worms and the soul.

She nestled into her father's big arms to listen, the warmth pulling them into that place reserved for the best memories. She was only an infant when the orphanage offered her to Arkady. The butcher's house was on the grounds of the Russian Academy of Medical Sciences, a part of its bustling commissary for doctors and professors. The prestigious institute had a small, odd orphanage used for studies on children, and Arkady was well known to the strict nurses. He would give the children candies on their walks to the biological testing center.

But Catherine was special. She developed polio, which was the only reason he was allowed to adopt her, they told him. *Defective goods.*

"No one else wants her," he was told by the head of the institute, Dr. Neiman.

"Defective like me," the butcher added.

As her disease took hold, it twisted her as well. She started to get made fun of at her new school. Arkady took it upon himself to teach her in his butcher shop. In the early years, professors' wives could get extra fat on the top cuts if they brought breast milk in reused bottles. They would take turns to feed the sick little girl of the popular butcher.

Catherine grew older. She would do light chores, but Arkady never taught her to cut meat. Blood was a poor man's work. She was his "Princess." It was a nickname that began at the orphanage, the only sweet thing to come out of the dour institution with her. He would orate to her, chopping great hunks of flesh, and she would work on her father's homework in chalk beneath that day's specials. No matter how busy it got, he always had an eye on her.

When she was six, Arkady was recruited once again. He told them he didn't want another child; however, this time they had a real job offer for him, if he was interested. The payment was ten times his government allowance. They told him he had skills that were valuable, and he would get to travel. The butcher had no idea what those skills could be, but he wasn't about to question them. Any sort of work association with the institute was bound to increase his eligibility as a bachelor. Blood had a way of staining everything.

On his trip, he would travel as a wealthy politburo party member vacationing with his daughter—a ruse Catherine loved, pretending to be important. They would scout by day (seeing the great sights and cemeteries). By night, they would plunder the world of its greatest intellectual riches. Under every type of sky, they worked, boring holes into chapel floors in France, cracking crypts open with crowbars, sneaking into hospitals, houses, and mausoleums. Catherine would sit, dead silent like she was taught, and listen for intruders as her adopted father would do his grim work.

He preferred the recently dead. Arkady could relate to cutting meat. It was the old churches, the sacred places, like Westminster Abbey, Notre-Dame,

Shinto shrines in Japan, that scared him—the human dust filling his nostrils with dread in the dead of night.

Catherine was his talisman, always a willowy specter in the near distance, protecting him. When he pulled bones from the ground, it was like Christmas for her. They would cheer and talk of the next adventure on their way home.

In the end, it wasn't that difficult. The dead, even the titans of our species, are all but forgotten once they are shuffled into the ground. The monumental gold that lay in their bodies—in every cell—was still mostly overlooked by the world. The Russians were the first to covet the value of these desiccating DNA strands. And Arkady was the one who was chosen to collect them.

But now, it was all over. He was home. Catherine was back asleep in her pauper's bed. And soon, they would be paid in full, completing their transformation from the town monsters into a prince and his princess, wealthy beyond their wildest graveyard stories.

He organized the vials once again, trying to put his proudest achievements front and center—Einstein, Galileo, Da Vinci. He placed Isaac Newton alongside them. The tooth, and the tiny bit of godlike DNA it represented, was the crowning piece he had been in search of for two years. He started to clean up the rest of the desk, picking up some of Catherine's toys and her hairbrush. He looked at the hairbrush, holding it up to the light. In it, her golden hairs sparkled. His princess. An idea swept over him with a smile. He took one of the few empty vials and put Catherine's hair into to it. He wrote on the label, Catherine the Great, after the famous Russian monarch. It was his own personal memento, a father saving a lock of hair. He brought the vial with him over to the fire to finish his brandy, putting it on the mantle.

***

It was hours before the car arrived, its headlights covered in snow. Arkady was sound asleep in his chair; the fire, a low warm ember.

The tooth fairy had finally arrived for its prize. A man emerged from the car and entered the shop quietly, the wind and cold sweeping into the room with him.

A gun was drawn, and then a bullet exploded inside the butcher, fate violently mingling with biology inside his chest. The man collected the vials, his grimace growing into delight with every label.

"You did good," he said to himself.

He stacked them into a leather case. It was only when he had finished that he saw Catherine, watching from her door.

"Hello Catherine," he said after a moment, his finger questioning his gun at his side. "Hello, Dr. Neiman."

Silence.

"Will you help me put these bottles in my case?"

Catherine nodded. She walked over to him and carefully helped pack the bottles inside, trying not to look at the blood seeping into her father's shirt next to her.

Once they finished, Dr. Neiman asked Catherine if she wanted to come back to the institute to live. She started to cry but held out her hand.

As they left, he noticed he missed a vial sitting on the mantle. *Catherine the Great, a famous Russian indeed,* he thought. She wasn't on the list they gave the butcher. Arkady must have used some of his own initiative and added to the collection on his own accord, Dr. Neiman assumed. He inspected the dead man, a flash of guilt swept across Dr. Neiman's stomach. Arkady *had* done well. He added the vial to the case, took Catherine, and left the door open on the way out.

Snowflakes teased Arkady's exposed feet.

THE RAPTURE OF THE DEEP

The Gulf of Mexico
Present Day

The oil platform waited patiently in the sun, its silhouette cut against the sky. On most days, the beast was a marvel of industrial fortitude, slurping oil up a 2,000-foot straw.

Today was different.

Flecked gray equipment and muscle sat idle. Laughter replaced the usual scream of metal-on-metal work and bitching. Roughnecks, drillers, and tool pushers dotted the top deck for the unofficial Memorial Day Steel Beach party. The rig supervisor planned maintenance for the holiday while a skeleton crew made retrofits in rotating shifts. The parent company knew of the stoppage, but the faux sense of breaking the rules increased efficiency the rest of the quarter. Even still, the ants at the picnic got only nonalcoholic beer.

On the helideck, volleyballs flew, cuts of meat cured in smokers, and guys bullshitted about diving off the drill deck. Below the rig, a geologist zipped around in a kayak retrieving volleyballs.

Jimmy Jones, however, was another three hundred feet down, marinating in a saturation dive suit. Unable to name Creedence Clearwater Revival's second album, he got stuck welding a new blowout preventer valve on the wellhead. Dangerous stuff. After the Deepwater Horizon disaster spilled five million barrels of oil into the Gulf, every company upgraded their rigs against a similar financial tragedy. This was Jimmy's task, and on Memorial Day weekend. *Dangit.*

Jimmy rushed. He knew it. In the dive room upstairs, his golf clubs leaned against the monitor wall alongside five hundred Costco balls. Holger, his dive tender, walked him through the final instructions on the installation. The room looked like a bad used-record shop. Obscure Norwegian rock paraphernalia could be found in every nook and crack. In the corner, there was a blow-up sex doll with dive gear and a sign that said OFF LIMITS. Holger fit the bill, too—overweight with long sweaty Goth hair pasted behind his ears. His glasses were the only thing that suggested decades of precise technical work.

"Come on, JJ, it's right there," Holger said. He used his best yoga voice to relax Jimmy.

Ever since Konstantin Khrenov invented underwater hyperbaric welding, people were paid well to risk dying underwater. Drowning, exploding, imploding, crushing, and electrocuting make the list of top workplace hazards. On the flip side, you could afford five hundred Costco golf balls. Jimmy just liked the stress, although he wouldn't admit it.

And the dark. The arc welder threw an electric blue light along the length of pipe, giving the whole world an eerie, alien feel. Every year, Jimmy certified to go deeper. He was nearing the limit for a human, even for the great Jimmy Jones.

Jimmy could taste metal in his mouth. *No bueno.* Shielded arc welding requires a waterproof electrode at deep-sea depths. It creates a magnetic field with alternating current. Secondary current sometimes flows back through the tissue of the welder, breaking down any dental amalgam in the mouth. This indicated that the system was juiced. Following the hint comes hydrogen and oxygen bubbles and then an underwater explosion. Jimmy had an attentive mother who encouraged good dental hygiene, so he ended up paying a confused dentist to give him fillings in eight healthy molars.

Jimmy ran his tongue over his teeth and eased back. He wanted to hit balls.

Done and done, the weld sealed. He uncapped his underwater sharpie to tag it with his initials. It was a new company requirement to promote ownership of work, as if he were in grade school. No one would ever see this, he thought, just a few of his fishy classmates.

Holger got on the com. "Nice job, Jimmy. Two more." Jimmy always forgot about the camera.

Holger dropped a needle on a vintage record player rigged into the com. Creedence Clearwater filled the void below.

Jimmy sank deeper to the next welding problem with a smile, pulling three hundred feet of hose with him. When he clipped in, he heard something unfamiliar under the music: a boom followed by rhythmic pounding on the pipeline leading to the coast.

The music and the deep-throated bubbles of Jimmy's regulator made it difficult to hear. "You catching that, Holger?" he asked.

Again, the boom. *Boom. Boom.*

"Turn that shit off," Jimmy said.

In the dive room, Holger spotted the gauge next to his HITS "R" US coffee cup. The oxygen saturation needle had dipped.

"Jimmy, your O_2 is low. Is your hose caught up in something? Nitrogen is climbing," Holger added.

"You hear that?"

"What's up?"

"Holger? You hear, man?" Jimmy repeated.

"Nope. Just a lot of thumping bass. Hey, we are going to wrap this up. Get you drunk on fifty bottles of O'Doul's." He put away his black nail polish and blew on his nails.

There was no response.

"JJ?"

Silence on the line.

"Jimmy, you listening to me?"

At sea level, air is almost 79 percent nitrogen. The remaining 21 percent of oxygen keeps your bits working. If alien PhDs evaluated our planet from afar, they would classify humans as nitrogen breathers on a nitrogen planet—except we don't really use nitrogen. The element has minor use in the human body, other than trying to kill us in bizarre ways. Under the ocean's extreme pressure, the nitrogen in the air we breathe has nowhere to go. It compresses in our tissues, storing up for a nasty coming out party.

One side effect is the bends. As old-timey divers painfully discovered, when you quickly ascend to the surface—where the pressure of the ocean is no longer threatening bodily functions—the accumulated nitrogen releases in a rush. In dive classes around the world, instructors use fresh bottles of Coke to demonstrate. Under pressure (with the cap still on), the liquid looks lovely, still, and golden brown. But when the cap comes off and the pressure releases, bubbles appear, creating the effervescent awesomeness we all love.

When your body is the bottle, the effervescence is much less appealing. Severe pain, injury, and sometimes death result if divers don't decompress at the proper rate. Sudden decompression is like shaking that Coke bottle and letting it explode in every vein of your body.

Holger stood. "J, I am calling it before narcosis. Let's go. First recompression at one hundred feet," Holger said.

"Stop talking," Jimmy replied.

Holger started up again, but Jimmy turned off the com so he could sit in silence and listen.

Another side effect of excess nitrogen in the body is nitrogen narcosis, or the "rapture of the deep," as Jacques Cousteau called it. The excess nitrogen in your brain makes you feel drunk and euphoric, similar to nitrous oxide in the dentist's office, another unfun place to have fun. In extreme cases, you can hallucinate. Divers have taken off their gear to feed the fish and even swam the wrong way into an abyss. Often, they stop doing anything. Death is hard to avoid when you forget how to swim.

Jimmy held his breath, wanting to stop the noisy, gurgling bubbles from escaping his helmet for a second. He looked out into the blue darkness, feeling lightheaded. He could hear it loud and clear now. Whatever it was, it was getting closer. He lit his welding torch to see more. A tiny speck of light. Nothing. Bubbles.

Then he saw it.

An army of sea creatures approached him in a vast wall of life. At first, they appeared in the distance but grew quickly in stature. The infantry led the way, pale glowing shrimps by the millions, tiptoeing en masse toward the rig and Jimmy. Their front was a mile wide, curving through the deep rock and silt trenches cut into the ground. Puffs of smoky fires squirted up when dive-bombing skipjack tuna snapped shrimp out of existence. A silver frenzy of swordfish preyed on the tuna. Above them, the wall of life continued, with wave upon wave of sea life stacked up to the sunlight. Box jellyfish the size of blimps anchored the attack, their tendrils providing cover for hundreds of reef fish. Turtles skimmed the legions in long, looping swoops. They headed in one direction. Jimmy.

As the parade approached, it reminded Jimmy of those Disney cartoons where every size of beast, large and small alike—birds, insects, and hooves—

flee from a forest fire or a dinosaur or hunters. It didn't occur to him yet that they, too, might be running from something.

A school of colorful tropical fish was the first to arrive, swirling around the struts of the oil rig, transforming the filtered light into an insane kaleidoscope of color. Every color of the neon rainbow shimmered above his head.

But something didn't sit right. Jimmy struggled with the tightening in his gut as he tried to manage his thoughts. The reef fish were too big, comparable to the size of cars, and some even more substantial. When one of them bumped Jimmy, he realized the huge fish was not a mere feeder fish. It was the king, a great white shark painted to look like a reef fish. With electric blue stripes, Night-Glo green circles, and iridescent oyster sheens, the shark was not the gray shadow of nightmares. It was delightful.

Jimmy watched in awe. Another shark was translucent, its organs visible beneath transparent skin. In front of its head swung a glowing proboscis lure, a fleshy, false fishing line to catch prey. Only a handful of small, deep-sea fish had evolved that adaptation, miles from the light of the sun. *Well, now, this shark too*, thought Jimmy.

A distracted tuna got too close to the shark. The great beast chomped, leaving a crimson cloud in its wake.

Jimmy laughed and turned back on his com to tell Holger.

Holger crackled into the scene, mid yelling rant. "Buddy, heck, talk to me! Anything!"

"It's a zoo down here, man," Jimmy reported back.

Holger collapsed into his chair.

"Some kind of crazy great whites, all colors and everything," Jimmy added.

"Yeah, kid, okay. *Puler deg Herfra*," he said swearing in Norwegian. "Let's get you up."

"Some big-ass shrimps too, like a foot long. Heard of foot-long shrimp?"

Holger clipped back, "Yup. The girls are waiting, time to hit balls kid. You are off the clock," he added.

No response.

"Jimmy?"

Impossibly large turtles, thirty feet each, lumbered out of the liquid haze. They filed past Jimmy, who was speechless. They ignored him, speedily weaving through the base of the rig like they had just escaped his father's kitchen pot. Each turtle was both blue and red, the colors split down their centerlines. Blue on the left, red on the right. It was this detail that made Jimmy realize something was wrong. It was not the neon sharks or the millions of fleeing animals or the fact the turtles were the size of Greyhound buses. No, it was that these turtles were all blue and red, like someone had designed them that way. It was this little detail that flipped the switch in his brain, elevating his terror alert level from one to ten.

The turtles were in a hurry. Come to think of it, everything was. The shrimp swarmed over the blowout preventer. Jimmy struggled to unclip as they ran over him.

He was not fast enough. They were in the millions, stacking one upon another as they tried to escape the growing blackness, burying Jimmy deeper and deeper in their squirming mass and oil. He finally unclipped and tried to swim away, but it made things worse. There was nothing to stop him from sinking further into the shrimp, their little feet becoming an escalator, pulling him down into the viscous oil now spewing into the ocean from the oil rig.

As he disappeared into the writhing, growing blackness, he felt the anesthetic urge to fall asleep, a sensation at odds with the horror coursing through him.

***

Topside, the party grew. It was loud. A helicopter arrived carrying girlfriends and families. A roughneck named Brian McInnes waved it in, clearing the platform so the chopper could land. He was the impromptu flight director and party planner for the afternoon. This was his sixteenth steel deck party at sea, starting with the *Stennis* aircraft carrier right after the Iraq War. He adjusted his chef's BBQ KING apron and chewed on a cheroot. He knew what to do: beer, food, girls, and volleyballs. For some reason, the volleyballs were vital. And the girls.

Over the thunder of the blades, something gave him pause. The rig shifted, causing everyone to take a half step. The women in the helicopter opened the door when it got close to land. Their smiles turned to concern when they spotted the looks on everyone's faces. McInnes called the aircraft off at the last second, yelling into the walkie over the rotor wash.

Silence soon fell on the helideck. The sound came from the black sea below them. McInnes peered over the edge to find the source of the ominous *thrum, thrum, thrum.*

In such a familiar place, sounds were like friends: you knew which ones to trust. He had never met this particular foe and regarded it with suspicion. In threes it came, louder each time. Something was not right. "Inside!" he yelled.

Thrum, thrum, thrum. The slightest change in the pitch of the drill can spell doom to those not acquainted to the acoustic subtleties of a drill platform at sea. In 1982, the Northern Ranger oil platform sank in a severe North Atlantic hurricane. The world's largest platform announced the end with a single whine of escaping gas. Had the crew heeded the odd scream whistle, some may have survived or at least tried their sudden fate in the open waters of the Atlantic. Instead, eighty-four men perished in the resulting explosion. The 25,000-ton behemoth sank in seventeen minutes. They say when a canary dies, somewhere a miner runs. McInnes knew enough to run.

Too late. The whole world tilted, the oil rig's legs buckled under the ocean's skirt. On the helideck, McInnes was one of the last to lose his grip, falling to his death alongside smoked ribs and sausage. Holger was in a stairwell when it flooded. The kayaker died trying to save someone swimming in fire.

Jimmy Jones was under a mountain of falling, twisted metal.

He was still alive.

BOOK ONE

THE UNCERTAINTY PRINCIPLE

Alastair Albert Mayes doodled in his physics notebook, a smirk on his face. With dopey eyes and shaggy hair, he had a distracted charm that blended seamlessly into the background of the dimly lit science lab. He molded into his chair, desperate to not make eye contact with anyone; his body was seventeen-year-old soft, like clay yet to be formed into a thought.

Alastair struggled not to laugh. He knew he couldn't look up, because if he did, if he looked at Leo, he would lose it. With summer around the corner, he just wanted to get to the finish line without getting in more trouble. Two desks over, Leo's shoulders shrugged uncontrollably with suppressed laughter, though he managed through sheer willpower, and pressed lips, to offer his theory to their exasperated physics teacher.

"We don't smell anything, Mr. Simmons," said Leo. "You might be imagining it? Perhaps you have synesthesia?"

Mr. Simmons ignored him, wandering around the lab, triangulating the source of the putrid smell wafting through his classroom.

"It's when the wiring of your senses gets crossed up," Leo continued, dangerously, "and you see colors when you hear music or taste things when you touch objects or—"

Laughter leaked out of Alastair.

"I know what synesthesia is," Mr. Simmons snapped.

The smell lingered, but class kept on. Zack was at the front, giving a presentation on the Poincaré Conjecture. New to tenth grade, he was the smartest among them despite being four years younger than everyone and painfully shy. No one paid attention to Zack, and as usual, it was Alastair's fault.

Zack mumbled again. He had struggled with a problem in his proof that one of his teachers had pointed out. The tweak required Zack to create a whole new field of mathematics seemingly. He tried to explain it to the class and then just gave up.

"And with the final transformation, Poincaré's Conjecture is true and verified," Zack said, testing the class's attention. Poincaré's Conjecture was one of the world's most famous, intractable math problems.

"I solved it," Zack said. He hadn't most likely.

Someone snickered, infuriating Mr. Simmons. The class was off the rails now. The teacher turned slowly, intent on having a target for his growing rage. He approached Alastair's desk.

Alastair doodled in the back of his physics book to avoid eye contact.

"What are you drawing?" asked Mr. Simmons.

Alastair felt the heat of his teacher's body, desperate not to let it uncork an explosion of laughter. "Huh?" Alastair closed his book.

"May I see?" Mr. Simmons used a ruler to lift a page.

Alastair reluctantly opened the book. He had drawn a decent portrait of a girl's face.

"It's well done," Mr. Simmons said, honestly.

He wasn't a bad guy underneath all the academic armor, thought Alastair. He was just tormented.

Like Alastair.

Truth was, Alastair wanted to succeed, but he was too proud to share his struggles with the academic demands, so he feigned indifference and hid behind idiocy. Sometimes he wondered if the Honors program had made a mistake letting him in. It was possible. Human error seemed to be the theme this year; however, most of the time, he did not admit to being this self-aware. He just messed around instead, challenging the universe to choose his future for him.

Mr. Simmons realized the smell was much worse in the neighborhood of Alastair's neighbor, lab partner, and friend, Milk.

Petite and pretty, she had big Afro hair and cute glasses. She was the only African American kid in the class, but she leaned into sticking out rather than hiding. By far the most confident among the group, she was also the most radiant. With her politically astute smile, blistering academic papers on the US government's organizational behavior—it was structurally doomed to fail as a function of complexity and time—and an addictive enthusiasm for arguing, she was a defiant, intellectual powerhouse in thrift store clothes. Everyone called her Milk; it was her nickname, and she swung a stick at you if you called her Martha.

She was as stiff as a rail now. And grossed out by Mr. Simmons invading her space with his sniffs. There was silence in the room.

"I have a theory," Zack peeped.

Behind Mr. Simmons back, a chorus of eyes and heads shook, indicating for Zack not to say anything.

Zack didn't pick up the social cues. Being on the spectrum, he never did. "Have you considered that it smells the worst on cold days?"

"Have you considered that it smells the worst on cold days," Mr. Simmons repeated. He looked up. There was a heating vent in the ceiling. He pushed Alastair aside, using a chair to stand on the desk.

Alastair watched Mr. Simmons's heel twist into his drawing. He tried to pry it off.

Milk caught his eye and looked down at the picture, seeing what he had drawn for the first time. Her eyes widened. She mouthed, *Katherine?* She glanced at Kat, who was at the back of the class, watching them.

Embarrassed, Alastair ripped it out from under Mr. Simmons's foot and put it in his bag.

Mr. Simmons pushed open the heating vent and popped his head into the overhead ceiling panels. The smell overpowered him. He dry-heaved as his head emerged inside the ductwork. There it was: a box.

Mr. Simmons took the box down and put it on the desk. Inside, there was a dead cat with a little pin on it that said, *Say my name.* It was one of the cats used for the biology dissection course the prior week.

"Heisenberg," said Mr. Simmons. "Continue Zack."

The dead cat was not only a reference to Schrödinger's famous quantum physics thought experiment involving Heisenberg's uncertainty principle—a cat, a box, and a radiation pellet—but also, it was a reference to *Breaking Bad.* Heisenberg was the name of the meth-cooking teacher who kept a burner cell phone in the ceiling of his classroom. The series was a favorite of Mr. Simmons, and he would quote it daily. He left the box on Alastair's desk.

"I expect more from you Alastair. At least make it difficult next time."

The smell of the cat's decay was intense. Now everyone was pissed at Alastair. And worse, the joke had fallen flat.

Alastair stared at the cat. It was like his life, a visual metaphor for his time at Union High School.

And he didn't even get a laugh: even his pranks were dumb now, apparently. The bell rang. Everyone escaped, like air whistling out of a deflating balloon. The kids filed into the hallway, mixing in with Gen Pop, as they called the non-Honors students.

Union High School was an average American high school in most ways, but the Honors program was a special track and attracted applicants from around the state. The program was a spacious, incredible place to learn—for a very few—and it rivaled some of the best colleges in America; however, it was still full of teenagers, which meant, it was still high school.

As much as Alastair wanted some breathing space, he didn't want to be kicked out of Honors, truly. He wanted to leave on his own accord—hence, the constant acting out. He never just stood up and said it. The truth only leaked out in attitude.

The two academic tracks at the school couldn't be more different. The standard academic track was like anywhere else in America, a mix of hormones and hazing—teenagers learning their first hard lessons about all the ways they will fail when they are adults.

It wasn't that Gen Pop was the worst track in the world; it was just that the Honors program was so good. Union High School had been the recipient of an enormous corporate education grant for the creation of a specialized, college prep program for select students. Part of the deal with the local government included a thirty-million-dollar gift to the local high school to promote individualized research. At first, the program was focused on just science, but soon, it expanded to involve everything, including the arts. The specialized track had been in place for over a decade and had lured top professors away from colleges by using a combination of astronomically high salary offers and promises of academic freedom. Only twelve students per year were admitted from across the state. And in the last five years, the first graduates from the program started placing at top colleges and internships, finally giving the school the recognition it deserved. People moved to the area to apply. Everyone wanted in.

Except for Alastair. He wanted out. So he didn't end up like the cat.

THE BUDDHA

Jimmy woke up on the ocean floor with a problem.

All the sea life seemed to be gone. The oil rig had clearly sunk. He was still breathing. These were the only three facts he could put together. He squeezed his eyes and tried again, slowly coming out of a fog.

One more thing popped into his head. Whatever was going on, his life was on a short leash, literally and figuratively. He checked his O_2. *Fine.* Nitrogen. *Fine.* The oil rig's oversized oxygen tanks had clearly survived the plunge and were still feeding his tubes, assuming they weren't leaking somewhere. He tightened his valves and adjusted his kit.

Options, JJ. He knew he couldn't simply ascend. With no decompression chamber at the end of the trip, he wouldn't survive the recompression, dying of the bends, or worse. And that was even if the hoses could still reach to the surface. He could see they were wrapped around the base of the rig, coiled around him. He was pinned to the ocean floor. By his calculations, even if he did ascend, he'd run out of hose halfway up and be stuck at 150 feet underwater, like a balloon on a string tied to the sea floor. And like a balloon, if he risked a fast ascent with no oxygen from there on up, his lungs would pop.

Jimmy considered the third and final option. He was still being fed oxygen. That was a fact. He would have to wait it out until the company sent down submersibles to inspect the site, which could be hours or days or weeks, depending on what was going on topside. It was a race between him, the remaining oxygen, and fate.

Jimmy believed it was possible he could survive long enough. As a result of his profession, and hundreds of hours of tedious study to get certified, Jimmy was a veritable expert in the macabre science of underwater emergencies at depth.

In 2013, a twelve-person tugboat sank while trying to stabilize an oil rig off the coast of Nigeria. Eleven of the crew members died. Harrison Okene, the cook, lived. While the boat sank one hundred feet to the bottom of the ocean, he managed to find a four-foot air pocket in the terrifying rush of water. Sixty-two hours later, divers were sent to assess whether or not the boat was worth recovering. He was discovered. He was as shocked as they were.

Ironically, it was the horrifying depth that saved him. The air bubble he lived in was only four feet high. Normally, someone would need over one thousand cubic feet of air to survive that long. It seemed to be a miracle until a group of scientists calculated that at that depth, oxygen is compressed by a factor of four, and water absorbs CO_2 more efficiently, carrying away his poisonous exhales. They also calculated that he had only minutes to spare once rescued.

Jimmy factored Mr. Okene into his grim calculus. People can survive, he convinced himself, slowing his breath. Nothing scrambles oil companies faster than an oil leak at the bottom of the ocean. It is a PR disaster certainly, but more importantly, with every minute of the gushing gold, the company loses a fortune.

They would be coming, but when?

***

Jimmy waited. He slowed his breath to once every thirty seconds, refusing to fall asleep, knowing his body would greedily devour his oxygen while he was unconscious.

He sat, Zen-like, waist deep in oil, a stone Buddha deep beneath the sea awaiting salvation. As his brain sipped oxygen, he found nirvana.

When the submersible robot passed him, his legs and arms were still crossed, his chest rising and falling, silently heralding the end of the world.

THE INTERNSHIP

Alastair's parents were at the end of the hall outside Principal Lazo's office. Even from there, he could see the look on their faces.

Guilt.

Every time he got in trouble, his parents looked guilty, as if his failures were their fault. It was a self-blame attitude that he had inherited from them, and he hated it. They always took responsibility, no matter how much he blew it. And the more they blamed themselves for his failures, the more he wanted to push it, to see at what point they broke and blamed him. He had yet to get there, but he hadn't told them that he wanted to drop out of the Honors program in twelfth grade—so he still had a shot at completely disappointing them.

Alastair sat down next to his parents. He didn't say anything. His mother had a soft edge about her; the kind of woman who never seemed strong, but no matter the hurricane force winds around her, she would always bend, like a willow, and never break. His dad was a nervous wreck. He hated confrontation, and he looked like he was the one in trouble.

Leo didn't have it so easy. Sitting directly across the hall from Alastair, his parents chewed into him, talking about expectations.

Alastair had been a sidekick to Leo's successes for years. The girls in the school quietly swooned over Leo's olive skin, long hair, and prowess on the football field. Alastair was always at his side or behind him. "Like background radiation after the Big Bang," he once told Leo. They got in a lot of trouble together on the team, but more than anything, they laughed, and they were friends, but now his stunt had gotten Leo, and everyone, in trouble.

The hallway was littered with complex parent-child relationships, all unraveling in whispered conversations. It seemed to Alastair that the entire class was there.

He couldn't help feeling like they all were talking about him. There were enough furtive glances in his direction that he sensed he was the problem.

And he was.

Principal Lazo emerged from his office with some families and called his next four victims. "Alastair, Leo, Milk," and as an afterthought, "you too, Kat."

Alastair hadn't seen Katherine. She was alone on a far bench, curled like a suspicious cat. Her eyes were soft and hid behind long, sun-blonde hair. She had dated Leo briefly but still maintained a cold distance that felt odd in such a small group of friends. Everyone had a crush on her, including most of her teachers, and she stuck out for her sheer beauty, but no one worshipped her more than Alastair. He glanced at his drawing of her and tucked it away. His father took it, crumpled it up, and threw it in the basket on the way into the office.

They were slow to enter the principal's office. Milk led the troops like usual, even though they were headed to an execution. "You too, Alastair," she said, kicking his leg on the way in. Kat was the last one in.

Principal Lazo had an amazing office for a public school official. Glass, aluminum, and books twisted through the modernist facades. The space felt more like a CEO's office than an educator's, with all the power it suggested and none of the warmth. There were only a few hints of the sixties paraphernalia that used to adorn the old office. It didn't feel like Principal Lazo's vibe at all, thought Alastair. The educator had always cut Alastair some slack, but in the last year, he had hardened, like his new office.

In the sun near the window, a sealed bottle garden sat on a wood pedestal. It was three feet around, a new addition to the office. Leo's parents admired it, in an attempt to suck up. Inside the large glass bottle, a vibrant plant grew in moss and dirt. There was a faded etching on the inside of the glass. Moss had turned the etching green, giving it a nice decorative look. It said, GENE-E CORPORATION.

Principal Lazo came over to admire the diorama. "It is a perfect ecosystem. The bottle was corked and sealed over forty years ago. And still, the spiderwort plant grows. The water is absorbed and exhaled as oxygen and moisture during photosynthesis. Then the water condenses on the glass until it is absorbed again. Endlessly. It is a beautiful thing, don't you think? Sun, water, and DNA in a perfect dance."

Something struck Alastair as he peered at the glass. "Unlikely," he said.

His mother pinched him.

There was no reason to start an argument, but Alastair was itching for a fight. "Gene-E Corporation was founded in 2000. You said this was sealed forty years ago, and yet the etching is on the inside. See the moss? So I see three options. It is not forty years old. It is not a true sealed ecosystem. You just water it daily, which is the likely solution. Or Gene-E Corp was secretly founded forty years ago, which it wasn't. So which one is it?"

The principal's face broke into a thin smile. "All your observations are correct Alastair. But there is always another option if you know all the variables in play. This bottle was indeed sealed forty years ago by the Gene-E Corp as a gift. And it is true the corporation was founded in the year 2000. It did not exist forty years ago. So what is the one variable, other than perhaps that I am lying, that is still in play?"

"None. You are lying."

"We shall see." Lazo gestured at the parents. "May we get to the matter at hand? Please find a place to sit, Alastair."

"Either way, it is not forty years old," Alastair added. "So it is not that impressive."

"Sit down please," said Principal Lazo, exasperated. "Please."

As he passed Kat to sit down, she gave him the drawing of her that his father had thrown in the trash. She had recovered it. "Thought you'd want this," she said, with a smile.

Alastair was unsure if she was being sarcastic or nice, so he went with a relatively safe, "Thank you," and sat.

The lecture was on script. Expectations. Performance. Gratitude—the three rules of the Honors program at Union. If you didn't adhere to them, you would be kicked out of the accelerated program and into the standard curriculum, which was a death sentence according to some of the snobbier teachers.

Principal Lazo was on point today. "Gratitude is the key to unlocking talent, realizing how lucky we are to have a school like this, for you. And"—he paused to drink some coconut milk—"I called you all in today because things are going to be changing."

Alastair sunk in his chair. *Here it comes.*

"We are graduating your class a year early."

A shock wave rolled through the students, electrifying them.

The parents looked like a train was going to hit them.

"Your postgraduate study year will start in eleventh grade instead of twelfth. And your summer internships with Gene-E Corp will start this summer."

Part of what made Honors special was that the final year of high school was treated like a postgraduate year of independent research, where the students were allowed to study whatever they wanted. The core curriculum ended in eleventh grade, and they graduated in a small, private ceremony.

Everyone looked forward to it, and it was often a carrot dangled out in front of them when they were being punished by studies in the earlier grades. Now it seemed like their graduation from the core curriculum was happening a year early.

Alastair was in shock. He knew his class was full of troublemakers, but this was an unprecedented move.

Milk cast a smile at her father. He wasn't as enthused. He looked worried.

In fact, all of the parents did. They sneaked glances at each other.

Finally, Alastair's mother spoke up. "Are you sure they are ready for ... graduation?" Her emphasis on the word "graduation" caught Alastair's attention.

"Yes," said Principal Lazo with a cough. "And the internships will start immediately after this year. No break."

***

That night, Alastair had a hard time figuring out how to modify his cap and gown to give it some personality for graduation.

He needed to celebrate. Honors was over. Somehow, he had gotten what he wanted without having to ask for it, although, he hadn't told his parents he wouldn't be going on the internship yet, so that still worried him. He resolved to tell them over dinner that he wanted to do summer league football instead.

Alastair went downstairs. The steps creaked. The townhouse was tired; yellowed wallpaper was littered with various awards he had won when he was younger.

The whole place felt like yesterday to Alastair.

He wore his graduation outfit at dinner, his sleeves rolled up for chicken tikka masala. His parents weren't talking, though the fact they made his favorite meal meant they wanted to.

"What's up? Aren't you happy for me?" asked Alastair.

"Sweetheart, we always are," his mom said, "but ..."

"But? What but?"

"Just know, that whatever happens at graduation tomorrow, we love you."

Alastair didn't know how to react.

"And we're sorry."

He looked at his dad, who pursed his lips before sliding in another bite.

"You're sorry?" said Alastair. "Huh." He left the table but then returned to get his plate so he could finish dinner in his room.

Alastair's father made to follow but stopped short when Alastair's mother touched his arm, sitting him back down. They ate in silence.

THE BERMUDA TRIANGLE

At the site of the oil rig disaster, the rescue helicopters arrived slowly, like mosquitoes at a campfire. Volleyballs floated on the water, some of them on fire. Search and Rescue divers dropped into enormous swells swept hard by hurricane winds. Young, brave men swam mightily for people who would never live. Boats arrived. Officials stayed behind the microphones.

Another storm roared in just as the rescuers decided there was no one to rescue. The recovery boats moved to shallower water to drop anchor and wait it out. Quickly, the media focused on the story of the three girlfriends who watched the whole, tragic event unfold from the helicopter. After the rig sank, the pilot had tried to get close enough to save one man, but the oil rigger ended up drowning at the tips of their fingers in the rotor wash. Despite witnessing the fiery cataclysm, it was the saucer eyes of the sinking man that lingered in the girls' minds. One woman jumped out of the helicopter after him, but she was too late. Field reporters ate her up on shore, their eyes glistening with front page headlines.

This was all before the news of the airplane crashes hit the wire, and the mosquitoes were off to Corpus Christi. While a rig sinking was capital-B *Big stuff* for the ravenous news hawks—especially with another oil spill brewing in the Gulf—airplane crashes scare Americans. When three planes go down simultaneously, it is time for lots of serious-faced conjecture. Terrorism is much better for business.

With the pressure from the media alleviated, the oil company didn't have to move quite so quickly. They balanced their short-term oil losses against the loss of more expensive equipment; some gray-faced risk manager decided to wait out the end of the storm. "And lives," they told the press that had stuck around. They didn't want to lose more lives for what was simply a recovery and inspection operation, they said with solemn hands.

During the final press conference, the oil company announced they had managed to staunch the flow. In the process, they discovered that a sudden change in the grade of oil was to blame. While variations were normal in the consistency of crude oil, the oil they were measuring was nearly 80 percent less viscous than previously modeled. They couldn't explain why the oil was suddenly so refined, hypothesizing that they may have punched through the younger deposit into one that was suddenly a million years older.

Although they had lost a great deal of money in the rig's sinking, the business suits were internally very excited. The refined crude was worth much more, and by their new flow calculations, the deposit was massive, extending well under the coast. There was never a mention of Jimmy having been below the surface during the accident in the official report.

At the site, the weather had moved on with the rest of the world. The sea was calm—seagulls picked debris out of the oil slick. On one of the recovery ships, there was light chaos. They had lost contact with one of their small scout submersibles at depth. After some tense moments, the computer found its location beacon. It was at the surface and must have somehow come un-tethered.

They deployed a skiff to retrieve the submersible drone. As the two graduate students headed over to find it, they spotted a body floating a good distance away. It was white and bloated. But something didn't seem right when they pulled up to it. They used an oar to turn the figure over.

It was a blow-up sex doll, the one from the dive command room on the sunken rig.

The doll was roped to the missing submersible, riding it like a six-figure cowgirl. The robot had been stripped of most of its gear, leaving just the external oxygen tanks for floatation. Its cable was cut, and its emergency beacon was flashing.

Big black block letters were written across the sex doll's back in Sharpie. *I am alive, you idiots.*

Next to the letters, there was an arrow pointing straight down.

***

In the hospital, Jimmy couldn't make heads or tails of what he had seen underwater. Having left such a surreal place, the banality of the beige room—stacks of folding chairs stored neatly in the corner—was confusing.

The more he told his story to the officials, the more he agreed that he must have been hallucinating as a result of—officially—"a diminished flow of oxygen due to the imminent catastrophic failure of the rig." Jimmy didn't care that the timelines didn't add up. At first, he decided to let oxygen starvation be his easy way out of the hard problem facing him. Yet he knew, deep down, it had happened; he hadn't hallucinated. He couldn't prove it or explain it. So, in the beginning, he tried to drop it and agree with them that his mind probably conjured up the monsters.

But it wasn't Jimmy's style to let things go. *Was it?*

While the rest of the world moved on to the airplane crashes, Jimmy stewed in the truth in his hospital bed. It started as a gentle gnawing in his belly and kept spreading until he couldn't stop obsessing about what he had seen and what it meant.

It didn't help that everyone seemed more interested in the mystery behind the plane crashes at this point, which was running on an endless news loop on the TV. In absence of details, "experts" were asking if the accidents had something to do with the famed Bermuda Triangle.

Jimmy turned the volume up.

The triangle covered 1.5 million square miles of the Atlantic Ocean, its vertices touching Miami, San Juan in Puerto Rico, and the island of Bermuda in the north. Over the centuries, hundreds of mysterious events had happened there. Sinkings, disappearing boats, ghost ships. Lost time. Plane crashes had taken place in the zone, including Flight 19—which started it all—the squadron of five fighter planes that flew out of existence on a blue-sky December day in 1945. Once the Bermuda Triangle lodged in the public's mind, more and more accidents were drawn into its mythic net. Everything was explored as a cause—from stories of the legendary Atlantis civilization and aliens to more mundane possibilities, like methane hydrate deposits and the powerful Gulf Stream oceanic current.

"What do you make of this triangle stuff?" Jimmy asked his hospital roommate. Jimmy knew he was reaching, searching for anything that could explain what he'd seen and help prove it wasn't his fault. The blowout preventer he had been working on was now buried under thousands of tons of steel. It was now Jimmy's word, which wasn't worth—

"Hogwash," the ailing elderly man answered. He was in for an appendectomy and was annoyed that it took seventy years for the thing to poop out and ruin his day.

Hogwash. While one TV science expert argued the Memorial Day events happened outside the triangle, two others were arguing for a bigger footprint for the triangle in the Gulf of Mexico. The first scientist argued that the triangle was not, in fact, any more dangerous than the rest of the Atlantic. For example, the actuaries at Lloyds Bank of London didn't care to charge more to insure safe travel through it.

The two conspiracists countered by saying that in recent years, the size of the triangle had indeed expanded. The original triangle was too small, and the events were spreading. *You just don't want to see the truth.*

The more the TV droned, the more the Bermuda Triangle conspiracy grew roots in Jimmy's mind, plumbing his childhood. Ever since he was a kid, Jimmy had enjoyed stories of the Bermuda Triangle, told to him by his conspiracy-obsessed father. He dug a good mystery, and the Devil's Triangle had been his gateway conspiracy into a whole world of his dad's hidden beliefs. Bigfoot, the Illuminati, false flag attacks—and more recently, government weather seeding experiments using chemtrails on commercial airliners—had all been the stuff of lectures and mythology at the family dinner table.

Growing up, it'd been fun, but as Jimmy was almost twenty-four years old now (and dealing with enough bullshit in the real world) the whole thing became ridiculous. And it drove a wedge between him and his father. It took him until he was in his twenties to see the crazy in his dad; however, enough of it had taken hold to harbor a sour curiosity about all things conspiracy.

These Bermuda Triangle experts had a point. Until they didn't. And then they did again.

Jimmy turned off the TV. He was running his own internal debate now. Should he tell someone what he saw? He wanted to work again. He measured the two futures and chose the one that didn't rely on him becoming a crackpot, like his father. He finished his last Oreo and decided he would never speak of what he saw underneath the oil rig. It would sink with him.

***

A recovery technician watched the feed recorded by Jimmy's camera. Jimmy's work on the blowout preventer was peerless. And noted.

The video footage of the turtles was remarked upon, but their incredible scale and vivid colors were lost on the technician. The feed was in black and white. The footage murky.

The tape was labeled and put in a box, never to be seen again.

THE GRADUATION

At Union High School, the Honors class got their own graduation. It was a private affair. Only parents were allowed to come; it had always been cloaked in secrecy. Even siblings were not allowed, though none of Alastair's classmates had siblings, which was odd in itself. The special event was a final step before the independent research year funded by Gene-E Corp, the corporation behind the lavish donations to Union High School. It was an odd cart-before-the-horse event.

The warmly lit auditorium was lavish, with stadium seating. Twelve desks were built into the slope for Honors lectures.

Up front, there was an old tooth on display, brilliantly lit behind museum grade glass. Alastair walked by it, curious. He tapped on the glass, testing its quality, before being shooed away.

He couldn't decide where to sit. Did he want to be close to the lectern and therefore within eye contact of the speakers or near the back, closer to Leo? He figured this was only ceremonial, so he opted for the back, like usual. It was also the farthest from his parents, who had continued to be cryptic all morning. He slumped into his chair.

Leo kicked his leg and sat next to him. "What's with the drama?" Leo whispered.

Pools of light illuminated the desks in the large, darkened room, giving it an ominous feel. Alastair shrugged and pulled a red laser pointer from his pocket, pointing its beam toward a pair of people on the stage.

It was Alastair's parents. Next to them were the school's faculty and other parents in front of a huge screen and podium. Also on the stage were some of the Gene-E Corporation donors Alastair had seen at official functions over the years. The postgrads from prior years leaned against the wall at the back of the room. Ms. Yaektova took the podium.

"Hello, parents," she said. Alastair watched her with suspicion. She oversaw the academic curriculum in the Honors program and was universally disliked. She had a coal miner's feel about her, thought Alastair. Her arms were built for carrying rocks, or students, and crushing them. In her sixties, Yaektova was a product of proletarian Russia, with a thick accent and an even thicker Eastern Bloc attitude, despite having been washed through decades of American life.

"Hello, Katherine," she said.

"Hello mother," Kat answered.

She couldn't be more different from her mom, thought Alastair.

"Hey, Kat ..." Alastair said to her as a prelude to asking her a question. She ignored him.

Leo spoke up loudly. "Hey, Kat!"

She glanced at him and Alastair. "You'll get a kick out of this," she said cryptically and then disappeared back into herself. Even now, she looked sultry when she sulked.

"Let's begin," Yaektova said.

On a table next to her, there were twelve thin leather-bound books. A group of teachers picked up the books and headed to the desks to give one to each student. Alastair's mother took her husband's hand, her lips pursed. The books were ceremoniously placed in front of the students. Alastair was one of the first to get a book. The leather was rich and soft with a fat strap latched over the cover.

It had a name embossed on the front: *Albert Einstein.*

Alastair was not sure why he was given a book about Einstein, but it didn't surprise him. The faculty had decided a long time ago that Einstein's work would be one of his primary tracks in physics. Before he was burned out and gave up on school, Alastair was pressed to spend his free time noodling on different versions of Einstein's theory of universal gravitation, which the great scientist had been trying to crack when he died.

He started to open the latch when Yaektova instructed the students not to open the folios yet.

As more books were placed on the desks, it was less evident to the other students why they were getting that particular one.

Milk's book thudded down. On Milk's cover, in gold letters, it said *Martin Luther King Jr.*

Every time a book was placed on a desk, the name on the book flashed up on the big screen at the front.

Next to Milk, Marie got her book: *Marie Curie.*

M-L-K? Milk mouthed to Leo.

Leo flashed her the cover of his folio: *Leonardo da Vinci.*

Behind him, Zack looked like a little mouse at his oversized desk. When his book arrived, it said, *Isaac Newton.*

Zack opened it, disregarding Yaektova's instructions.

More names flashed up on the screen next: *Charles Darwin. Sakichi Toyoda.*

Alastair glanced at his classmate Charlie and his adopted Asian "twin" brother Sakichi. They were the same age roughly, and equally annoying, but for once, neither of them were speaking.

When Kat's book landed in front of her, she didn't look down at it, but Alastair could see what it said. On the big screen, the name *Catherine the Great* flashed up.

"Zack, please close your book, you will understand in a moment," Yaektova urged.

He ignored her. He kept reading until a teacher walked up to him and whispered in his ear. When he still wouldn't stop, she took the book and held it in her arms, standing next to him.

There were more books, twelve in all. Once the last book was distributed, Yaektova began.

"Welcome to Honors graduation. Parents, faculty, Principal Lazo, I would like to introduce some members of the Gene-E Corporation board who have joined us today," she said.

The board members' somber gray suits and sallow skin created the sense that they were all produced in the same factory.

Another reason to avoid the internships, thought Alastair as he scanned their faces.

The students clapped feebly. Gene-E Corp officials were trotted out at every event to make sure the kids felt indebted for the rest of their lives.

Yaektova didn't waste any time. "Thirty years ago, our benefactors at Gene-E Corporation purchased samples from a DNA library owned by the

Soviet government. It represented tissue and biological material from some of the greatest geniuses, scientists, artists, and leaders in the world."

She paused, taking a drink, looking nervous for the first time in her life. She shuffled papers, looking out across the young audience.

Alastair watched Kat in the awkward pause.

And she watched her mother closely.

Milk mouthed to Alastair, *Weird.*

He agreed. This was an odd way to start a graduation speech.

Leo looked confused too. He toyed with the strap on his book.

"The goal was to create twins of those great minds, to resurrect their DNA and reexpress it in the world in new and amazing ways." Yaektova paused again, leaving silence in the room.

There was not a sound, everyone was holding their breath.

"The twelve of you are the product of that dream. Twenty years ago, your parents were chosen for a unique in vitro fertilization program. Unable to have children, they were given you as a gift to gestate. All twelve of you are identical genetic clones of the people whose names adorn the books before you. It is a great legacy you have inherited. It is your journey alone to go on, to discover what it means to you. But within your DNA, your exact chemical expression, greatness was once born. And we hope, with the help of the Gene-E Corporation, greatness will be born once again." She then stepped aside.

The theatre darkened for a video presentation.

Milk had her arms stretched out. Like she was holding back two walls that were going to crush her.

"Charles Darwin teased out the basis for all life and its evolution through observation and logic. Isaac Newton unraveled the motions of the stars and gravity, creating calculus in the process. Marie Curie discovered radiation in a world dominated by men. Albert Einstein"—everyone looked at Alastair—"found his own path, peered beyond the classical world discovered by Newton, and teased out some of the most profound secrets of our universe."

Alastair's face felt numb.

His mother wasn't his biological mother. She had lied to him his entire life. He looked around; his classmates also seemed like they were a mess of different emotions.

The video continued on, listing the accomplishments of Leonardo da Vinci, artist, scientist, and consummate Renaissance man; Sakichi Toyoda, the industrialist who transformed Japan and founded Toyota Motors Corporation; Thomas Edison, who invented the lightbulb; Catherine the Great, who ushered Russia into the modern world; and Martin Luther King Jr., the political firebrand whose life was cut short.

Alastair felt all these things—fear, rage, confusion, betrayal—but on the outside, he was stone-faced, the emotions a wild swirl beneath the surface. He locked eyes with his mother, who also was motionless but with tears on her face. Alastair knew she wanted nothing more than to run up and hug him, and he wanted nothing less.

The video was over.

Milk already had her hand up.

"In a moment," Yaektova said. She began lecturing again. More talk of expectations, promises to succeed, and gratitude.

Alastair didn't hear anything Ms. Yaektova said now. He was caught in his head, unable to look at his mother anymore, chasing dimly formed questions that could never be answered.

Leo flipped open his book. Inside it, there seemed to be an original page from Leonardo da Vinci's sketchbook.

"Before you is a folio, our gift, and Gene-E Corp's gift to you on your graduation. Inside—you may open them now—are original, seminal works from each of your predecessors. They are priceless, some worth millions, and they are yours to keep, as a reminder of the legacy you have inherited. While we would never expect you to live up to the greatness in these papers before you, let them serve as an inspiration to your own intellectual pursuits."

Alastair opened his folio. In it were handwritten pages from Einstein's *Annus Mirabilis* papers, the miracle year in which he first expressed special relativity.

And there, on one of the pages, $E = mc^2$. Alastair stared at the simple equation upon which the entire universe spun.

He felt small.

He turned over the folio. On the next page was a sticky note. It had his mother's writing on it. It said, *I'm sorry.*

Yaektova finished up. "Your internships start in two days. This year, you will be split up, and you will not have a choice of projects within the Gene-E Corporation. Five of you, who focus on physics and chemistry, will be headed to our Texas facility. The other seven, who focus on life sciences, will head to

North Dakota. Your parents have all of the information. Congratulations. I am proud of every one of you. I can answer a few questions, which I am sure you have."

Eleven hands shot up.

"Questions. Questions. Questions. Alastair," she said.

"Are we the only ones?" he asked.

"Yes, every student who has ever gone through the program is, like you, a genetic twin of someone great. However, there is only one of each of you. There are no other Albert Einsteins, nor Leonardo da Vincis. You are all unique. This is a very special class."

At the back of the room, someone coughed.

Yaektova corrected herself. "Except for Zack. Isaac, who is with us today, is also a genetic twin of Isaac Newton." She motioned to the back of them. "We did a redo with that one," she said.

Alastair turned around. The other Isaac was tall and older than fourteen-year-old Zack. He was in his early twenties. His insect stick-thin demeanor cast a narrow shadow on the wall. Alastair never liked the older postgrad, and now he liked him even less. He was obnoxious enough without the new and improved heritage.

"He has been working with us at Gene-E Corp for a while now. With great success. Like you all will someday, possibly."

Looking back and forth at the two supposed doppelgängers, Alastair didn't think Isaac looked much like Zack. Isaac was incredibly well dressed, obnoxiously so. That and his age made it seem like he couldn't be more different from Zack.

"Hello, brother," Isaac said to Zack.

Zack didn't react, turning back to his folio to look through it.

Did he have a twin?

Were there thirty more little Einsteins running around in diapers somewhere?

"Any other questions?"

"I got one. What the fuck?" Milk said.

"That's not a question."

"Yes, it is," she said. "What. The. Fuck. Question mark. Martin Luther King Jr.? A dude."

"You have both of his X chromosomes, making you female: XX instead of XY. Anyone else?"

"I got one. A different one," Milk said.

"Okay."

"What the fuck?" she yelled.

"That's the same question. Katerina?"

"Are you aware of Gene-E Corp's criminal abuses and the Cornerstone Project?" asked Kat.

"Another question."

The questions kept coming.

THE TURTLE

No one came to visit Jimmy at the hospital. Ex-girlfriends, ex-fiancées, old buddies, relatives—relatives!—they all stayed away. It was a dark, Texas harbinger. The idiots really thought it was his fault. Text messages gave people cover, but the excuses were horseshit. And those who said they would visit, didn't show up, even if they said they would, with a bullshit afterthought text message.

Jimmy stewed in his hospital bed, waiting to be discharged, listening to the hushed hints of tragedy in the halls. An engineer from the oil rig survived the fires and was on a different floor. On the way out, he visited her in the burn unit with what he could buy at the gift shop from the change in his pocket, but she was in a medically induced coma and wasn't allowed to have the flower, so he dumped it into the trash instead of giving it to the nurses, suddenly feeling angry again, unsure if the oil rig sinking was his fault.

Deep down he knew he had welded the blowout preventer successfully, but with the severity of his coworker's condition and no one to talk to, Jimmy's doubts ricocheted around his mind. They amplified and swelled into righteousness and then sank back into guilt, then doubt—and then twisted down there back into anger, eventually rising up like acid in the throat to start the cycle over again as he sat in the hospital cafeteria waiting for his taxi. He had really liked his job, the friendships, the expertise, and now it was all gone. Just because—

He had seen something.

He knew no one would believe him. He risked being the crazy guy. He hated the crazy guys. It was moral weakness to not own up to your screwups in Corpus Christi. Jimmy prided himself on his individualism and no-nonsense, honest work ethic. It was actually easier and more socially acceptable to pretend he made a mistake with his welding than to blame monsters, but both carried heavy liabilities. Admitting a mistake that didn't happen could lead to legal troubles; however, blaming monsters would turn him into his father, a crackpot who believed in conspiracies and the bogeyman. Given both options, Jimmy preferred being a legal pariah.

As he left the hospital and got into a cab—why did no one come to pick him up?—Jimmy was still at the bottom of the rig, running out of air. The night through the fly-caked taxi's windshield was another form of anoxia: this one spiritual. He considered getting his hair cut. When he was on the rig, he never shaved due to superstition, having survived his very first rotation with a long, ratty beard and hair to his shoulders. And the girls loved it when he came home grizzled. And then they loved it just as much when he shaved clean and cut his hair "for them," revealing his boyish looks.

When he was on land, Jimmy lived at his father's house in a sprawling housing tract on the edge of Corpus Christi—a brilliant white stucco mirage that pushed ever outward into the rust, heat, and death of Texas. The housing development held a unique kind of poverty—a poverty of spirit—specific to the American South. Banks and insurance companies owned the maze, having built a thousand paper walls out of promissory notes and sadness.

Jimmy couldn't find the house, circling the endless blocks with an increasingly suspicious taxi driver. The man looked into the rearview mirror at Jimmy's long hair and matted beard and then asked Jimmy if he actually had a home.

"Just drive, asshole," said Jimmy.

Jimmy gave up on the cab, forced out. It was too expensive to keep the meter running anyway, when he had only seventy dollars in his bank account, and that would get consumed by overdraft fees soon enough. While he had been on the rig for months, and would usually have a large paycheck on his arrival home, Texercon had held his last month's pay pending the litigation, and his father's medical bills had been chewing up the money prior to that as fast as he made it.

Jimmy knocked on doors to see if someone knew where he lived. Strangers answered. They didn't trust him, eyeing him warily. An hour later, after crossing perfect lawns, then brown lawns, and then empty lots, Jimmy spotted his father's Welder's Local Union 211 sticker in a window.

The drapes were drawn. The door was unlocked. Inside, it was dark, darker than beneath the oil rig. As he entered, Jimmy felt his throat constrict again, shortening his breath. He had been suffering bouts of claustrophobia on and off since the moment he was dragged back to the surface of the world, bobbing lost on a new ocean.

He knew he would never dive again.

Jimmy usually came home with his golf clubs and duffle bag, chucking them onto the couch, flicking on the lights for a brief visit before he headed back out to sea. But today, his golf clubs were at the bottom of the gulf, and he kept the lights off. He went through the dark of the living room, trying to find his father amid garbage that was strewn everywhere. Stacks of research, obscure science-fiction zines, food containers, and cryptozoology conference pamphlets littered every surface, including the floor. It was worse than it had ever been.

His father, Cayce Jones, was a hoarder, a habit that grew out of the man's obsession with conspiracy, as if the search for hidden truths and monsters necessitated its own personal, dark mythological cave. Typically, when Jimmy returned from an extended job, he cleaned his dad's house, top to bottom. However, this time, he knew he wouldn't have the energy.

Blankets hung over the windows, one of which held a swamp cooler blowing musty air into the space. The air conditioning had gone out last time he was back, almost a year ago, and only mold had grown in the absence. Everything else was a subtraction.

Including his father.

In his early seventies, Cayce was named after the true story behind the train engineer immortalized in song and film. While popular myth told the story of the great "Casey Jones"—whose skull was crushed, and his arm torn off, while stopping a train full of families from barreling into another train—the truth was murkier. The engineer's real name was Jonathon Luther Jones, and he was from Cayce, Kentucky, so people called him "Cayce" Jones (also pronounced Casey) to distinguish him from the other Jones working the line—the first mistake of the runaway myth. Also, historians were pretty certain the disaster was of his own making. The real engineer possibly missed the torpedoes, small explosive devices left on the line that night to warn of the stopped train ahead. So the truth was much more complicated than the myth, and that was why Jimmy's grandparents chose Cayce as the name for their son, to make a point about bullshit.

Jimmy's grandparents wanted their son to search for the truth in life and not be led astray by what other people said, by music, or by other fancy stories. It was the devil's work, and it was as if the legend (and the truth) of Cayce Jones was truly biblical, a sermon on the tragedy of the blue-collar life, which was hard, nasty, and honest in their eyes.

Of course, like many parents' good intentions, the unique naming had the opposite effect on Cayce, passing down a taste for distrust through the generations. Decades later, the search for "truth" had metastasized into "truther," and he had a hunger for conspiracy, false-flag events, and cryptozoology—a new sort of modern-day myth chasing.

Jimmy flicked on another light, and there he was, Cayce Jones of Texas, in a recliner in the dark next to an oxygen tank for his lungs. He smelled of Vicks VapoRub, and he was naked, a loose collection of bones held together by a taught bag of skin. Cayce had a wet hand towel on his lap with ice on top of it, cooling his balls.

"Heard you sunk the rig," he said to Jimmy, eventually.

Jimmy went into the kitchen to look through the fridge. His dad followed him and stood at the kitchen door now, naked, the towel on his shoulder, clutching his oxygen bottle to his chest, sipping air through the cannula in his nose.

"Heh," Cayce said.

"Guess I did, if you say so," said Jimmy. He made a sandwich, adding mayo because his father had a shelf full of Hellmann's bottles for some reason.

"Did you?" said his dad.

"They say I did, I guess." Jimmy handed his father the sandwich. "You need to eat."

"I hate mayo," Cayce said and tossed it in the garbage.

"Then why—" But Jimmy gave up on the mayo.

And that was it. The rest of the conversation would play out in their heads unspoken—a dialogue about trust and love and faith between a bitter father and a broken son, a father whose own pride as a welder had been knocked down into a chair and tied to an oxygen tank on land.

They sat in silence watching *The 7th Voyage of Sinbad*, the 1958 Ray Harryhausen monster movie with giant stop-motion scorpions. Watching a random TV movie was always a signal that they needed to talk but couldn't, so the movie did the talking until one of them found a way to begin. Finally, after the beer was finished and the stop-motion Cyclops had been blinded, Jimmy broke the silence during a commercial break for Gold Bond lotion.

"I saw something, Dad. Under the rig. Giant things."

The room was silent, listening.

THE SECOND ONE

Albert Einstein, the second one, wasn't born yesterday.

This was all bullshit.

At Alastair's table, everyone spun, but the parents talked the most. Guilt worked their jaws, explaining themselves, their decisions, and their *pride* in all of the kids.

The Spaghetti Factory was mottled with other families but none like this table. Alastair's mother spoke, reiterating the theme of this, their graduation dinner: "You can be whoever you want to be." But the more the parents echoed the sentiment, the more it was obvious it wasn't true. They had been branded ... forever. Lied to.

Everything they loved at their school's elite program came with strings, money strings. And it always left some distaste in their mouths; however, it wasn't until Milk stumbled on Gene-E Corp's Cornerstone Project that there seemed to be something more sinister behind their beneficence. They'd thought something weird was up, and now they knew what.

Leo tried to put a stake in the ground. He thought they should go on their internships at Cornerstone despite the intense betrayal they all felt. To Alastair, it felt like a salvo from his eternally curious friend to trust that "everything will be all right." To Milk, who was eternally suspicious, she made it clear it was about the dumbest thing they could do.

Leo and Milk were trading barbs back and forth as Alastair juggled a football under the table, losing patience.

Alastair thought how much Milk was actually like Martin Luther King Jr. in a weird way. Her name, Martha Lexie Klein, was a clue, hidden all these years. They even called her MLK, her initials, for a long time, until she eventually morphed into Milk. Of course, no one would ever be able to spot the clue.

But she certainly knew how to command attention. Alastair had been in Milk's friend zone for three years despite all his attempts to escape, occasionally testing its depth with the odd comment or flirtation, but he never found the bottom. Sometimes she felt like a sister, but most of the time, she was the most electric thing on earth.

But now, she was about to blow a cork. Leo was working her up.

"I am going to the bathroom," said Alastair, dumping his football into Leo's lap unceremoniously. Alastair walked the length of the restaurant, everyone watching him.

"Hey, Einstein," Leo said.

Alastair turned. Leo hit him with a perfect throw. Alastair caught it at the last second. There were no real complaints at Alastair's table. They knew what Leo was trying to do.

"Leo," his mother chided him as a manager walked up.

Alastair went into the bathroom still holding the ball.

Inside, Zack washed his hands.

"Albert Einstein and Isaac Newton, together again," said Alastair.

Zack smiled. "Not really."

"No, I guess not," said Alastair.

"They lived in different time periods."

"I am aware." Zack was always so literal. It was one of his spectrum superpowers. Alastair spun the ball on its tip on the sink.

"Why are you so upset?" Zack asked. It was a rare question from the fourteen-year-old. "You are still you."

"Are you seriously asking me that?" said Alastair.

Zack left the room.

Alastair washed spaghetti off his forehead, looking at himself in the mirror. It was the same soft face, but now it seemed imbued with something else. For a moment, it felt counterfeit. He couldn't shake the feeling. Someone else, across the chasm of time, was looking at him with his own eyes, speaking to him. He felt disconnected from his own story. And then his face popped into being him again, round and unremarkable. He looked into his eyes, searching for the feeling again.

The hot water of the sink steamed up the mirror. He swiped $E = mc^2$ into the steam. It faded away as soon as it was written.

***

"Everything, everything could happen!" Milk said. "I'm not going to Texas. And neither are any of you." She sat upright in her chair. Alastair returned to the table.

"You ready, Alastair? This is for you," she said, like a coiled spring ready to attack. "One!" She thrust up a finger, looking at her classmates, pausing for effect. "Gene-E Corp bought shiploads of unprocessed plastic from China, all through military bulk requisition channels to cover the purchases. Based on daily manifests posted in /b forums, the port in Corpus Christi has seen over 5 *billion* dollars' worth of plastic shipped through it this year alone, all before being trucked to the middle of nowhere Texas on the Gulf of Mexico coast. And it's not just plastic."

"Plastic could be—" Leo began.

"OMG! Two! Cement. Cornerstone is consuming insane amounts of cement, gravel, dirt, copper, and wiring, all that stuff, causing a shortage that has driven up the cost of commercial grade construction materials across the Southwest. *Millions of tons.* The drain on the market has slowed construction across the world, including on the second canal they are building in Panama. /b spotters count over 500 truck shipments every Tuesday."

"What is /b?" Alastair asked.

"4chan," said Leo.

"What's 4chan?"

"Pay attention," Milk said. "Three. After the last election, the CBO—"

"What's the CBO?" Alastair inquired again.

"They requisitioned a large portion of the Pentagon's black budget," said Milk leaning into the table, "shifting money into the science administration budgets. And *for the first time in history*, a President attended the closed-door administrative session. And only a few weeks later? The Pentagon canceled the Joint Strike Fighter program's next phase, recalled *all* of our nuclear submarines back to their ports, save one. And, most worrying, lithium production has skyrocketed, but it can't keep up. To what?"

"Budget cuts," Leo said, less confidently.

"I'm with her," said Alastair.

"For what, Leo? *For Cornerstone*. And this is the one that freaks me out. Four. In Corpus, there's been a metric suck-ton of scientists and engineers showing up. After landing at the airport, they stay at a hotel for like one day and then disappear south to Cornerstone, never to return. Never ever ever. Hundreds have taken this one-way trip—architects, engineers, physicists, contractors, and mathematicians. And they aren't just Americans, Varsity, they come from *all over* the place. Which is how /b spotted it. There were too many people trying to order breakfast at Denny's in broken English. Like seriously, that's the level of messed-up-ed-ness."

It was a conspiracy theorist's dream, which meant that everyone else thought it was a bunch of bull—people seeing patterns on a Rorschach test. It didn't help Milk that some of the crazies started claiming they saw Bigfoot, Chupacabra, the Mexican vampire monster, and all sorts of other weird blue and red animals stalking the nights and waters in southern Texas.

Leo took a tactful approach. "I admit it's weird stuff, but what better way to find out than to take the internship and poke around?"

Milk finally shut up. "That's the first intelligent thing you have said." The chance to know more about the black site had landed.

"So, the lies and hypocrisy will be exposed?" he added facetiously.

"You are an idiot," she said. She crossed her arms around her chest, like she was trying to hold onto something too heavy.

"I'm with Milk," Alastair said. He tossed a breadstick at her. She let it bounce off her arms, instead of catching it.

"How else are we going to find out?" said Leo. "Think about it, Alastair, we have to go on the internship. It's not like we can just graduate and do what? Work at Waterworld? You are Albert Einstein. I'm Leonardo da Vinci."

"You *are not* Leonardo da Vinci," a few people said simultaneously.

"I am. *I am* Leonardo. Nature is deterministic. We are just software and hardware machines and my machine is exactly like his. *Exactly*. We have the illusion of free will, but everything about us starts with those 3 billion base pairs of amino acids, right? The way we react, our emotions, our strength, our weaknesses. It is all pre-determined by our DNA. It just needs to be expressed into the real world. Aren't you fascinated by what it will be like? What new things we can do, now that we know? It's like you just discovered your crappy Ford Explorer is a Ferrari. Let's take these minds for a test drive, right?"

"It's not crappy," said Alastair.

"It is." Leo poked Alastair's chest. "Albert Einstein," he said. He went around the table, pointing at people. "Charles Darwin, Thomas Edison, Marie Curie, Catherine the Great. *Isaac Newton, for God's sakes.* Emilie Chatelet. Lucien Freud. We are all potential greatness that needs to be expressed," said Leo. "And the path of least resistance right now is Gene-E Corp. They have a plan for us; it's obvious. Aren't you curious?"

Milk nodded.

"And, we will all be living together," Leo added. "It's going to be fun, I promise."

"It won't be fun," Milk said.

"And necessary," said Leo.

"OK," Alastair replied, falling into line behind Leo like usual.

The dinner was over suddenly. Alastair got up from the table and headed outside, trailing the others. At the same time, a woman in a deep corner of the restaurant also got up and followed him. She was in her early thirties and despite her beauty and expensive clothes, she was invisible somehow. She moved in a way that didn't attract any attention, like a lightbulb that, when on, burns with fierce energy, but when off, is grey and nondescript.

When the group of friends stopped suddenly on the sidewalk, arguing, she tripped and fell into the middle of them. Her ankle twisted on a cement bump.

Leo helped her up, though he didn't stop his argument with Alastair. The contents of her purse spread out on the ground: tissues, makeup, and some Pokémon cards. A gun. The woman stuffed everything back down into her purse before anyone noticed, and then left, saying nothing, her invisibility somewhat intact.

***

The kids said their goodbyes to their parents and headed next door to the local used bookstore, descending into overstuffed aisles to find books, all the books, about their namesakes. They lay on the ground, spreading the tomes out, devouring them. Kat flipped through her phone, bored. Leo sat cross-legged on the floor with a giant coffee table book about Leonardo da Vinci in his lap.

"Listen to this, Kat: *Why did nature not ordain that one animal should not live by the death of another? Nature, being inconstant and taking pleasure in creating and continually producing new forms, because she knows that her terrestrial materials are thereby augmented, is more ready and swift in creating than time is in destructing.*"

Leo flipped through the book on what his DNA had previously accomplished. "And this: *The water which you touch in a river is the last of that which has passed and the first of that which is to come. The same is true of the present moment: life well spent is long.*"

As Leo turned the pages, masterpiece after masterpiece flashed by: inventions, helicopters, gears, weapons, anatomical drawings, the Mona Lisa, the Codex with hundreds of pages of profound philosophical insights. "I have to get organized," Leo said, half to himself.

***

Alastair browsed the used comics section. Kat came up to him.

"I know how you feel, you know," she said.

"I am sure you do," said Alastair. He was not used to chatting alone with her. She rarely, if ever, said what she was thinking, and any direct conversation always made him feel uneasy. Kat never made small talk. When she did, it was mildly terrifying.

"I do." She thumbed a comic. Alastair watched her out the corner of his eye, like you would a raccoon if you were locked in a dark garage with it. "I feel like me," Kat added. "Not someone else." She stopped, clearly waiting for Alastair to respond.

There was a long silence.

"Aren't you going to get any books on yourself?" he asked.

"Not interested. Not sure why everyone is buying into this so much. You should think about that."

It was a hint. Alastair knew Kat well enough to take whatever crumbs she offered.

"You're more like Einstein than me," he said. "At least you get great grades."

It was a common myth that Einstein was a C student, created by the fact that one of his teachers said he would never amount to anything. He refused to memorize his multiplication tables, instead wanting to do the math from scratch each time. He still got As.

"You get good grades," said Kat.

"Not Einstein good."

"Not Einstein good, I guess," said Kat. "But that's cause you can't get out of your own way."

"Am I meant to? Is that actually important?"

Now it was Kat's turn to pause and consider.

Leo bounced up like a Labrador. "I could get used to being called Leonardo, I've decided," he said. "Could you—"

"Fat chance," said Kat, cutting him off.

Alastair welcomed the intrusion.

"We are going to be rock stars, you know that right?" Leo added.

"You heard what my mother said," Kat said. "This is our greatest, most precious secret to keep," she said, quoting Ms. Yaektova's lecture at graduation.

"There is no way this is staying secret," said Leo. "I am telling you, we could be on the cover of Rolling Stone magazine tomorrow, with millions of Youtube subs. Leonardo. Da. Vinci. Tik Tok. Instagram. I wonder if I Twitter would give me the verified logo."

Kat looked like she was going to barf.

"What?" said Leo. "I'm just saying."

One aisle over, the invisible woman from the Spaghetti Factory browsed quietly, listening.

"It does explain why you are such a good artist," said Alastair.

"You too. You have one of the two greatest brains in the history of the world," said Leo. "Think about it. And who has the other greatest brain?" Leo asked Kat, expecting the answer to be himself.

She pointed down the aisle. Zack was on the floor reading a book about economics. "That guy. I. Zack. Newton," Kat said, emphasizing every syllable.

Zack looked up when he realized he was being watched. "Hi," he said and went back to his book.

"Guys, you have to admit, this is pretty awesome," Leo said. "We are like superheroes."

"Enough. You really like this, don't you?" said Alastair. "You just think it is going to get you laid."

"Of course I do. All of us, even you. Do you know the amount of—"

Milk joined them with a ton of books in her arms.

"Ms. Martin Luther King, everyone," said Leo, "how's that for a head-line."

Everyone abandoned Leo for the check out.

The bookstore closed. They said their goodbyes and arranged to meet before their flight to Gene-E Corp the next morning.

"I'm going to walk home," Alastair said, separating from the group. He wanted some alone time.

***

Alastair walked home the long way, through old trees and shadows. The street was quiet except for night sounds. A distant car alarm. The odd street sweeper. The ordinariness of it calmed Alastair's mind.

"Albert."

Alastair slowed. A woman sat on a bench in a well-lit area. He didn't say anything, considering her.

He didn't know her.

"Sit. Please, would you join me?" the woman requested in a pleasant British accent. She was well dressed, designer clothes, tasteful, and seemed friendly. So he sat down. He was in no rush to see his parents again. Their guilty faces exhausted him.

"My name is Alastair."

The woman patted Alastair's leg. "Are you not Einstein? In time, perhaps?"

"Trust me. It's Alastair."

"In time. My name is Sephora Neiman."

Under her British accent, there was a hint of Russian.

BOOK TWO

THIRTY SECONDS AND COUNTING

The room had the feel of an accountant's closet. Too many filing cabinets were stuffed into the small, drab space. The artificial light was an off-yellow puce that stuck to visitors even after they had left and moved on, like the chill that stays with you after a visit to a graveyard.

Paul Summers sat on a folding chair pressed into the corner with two subordinates stacked behind him. He was smoking, which made the room that much more unbearable, but no one said anything. Their boss had the crush of the world on his shoulders, and if he wanted to give himself—and them—lung cancer, they were fine with it. They would go to the grave with him, spitting blood.

The group watched the Joint Chiefs of Staff video conference on a cheap monitor. Silent. Three others sat on Paul's desk, their legs akimbo between cluttered shelves and boxes. The group had been working for weeks on end. Their suits were disheveled, their eyes dark circles of professional regret at being buried alive under a mountain of paperwork, secrecy, and cold calculations on death tolls. Game theory had taken its due on their souls, leaving them empty at the most important moment of the project to date.

Teigen Ralls, Gene-E Corp's loud founder and CEO, was updating America's military brass on Cornerstone's progress. His big potbelly filled the bottom of the screen, bouncing up and down in rhythm with his oratory. He wore a shirt that once fit him, but now the buttons bulged out in protest—the physical manifestation of id and ego, a man with a massive appetite for beer and the impossible. And while his enthusiasm was once infectious, seeing the infamous titan in such a contrite position had become awkward. The worse the situation, the better it was. The louder his talk, the greater the possibility. And usually, Teigen Ralls was right. Until now.

A commuter flight out of Denver had forced the meeting. It never arrived, falling and then disappearing into thin air, or the thin future, depending on how you looked at it. *Somewhere*, thought Paul, *the president is also watching this feed.*

"The NTSB issues seem to be isolated," Ralls said in his sweaty, flushed manner. "We are looking at new flight paths out of Corpus." His confidence was still there, but he seemed to be cracking under the pressure of each successive update demanded by the Joint Chiefs of Staff. Ralls knew the government was looking to remove Gene-E Corp from the project and go full dark with it. Ralls had been fighting to contain the leaks and keep the project in his purview.

"We've had to widen the COA and include the board of the FAA to slow down the release of information on the Corpus Christi anomaly."

"Anomaly?" asked one of the Joint Chiefs."

"The plane accidents, General," Ralls said, not flinching. "And the oil rig sinking. We think they are related."

COA, Circle of Awareness, thought Paul with a sad exhale. It was a catch-all term Ralls came up with to describe the amount of people who were aware of some aspect of the project. Because Cornerstone had started in the commercial sector with the Gene-E Corp discovery, it did not have the Manhattan Project–level secrecy the situation currently demanded. It was also much harder these days for a big government project to stay hidden. COA was designed to deal with shades of secrecy, leaks, and misinformation. Much of Paul's office spent time trying to understand and calculate the likelihood that any one event would trigger a tipping point in public awareness.

"The scattered reports of animal sightings south of Corpus are contained. The breach in the ocean nets from cycle 38A have been repaired. Ferromagnetic ants are the only worry right now, but they seem to have settled in below ground. We don't expect them to be a problem."

In the early days, Paul had championed a new approach to secrecy called Alternate Reality Flooding (ARF), huge data dumps onto the internet whenever there was a leak. The logic was that it was easier to bury a secret in plain sight than it was to try to disappear it. Plus, all of the search engine companies were now in Cornerstone's COA, able to direct queries about "areas of concern" to mundane and misleading results. In the beginning, the search companies would receive a government memo about a tweak to their search algorithms every few months.

Now, it was daily. A classified memo would go out, and the internet would present a slightly different version of reality, consistent across all search sites. Everywhere. The basic premise of ARF was that no one experienced anything firsthand anymore, and if the filter between what happened and what is presented can be controlled, nothing would bubble up. It used to be that you wanted someone to bark up the wrong tree. Now, with ARF, there were too many trees to bark up, so no one bothered. The truth was lost in a forest of nothing.

But Paul knew Cornerstone was getting too big to hide. Even under the avalanche of misinformation and management by his office, it was starting to show its hem, as Paul had predicted in his very first white paper on the insane project. And these days, the puppet master, Teigen Ralls, had to dance more and more.

"And what about the reports of a multiparty incursion south of the central dam?"

"Just some lost workers from the drone survey."

"Who shot two of our guards?" replied the joint sec aridly.

Ralls stalled. "I will look into that, sir," he said.

He was a good salesman but a bad liar, a combination you didn't often see.

"We have another time cycle in two days in conjunction with the arrival of alpha class. We have moved up their graduation, and they are now aware."

Paul dropped his head, running his hands over the back of his neck, massaging his shoulders. "Chattel," he said to no one.

The military brass sat stony-faced. Ralls finished his briefing with all the discoveries and promises of Cornerstone. He outlined the benefits to mankind that Isaac's discovery had already created despite the nuisances and minor setbacks they had encountered.

The Joint Chiefs thanked him.

"The CBO will draft budget considerations," he added.

The feed cut out.

Paul turned to his team. "Well?"

"He didn't mention the oil," someone said.

"I know. It is a prob—"

His phone rang before he had a chance to finish.

"Yes, I was watching."

Pause.

"Yes, Mr. President, I am concerned."

There was another long pause. The president was a slow talker.

"I understand." Paul hung up, lost in thought.

"Well?" someone asked.

"The president is worried about Texercon. They know about Cornerstone now and are lobbying hard for the technology. He said it is one thing to bully a search engine run by forty-year-olds, but it was a whole other thing to force a multi-billion-dollar oil company to ignore how a mostly valueless oil deposit grew overnight into a massive deposit of high-end crude oil stretching the length of Texas. He thinks he can control Texercon, but he's worried about the other multinationals, particularly the Russian-backed petrochems. They are sniffing about, drilling test wells."

Paul stood up, stretching his back. He lit another cigarette.

"The president wants me to go down to Cornerstone to assess Ralls and for us to deliver a report on whether the government should assume all control over the project and go dark. It needs to be done in three days."

"I know," he said, reading their looks. "Figure it out, and please, write it in English, and short sentences. But this time, start with the dangers, not the opportunities."

Paul collected some papers on his desk, shoving a bunch into a trash can. "I am sorry, but as we go, so does the president."

They scurried out of the room with the dry fuel of pride in their steps.

TWENTY-NINE SECONDS

Jimmy didn't want to tell his father about what he saw under the rig. He knew the story would light a bonfire in his dad's mind, kindling an already unstoppable obsession for monsters and conspiracy, but Jimmy was drowning, and he needed a parent.

Inside the dark house, opposite the suspicious wraith of a father, Jimmy wove a tale about millions of shrimps, precision arc welding, blow-up dolls, giant neon sea creatures, translucent sharks, bus-sized red-and-blue turtles, and meditating at the bottom of the world, chest deep in an impossible, mind-bending horizon of dense oil, turtles rising and falling beneath it like they too were drowning in slow motion.

When he finished, his father didn't react.

Jimmy listened to the low hum of a fan like it might instead have some fatherly insight on the matter.

"Need some thinking juice," Cayce said, turning up his oxygen. Then, he said, "Bullshit, kid."

They argued until they both shouted. Cayce understood nitrogen narcosis, he said, having experienced it himself as a Navy ordinance diver training a support Clearance Team off the coast of Vietnam. Recovering deep-water anchors, he had imagined he was being chased by the Vietcong underwater, bullets flying by him from underwater foxholes. It was very embarrassing to be dragged up to the surface by his men. He never lived it down during the war, which quietly enraged him at the time and openly enraged him later, driving his intense hatred of the military.

Cayce pressed Jimmy on the blowout preventer. If it fails, it can sink an oil platform. Cayce wanted to know exactly what Jimmy had done wrong.

Technically. For the moment, Cayce's disapproval as a father and as a former commercial diver outweighed his obsession with conspiracies. His son had become the scapegoat on the local Fox News, and Cayce needed his own underwater ammo for when he saw his welding buddies.

But more importantly, he wanted to know why Jimmy was lying, he said. After nitrogen narcosis, if you survive it, the truth is evident. But for some reason, Jimmy refused to cop to it.

Vietcong cannot breathe underwater despite their intense ability to survive trying situations. There was no question what happened to Cayce.

"It is moral weakness to lie to yourself. The worst kind of lie," Cayce said, living up to his name and the hard truth about life his parents had taught him. "Why did the oil rig get sunk then?" he said. "I need an answer."

Jimmy ran his fingers through his hair. "You believe in all of this Bermuda Triangle crap," said Jimmy, "so why do only you get to be the expert on unexplainable things? I am lying to myself? You do it all day long."

"Because *you are* my son, that's why. We're screwups. And I've been one for longer. So I have seniority." Cayce went to get up, but the yelling had weakened him.

Jimmy deflated, the anger dissipating. "I didn't sink the rig," he said softly now. "I just happened to be under it when it did. There's a woman, a real nice girl in the burn unit, and she has it much worse than me, but my weld was perfect. And I really saw those animals. They were monsters, giant turtles, like in *Sinbad*, sort of," he said. "Enormous things. Ten times as long as me or you. And they were blue and red, split right down the middle. Like they were designed that way."

"Blue and red?"

"Right down the middle."

"Like they were designed?" repeated Cayce. He stopped talking, the look of disappointment in the creases of his mouth.

Jimmy knew that look, his father's look. *How does he have so much power over me?* He glanced around the house, as if seeing it for the first time again. It was trashed, literally, with garbage everywhere, stains on the walls, and his father's yellowed, nicotine-stained fingers. He couldn't look in his eyes yet. It all made him so sad. His father had once truly been a great man.

It was no use trying to convince him, Jimmy suddenly realized. He was too far gone. There was no safe harbor for Jimmy here anymore after years of being lost at sea.

"A blue-and-red turtle, you say?" Cayce said, getting up on his second try. He went through the darkness, headed down the hall, his oxygen tank slowly in tow. Jimmy followed, wanting to give up on the fight and find a way back to the conversation. He didn't need to win anymore.

"Why don't you have any lights on, at least?" said Jimmy.

"Because you can't afford the bill."

It wasn't fair, but Jimmy knew that the rest of the conversation would be him conceding to everything his father said.

"I thought you were dead, okay," his dad barked, causing another fit of coughing.

"I should have called you earlier," Jimmy said, fast-forwarding to the next phase of the conversation where they made up.

"Get off." Cayce went into the garage, which was a converted workspace. Animals in various states of taxidermy hung from the wood rafters. Skeletons sat in containers of bleach, the ligaments and flesh slowly dissolving their bonds. The organization and attention to detail was at odds with the hoarder house that surrounded it.

Jimmy noticed the windows were covered in tinfoil now, which was new, and not a good sign for his father's mental health. Slits had been cut into them to let in shafts of light into the dark space.

After he had retired, Cayce had combined his interest in hunting and taxidermy with cryptozoology. Late into the nights, he created fantastic beasts out of multiple animals, posing them into absurd scenes, and then selling the Frankenstein pieces at conspiracy conventions and online. He made the front page of Reddit once with a rocky tableau featuring a jackalope—the mythic North American jackrabbit with antler horns—in a mortal battle with a skeletal dog with three heads and chimpanzee arms. His most famous creation was the manimal—a real human skeleton combined artfully with the bones from a dolphin and a tiger to create a skeletal warrior.

Cayce's passion for monsters—the stripping and boiling of flesh off skeletons—unnerved Jimmy. However, it was a productive form of crazy that kept his father away from the conspiracy forums online, which were much more terrifying, so he put up with it.

Cayce turned on a desk lamp and used some tongs to reach into a giant boiler pot that was simmering on a stove. Jimmy winced. He never knew what his dad was cooking up. Heads had come out of that pot before. A turtle shell emerged from the steam. It was about a foot wide and two colors, red and blue, bisected down the middle.

"Red and blue," said Jimmy.

"Yup."

"So you believe me?"

"I bought it yesterday at Conspiracy Con, down at Mayfield's Mall."

Nicknamed ConCon, the conference had been shut down in previous years due to lack of organization, but with a new influx of mysterious cash, the "Coachella of Conspiracy" was back on its feet, traveling through the Southwest, renting abandoned malls because they were cheap, trading on fear, wild conjecture, and loneliness for a hundred bucks a speaker.

"When?" said Jimmy.

"Yesterday. It's still going. I was going to make this into a chest plate for an Asian battle raccoon and sell it on the last day."

Jimmy ran his hand over the shell. The colors didn't look like one of his dad's typical crypto fake jobs. The shell itself was red and blue, not a coating or paint. And it seemed old. Jimmy took a screwdriver and chipped a barnacle off of it. The red continued underneath the barnacle. Then, Jimmy made a gash into the shell with the screwdriver. The red went down into the scar as well.

"I paid for that, you know," said Cayce.

On the blue side of the turtle, it was the same thing. The color went all the way down. It wasn't a paint job.

"You bought this yesterday?" said Jimmy.

"There was a fellow there selling a whole bunch of them he found on a beach somewhere, going on about Cornerstone. He thinks they are juveniles."

Jimmy turned the turtle in his hand, feeling his sanity drain back into his body. He took his first real breath in days.

"I didn't sink that rig," Jimmy said.

"I know, kid, but everyone else thinks so, so what's the difference?"

TWENTY-EIGHT SECONDS

In the beginning of Cornerstone, Paul slept on a couch at the Pentagon. He found one in an empty office and would catch what sleep he could during the insane first few months. His policy papers were deciding the course of American history, he knew. And going home—the commute, the shower, the kiss on the cheek, and the drive back—seemed to be an irresponsible use of time. In usual Pentagon fashion, no one disagreed. He was a rock star in the halls, and when his staff quietly shuttled in a real bed for him, furniture for clothes, and softer lighting, no one complained. It was the Pentagon's cold kiss on the cheek.

Paul hadn't left the building in weeks. Now, he was hurriedly packing to leave. A four-star general showed up at his door.

"Permission to enter?" he asked. General Ed Manders was in full military dress. He might as well have been walking onto the bridge of a destroyer instead of a makeshift bedroom.

"Oh, okay," Paul said, trying to clean up his bed. "I get it. I'm really sorry," he said.

"Continue packing. I just came for a chat," he said, sitting on the bed. "I like what you've done to the place."

"Well, I—"

"It's fine, of course." The general spotted a poster of Cardi B taped to the ceiling. "She's a great actress."

Paul's staff had taped it there. "She's—"

"Do you have any projections you expect to report back on?" asked the general.

Paul was happy to get back to the subject of Cornerstone. "I'm going in open-minded."

The general considered this. He was measured. "Please don't. It's that type of thought that got us here, I think. Sometimes decisions, once they are made, can't be unmade. And a lot of people in this building want the project to succeed, but you are the one person the president listens to," he said, glancing at the poster. "If you think, for a second, that Cornerstone is a danger to this country, or planet ... get back here, write one of your papers, the *last* paper on the subject, and kill it. For good. Okay?"

"Okay."

"We have never used a nuclear weapon in war since the last time we had to. America chose not to use them because of little white papers written by guys like you"—he looked around the room—"living in the Pentagon. We don't want to use one again. And certainly not on our own soil. Your words have power. You can stop this if necessary. Don't listen to anyone but yourself. Obtain the details and get back here."

"What about the kids?"

"The kids are a distraction. Cornerstone is already out of control. It doesn't matter who they are—or were—they are still just teenagers. They won't fix this mess. It is up to you."

Paul went back to packing.

"How long is your flight?"

"Three hours. Layover in Chicago."

"New plan," the general said.

Two drivers were already at the door.

"Make sure Mr. Summers's luggage gets to the base," he said. "They will look after you."

"Yes, sir," said Paul.

"The last paper."

"Yes, sir."

"Ikea?"

"Pardon?"

"Your furniture."

"I'm not sure, sir."

"It's your job to know. Always have an opinion."

"Ikea it is, sir."

"I like it," he said with one last look around the room and left.

Paul had never been in a presidential motorcade, but he knew he was a target, and considering how protected he had been inside the Pentagon, it made sense. The government's paranoia extended out into the real world. The city of Washington streaked by in a blur of rain and blue-and-red lights. He was in the Beast, the president's limousine. Built to withstand a mortar and aerial assault, it weighed over ten tons with doors heavier than those on a 747.

Next to Paul's hip, there was a hermetically sealed compartment containing the entire first family's blood, in case of a transfusion en route to the hospital. It was the safest mode of car transportation in the world, even at eighty miles an hour in the rain, ripping through red light after red light.

A voice sounded on the intercom: "You have a call. Would you like to take it?"

He couldn't imagine no would be a satisfactory answer.

"Paul! Hey, man, how's it going? I heard you were coming down for a visit." The audio in the limousine was flawless; it was like Ralls was sitting in the vehicle with Paul.

Paul was glad he wasn't.

"The president asked me to come down for another evaluation," he said.

"I know, I know. You are more than welcome."

"This time," he said.

"Yes, this time, we have a much better grasp on things."

"What about the crash?"

"That's their fault. The NTSB knew we were closing down the aerospace."

It was never Ralls's fault. *A terrible trait for a leader*, thought Paul. Especially when everything was going wrong. He was always that way. It was surprising that Ralls had maintained control of the project this long, a measure of how good a salesman he was and how poor of a scientist.

The initial discovery had nothing to do with Ralls, though he took credit for it. A graduate student in his lab found a new way to do a somatic transfer of nuclear DNA in a study on how to diminish antibiotic resistance in pigs. Ralls, to his credit, realized that the technique solved one of the most confounding hurdles faced by companies working with human stem cells. The graduate student went back to graduate school, while Ralls went to investors. He originally called his company Genius Inc., a not-so-subtle nod to the aims of the start-up that would eventually gobble up the Pentagon. After a few branding studies were done, the name changed to Gene-E Corp, a play on the word *genie*. "The E is for Einstein," Ralls would tell anyone with money who would listen.

He would begin his elaborate presentation with the most shocking fact: cloning humans is not illegal at the federal level in America. Fifteen states have laws that ban the cloning of human DNA, mostly due to advocacy by the religious right. More importantly, thirty-five states have no laws regarding cloning at all.

At first, Ralls's business plan was to offer commercial services to recently bereaved families who lost babies and wanted to clone them, much like pet owners who can pay to clone their recently deceased furry loved ones. But no matter how many anonymous marketing studies he did, religious people saw it as playing God. Baby Jesus needed to stay that way, dead.

Ralls soon realized that in playing it safe, he was actually taking the riskier direction. Even though laws weren't on the books yet, he sensed that if he went wide with his discovery, they soon would be. He needed to make his product more valuable, indispensable. Hence Gene-E Corp, the first company to attempt to resurrect the greatest minds in history, selling its wares directly to the US military. Cynical but savvy.

After he had secured an IFB (Invitation For Bid) from the Pentagon, Ralls quickly raised the millions necessary to buy the DNA samples. The largest group came from the defunct Academy of Medical Sciences in Russia. Despite the amount of money required to buy the DNA, Ralls always maintained that it was all in the name of science. Not that the Russian oligarchs behind the sale cared. DNA was just another commodity they were willing to sell to the highest bidders when the Iron Curtain fell and Russia found itself on Craigslist.

Twenty years later, Ralls and the US Government were finally seeing a return on their billion-dollar investment, the Cornerstone Project. And it was Paul's mess to figure out whether that was a very good thing or a very bad thing.

Ralls finished up his sales speech. Paul knew better than to stop an orator midstream. It wasn't worth the petulance on the other side. He let Ralls wind down with his narcissism intact.

Ralls ended like he began. "It's a beautiful thing."

"Do the children know yet?" asked Paul.

"They are not children. And yes. They are excited about the possibilities."

"Not that. I mean about the internship? Have you told them exactly what that entails?"

"No, they don't know that yet."

"When is the next cycle scheduled?" asked Paul.

"In three days. Tuesday," Ralls replied. "More than enough time to get them ready."

Paul doubted that. The fact that Gene-E Corp had managed to resurrect the likes of Einstein, da Vinci, and Newton was a parlor trick compared to what the Cornerstone Project had in store. "It is one thing to raise a genius, but it is the by-product of the genius that matters," Ralls would say. He sold the government over twenty years ago with that mantra, and now mankind stood on the precipice of his spin.

"What would happen if you gave Isaac Newton a particle accelerator?" Ralls would ask his wide-eyed investors.

Bad things, apparently, thought Paul.

"I heard there has been another species sighting outside the Crypt," Paul said.

"Just a commercial diver from the Texercon oil event," Ralls said, hedging. "Saw some odd sea life. Nothing important. It actually helps us that they are conspiracists."

"His father is making a lot of noise online, as well."

After a long pause, Ralls said "I didn't take you for the conspiracy bulletin board type. Maybe you can chat with them. Offer them a job?" Ralls said. "And please don't call it the Crypt," he added.

Paul realized his slip. The Crypt was a nickname his staff called the project after everyone started dying.

"What would you like me to call it?" asked Paul.

"The Naut, of course," said Ralls.

The Naut. The words hung in the air.

Paul had never heard the name before, mostly using "the biosphere" when describing the project in formal settings. He knew what "Naut" was short for, but the word still carried the air of mystery.

"Will you talk with them?" said Ralls

"Is that what you want?"

"I want to offer them a job. That's all. In the Crypt, as you call it."

Now it was Paul's turn to be quiet.

TWENTY-SEVEN SECONDS

When the class arrived at the regional airport for their internships, two of Gene-E Corp's jets were waiting for them. Both 747s had dramatic Gene-E Corp logos emblazoned in red and blue across their length. One airplane was headed to the Cornerstone facility outside Corpus Christi, Texas, with Leo, Alastair, Milk, Zack, and Kat, while the other airplane would soon disappear to North Dakota with the rest of the class.

Paul watched Kat and Milk board with Zack, while Leo rolled around on his BMX, checking out the undercarriage of the airplane.

Alastair was missing.

On the plane, each kid had their private sky couch with their "names" on placards. Leo grabbed his sign and put it in his pocket. He leaned into the soft leather and angled out the computer mounted on a swivel arm to his right.

Once they were settled, Teigen Ralls came on board. Paul was behind him.

Ralls introduced himself to the crowd, though the kids all knew who Teigen Ralls was—Gene-E Corp's loud founder and CEO who financed their school. His big potbelly filled the aisle, bouncing up and down in rhythm with his small talk and glad-handing, like the kids had just won the state championship. And while his enthusiasm was once infectious to others, seeing the infamous ogre trying to fake enthusiasm was awkward. The worse the situation, the better it was. The louder his talk, the greater the possibility. And usually, Teigen Ralls was right. Until now.

He puffed up and started his speech, talking to the kids like they were ghosts that had returned from the dead (and weren't teenagers from Ohio.) It was his subtle use of the second possessive—you, your, yours—that was eerie. "Zack, when *you* discovered gravity, it was …"

It was one of his weaker performances, thought Paul.

Ralls was losing his audience. He seemed distracted. His eyes flicked to Paul every so often. And then to Alastair's empty seat next to him. He checked his watch. "You will accomplish great things once again," he said.

Paul sensed worry. Or stress. *Or was it guilt?*

Ralls finished up and then sat down on Zack's armrest, attempting to chat with the unchattable boy.

"Where's Alastair?" Leo whispered to Milk.

She shook her head; she didn't know.

His seat was empty, the little placard that said EINSTEIN unaccompanied.

***

Two hours later, the seat was still empty. The 747 baked on the runway, and the hot pockets inside started to warm up. Ralls was testy. He had been on the phone with the school, Alastair's parents, the local police, and hospitals. But Alastair was still AWOL.

"We're leaving," Ralls said to the pilots, pushing his big frame into the cockpit.

Paul came up to the front. "Are you sure?" he asked.

"We can't wait. We have to make this cycle," said Ralls.

The plane started moving.

"You could push it a day, there is no reason to rush, is there? Considering the flip side?" asked Paul. He was less concerned with Alastair and more interested in seeing Ralls's reaction to his suggestion.

"We must fire on Tuesday. There is no option. Einstein or no Einstein. History is bigger than any one man," said Ralls.

"Or boy," added Paul.

"Yes. Or boy," Ralls repeated.

The engines roared to life. Ralls stood square in the aisle, eating nuts, as they lifted off for Texas.

TWENTY-SIX SECONDS

Jimmy arrived at ConCon with his hands in his pockets, as if it would protect him from the intense idiocy he was about to sludge through. The bimonthly crazy town conference was held at Mayfields, an abandoned mall that had been popular in the seventies just far enough from civilized society to be ignored for the day. With the rise of the big-box stores and Walmart, the traditional building had slowly emptied out over the years, leaving aging retail decor, a few seasonal pop-up businesses, and clearance shoe retailers in between the empty storefronts.

And a bunch of crackpots.

Outside the mall, conspiracy fans swirled in the parking lot under aging halogen lights, waiting for the event to open. There were Flat Earthers, creationists, paranoid schizophrenics, 9/11 Truthers, Sandy Hook False Flaggers, those who believed in chemtrails, who believed in the Illuminati, who were against anti-vaxxers and cryptozoologists alike.

None of them trusted each other. At ConCon, it was sort of like trying to organize anarchists; there were structural deficiencies to throwing an event.

Jimmy saw someone walk by with an amazing model of the earth as a big, flat disk held up by a muscular modern day Atlas, Sydney Shenton, founder of the International Flat Earth Research Society.

It was a trying group, thought Jimmy, not because their beliefs were often insane but because they often were successful at making sane arguments, and you had to hunt for the logical inaccuracy in a field of logic bombs. A whole conspiracy could obviously be nuts—the earth is not flat—but if you got into the weeds, there were often long, unbroken chains of reason, which led to absurd places.

It was infuriating.

And some, like Jimmy's father, were brilliant at forging the chains that imprison weak minds. Throw in the occasional mental illness, confirmation bias, the power of the internet to amplify people with similar beliefs, and Texas stubbornness, and you had a truly challenging group on the sunny morning. Of course, like all families, some were worse than others. Even the people who believed President Bush's family were lizards thought the Flat Earthers were idiots. The two camps would often break out into fights at the coffee stations.

Cayce unpacked his creations. He had used his acetylene torch to neatly cut out the side of his van so the panel could hinge up and out "professionally." Inside, sloped shelves displayed his taxidermy monsters for sale, luring a grab bag of people with questionable psychological profiles.

Jimmy watched his father set up, sadness creeping into him. He was afraid of becoming his father: out of a job, sick, and bullshitting people for a couple of bucks. Cayce Jones wasn't always obsessed with conspiracy, his mythic name notwithstanding. It began during his grief over the death of Jimmy's mother, who died during a hysterectomy. It was a real medical conspiracy made more complicated because Jimmy's mother was part of a long running government fertility and surrogacy study. The study had extra layers of legal protections surrounding patient anonymity, so Cayce never got an answer. And soon, she faded into myth as well. When Jimmy was in middle school, Cayce's conspiracy theories, and the conferences, seemed dangerous and, as a result, fun. The myths, the monsters, and the allegations of cover-ups made the world interesting. But as Jimmy got older and started excelling in school, the falsehoods his father raged about with Jimmy weighed him down and embarrassed him.

Cayce argued with someone now, getting a lot of attention for his bullshit Snaketopus, a collection of eight snake skeletons that had been arranged together with a ferret's skull to form a sort of bony octopus nightmare.

The customer bought the Snaketopus anyway, conceding that in the antipodes beneath flat earth, it made sense that there could be adaptations that favored bony octopi.

"Thirty bucks," Cayce said to his son with a big smile. "That'll pay for something."

"How much did the skeletons cost?"

"Forty," Cayce said, laughing.

A guy limped up, wafting the eighties with him, cash in hand. "Hey kid, heard you sunk that rig out there," he said. He wore a Vietnam hat and looked at the creatures on sale suspiciously. "Steve's boy died on it, you know."

Jimmy had been friends with the man's son in high school. "I know, sir," said Jimmy. "Real sorry about that."

"I'm sure you are. Probably more Cornerstone bullshit. You got any more of those squirrel things?" the man asked Cayce. "I thought you'd be in graduate school or something by now," he said to Jimmy, "till I heard about the sinking and your name on the news. Didn't know you went into diving like this shithead."

"We're done," Cayce said, slamming shut the van. "No more snakes today. Let's go find that turtle guy," he said to Jimmy.

As they approached the front of the mall, another man stepped up to talk to them.

"I'm closed till after lunch," Cayce said, his free hand already up.

The man was trim and stood still despite seeming like he was in an incredible rush. He introduced himself as Paul Anthony Michael from the Pentagon. "Can we chat?" he said. "You are Jimmy, right? The diver?" Paul said, double-checking photos he had on his phone to make sure he had the right person.

Behind Paul, Jimmy could see a military vehicle parked at the curb and two men watching them closely from a distance.

"You have three first names?" said Cayce. He added that he was suspicious of anyone with three first names, saying they were usually serial killers.

"I guess I am sort of, depending on how you look at it. I'm with the government," Paul said, trying to be funny. When neither Jimmy nor Cayce reacted, he added, "I'm with Cornerstone."

***

Jimmy eyed Paul warily as he stuffed fried onions into his face.

Paul apologized for being so hungry, humblebragging about the lack of snacks in the president's limo earlier in the day. They were at a diner, and the fried onion had arrived at the table, signaling it was time to talk.

"I want to know what you saw. Under the rig before it sank," said Paul.

Jimmy didn't say anything, weighing in his mind if he could trust the man. His instincts said no, but he didn't know what else to do. This man clearly had information, and more importantly, Jimmy needed a job, so he broke his general rule about prying assholes and started talking.

And talking—about saturation diving, perfect welds, black oil, hallucinations, and aliens coming to gather his soul.

Paul had his phone out, recording.

After Jimmy was done, he waited for a response from Paul, but the man instead took a long sip of his coffee, thinking.

Then, Paul seemed to make a decision and said, "We are looking for a deep-water diver at Cornerstone. A guy like you who can go deep, a full saturation dive, but also knows technical cave diving. We have a problem, and maybe you can fix it."

"My skills weren't much use last time," said Jimmy.

His father was silent on the topic.

"We'll have your back. You won't be alone down there."

Jimmy laughed but then looked at his dad, expecting support, but Cayce was dead serious, studying Paul's face. Jimmy looked at his plate, thinking, gathering his thoughts.

"Down where?" asked Cayce.

Jimmy had performed some of the world's most dangerous cave dives as part of his reckless chase to earn the most extreme diving trophies. He had been stuck, head down, far beneath the surface of the earth, shoulders wedged in flooded cave tubes, wiggling through small holes, moving his sidemount oxygen tanks between his legs. In Belize, he connected the world's largest two cave systems by swimming one way through increasingly smaller lava tubes, on the suspect assumption that the oxygen tanks he staged in the other cave system would be there when he found the connection.

It was a suicidal hobby. Though he never boasted about it online, others did. And he read every comment. His dad secretly printed them out on old, yellowed printer paper.

"We have a cave system we need to dive at Cornerstone. It's deep, and we don't know where it goes, but we need to know. And seeing as you are already somewhat familiar with what we are dealing with, we thought it might make sense to hire you."

"Cornerstone's military base is just west of Corpus Christi," said Cayce. "It ain't secret, we know about you, and there are no caves on the coast there, its flat as a pancake. So stop lying to us. We're from Texas. We invented bulls and shit. And this is some A-grade government bullshit," he said, twisting to Jimmy. "He just wants to silence you. Make you sign a bunch of contracts. Shutting us up."

"Actually, I want you both to sign my contract. And work for us."

It was the first mention that Paul was interested in his father as well. Though Cayce was once just as much of a diver as his son, this revelation skipped Jimmy's alert level up.

"Huh," said Jimmy, not hiding his suspicion.

"I'm not the one saying I saw monsters in the Gulf," said Paul, losing his warmth, matching Jimmy's temperature. "To be honest, it sounds like a lot of *bullshit* to me. Not sure why anyone would ever hire you with such a cocka-mamie story." It was a threat from the man from the Pentagon.

Cayce asked for the check.

"Can I tell you at least the basic terms?" asked Paul.

"You'd like to," said Jimmy.

"Ten-year guaranteed contract. Two million dollars. One million on signing. And if you don't want to do the dive, you keep the million, which also pays for your silence."

"You're trying to muzzle us," said Cayce. "That's what this is about."

"A part of it yes, a part of it no," said Paul, stirring his coffee.

Jimmy put a hand on his father's arm, pulling him back down to the table as he got up. "And for dad?"

"Same deal. You will need a dive tender," said Paul.

"It's too much money for this to be legitimate," said Cayce.

"We have all the money in the world. The government prints it. But there is only one of you. And we have a problem."

"Four million," said Jimmy.

Paul paused, smiling. "Yes, four million, two each."

Paul took out two contracts from his briefcase. He fished for a pen in his jacket pocket, putting a polonium vial he had received from Teigen Ralls onto the table, among other effects, absentmindedly. It was a sample recovered from a presumed Russian poisoning of a Cornerstone scientist. When Ralls gave it to Paul, it wasn't clear why.

"What's that?" asked Cayce, glancing at the vial.

Paul picked it up and looked at it, his eyebrows shooting up for a second. "Vitamin D extract. I don't get much sun at the Pentagon."

Paul put the vial back into his pocket and spread out the contracts, using a highlighter to mark up the key details for them to read.

"Where do people sign?" said Cayce.

"There."

"I don't sign things," said Cayce. He turned to Jimmy. "There is no job. This is just because we made a big stink online. Because we are going public. They are listening to us. Signals in the noise they have to snuff out."

"It's true that you two are a problem for Cornerstone," said Paul. "A thorn in the lion's paw, and we are trying to keep this quiet for National Security. But you," he pointed a French fry at Jimmy, "genuinely have skills I need."

"I don't need a dive tender for cave diving. It's not hose fed," Jimmy said.

Paul said he was being nice. He didn't want Cayce really.

"You are not smiling with your eyes," said Cayce, "which means you are lying. Or you are a serial killer. Which is it?"

"People die at Cornerstone, so maybe both. But if you ever want answers, Jimmy, I represent that. And you can have both the money and the truth. Or you can leave. No truth. No money. And never be taken seriously again in your life, like your father."

"Listen," said Cayce, "this man is not what he says he is. What does he want us for? As if the US military doesn't have divers. Or welders? They just *happen* to want to hire a diver and an old sick man as his dive tender. This is bigger than us. And we are making noise. They want us to shut up."

"That's what I said," said Paul. "It's not a conspiracy. It's literally what I said. Right now, I want you to shut up."

"But there's more you're not telling us," said Cayce.

"Once I leave this table, you will have nothing. No more information. No money. No job. You will be on the outside."

"We are not going. We are going to expose you. And whatever you are engineering down there," Cayce pointed his fork at Paul now, like he would stab him if he moved or said the wrong thing.

Jimmy had been listening the whole time.

"You won't be seeing anyone until the entire term is up, all ten years," said Paul. "But we will pay for accommodation, living expenses, and everything else while you are on the base. It's like one of your contract jobs on a rig," he said to Jimmy. "We own you for the duration, due to secrecy."

"Ten years?" said Jimmy. "Lot longer than six months. I'd make a million on my own over ten years."

"If you ever get a job again," said Paul. "I'd tell you more, but you will have to see for yourself. And it's two million dollars. For each of you when you are done. The first million is for the confidentiality."

The waitress showed up with the salad, it made for an awkward moment when no one acknowledged her, everyone staring at Paul. Eventually, she stared at him too.

Jimmy looked at the highlighted number. It said two million dollars. "So if we say no to the job, we get to keep the first million, for the confidentiality?"

"You won't say no," said Paul. "As for the confidentiality, we have a breach of confidentiality clause for that with a fifteen-million-dollar penalty, though probably, you would just go to jail for life."

"Hmmm," said Jimmy. "Health insurance?"

"Yes, world class, for your father and you."

"What about a pension?" asked Cayce. "Could use that too."

"Don't push it. We have a lot of money, no end of money, mountains of it, but we have more problems."

"I'll do it," said the waitress suddenly. "I want to work there."

Paul took the salad from the waitress so she would go away. "And you two are one of those problems right now. I am offering you the chance to save your lives, to transform them, and for an adventure of sorts." Paul patted his coat pocket. "Or we have some tea and say our goodbyes. Your choice."

He wiped up the last of the dipping sauce with a final onion slice, adding, "I am actually a nice guy, you know. But I have my limits. I need your answer right now, or I am walking out of here. Two, four, million dollars," he said, pointing at Jimmy then Cayce. "Make your choice."

"What the fuck," Jimmy said, "are you buying for four million dollars? Like seriously. I am good, but—"

"I am buying secrecy and two disposable American lives, which are on a fire sale right now."

"Could have had me for fifty K," said Cayce taking a bite of food.

***

Alastair sat outside his coach's office, football in hand. Since slipping into the school, he had waited for over thirty minutes.

"Ball," Coach Schoeffel said. He pointed at a chair. Alastair sat and handed the football over. Schoeffel went to work on some papers; he hadn't made eye contact yet. The coach was in his usual uniform of a tattered brown cardigan and Chuck Taylors.

Eventually, Alastair spoke. "Coach?" he asked.

"Yes, how can I help you?" he said.

"I want to play football this summer, in summer league," Alastair said.

"And?"

"I wanted to see if it was okay with you."

"Why would it not be?" he asked. He looked up at Alastair for the first time.

"Well ..." Alastair wasn't sure what to say. He had the sense that this would not be the last time. He got easily tangled in his thoughts.

"What about the fancy internship?" Schoeffel asked.

"I am not going," Alastair said.

"Why not?"

"You wouldn't get it."

"Try me, Einstein," he said.

"I am Albert Einstein, and Gene-E Corp expects me to—" Alastair stopped suddenly, realizing what Schoeffel had said. *He said Einstein.* Mr. Schoeffel hadn't been at graduation.

Who else knew?

Alastair understood instinctively when he had to wait to allow Schoeffel to have his moment.

"Well, first off, you are not Albert Einstein," Schoeffel said, after signing a few more papers. "You are Alastair Mayes, so let's get that straight for now and forever. Secondly, I don't care who you are. If you don't know who you are, you're nobody. Got that? Especially if you can't run a post route for the life of you."

"Yes, sir," Alastair said.

"But, let's suppose you can, and you had a shot at a postgrad spot on varsity, why?

"Because I love football," Alastair said.

"No, you don't. You hate it. Why?"

Alastair wasn't sure what to say.

"Because it makes your teachers angry that you play. Because it is violent. And you can get a chronic brain injury, especially the way you tackle headfirst. That's why, and you know it, but anger's a piss-poor reason to play football," Schoeffel said.

It was true. Even still, Alastair struggled to understand why only he and Leo were banned from football for the first few years of high school. He knew now, of course, but then, it had taken a titanic and public struggle to be allowed to pull on the pads.

"Here's the thing," Schoeffel said. "They had to tell me. I wouldn't shut up about it because I wanted Leo on the team, but you need to figure out who you are. And what you want. I have my opinions, but you need to figure out yours. I hate that they told you the truth. I know there was debate about never telling you kids at all and letting you discover your own paths with your own skills to unlock and discover, guided by their—our—invisible hand."

Alastair shifted in his chair.

"But," Schoeffel continued, "you know now. And the truth is yours to keep. If you let it control you, it'll ruin you. Or you can own it and be whoever you choose to be."

Who else knows? Alastair wondered. He couldn't let that go. He already had too many people disappointed in him. He didn't want to add more.

"How long have you known?" Alastair said.

"Ever since I forced Principal Lazo to explain why you and Leo were so special that you weren't allowed to play. He wanted to protect your brains, but he didn't think about protecting much else. I won him over on Leo and got you too." Schoeffel smiled. "Like a free cup with my order."

"I'm not even a free toy?" Alastair joked. He always admired Schoeffel because the coach seemed to be the hardest on him at practice.

"Nope, a free cup, at best. If you want to play this summer, then try out, and we'll see if you make the team. I am not going to hand it to you because your twin brother discovered the speed of light. *You* are still slow as shit."

"Technically, he discovered that light is a constant speed and that its square multiplied by its mass equals its energy. Ole Rømer was the first to figure what that actual speed may be."

"Well, whatever, Einstein," he said with a laugh. "So football it is. What else are you going to do with your time?"

"You are okay with it?" said Alastair.

"Why not? It's your life."

Alastair didn't trust that his coach meant this. He could be so inscrutable. "What are you going to do if you don't make the team?"

"I got a job offer, but I turned it down," said Alastair, thinking back to the woman on the bench.

"I am sure you did. There is more than enough time for the world to exact its tax on you."

"Or I've always wanted to work at Waterworld, that fire-and-water stunt show at Universal Studios. That looks like a cool summer job?"

Alastair got up to leave under his coach's withering gaze.

"Hold on," Schoeffel said. He wrote something down on a piece of paper and folded it over. "Promise you will never read it," he instructed, handing it to Alastair. "Say it: 'I will never read what is on this piece of paper, no matter how much I doubt myself," said Schoeffel.

"I promise," Alastair said.

Schoeffel went back to work, indicating to Alastair that the meeting was over.

Alastair walked down the empty school hall. It felt foreign to him now for some reason, when only a week ago, it was his whole world. He opened his wallet and looked at the folded piece of paper, but didn't open it, only sensing its talismanic draw. His coach could be so cryptic at times.

He bounced his football against the wall with a quick flip of his wrist as he walked, but when he tried to catch it, he missed. Like usual.

He watched the ball roll away from him. By the time he got to it, he realized he was in front of the trophy case for the football team. There weren't many pictures of Alastair, but Leo was everywhere, clearly the star. Next to the largest trophy, there was an oversized photo of Leo diving into the end zone.

Alastair felt the ball in his hand. A cold wind pushed through the hallway. Schoeffel walked down the hall, away from Alastair, leaving him alone with his thoughts.

Alastair left the ball on the ledge in front of the trophy case and ran out of the school.

***

Ralls stuck his red, fat face into the cockpit. "Turn around," he said.

The captain said, "Can't yet. I have to file a—"

Ralls threw a handful of nuts at the pilot. "Turn around! Now!"

"—a change of course at the next ATC handover. Copy that Mr. Ralls. We'll wing it for now."

Ralls left the cockpit.

"Requesting emergency flight plan change," the pilot said into his headset.

ATC responded, "What's the emergency 159?"

"We have a hole in our fuselage, sir."

"Jesus, what type of hole?"

"An asshole. Client issue. We're headed back to you Springfield, 150."

The copilot chuckled.

***

Alastair stood on the tarmac with a duffle bag slung across his shoulder. He watched the 747 land and come to a stop on the private airstrip.

He could feel the heat of its engines turning toward him. It made him feel like a magnet, pulling the aircraft out of the sky and down to his feet. He had the power to turn around a 747 midflight. *What other powers lay ahead?* he wondered.

He could see his classmates silently peering out of the windows. The door opened, revealing Ralls.

"What happened?" Ralls yelled over the scream of the engines.

Alastair boarded.

"I hate football. That's what happened. Hey, guys!" Alastair was happy to see his classmates, but other than a few glares, most of them weren't looking at him. Alastair took a seat, quickly catching on to the mood.

"You know what, Whine-stein?" asked Kat. "At some point, no one's going to wait around anymore for your angsty bullshit."

"Whine-stein?" said Alastair, laughing, impressed.

"What the hell, Alastair?" said Leo. "We were halfway there!" He reached out across the aisle and hooked elbows and hands with Alastair.

They were back in the air. Alastair reclined into the soft leather seat. His head pressed into the Gene-E Corp logo behind his neck.

"It's going to be a good summer," he said, exhaling for the first time in weeks.

TWENTY-FIVE SECONDS

The nations were expected to forge a historic alliance with each other tonight. Sephora Neiman's hubris led her to think she could broker it. Oxford-educated by way of both wealth and intellect, the British Gas Consortium executive had Middle Eastern opal eyes and weedy legs that distracted men and boys from her clever mind. At thirty-three years old, she was the youngest CEO of an FTSE 50 company, and she wore decorum like a soft glove when discussing matters of corporate and national UK concerns. It was Sephora's idea to hold the meeting in Austin, Texas, where the oligarchs that ran Russia liked to play after New York and Miami. Sephora had recruited the help of the embassy to throw a charity event as a cover for the unlikely assortment of guests.

And it was close to Cornerstone.

As the former undersecretary to the United Kingdom's chancellor of the exchequer, Sephora was the highest-ranking representative of the British government at the meeting. Though raised in London, she had a Russian background herself. Her father was once a high ranking doctor and geneticist with the Russian government before moving to London in the 1970s. Dr. Neiman wanted to escape Russian "corruption" as he called it. Or perhaps, to promote it abroad.

Though thoroughly British by birth, Sephora grew up in the shadows of the former Soviet Government and knew how to operate in them, when it was convenient for her.

And tonight, the cabinet and House of Lords wanted to keep at arm's length from the "technical relationship" the countries were forging at lightning speed, so Sephora, seven senior BGC executives, and twelve former Russian thugs turned power brokers turned philanthropists were left to decide whether they would officially try to undermine the United States' greatest scientific and military gambit since the Manhattan Project.

Or not, thought Sephora.

After interminable bickering over Crimean port leases, the men wanted to begin. "We do not need to wait for Brother. He is a criminal," one of them said—ironically.

"Let's wait, shall we not? He is close," Sephora said with finality. She could command a room with her smile alone; it was like a brilliant spotlight when it was on, but the second it disappeared, you were left feeling cold.

"I'm not close. I am here!" Petyr said, slapping Sephora on the ass as he entered the room. Once Petyr crossed the threshold, everything changed. Handshakes. Smiles. Suddenly, the men played friends with each other, like a room of children who fall into line when their father comes home.

"What is this about some American bullshit time machine?" Petyr asked.

Sephora knew that Petyr knew full well what was at stake. His compatriots didn't yet. *Petyr plays dumb so he can be in a position of trust to convince them if necessary*, thought Sephora. Weeks earlier over lunch and laughter, Sephora convinced him that as the largest shareholder in Russia's petrochemical industry, he would be bankrupt in months if he didn't join forces with BGC to stop the Americans, or at least slow them down. Everything Petyr had built—in fact, everything Russia, India, China, Britain, and the rest of the world had ever built—would be overwhelmed in short order.

The British government had disastrously taken a wait-and-see approach, and now it was up to the power brokers of the gas and oil industries to flex their might. They had the most to lose. And Petyr was the linchpin in Russia.

But that was two months ago, and the situation had gotten dire since they last spoke. Now they had days, not months.

Everyone called Petyr Hirsch *Nash Brat*—"Our Brother," in Russian. By modern standards, he was an oligarch, but unlike the early American twentieth-century robber barons, and all the other newly minted oligarchs spun out of the turmoil in Russia, he was *not* working hard to transform himself into a well-respected philanthropist.

He still bought jewels in bulk: thousands of low-grade diamonds filled bowls like candy at the doors of his various wolf sanctuaries. Guests would take some as they left, at first sheepishly and then greedily over multiple visits, as they discovered the bowls of Our Brother's wealth had no true bottom.

"One fist," he would yell with a drunken roar from the top of the fire-smoked stairs in the soaring wood palaces. And then he would laugh at their greed and chase his children around the fire, wrapped in bearskin, waiting for his next prey to arrive for the weekend. He knew it was very James Bond of him, which he did on purpose as the Russian "oligarch."

Stereotypes have value when you can weaponize them. They blind people to your true motives.

There was a practical side to Petyr's flourishes with the jewels. It was very hard to eyeball their true value, and as a result, they were great for bribes. Fifty stacks of ten-thousand-dollar bills could be counted and negotiated over. Five hundred thousand dollars in diamonds, however, could very well be worth $150,000 or $1,000,000. But to the beholder, it was always treasure. Petyr had a jeweler on staff whose sole job was to sort the jewels by quality, putting all the flawed diamonds into slush piles for bribing down at the ports and for replenishing the bowls. Sometimes, Petyr purposely let a real gem out so his "treasure hunters" kept coming back for more. But for the most part, he resold the top jewels back in New York at a profit.

Sephora fingered her diamond necklace. Even she had her weaknesses. She glanced at Petyr as he finally settled down at the large conference room table.

"You wouldn't mind, would you, Mr. Hirsch?" Sephora asked Petyr. She nodded to a security guard who had been waiting near a wall.

"Not at all," Petyr said, clearly amused at her use of his last name. The man approached Petyr and ran a device over him in search of surveillance tech. Petyr had a problem, and Sephora knew it. His house was bugged, his estates, his cars, even his bed. For fun, Petyr would put on a sex show for the spooks in the walls. With a wealth similar to some countries, he was part of a standard list of entities—again, mostly countries—that were too large not to eavesdrop on.

It was only fair, she thought. The doors closed and she began.

Sephora knew Petyr was aware of the details, but nonetheless, she started from the beginning. She had not won over her entire audience yet. They weren't as easy to beguile now that fear had them by the throats. She felt Petyr quietly watching her like a machinist watches a lathe cutting steel.

"My company's engineers were the first to discover its existence in the Gulf of Mexico. Something new and curious. Our central oil deposits aged suddenly by over a million years last March. There is no geological model for the change. And then, more reports. The widely reported plane crashes and stories of strange creatures in the waters outside Corpus Christi. With the help of MI6, we have managed to unpack the last few years of the American project called Cornerstone."

She paused to take a sip of water. The men were rapt. She walked to the side of the table, her legs slipping past their glances.

"What we know is this. Cornerstone is a particle accelerator but infinitely more powerful than CERN or even their failed SSC collider planned in Texas in the nineties. When it is turned on, the energies of the particle accelerator create a relative time difference between *here* and *there*. For every minute here, there, on Cornerstone's property, three years pass. This includes a stretch of ocean that is encircled by the particle accelerator's buried ring, an area of about fifty square miles. And for every three minutes that pass for the rest of us, at Cornerstone, almost ten years pass. In the space of the time I have been here, the Americans can squeeze"—she checked her watch—"forty years" worth of research. Or manufacturing. Or weapons."

"In twelve minutes?"

"Yes." She let that sink in. "The Americans can control the relative flow of time."

"Ten years is not millions of years," said one of the more quick-thinking men. "What of the oil?"

"Last year, for reasons we don't understand, they left the accelerator on for eight months. It was after that that we noticed the change in our oil deposit south of Charleston. Also, it was then that new creatures started to be spotted in the Gulf and on land. Two children were killed in a nursery playground. And the ecosystems surrounding the gulf marshes all started dying due to an ant infestation. The ants were bright blue and magnetic in bulk. There was a clampdown on media reports, but things still leak if you are looking for them like we were.

"Anyway, the oil, it is useless to us. We don't own the rights there. You do. And it is not the local oil we are worried about. The US is preparing to put a collection of their top scientists and researchers into Cornerstone to live and study for ten years. On the top of their list is energy independence. Cancer, medicine, and military research are all part of the plan too. But energy is why you are here. Our livelihoods in oil and gas will be over if someone walks out of there with a solar converter above 90 percent efficiency. Or the battery tech to store it."

She continued. "On Tuesday, when the accelerator fires next, it will take only three minutes for us to be another ten years behind. The following Tuesday, ten days from now, it will be twenty years. We will never catch up, nor will the rest of the world. The Americans have already made use of this technology. In two weeks, twenty years in 'the biosphere,' as they call it, they built the living and science facilities that will support the researchers who will be trapped there for ten years of their life."

"What can we do?" Petyr asked, playing naive.

"I tell you all this because the combined wealth in this room is needed. We have successfully built our own accelerator through a multinational effort." She paused again and took another sip of water.

Sephora didn't believe the men needed to know the true nature of the young scientists who were going into Cornerstone. Nor did these men need to know about the efforts to create a competing genetics program. The only thing that mattered was catching up on the tech before it was too late.

"Our accelerator is hidden, but to keep the flow of bribes going, we need another truckload of billion-dollar bonds to appear. Quietly and quickly." She continued.

"The Americans, we believe, know about this. But before your money evaporates next week, or the week after that, or after that, we want to use your"—she paused, trying to pick her words wisely—"financial infrastructure to catch up. China is work for hire. Russia and the UK are bearing the brunt of the cost for now. But we can't hide the flow of money for much longer. The Russian government sent us to you. To avoid war if the Americans find out. Your government has agreed to funnel the excess funds needed through your petrochems. As will we. And India. It is the only way to move this level of money without the Americans taking notice. You seem to have perfected the billion-dollar black market for dark money, and now we need your infrastructure. Not your money. You will have a stake in everything we produce. But it is all contingent on you saying yes tonight."

There was silence.

"You are asking to funnel your money through us?" Petyr asked, feigning ignorance again.

"Yes, and we expect, once you see what is at stake, you will also expend every penny of your own money to ensure the survival of your empire."

Petyr laughed. "Every penny. Of course," he said sarcastically. "This is ridiculous. Of course not," he added, playing the rube. The audience was rapt, motionless, while Petyr pointed out all the hurdles to such a scheme.

It's working, Sephora thought.

Sephora knew the men in the room. After decades of graft and theft, they would relish the idea of siphoning hundreds of millions off this new flow of cash. Regardless of whether they believed her explanation of the threat to their businesses, most had already decided they would only let a trickle of money flow back into the black hole of the Chinese labor force, making sure to pocket most of it themselves. She knew that greed would hook them in, and when they saw what the Purity project really was—and what it was capable of—their money would also gush into China like the Yangtze River.

"But what about this Tuesday, if we say yes?" one of the men asked.

"My men are on the ground in Texas already. They will slow the Americans down," said Petyr, suddenly turning dark.

The ruse was over. No one was surprised. They all knew how Petyr was. Except for Sephora.

"Inside?" she asked. This was a surprise to her.

"Yes, this is a two-front war. We must stop them while we arm ourselves."

"This is not a war. This is about money. Your money. And BGC's money," she said.

"All money is a pretext to war, Sephora," Petyr said. He got up and walked over to her, standing behind her chair, his oversized hands on her shoulders. "If we stop their fancy young scientists, then there are no worries for now, okay? You made that clear months ago. And we take our turn with our accelerator. You don't need to destroy the entire project; we just need to take out a few of the links in the chain."

"And who are you referring to when you say 'links'?" Sephora asked, pulling herself away from his massage, turning around.

"Stop. Bang. No science. No kids. And then we all get more jewels," he said, "like your necklace, perhaps."

TWENTY-FOUR SECONDS

Alastair found Milk hanging out in the back of the plane. She was dressed in fuzzy Christmas pajamas. She thought it would relax her, but now the cold air made her shiver, amplifying her anxiety.

"You know, peanuts are not nuts. They are legumes," she said randomly.

"I'm aware," Alastair said, squeezing past her to get to the bathroom. "You okay, Milk? You seem a bit stressed." He closed the door.

"Did you know the 747 has over six million parts? There are 171 miles of wire stringing this thing together in the air. Doesn't that worry you a bit?"

"No," Alastair answered from inside the toilet.

"171 miles."

"You mentioned."

"I just don't like closed systems. Humans are terrible at complexity."

Milk demanded intellectual attention even before she found out she *was* the famed orator and leader of the civil rights movement. Unlike her classmates, who had a tendency to lean into their teacher's challenges, Milk always poked around assumptions, pushing everyone to question the question. Not the answer. It made her mind razor sharp, but as a result, she always seemed to be in some other eddy, churning ideas that no one—other than her—wanted to chew on. But she also had an odd way of always being right at the wrong time, like on a flight during heavy turbulence.

"It should worry you!" Milk exclaimed. "This is a linear system. All six million parts need to be correct—perfect—for the thing to work. There is nothing organic about an airplane. Half of the parts are fasteners. Sure, you can put a lot of them in, make sure they are tight, build with some redundancy, but that doesn't account for conceptual mistakes, right? That's a lot of little things, a million moments of human logic, holding together a big thing. No wiggle room for unlucky days, spilled coffees, late parts, dead ends. One bolt breaks and the whole wing could shear off. Rip right off. Humans aren't smart enough to figure out that much complexity."

The turbulence got worse. Alastair held on to a handle in the bathroom to stay on the toilet. With a big bump, he accidentally yanked it off the wall.

Milk steadied herself. "An eagle's wing can't rip off midflight," she said. "Complex systems that evolve through conflict and generational change have the ability to adapt to shifting environmental pressures. They have checks and balances so the system can absorb shock and sudden failure. But we are terrible designers. And we trust this thing. Why? Because the plane didn't spiral to its fiery death on its last trip from Tulsa?"

Alastair knew that Milk understood exactly why, how, and when planes stay in the sky, but this was part of her process of dealing with anxiety, and as her friend, he would just strap in and go on the intellectual ride until her anxiety faded. Sometimes, late at night, it would lead to interesting places.

"Yes, that's exactly why," Alastair said, attempting to reattach the handle.

"The past is a terrible prediction for the future when it comes to complexity."

"It's in the air now, and odds say it will remain in that state," said Alastair, emerging with the handle behind his back, not sure where to put it.

"Until it doesn't. Shearing events are zero-sum," countered Milk. "They either happen or they don't. There is no middle ground. Zero or one. A bird's wing gets sore or hurt or loses mechanical lift with injury."

Alastair finally maneuvered himself over to the galley without Milk seeing the broken handle.

"It's analog, it doesn't rip off because some eagle mechanic had a fight with his wife the night before," Milk continued. "Or padded some insulation wrong or used centimeters instead of inches after a shitty football game in Buffalo or—"

"Does your brain ever turn off?" Alastair asked, finally dropping the handle into the galley's garbage.

"No. Nor does yours, and I think that is—"

Kat walked up with Paul from the Pentagon. He had been chatting with Kat for a while, until she got bored and was looking to foist him off on someone else.

"Hey, Kat," Milk said, ignoring Paul, continuing her train of thought to Milk. "I just prefer nature. I guess I'm wired that way."

"You freaking out again about flying?" said Kat.

Milk had a very famous meltdown on a trip to Washington, DC in tenth grade. "No," Milk said, sliding to the floor to sit out some turbulence.

"This is Paul," Kat said. "He is from the Pentagon."

Paul introduced himself.

Behind Paul's back, Kat made a face to Alastair, eyeing Milk.

Alastair got the message. He poured her a cup of hot tea and joined Milk on the floor. "The Pentagon?" he said.

"Don't mind me. I'm just here to get to know you guys," said Paul, as if they were friends. "Can I hang out?"

"No thank you, Mr. Pentagon," said Milk. "I thought we were going to Gene-E Corp's headquarters. What's the military got to do with that?" The question was actually directed at her friends.

Paul didn't respond.

After an awkward silence, Milk picked up the earlier thread. "What makes my brain so special? It is organic. Flexible. I am an evolved system with a particular version and model number: off-brand Martin Luther King, luxury female edition. Millions of years of evolution perfected him and then me."

Paul laughed.

Milk flushed with anger.

"You know how many people are in the air above America at any given point?" Paul asked.

Milk wasn't taking the bait.

"Sixty-one thousand. Do you know why I know that? I know that fact because of 9/11. There were fifty-eight thousand Americans in the air, and three planes went down. So air travel isn't always that safe if the conditions on a particular day are wrong. I was agreeing with Martha."

"We still don't like you," said Kat.

Paul seemed to get the message. He left. "Nice meeting you."

"Do you have to be so intense all the time?" Alastair asked Milk. "You do realize it makes our lives more difficult most of the time."

"Yes, I do," said Milk. "You laugh at me about being scared of flying, but if Martin Luther King were here, he would freak out about this plane. Because *I* freak out about this plane. Where is the choice in that? I *can't* be any different."

"Well you are," said Alastair.

"We are not *built* for this time period. This is a disaster. We should not exist. We died. Our DNA is outside its time period. Out of historical context."

"It's not like humans have evolved in the last few centuries, what are you talking about?" Alastair said, getting tired of the conversation finally.

The galley tilted into a hard descent. Milk instinctively grabbed Alastair's hand. He gripped it as a concession, the argument quickly draining out of them in the warm press of their palms.

Kat glanced at them.

An announcement came over the PA. "Please take your seats, we have an emergency stop."

"I'm just with you. That's all I am saying. This is a bad idea," said Milk. "And wherever they are taking us will end poorly."

"Why can't you ever see the good in a situation?" Alastair asked.

"Do you really want me to answer that?"

"No," Alastair and Kat said simultaneously.

TWENTY-THREE SECONDS

When Sephora finally got to the used game store, it was past 11 p.m. She hadn't had time to change her outfit. Since Petyr's dramatic reveal that he had men inside the American project, she had been working hard to improve her plans, determined to get into Cornerstone. She pounded on the door to the store, out of place in the dingy strip mall parking lot.

"He's upstairs," the clerk managed, letting her in. He watched her legs go up the stairs. Dressed in her trademark Louboutin heels and a short $1,500 skirt, Sephora was alien (and confusing) at that late hour.

Sephora found Isaac alone at a gaming table. His Pokémon cards were out for battle. He didn't say anything at first, picking at his wrist with a heavy metal wire. When he dipped it into an ink bottle, Sephora realized Isaac was tattooing himself.

"Ouch," she said playfully.

He wiped away the blood and black ink to show her what he had carved into his skin: F = ma.

"Force equals ..." he started.

"Politely?" she interrupted him, sitting down.

"Force equals your turn," he said curtly, flipping over a Pokémon card.

"Can we talk first this time?" Sephora asked.

"No. Evolutions, go."

"Isaac. Eye contact. I dressed up for you."

"You look nice. First, we play, then we talk," he said.

The delay was inexcusable. Somehow, Sephora's entire world came down to satisfying the whims of the gaunt, unpleasant man-boy in front of her. Sephora reached into her purse and pulled out her collection of rare Pokémon cards. She laid down a Charizard Mega X. "Flare Blitz attack, 120 damage points," she said.

"I like your perfume," Isaac said.

"Thank you. Compliments are good *and* so is eye contact."

It was a typical routine. She would coach him on passing as socially normal; he would teach her Pokémon skills.

And state secrets.

Tonight, however, she was in a rush and didn't have time to play his usual games.

Time mattered, especially now. Petyr had laid his gambit. Fortunes could be won or lost in days, and she didn't want to be burned again.

"Things have changed. Gene-E Corp has moved up the graduates, and they're on their way to the site. They are to be put inside the accelerator this Tuesday," said Sephora. "Correct?"

"Ish," said Isaac. "Zack could almost be the same age as me by Wednesday then. QED. You can bug him. And leave me alone."

"Do you remember the sequence?" She was tired of him.

"Yes, Sephora Neiman."

She had never told him her real name before. Was that a threat? She laid down a new card. "Pikachu, illustrator's subway edition. Number two."

It had been nine months since her team had discovered that America's prize possession had a hankering for Pokémon. To befriend him, her company had spent thousands of dollars purchasing ultrarare Pokémon cards on eBay. Sephora flew in every Thursday for six months to attend a weekly Pokémon gaming night on the outskirts of Corpus Christi. She made enough bad trades early on to catch Isaac's eye and eventually his friendship. It was odd for a thirty-something woman to be playing Pokémon, but she knew to dress down or come in cosplay. People bought her story of being a Pokémon freak, albeit a clueless, rich one. Isaac relished swapping his valueless cards with her.

It wasn't long before Isaac realized she was not a Pokémon fan and had other reasons for being there. But she had learned his private language and would argue Pokémon with him well into the night, having studied it on her transatlantic private jet. It wasn't easy keeping up with his mind. But she did, so he started to share secrets.

"Another stupid move," he said.

"Eye contact," she said.

"You know that the new Broken Heavens card series has been delayed," he said.

"Yes," she answered. She took his hand and turned his wrist hard, looking at the formula. "What if you come up with a better formula?" Sephora asked.

He jerked his hand away.

As usual, their conversation was a game of cat and mouse. She would switch rapidly between the two, from domination to submission, to keep him on his toes.

Isaac finally softened under her glare and then looked away. "I want my own team, my own house, Baroque-style, and no one speaking Russian or Chinese to me. It has to feel like his home. Only British people, like you."

"Because Isaac Newton was English," she said.

"Because I am genetically English. And I want to recreate his conditions for genius. And I get to publish everything in my name, Isaac Newton, no coauthors."

"Who would share authorship with you?"

"And—"

"First, we must get Cornerstone offline." For once, she wanted him to slow down, cutting him off. "I have figured out how to get in, myself. This will give us some space for you to solve the time leaks. You did it once. All you have to do is create the magic trick again."

"I will solve the time leaks."

"A Russian team has already infiltrated the Cornerstone property. They are surviving but barely. If you can get them inside the barrier dam by Monday, they will blow it, and the entire ocean, into the property just as the time cycle starts."

"And the kids?"

"It's up to you to keep them out. But we are not interested in them," she said, lying poorly on purpose. She hoped he would pick up the thread. "The Americans are very shortsighted in using this power for pure science research with a bunch of untested kids, famous or not. We want to catch up, that's all. And we have our own plan."

"I also want an entire, perfect Pokémon collection."

"Some things even Isaac Newton can't have," she reminded him, reaching into her purse.

"Everything, including all the cards in your purse right now," he said, "that they bought for you for me."

This time, she didn't pull out a card. In her hand was a clear plastic envelope full of tiny, insect-sized drones.

"It is a flying swarm," Sephora said. "You can download the barrier dam lock codes via Bluetooth. Your phone will work. Only one of the insects needs to find the team. There are more drones waiting for you at your apartment. Other types, too, as backup."

"Can I put any codes on them?"

"Yes, but keep it simple, the team inside is trained for one purpose. And it is generally unpleasant. You will need to be inside the biosphere when you release the drones to avoid detection."

She turned the drones on with a flick on her phone. The flies jumped into the air, indistinguishable from their natural counterparts. She swiped her finger around, and the flies danced to the motions.

"Like I said, the drones will find the team for you, so you don't have to risk contact. But you do need to be on the inside. These things won't make it past the electromagnetic barrier shielding without frying."

"They won't let me inside the biosphere since the accident," he said.

"You're smart, figure it out," Sephora said, playing the mouse once again. "I did. Your turn."

"How about I take the kids on the safety tour on Monday? I could join them for that briefing."

"My thoughts exactly, Isaac. Smart."

"Yes, I am," he said, rubbing his wrist.

"Of course you are," Sephora said. "And soon, the whole world will know it."

TWENTY-TWO SECONDS

Corpus Christi, Texas
Predawn

They touched down with a jolt.

"We're changing planes. Safety," Ralls explained.

"See!" Milk said to no one in particular, as if this justified hours of anxiety.

Ralls was tired of the bickering and Milk in particular. He wanted to be there already and regretted not taking his own jet separately. Now that he had mastered time, terrestrial delays and waiting for people had become interminable for him.

The kids spilled out of the plane with Gene-E Corp blankets wrapped around them. The tarmac was hot, washed with jet engine, humidity, and fuel. The air had a fetid smell from a nearby cattle ranch.

"Your bags will follow, this is our transpo for now," Ralls explained.

They cleared the huge wheels to see a large prop plane.

"No, not happening," said Milk, slowing her step.

The rest of the kids boarded the plane.

Once Ralls settled inside, he looked out and saw Milk still standing in the same spot.

A figure approached her from behind. The heat deformed the body. It dipped in and out of a slice of air, until eventually, the apparition ascended the stairs and entered the cabin.

"Everyone, you remember Dr. Isaac Newton?" Ralls asked.

Isaac smiled as if he was aware of every muscle in his face.

"Alastair, will you please get Martha?" Ralls instructed.

The flight attendant offered to take Isaac's satchel to the back, but Isaac clutched it like a teddy bear. Ralls smile was strained. "Sit," he said.

Isaac was never easy, thought Ralls. When Isaac was finally born through a surrogate, Ralls thought he was at the finish line; however, he quickly realized that the true marathon had just begun. This great mind needed burping, feeding, and raising. It became apparent that while a genetics firm backed by billions in military investment makes for a great start-up, it also makes a terrible parent.

The mistakes started immediately. At first, Ralls brought the baby to Pentagon meetings for fun. The men would poke and pinch him, talking about their own grandkids. Ralls made sure he was legally Isaac's father, but when colic made Isaac a fussy, unpleasant mess, Ralls left him to Gene-E Corp's growing staff of nurses and professors in child psychology.

In the hands of the professors, every moment of Isaac's childhood was managed like a software beta release. Key developmental dates, accelerated nonstop educational milestones, and white lab room testing every month since birth created an incredibly unnatural environment for a child. Ralls realized that now.

Isaac didn't see another child until he was two years old. And worse, adults talked to him like they were his equals, even when he was throwing spoons full of applesauce at them, still just a toddler, no matter the future (or past) pedigree. When Isaac grew and started to rebel against the extreme rigidity of his life, the adults decided they had to tell Isaac who he was, despite the risk. The investment, expectations, careers on the line, and possibilities for greatness proved more important. Ralls told Isaac he would become "a great partner" in a grand experiment.

Isaac was ten.

It worked, at first. By then, Isaac was allowed to play with toys. And Pokémon. Everything seemed to be working out until Isaac discovered that Ralls had been given the green light to "have more children." Isaac withdrew.

Ralls took the Pokémon cards away when he couldn't get Isaac to stop obsessing over them instead of focusing on his studies. Then he fired his primary nurse—the only true parent Isaac had known—and brought in more PhDs to accelerate his learning. It was a slow rolling disaster.

Now, Ralls thought, he would finally make it all right. The small plane climbed into the sky, buffeted by winds as it passed over the Gulf waters below. Isaac flipped through his perfect set of Pokémon cards. Alastair and Leo played games on their phones. Ralls looked at the plane full of teenagers.

The risk of raising another Isaac took Ralls and his investors to the other extreme. When "the twelve" were born over the course of one stressful year, the children were given to parents desperate to adopt, parents who valued education and love. The children would be monitored, certainly, their fantastic education paid for, nurtured by teachers who knew the truth. Still, Ralls had learned the hard way that, famous or not, these kids still needed normal upbringings. He had to let them into the wild to grow like weeds—unaware of their heritage—before he could cultivate them, even if it meant a plane full of unruly, opinionated teenagers. At least they seemed normal, if that was even possible for a group with an average IQ of 171.

Now, hopefully, they would fix Isaac's mess once and for all.

***

It was dusk when the plane banked toward the coast. Early morning filled the interior with a golden glow.

Alastair looked out the window, squinting past the rising sun. There was a wall structure—a vast circle carved into the coast and land. The circle structure was so big that Alastair couldn't see its far side. What was even odder was that in the bottom of the circle, there seemed to be a jungle. The whole thing had the appearance of a flat salad bowl pressed into the desert, a portion of it pushing out into the Gulf of Mexico. Ralls sat down next to him.

The seatbelt sign suddenly illuminated. "What altitude are we at?" Alastair asked.

"Ten thousand feet. We should be there shortly. Can we chat for a second?"

"Hold on," Alastair interrupted. He grabbed a black marker from his bag and started to trace the shape of the circular enclosure on his window, bisecting it with lines and numbers. Then he lowered his tray table and started using it as a scratch pad for formulas. Black numbers and calculations soon covered the whole thing.

Ralls watched him notate. "Amazing, isn't it?" Ralls asked.

"That structure is over fifty miles wide," said Alastair, finishing his calculations. "The ocean pressure on that wall alone is ..." Alastair consulted his tray table. "That thing is holding back the entire Gulf of Mexico. How did they do that?"

"It's amazing," Ralls continued, "that despite being a certified genius, you don't know the difference between a dry erase marker and a Sharpie."

Alastair looked at the marker in his hand. He tried to rub the lines off the window. It was permanent.

"Oh shit! Sorry, Mr. Ralls. I can pay for it. I think," Alastair said.

"Once you are done with your internship, you will probably be able to buy ten airplanes. You can repay me then."

Alastair looked back out the window. "What is that thing?"

"Look, I need you to be on board tomorrow. There are a lot of changes coming, and they'll listen to you."

"No one listens to me," said Alastair.

"They do. They just don't admit it 'cause they are all smart-asses. I know you are a leader. Leaders make hard choices. Wise choices. Okay?"

"Okay, Mr. Ralls."

"Actually, please call me Dr. Ralls."

"Ah, Doctor. Got it."

Ralls went to the cockpit, passing Leo's seat with a sigh. Leo drew in his sketchbook, attempting to copy Leonardo da Vinci's *Vitruvian Man*, the world-famous illustration of a man reaching to the edge of a perfect circle. Leo had added his own touch: long schlongs in various positions, from flaccid to erect, matching the angles of the man's arms and legs. Under it, he wrote *Homo Erectus*.

Alastair grabbed Leo's head and twisted it to the window.

Leo pulled down his headphones and looked outside. Then he turned back to look at Alastair with a blank look on his face.

Alastair gestured with a nod to Leo's sketchbook.

"Might be handy," Alastair said.

Leo flipped to a new page and started to draw. While Leo's *Vitruvian Man* was a middling rendition of the original, the speed and accuracy at which Leo could record what he saw below was impressive and beautiful. Leo's illustrations grew into an ad hoc map of the giant, circular, jungle enclosure. The ecosystem sunk below the desert, as if someone had buried a vast ecosystem five hundred feet below sea level and then wrapped a big wall around it to protect it from the desert heat.

The plane passed over the top of the barrier wall. Giant metal wires and sentry posts gave it the look of a military outpost, but weirdly, everything faced into the circle. It seemed to be guarding what was within rather than protecting from prying eyes outside.

On the other side of the wall that held back the Gulf, where there should be more water, a huge drop-off revealed a jungle, as if it had once been growing on the sea floor until someone drained the tub. A lazy river ran at the base of the giant wall and then cut inward into the jungle. Water poured from sluice gates high above the floor, feeding the river at odd intervals.

"You see that? The numbers?" Milk asked, joining them.

On the inside wall, giant red numbers the size of buildings counted off sections into the hazy distance.

Leo denoted the nearest number in his sketch: 176. They both could see where the numbers counted up by twos to 180 and then reset to zero and then started counting up again.

"How big do you think each section is?" Leo asked Milk.

"I can tell you," Alastair said. He added some calculations to his tray table. "About three-fourths of a mile."

Leo kept drawing. Soon a mountain appeared on his map and then thin highways, most of them in ruins. The odd building flashed by below, their shapes outlined by younger forest growth.

The whole thing also reminded Alastair of the toy glass biosphere in Principal Lazo's office; except, where a single piece of wood or some moss would be the main features in the diorama, in this enclosure, giant rivers twisted through canyons into waterfalls that disappeared into holes and never emerged. Every type of biome seemed to be represented: a small section of ocean, rivers, deserts, deciduous forests, farming tracts, and above all, impenetrable jungle, all packed into one tight space, as if it were under glass with desert and ocean surrounding it.

None of this prepared Alastair for what he saw next. Alastair had spent the morning watching oil rigs scroll by below, sparkling in the gulf like elaborate miniatures placed by a giant. He even saw the oil rig from the news that sunk due to diver error, ringed with salvage boats.

The plane banked hard again.

Now he saw one last oil rig, this one well inside the barrier wall. It was still a mile from the old "shore," so it would have been originally in hundreds of feet of water. Its long, thin legs were exposed now, but it was still standing, giving the whole thing the appearance of a rusting tin soldier teetering on stick metal legs, peeking over the wall.

As the plane dipped lower, arcing around the rig, things got weirder. The massive structure was covered in jungle vegetation, flowers, and sea life—a mini Eden paradise in the sky. Huge, thick vines the size of tree trunks twisted up their legs, like snakes trying to consume the ever-vigilant soldier.

Leo was also glued to the window. He made a note of the nearby section: 6. "Hey Kat, you awake?" Leo asked.

The whole class now peered out the window at the strange sight. Milk came to Alastair's side of the plane to get a better look. She sat next to him, leaning over him to look out and down. He became more aware of her pressing into him than what was going on below.

For the first time since they knew each other, no one could think of anything to say.

***

The plane crabbed sideways, landing on an ad hoc runway in the Texas desert not far from the barrier wall. When Alastair got out, wind plastered his shirt to his chest.

"The site creates its own weather," Ralls yelled over the wind. He waved over a sprinter van that waited for them.

Now that they were on the ground, the facility did not seem as imposing to Alastair. It was maybe four stories high. Alastair knew it plunged hundreds of feet on the other side, but from this vantage point, it seemed like a simple concrete dam with some utility buildings. After a few hundred meters, the walls got even lower and ran off along the dirt for miles in both directions, studded with lookout towers. At the top of the berm, industrial wire netting leaned inward on poles. It didn't seem designed to keep something out but, rather, designed to keep something in, like a zoo.

Gear was loaded into the van. Leo threw his bike on top of everyone's rucksacks and duffle bags.

They drove through a security checkpoint and then into the structure through some blast doors. Alastair expected to emerge on to a grand vista of the jungle he had seen from above, but instead, they took a right turn inside the wall and traveled down a well-lit vehicle corridor. The curve of the tunnel reminded Alastair of the stadium where he and his dad would see the Cleveland Browns every Thanksgiving. His dad would park in the cheap lot, and they would walk the entire circumference of the stadium to get to their even cheaper seats. The team didn't deserve a dollar more, his father would say as he bought another Browns hat for Alastair.

On the walls, big red numbers passed by every so often, counting down in twos. Vehicles came and went. They finally stopped at a glass lobby that looked like the base of a newly built skyscraper: art, couches, and security guards checked people in before they could use the elevators. It dripped with Gene-E Corp branding. When the kids got out of the van, Milk pointed out the number on the tunnel wall opposite the doors.

"Section 90," Milk said to Leo. "Each section is two degrees, I counted the sections. We traveled eighteen degrees of the circumference, I think. The other stops were at 74 and 82."

"Planning your escape already?" Ralls said with a genuine smile, holding the doors open for Milk.

"You've lied to us for years. Why should we trust you now?" Milk replied.

There was no emphasis or affect in her voice, just a simple truth spoke plainly, but it struck Alastair, elevating his heart rate. Alastair paused at the door. He felt the cool air try to draw him in.

"Too late now," Leo said, pushing him through the door. It closed behind them, revealing a sign: DEMONSTRATION ATRIUM.

They entered a big atrium shaped like a nautilus shell. A ramp wound around the center of the room, the spiral getting wider and wider as it descended to a big open area below. Leo hopped on his bike and pulled a wheelie down the sloped walkway, riding ahead of the group.

On the walls curving around the ramp were a collection of skeletons all posed alike, with morphing anatomy that captured the animal's evolution over time.

Milk examined them, carefully moving from one to the next. "What's with the fossils?" she asked Ralls.

"In time," Ralls said. He seemed tickled pink.

Paul followed in the back, watching Ralls closely.

"They are not fossils; they are bones," Milk said with an air of finality. "Recent bones. But everything is sort of backward," she continued. "They are birds, but their pelvises are tilted too far forward for flight. Each one more so than the last," she said, moving to the next specimen and running her hand over a vicious set of claws. "Also, they have five claws, not four."

"So?" said Ralls, like he was a teacher leading a student to an answer.

"So," Milk answered.

There were more on the way down. Walking skeletons morphed into skeletons that could clearly swim. Small, land-based animals took flight into winged skeletons. It was as if God had saved every skeleton, connecting the whole evolution of life in a display to show off to his friends.

They reached the end of the ramp and entered the atrium. Alastair finally got the view he wanted. Behind a giant wall of glass, the jungle stretched out before them, enshrouded in fog. He imagined it was how the Amazon looked, or some untouched primordial land, if it were not for the wall disappearing into the mist.

"Isaac, if you would," Ralls said.

Isaac retrieved a small potted tree sapling from a table covered in them.

"Last year, none of this was here," said Ralls. "It was just hardpan Texas dirt and a research facility studying high energy physics. Now it is something altogether different. Thanks to Isaac. Leo, may I?"

Ralls wanted Leo's bike. Leo hesitated. Ralls waited until he gave it up.

Ralls hit a button on a fob, and the glass wall slid away. The humid, fecund air hit Alastair. The smell of dirt, rotting vegetation, and the calls of birds and animals rooted the jungle in reality. Almost immediately, everyone's eyes watered. Alastair clenched his eyes. Something in the air made them sting.

"You'll get used to it," Ralls said.

Ralls rode Leo's bike onto an earthy plateau overlooking the jungle valley.

He took a handkerchief from his pocket and wiped his eyes, indicating he had not yet "gotten used to it." Isaac followed him with the plant and a shovel, his face buried in the cloth at his elbow.

Ralls brandished the small pot, ballroom dancing with it, and then planted the seedling in the ground with a shovel. Then he used the kickstand to rest the bike on top of the plant. He came back inside.

The glass wall slid back into place. Ralls stood looking at the kids, rubbing his hands. He checked his watch. It was almost 3 p.m. He nodded to someone behind the kids.

Alastair turned but didn't see anyone.

"It takes about three seconds to get up to relativistic speeds," he said. "Or seventeen hours inside there, depending on how you look at it," he added.

Before Alastair could ask him a question about what he meant about seventeen hours, Ralls counted down for dramatic effect. Always the showman.

A hum of power suddenly swept through the building. The lights dimmed. Outside, everything seemed to blur and then shimmer.

On the wall, a clock lit up with spots labeled for DAYS, MONTHS, and then YEARS.

An echoing *boom* shook the building and grew into a distant electronic scream. After a few seconds, the calendar clock climbed through seconds, minutes, and then hours.

The tree grew.

It was like a live time-lapse video but more beautiful and fluid. The seedling grew into a young sapling, gaining strength. The roots thickened into the ground. Soon it was a small tree. Its trunk grew through the center of the bike's frame.

After about only twenty seconds, the clock on the wall was at one year, and time was still accelerating. Now the tree had become a twisting ghost, maturing into adolescence. Ethereal branches reached upward in a hazy mist of movement. A limb caught under the bike's frame and lifted it skyward.

Alastair moved closer. His whole class soon lined up next to him, their faces pressed against the glass. The ecosystem for miles was twisting and growing and changing, in a fast-forward time-lapse, along with the tree.

Three years on the clock: the trunk was thick now, its bark aged with moss. The tree twisted and wrapped around the frame of the bike, swallowing it like slow-moving molasses made of wood.

Seven years on the clock: the bike had almost disappeared inside the ever-thickening tree trunk, the frame bending under the power of nature, the tree dancing to the symphony of time.

Ten years: the tree was now mature. The clock stopped. The shimmer faded in the room. The lights came back on. The glass doors opened back up.

It wasn't an illusion. Where there was once a small plant now stood a towering oak tree, the dancer frozen in its final repose, waiting for the applause after the hushed shock of the audience. Leo's bike was buried midway up the trunk.

Ralls went outside, inviting the others to follow. Milk stayed back, her hand over her mouth. Kat ran her fingers along the trunk of the tree, trying to find the parlor trick.

The bike's frame was now rusted and bent. The tires were flat. Leo tried to pull it out of the wood. He tugged, but it was clearly stuck, buried in the tree's growth. Alastair joined Leo, trying to yank it out.

"The sword in the stone," Isaac said. "Looking for a hero."

"I'm getting this out," said Leo.

Alastair wandered away. He spotted other trees on the plateau with objects embedded in them. One tree had a trumpet caught in the trunk, another had a rake. An axe. A chair. On a table, aging glass dioramas sat, clearly ready to be handed out as bribes to officials, like the one in the principal's office. Alastair remembered he pressed Principal Lazo on the diorama's mystery. At the time, he was trying to get a rise out of the man, and now, in context of all this, he felt a flash of embarrassment at how juvenile he had been. In that etched glass, the sweep of history was caught and turned into a trinket. It wasn't the first time Ralls had put on this show.

***

A cold wind blew across Jimmy. He looked up. The clouds seemed frozen in the sky, unnaturally, like someone pushed pause on a video. The quality of light in the jungle changed as well. The sky shimmered with an iridescent sheen that grew with every second.

Somewhere beneath the welder, particles chased each other in a burst of primordial light and hubris.

Time began to bend, a clarion bell calling on the universe announcing that man had broken free of its tyranny. The laws of nature groaned under the accelerator's insult, dragged and bruised by the great machine into a new compromise.

Jimmy considered the ten long years ahead of him and the silent promise made that he would save his father.

***

An ocean of decisions—ten years of life and death—tumbled into the future.

Jimmy changed like the tree, his roots burying themselves in the Crypt's soil with time.

Leo tried to pull his bike out of the full-grown tree.

Another airplane fell out of the sky. It was becoming a thing.

BOOK THREE

TWENTY-ONE SECONDS

Milk closed her mouth. *This is the end of the world.* Ten years had passed inside the enclosure in—

Only three minutes.

She began counting all the things that this technology would change but soon gave up. *It was everything.* The technology would spread like a weed. Knowledge always does. It can't be suppressed. She knew. And civilization would shatter. People would age and die before their parents, or generations of parents. Companies would leapfrog each other daily, the world constantly knocked off center by cataclysmic economic change. Wars would start and finish in days, with the military-industrial complex able to pivot in mere minutes, raise a new army or a battalion or, god forbid, a weapon in the space of a single meeting.

It all raced through Milk's mind. In every situation, you would have to be the first to move, or else you could never catch up. This would force aggression rather than political détente or social restraint as the defining strategy of war. Aggression. The end of the world. Milk saw it all in the gentle swaying of the oak tree.

"You idiots," she said, sitting down.

***

Paul had seen the trick before. He had grown tired of the display. He thought back to the first demonstration for the Pentagon. Ralls had a preternatural ability to condense the complexity of their discovery into a single bravado display. However, every time the accelerator was fired, they had ten years of repairs to do on the property, another example of massive waste. Those who committed to take the risk to stay inside and maintain the facilities were often dead three minutes later, lost from some accident in the decade that rushed by. And today, it was all to impress a bratty group of kids. The more time Paul spent with them, the more he realized they would never find, nor fix, Isaac's failure. Paul wiped his eyes, aware again of the stinging histamine reaction the alien ecosystem caused and the deadly mistakes they had already made along the way.

***

Alastair laughed. He recognized the physics at play. He had spent most of his senior year working on the Pioneer Anomaly. He never understood why his teachers had pushed him so hard into the work. He really didn't like physics. There was too much pressure to succeed, and it seemed pointless. NASA had given up on the problem. Why would he be the one to figure it out? Now it all made sense.

It was a famous challenge. Launched in 1972 and 1973, NASA sent two Pioneer probes on opposite one-way trips out of the solar system. Years later, the mission exhausted and the probes still supposedly accelerating, scientists discovered they were in fact slowing down.

No one knew why.

Alastair's teachers expected him to figure it out as his senior thesis. The true difficulty of the problem was that it touched on all areas of physics. It could be a question of dark matter, an invisible force dragging on the universe, showing its reach in the deceleration of the probes. Or it could be an applied physics problem—venting on the probes degrading their speed. It was messy, and Alastair hated that he was assigned some outdated seventies problem. It was part of the reason he wanted to play football so badly. No one let him choose what he wanted to study. He would either have to rewrite all of physics to explain it—and dark matter—or there was some completely random answer, like a technician's piece of gum changing the angular velocity of its spin.

Now he knew why they had him study it. It was all to prepare for this. Isaac, Alastair guessed, had somehow cracked quantum gravity, and Cornerstone was harnessing it.

"You figured this out, Isaac?" Alastair asked. "How did you—"

"Yes," Isaac replied. "At high enough energies, it gets pretty pedestrian."

"I mean, how did you solve for ... quantum field—"

"It has nothing to do with that," said Isaac. "You sound like a fool. Don't be ridiculous. You can't just use the word quantum and expect to sound smart," Isaac said. "I created my own mathematics."

"It's hardly—" started Alastair, but then he stopped, stuttering a few more words. He wanted to prove he could be a part of the conversation, but Isaac made him feel small and stupid, like his teachers often did when he didn't get some incredibly complicated theory fast enough as a kid. His mind raced in the background, on the physics, but running at the front was the flush of embarrassment, crowding it out, confusing him.

"Easy. Easy. There are still a few kinks to solve," Ralls said, shutting Isaac down before the pissing match got out of control. "You are going to have to play nice."

Ralls approached a large outdoor bench where there were several glass diorama biospheres. He handed the mini dioramas out to the kids. "You have complete freedom to choose your destiny here," Ralls said.

Alastair looked at his glass biome, making the connection to the jungle vista.

And the gift in Principal Lazo's office. Now he understood the question, "What was the one variable you haven't thought of?" It was time. Time can be variable.

"You grew the rainforest," Alastair said.

"To provide resources for those living inside. It took us eight months to finally grow an ecosystem that could function and survive on its own—oxygen, water, and all the nutrients for life in harmony. Before that, everything died whenever we turned it on."

"Including the people," Paul added.

"Yes, people too. We didn't understand the constraints in the early days. But we have solved that now."

"Somewhat ..." Paul's tone was contrarian.

"Yes, somewhat," Ralls said. "Time passes normally when you are inside of the biosphere. Had you been standing next to this tree just now, you would have to wait ten years for this door to open again. For us, it's just three minutes."

"Eight months on the outside or on the inside?" Milk asked.

"Outside," Ralls said. "Do the math," he added, smiling. "Every three minutes is ten years. For eight months—"

"What's so funny?" Milk snapped. "It's not funny."

Ralls dropped the fake smile.

"That's 1.17 million years," Zack said, piping up for the first time.

"Be precise. It was 1,171,200 years," corrected Isaac.

Alastair glanced at Zack, who, as usual, missed the insult coming from his older "brother."

"It was 1,171,200 years," said Zack, snapping back at Isaac, "and twenty-seven days. But it's a pointless detail to add after a million years, unless you were so insecure you wanted to show off you could do simple multiplication to a bunch of people who think you are an asshole." Zack looked at Alastair.

Alastair nodded back.

While the five kids were as different as possible, they were pack wolves when it came to protecting each other, even Zack.

Ralls continued, clearly wanting again to short-circuit the tension. "It took that long to get the ecosystem balanced, living and breathing on its own, independent of the rest of the world. Nothing other than light, as a constant, gets in or out. This means the ecosystem needs to recycle everything. And now, it is perfect." He wiped tears from his eyes. The stinging got worse. "Though we never exactly figured out how that happened, by what process. It's a bit of a mystery."

"A million years," Milk said to herself. "You just winged it."

"Like these terrariums," said Alastair.

"Precisely," Ralls said. "It sounds irresponsible, but it wasn't a completely blind experiment. We would get to peek each night, or every 7,800 years, and could make adjustments: more water, less water, pesticide spraying, occasionally controlled fires. However, because it was dark, we could only see so much with the floodlit drone surveys. I guess there was some winging it. It would have been quite dramatic if you didn't know what was coming. Seventy-eight hundred years of sun, then one night, the sun sets. It disappears. Poof!" he said, laughing. "A funny little quirk, don't you think?" he added.

"That's one word for it," said Milk.

There were other "quirks." The thousands of years spent in the dusk (and dawn) of the typical 7,800-year day created a lot of evolutionary hiccups,

Ralls explained. When the sun was low in the sky for millennia, animals' visual acuity and hunting skills thrived. Everything evolved to be slower and deadlier through poisons, guile, and intelligence. Finally, as the higher energy states gradually arrived after 3,400 years and the sun neared high noon on the outside, higher energy survival tactics dominated: speed, power, and physical domination. Energy levels in the biosphere swayed back and forth for thousands of years. This created an exponentially increasing weaponized nature, two survival tactics warring with each other over millennia, or each "day." By the end, their combined lethality made it the most dangerous place on the planet.

Or at least, that was the theory.

"You saw some of the new species on the walls when you entered," said Ralls. "Of course, we seeded and populated the property with thousands of animals and plant species we thought could be beneficial. We modified their DNA to visually tag them for tracking purposes. Blue—"

"And red," Milk said, finishing his sentence. "We know. You let 'er rip," she said sarcastically. "You realize they are getting out, right? Two children died."

"I heard. Again, there are quirks, tweaks that need to happen."

"How irresponsible is this?" Milk said to no one in particular.

"We want to grow our investment with you, giving you all the time, money, and resources to make similar discoveries that can transform the world."

"This is some sort of bullshit," Milk said.

"Actually, it's not bullshit. Look past the conspiracies and worst-case scenarios for one second and think of all the good that can come from this," Alastair said. He spoke more to himself than Milk now—a fire was lit in his mind, fueled by his insatiable curiosity and desire to prove himself after Isaac's insults.

"This summer, you'll have complete and utter freedom during your internship," said Ralls. "To live, to study, to test the boundaries of science *and* your special heritage. Cornerstone is your playground. Once you acclimatize, you will have the chance to present research proposals to the academic committee for projects you'd like to study with the accelerator. It will be similar to how time is booked on the Hubble."

"It is not bullshit," Alastair said, reacting to the way Milk was looking at him. "It's amazing," he added, with a little too much pleading in his voice.

"Just you wait. It gets *way* more amazing," Ralls said with a smile. "There are many more secrets. This is just the first magic trick. Would you like to see where you will be staying?"

***

The group moved on. Kat held back. She looked at the collection of skeletons again. Their twisting, shifting spines seemed more sinister now. Disorganized thoughts tumbled through her mind.

One set of skeletons swept into a separate room. The first skeleton by the entrance was about the size of a car, but over the course of ten skeletons, they kept shrinking and morphing until the last one was only about a foot long, a miniature version dramatically surrounded by its bigger ancestors. The larger skeletons were all posed to seem like they were in a dance around the smallest skeleton, which had its own podium with a light. There was a placard under it: *Ursus arctos horribilis.*

Its claws were much longer relative to its body than the bigger skeletons that surrounded it. The talons curved under its wrist like a third joint or limb. Or a wing.

She was glad it was under glass.

TWENTY SECONDS

The hallway reminded Alastair of Disneyland when you are stuck in an interminable line with a coughing kid, empty Coke cups, and grating music. The Imagineers have to come up with *something* to keep you occupied. Display after display seemed to go on forever.

Milk got stuck reading a long piece on a foam grasshopper species that had grown enormous in the Crypt during one cycle and then disappeared. It was a descendant of the African *rooibaadjie*, and in a grainy picture, its head cleared the trees. Its growth exploded when it became carnivorous, each cycle feeding on larger and larger rodents until it graduated to boars. It's black-and-red stripes give it the appearance of blinged-out Chevy Camaro, customized by a chop shop that specializes in weaponized grasshoppers. And the graininess of the long-distance picture made it look like whoever took the shot didn't want to get too close to it.

The further they walked, the longer the hallway got, dense with information and marvels. The walls also told the history of Gene-E Corp. Photos of serious men in boardrooms, oversized photos, dioramas, maps, and blueprints of the original Cornerstone construction site were all bathed in warm, museum-quality light. With every step, they were diving deeper and deeper underground.

Alastair felt like he was being swallowed. His initial enthusiasm was fading, like usual. Up ahead, Ralls orated Gene-E Corp's creation myth, focusing on his personal heroics. No one paid attention other than Kat, who kept stride with Ralls, stroking his ego with the odd "wow" so she could surreptitiously take photos of the diagrams and maps with her phone. Zack trailed them, reading a textbook while the rest argued about evolution.

"You just like to antagonize me, and it bugs me," Alastair said to Milk. "I'm sorry for calling you annoying."

"I'm just programmed that way. Apparently, I have no choice but to be annoying," she said with an unconvincing smile.

Alastair thought her feelings seemed hurt, which meant she was losing an argument and had resorted to secondary tactics. Milk was anything but annoying, actually.

"I grew up surrounded by you idiots, so I had to evolve and become annoying so you would pay attention," Milk continued with a real smile now. "You said that. You agreed with that, Alastair. Life never fails at getting the right answer to whatever environmental survival problem it is presented with. There is always a solution. Here's the thing: with real evolution, sometimes the solution might not include humans at all," Milk said. "Nature is agnostic."

"She's right, Alastair," said Leo, agreeing with Milk.

"Do you even know what agnostic means?" Milk snapped.

"Or those two kids that died," Alastair said. "Nature didn't include them." Alastair felt the need to agree with Milk's side now that she seemed less angry with him.

"Evolution doesn't care what survives," Milk said. "It is just programmed to make sure *something* survives."

Leo said, "Now, I call bullshit. We've been manipulating evolution forever. Look at the modern cow or the variety of dogs. That's selective breeding over time. No different than what they are doing here. They are just doing it more efficiently."

"He is not Albert Einstein," Milk said.

"I am. I realize that now," said Alastair. "I am Albert Einstein. Sure, there will be issues, there always are, but in the end, issues are controlled with a massive net positive for civilization. With a company like Monsanto, this thing could feed the world."

"Net positive," Leo agreed with Alastair again. He could be considered a swing vote if his vote ever counted for something, which it usually didn't.

"Monsanto?" Milk started counting on her fingers. "Dioxin. DDT. rBGH. PCBs. Aspartame. Agent Orange. *Agent Orange*, Alastair!"

Agent Orange was another favorite sparring topic of Milk's. They had heard about it ad nauseum after Milk was assigned the chemical for her senior project in organic chemistry. Starting in 1963, the United States military used Monsanto's newest herbicide, Agent Orange, to defoliate the jungles so they could see the enemy better. They claimed it would increase the accuracy of their targeting and protect civilian populations in the jungle from indiscriminate bombardment. Over 4.8 million people breathed it in, bathed in it, drank it from the rivers. The product was rife with Dioxin, known now to be one of the most toxic chemicals in the world. Children were born with severe deformities, their heads the size of warped watermelons.

"That was a mistake. I grant that. But it's been like that for every new technology since the dawn of time," said Leo, shifting his stance. "There are always kinks at first."

Milk leaned into him, her small frame threatening him. "A *million* disabled people. Kinks? And that was just an herbicide."

"It takes time, but eventually they get it right," said Leo.

"Who are *they*?" Milk said.

"Science."

"And what set of rules are *they* following? You talk as if everyone mucking about with nature gets together and decides what the right thing to do is with perfect vision and control over unintended consequences. It's a disaster."

"She's right, Alastair," Leo said, changing his mind. "It's a disaster."

"Leo, don't be a wuss!" said Milk. "A second ago, you were siding with Alastair. If you don't have anything to add, at least be—"

"Guys," Alastair said, slowing.

"—consistent," said Milk.

"He agreed with me," Leo said.

"Guys," Alastair said again. He had stopped walking.

"I don't understand how you can change your mind so often," Milk said.

"I guess I see all the possibilities," Leo said sheepishly. "I *am* the creative one."

"Well, it's unattractive."

"Guys, look," Alastair said.

They were in a new section. The hall was now full of oversized photos from *their* lives. The candid shots began when they were babies and included an elaborate timeline of all of their milestones, including intimate scenes from home, shot by their parents. A hush fell over the hall.

Placards under the photos told stories about the kids, observations on their odd personality developments, physical growth, intellectual milestones at school, and most intrusively, narratives about their emotional life—failures and fears only their parents should have known.

"Your parents are all very proud of you, okay," Ralls said, attempting to lighten the mood.

Once they finished their life stories, they soon read each other's. Milk browsed Alastair's preteen years.

"Taylor Swift?" Milk asked playfully. "No way."

In a photo, Alastair was twelve years old, standing backstage next to Taylor Swift, wearing a t-shirt with her face on it. Crying. Alastair's felt his cheeks go warm. Kat approached. He angled his body to hide the photo from her.

"Hey Milk, do you know what's Ursus Arctos Horribilis?" she asked.

"Grizzly Bear."

Alastair realized Kat had been missing the whole time. She was prone to disappearing, even when she was standing right there.

"That's not right," Kat said. "It's little." She held her hands up to show her how big. "Does Arctos mean arctic? Like a polar bear?"

"No," said Milk. "*Ursus* means bear in Latin. *Arctos* also means bear, but in Greek. *Horribilis* means. You get it. So technically the Grizzly Bear is called 'The Horrible Bear of Bears'. Kind of a way of saying King of the Bears. Why?"

"No reason," Kat said, folding her arms. "Taylor Swift?"

***

They had just turned into a new corridor when it hit the students. The pungent smell of decay. The stinging in their eyes returned, more potent as they approached the source. It nearly blinded them.

"Something's wrong," Ralls said. "Stop."

At the far end of the hall, workers removed a huge panel of glass, laying it on a utility 4×4. They had masks on. Five men with rifles faced out into the black jungle, protecting against something. Ralls ran over to them, his arm over his face.

Alastair watched his angry gestures.

Ralls returned with disposable hoods to wear so they could handle the air.

"The glass was compromised on the last cycle," Ralls explained. The kids put their hoods on. There was no other way around the breach.

When they got closer, they saw something that made them slow to a stop. The glass had deep claw marks in it, gashes that were almost three feet long.

"Leo?" Milk asked.

It looked like something had been scratching into the same groove over and over again, a concerted and durational effort.

"I concede," said Leo.

"Thank you for playing." For someone as verbose as Milk, she couldn't have summarized everyone's feelings more succinctly. "Anyone?" Milk asked, pointing to the next panel over.

Next to the gashes were dried red symbols written in angry red mud or blood—a circle with two parallel vertical lines through it and one diagonal slash. There was something written underneath it in scrawled symbols: U+0338.

"Anyone," she asked again, "know what this code means?"

Zack looked up. "That's not a code," he said before going back to his book. "That's a warning."

NINETEEN SECONDS

The kids weren't able to get more out of Zack. He had a completely different operating system than they did, and no amount of social pressure or lines of questioning could get him to disconnect from working on his formulas long enough to explain his comment.

Ralls left them to fetch a "surprise." They were in the cafeteria having a tense lunch. The space had a military feel, not nearly as lux as the demonstration atrium.

Paul took Ralls's absence as a chance to join the kids for a private talk. Before he could begin, Zack spoke bluntly.

"They are planning on putting us inside, aren't they?" Zack asked.

Paul looked at him.

The idea spread across the table, eyes opening wide as everyone contemplated the simple logic of it.

"We are still teenagers, and what better way to accelerate our output? We are still developing. I'm only fourteen."

Paul took fries from Milk's plate as a delay, thinking.

Milk was grossed out.

They waited for him.

"I guess we considered this at first," said Paul. "But Cornerstone is bigger than you now. It is such a powerful technology. If you were locked inside, we would only get the value of one cycle, ten years of your life, instead of letting you work on the outside with the research teams, crafting hundreds if not thousands of years of research."

He reached for more fries, but Milk pulled her plate away.

"Or that death machine is too dangerous, and you don't want to jeopardize our contribution," said Milk.

"That too, but the government has taken greater risks bringing you here. And we have a few major areas of concern right now for you to get started on." He licked his fingers and then spread out a chart on the table. "Consider this the first genius pop quiz."

On the first chart, there were columns of data.

INCIDENTS	OFF.H.SEC.CC	REPORT *	FAT. ^	CLASSF: ACCM
DL790	DL4345*	WN2892*	DL16	UA1010
AA5790*	WN280	DL4245^	DL3079	DL3309*
UA3780	WN1659*	DL3364	UA4075	DL5790
NK15	B6100*	UA3310	AA3344^	HA101^
F9204	F9205	F9206	UA11	WN2600

"Professor Ralls isn't a fan of you troubleshooting our problems rather than working on big-picture stuff, but the government has different ideas about what is important right now. You may have heard about the plane crashes in Corpus. Cornerstone caused it. We know why, but the problem seems to be growing further and further afield with every time cycle. The media hasn't caught on yet, but it will soon."

He flipped a page. Additional charts had flight departures and destinations, in-air flight time, actual on the ground durations, dates, and locations of first-reported incidents. It was a mess of numbers.

"Something is skewing the GPS time signatures in the airplanes that are used to calculate the instrument landings," Paul said. "Look at the times of day, duration times in flight, and the GPS signatures. Here, here, and here."

It was a giant meaningless jumble of numbers to Alastair.

"Most concerning is that this is happening now when the accelerator is *not* on," said Paul. "The NTSB is in the dark, but they did send out error corrections after the first crash, to no avail. We can't shut down the US airspace. Isaac thinks the problem may have to do with Einstein's conjectured gravity waves. They may be continuing to oscillate after we turn the accelerator off, leaving enough of a signature to skew instruments sensitive to time. Think of ripples in a pond. The rock is gone, but they keep extending outward after the event. Or a plucked string."

"Gravity waves," said Alastair.

They were the trendiest field of pure research since a team of Caltech and MIT researchers managed to directly observe the effects of gravitational waves from two black holes that collided 1.3 billion years ago. The gravitational impact left a signature on a phased laser array that shot between Livingston, Louisiana, and Hanford, Washington. The indirect proof supported earlier work on spinning neutrons, cementing gravitational waves as most likely to be real. It was popular to conjecture. Einstein struggled with the theoretical side of gravity waves for decades, alternately saying they existed and then they didn't exist. Ever since, people liked to fill the holes in his theories, like popular kids making sure their ringleader never looked bad.

"Every time we run a cycle, the effect's radius—the ripples—seem to grow," said Paul. "Planes are going down in other states, even on the other side of the country. And we don't understand the physics of why or how the effect could be traveling so far. Can I have a chicken finger?"

Kat handed him one.

"Isaac failed to solve it. The Pentagon has been no help," said Paul. "We even asked the MIT crowd, risking security, but we had to give up. There were too many foreign graduate students who would never make it through the security clearances. And so, it became politically expedient to graduate your class early to find a solution."

Paul kept eating off Kat's plate. The kids were more amused by his behavior than what he had to say.

"I'm not a physicist," Alastair said.

"Your brain is wired for this type of problem. We have faith that if Isaac Newton could create this mess, Albert Einstein can fix it."

Milk had her first real laugh in a while.

"Professor Leonardo Da Vinci, you got anything?" Alastair said.

Leo looked at Alastair blankly.

"Didn't think so," said Alastair.

"Well, GPS uses time as a constant," Zack said. "With your accelerator technology, time is neither a constant nor linear in relation to the satellites. It's no wonder the planes can't land accurately while it is on. You should have seen that coming. Why the problem persists after it's been turned off is ..." Zack paused.

"Exactly," said Paul. "A problem."

"I know why," Kat piped up.

For most of the conversation, Kat had been quietly looking at the chart.

"Katherine, is it?" Paul asked. "The Great?" A smirk played on his face as he waited for a solution to the gravity wave problem that had been plaguing the world's top minds for months and the original Einstein for his entire life.

"Apparently, your time machine hates Americans," said Kat. "And Delta in particular. Look at the airplane flight codes."

Alastair knew Kat used to fly a lot; her family moved to New York without her when she was in seventh grade, leaving her in Ohio. In the first few years, she was a frequent flier, but then the invitations started to dry up.

"This one here is DAL790. DAL for Delta Air Lines. And this here is UA1010, United Airlines 1010. Here is another DAL. This one as well. This grouping out of Houston is WN, Southwest Airlines. So, I ask you, where are the foreign airliners?" Kat asked, tucking her hair behind her ear. "Why aren't they being affected by this universal constant?"

Paul's smirk disappeared.

Alastair's respect grew. He knew better than to underestimate Kat. In ninth grade, he had been assigned to help her in math. However, it was quickly clear to him that she was razor sharp when it came to logic and lateral thinking. She just didn't care enough to study the straightforward stuff. They ended up mostly gossiping about their overbearing teachers—*Other older men who made the mistake of underestimating her*, thought Alastair—and they played video games.

"My guess is that after the first one went down, all the domestic airlines rushed their planes into maintenance to fix their GPS systems, adjusting them per the NTSB guidelines, like you said. Except the planes weren't broken—time was. And rather than realizing that the fundamental constant of time had changed—How could they? Who would be stupid enough to mess with time?—the engineers updated the GPS systems with faulty error corrections. And those software errors are flying all over now, flattening children and grandmas on runways. Meanwhile, the foreign airliners—the Krauts, Frogs, Canucks, and the rest—they have farther to travel for the suggested upgrade maintenance and therefore haven't made it back here to crash. So no foreign airlines on your little chart yet."

Silence.

Paul scoured the paper for any sign of foreign airliners.

"Still hungry?" Milk asked.

"Your time paradox isn't expanding," Kat continued. "The problems as a result of it are. And now you've got a bunch of airliners running around the country with bad, no good, horrible GPS. Human problem."

Silence.

"So hot," Leo said to himself.

"Katherine the Whhhut!" Milk said, giving Kat a high five.

Kat pretended to drop a mic and did a little dance.

Ralls walked up, wanting in on the party. "I'm glad to see you are having fun. It is fun, isn't it?" Ralls said.

"I think we have an answer for the plane anomalies," Paul said glumly.

"Well, perfect timing! Now we can focus on the positive. I want you to meet our newest class," Ralls said with a flourish.

With that, a bunch of barefoot ten-year-olds ran into the cafeteria, running up to the table in white Gene-E Corp jumpsuits, striped on either side with red and blue.

"Benjamin Franklin! Galileo! Niels Bohr, the second! Richard Feynman! Leonhard Euler! Johann Goethe! And more!"

EIGHTEEN SECONDS

"Where are the girls?" asked Kat.

"This time, there are no girls. All business," said Ralls.

Kat pursed her lips, pressing them together so her mouth would stay shut despite the insult. She was sick and tired of Ralls's misogynism and let him know it.

"How old are they!" Paul asked, jumping in when she caught her breath.

"Does it matter? Ten years old," said Ralls, deflecting Paul's anger.

"How did you keep them a secret all these—" Paul started.

"All these what?"

"All these years?" Paul said. "The money alone—"

"Years, it was only three minutes!"

"During the atrium demonstration?"

"Ten years is ten years. What a waste to just grow a tree, *n'est pas?*" said Ralls.

"These are humans, not toys in some experiment. It's completely unethical, unacceptable, unbelievab—"

"I think you'll find them delightful. They are easily amused."

"Unbelievable. That's a lot of uns! And uns are bad, Ralls," exclaimed Paul.

"Hello, what's your name?" Kat asked a little boy who offered her some blue apples.

"They don't speak English," Ralls said.

"What do they speak?"

"They don't, apparently. They can't speak, at least we think they can't. We are not sure when they separated with the adults over the ten years." Ralls smiled, his eyes betraying his thoughts.

Kat watched one of the ten-year-olds pee on the ground next to the salad bar. The other children sampled vegetables they clearly had never encountered before.

"Which one is Euler, the mathematician?" Kat asked Ralls.

Kat knew a lot about Catherine and Euler. Catherine the Great had invited Euler to Russia, and they were rumored to have been lovers.

Kat felt a deep connection with the monarch because she was nothing like her, and that served as a study in opposites. Empress Catherine was strong and thoughtful, socially enlightened, a pen pal with Voltaire, defeated Turkey and Poland in wars that redefined Russia's boundaries forever, acquiring South Ukraine and the Crimea, built the Hermitage Museum, westernized Russia's education system, and was the longest female ruler in Russian history. Despite all this, the ruler was trapped in history's amber by her sex and beauty, hence the rumor of illicit love with Leonhard Euler, another myth in a long line of lies conjured up by her enemies about her voracious sexual appetite. In that way, they were very similar.

"Why do you care?" asked Ralls.

And like Catherine the Great, Kat knew how to make men squirm. "We used to fuck." She shared that trait with her twin sister-in-time.

"I have no idea," he answered. "There were no adults left. The nurses, etcetera, they didn't survive unfortunately."

She pointed out the kid taking a piss.

Ralls scrambled to corral the child, avoiding Kat's glare. It was chaos, like a grade-school field trip had just shown up in the middle of the Manhattan Project.

Then Kat noticed their backs. The children all had deep scars all over their bodies.

"No wonder they don't talk," Milk said under her breath, sidling up next to Kat.

Kat tried to touch the child, but the kid flinched and pulled away. It was obvious to Kat that these kids' scars weren't just surface level. They had trust issues as well, and those, she understood intimately.

When Kat was thirteen, her foster father got a job in New York and decided to leave Ohio with her mother and sister. She wasn't allowed to join them. No matter how much she cried, she was to stay behind in Ohio with a new foster family. Her family never told her why, other than to say it was for the school. Her grades weren't great, she never kept up with the Honors class, and the sudden rush of puberty was not kind to Katherine or her teachers. She hated school. It just didn't make sense to leave her there.

Kat moved in with her Russian teacher, Ms. Yaektova, who created a Russian immersion program at home. Yaektova also taught in the high school, and Kat's parents thought it would ease Katherine's transition to the upper school.

Kat, of course, blamed herself and the world, raging until she learned the truth about her unique heritage. Her foster mother told her over breakfast one morning while pouring orange juice and serving runny eggs. After the shock, Kat understood why she'd told her. It brought her closer to her foster mother, but the longer she kept the secret about their true identities from her classmates, the more isolated she felt.

Then Kat's sister died in New York, hit by a messenger bike rider outside her grade school. Once her parents' grief settled into stone, the visits slowed down. The distance to New York grew with every year until Kat was legally emancipated and adopted by Yaektova as a formal convenience.

As much as Kat hated speaking Russian at home—no matter how small she felt when her classmates consistently outperformed her at school or how many fights she got in with adults—she never said a word about what she knew. It became so verboten, she sometimes wondered if Yaektova remembered telling her. It was one of the reasons she was sometimes so disliked at school. Her aloofness was her only protection against ruining everyone's lives, like the truth had ruined hers.

And like her dark story, she could tell something terrible had happened to the children around her. She also knew how hard it would be to get them to open up—sometimes scars go all the way down.

"Where are the parents?" Kat asked Paul.

"He has no idea. They're gone. Just the children were left. And he's happy somehow," said Paul, "because everyone died, except the mute, traumatized kids."

Finally, Ralls managed to get the children to pay attention to him using one of the oldest parenting tricks in the book: his iPhone.

Kat's vehicle was last in a long convoy of golf carts trundling down another endless cement tunnel. The children nestled in the back seat, watching a cartoon on Ralls's iPhone while Kat drove. Alastair sat in the passenger seat, rambling about Malthus' theory on population growth over time, clearly trying to impress her.

"What should we call them?" Kat said.

"Huh?" Alastair replied.

"The kids, what should we call them? I think we should call them the Lost Boys."

"You mean the movie? With Kiefer Sutherland? About the vampires?"

"From *Peter Pan*," said Kat. "The Lost Boys."

A child with a useless leg clambered up into Kat's lap. She pretended to let him drive, wrapping her arm around his waist instinctively. The feeling reminded her of her little sister, and it made her feel good.

"They don't know who is who, you know," Kat said. "They don't know their names. Or anything. They were, like, lost in time."

"Yes, I do," the kid in her lap said. "I'm Gally."

"Galileo?" Alastair asked.

"Where are your parents?" Kat asked. "The adults."

"What is an adult?"

"I am an adult. I am bigger and older. A bigger older person," Kat answered.

"With soft stomachs."

"Yes," she answered slowly. "We have soft stomachs."

Gally giggled again. "I know what an adult is, silly."

When Kat tried to get more out of him, running her hand over the scars on his arms, he left her lap to go watch more cartoons.

SEVENTEEN SECONDS

Ralls fumbled through a large set of keys, annoyed that a more up-to-date security door hadn't been put in yet per his request. *It's always the most awkward part of the tour*, he thought. Ralls finally got the door open, revealing a cavernous space filled with a massive assembly of wires, tubes, twisted cables, and color-coded piping. An insane machine stretched six stories high, weaving through catwalks and open stairs. Ralls thought it looked like a giant robotic eye looking into the future, with bent metal for blood vessels, gold wiring for the iris, and giant black magnets for the pupil. He never shared his interpretation, avoiding anthropomorphizing the already terrifying technology in front of his clients.

Alastair and his class filed in behind Ralls. The older Isaac joined them as well. The ten-year-olds remained behind in the golf cart, captivated by their handheld movie.

"Anyone know what this is?" Ralls asked. Hands went up, except for Kat's.

"Well, jeez," she said.

"Katherine?"

"It's the set from *Superman III*." Katherine had been obsessed by eighties movies after discovering *Sixteen Candles* as a teenager.

"Incorrect."

"Fancy, I thought it was the thing that ate Richard Pryor."

Ralls waited for her to amend her statement.

She didn't.

"Who's Richard Pryor?" said Alastair to fill the silence.

"A washing machine?" said Kat.

Ralls still waited, his frustration growing.

"It was actually Vera, the CEO's sister that got turned into a cyborg," Leo said. "In *Superman III*."

"You can still be sent home," Ralls said, his finger hung in the air, pointing at Kat. "Wherever that is. You wouldn't be the first to be excommunicated. You wouldn't, okay?"

"I assume it is the doohickey of the particle accelerator that you use to capture the collisions of the particles to see what they are made of?" Kat answered meekly.

"Precisely! Exactly!" Ralls said, fueled by his victory. "You are looking at the largest supercollider detector in the world. The energies captured by this doohickey here improve on the core concept design of the Large Hadron Collider in Switzerland. It crosses a relativistic barrier at much higher energies, closer to sixty TeV, so it can do some fancy Superman stuff, like you say. This detector is the terminus of the central accelerator loop." He waved them over to a schematic drawing of the property on the wall.

"Join me around the campfire. You can see there are three primary rings. The big loop is the perimeter of the time effect. The barrier wall is built directly on top of it—you saw that from the plane—and right now you're inside it with the accelerator loop underneath us," he said, pointing down.

The kids all looked past their shoes.

"The two smaller rings are buried underground and run counterclockwise to the large ring, one inside the barrier wall perimeter and one outside. They're used to accelerating protons up to speed from their initial injection points over here. And here. Helium-cooled electromagnets are housed here and here. They pulse an alternating electric current millions of times a second, timed to perfectly match each passing of the particle, giving the proton a kick in the pants when it goes by until the particles are traveling almost at the speed of light, about 99.99999997 percent. Right, Isaac?"

Isaac looked bored. "No."

"Care to correct me?"

"Nope," he said.

Ralls continued. "Along the entire circular racetrack, there are more liquid helium–cooled magnets every step of the way. These things rest at 450 degrees below zero Fahrenheit, colder than deep space. And we have more of the stuff, liquid helium—it's amazing—on this property than the rest of the world combined and then doubled. Pipelines crisscross the whole ecosystem, buried underground for protection. In fact, one of the hardest things about building Cornerstone wasn't the technology; it was keeping the purchases hidden."

"It's not colder than deep space," Isaac said, interrupting.

"It was tough hiding the purchases for a project of this scale because we were driving up the prices of raw materials. The tech was relatively straightforward. Had the same problem with helium that we had with plastic and ceme—"

"Hardest thing," Isaac said.

"Cement," Ralls finished. "Isaac's the expert. I ride on his coattails. Care to continue for me?"

Ralls waited for a response and then carried on.

"See you, doohickey," Isaac said and then left.

"The loop magnets bend the particles, keeping them centered in the vacuum pipes." Ralls watched Isaac exit out of the corner of his eye.

"Anyone know why the loop is so big? Why it needs a circumference of eighty miles?

Leo raised his hand. "The higher the energies, the harder it is for the magnets to bend the path of the particle, so a larger circle means the deflection angle is less."

"Correctamundo—the great Leonardo Da Vinci, reprogrammed to be a physicist. Interesting isn't it, what genius can do? I see your Hadron Collider assignment went to good use Leonardo. What did you get on it? Tenth grade, correct?"

"C," said Leo.

"Ah, it takes about five seconds to get the particles up to speed. Once there, the particle's time frame shifts with a Lorentz factor of 7,664, and the particle also increases in mass, growing sixty thousand times its size, which provides the heft to drag time with it, locally that is. When it finally collides with another particle, an eensy-teensy exotic particle similar to a strangelet is created or a microscopic black hole or both. We're not quite sure."

"Seems like an important distinction," Milk said.

"No, doesn't matter. It's the effect that matters. And how we stabilize it."

Ralls glanced at the door again. "Isaac's genius idea was to do something we call collision stacking. Instead of one particle collision, we create a parade of them, a mess of data—terrible for scientific research—particle after particle, colliding in a stream, like two rivers flowing directly into each other, creating an 'infiniton.' And we keep it stable at the collision point by feeding it with a continuous source of collision energy."

"You mean a black hole," Milk interrupted.

"And with each collision, the infiniton grows until, voila, it's not a black hole. And if it is, it's a miniature one." Ralls composed himself, then added: "It takes three minutes for the effect to grow, which is why that's the lower bound for how long we have to wait on the outside for the tree to grow up."

"And ruin my bike," Leo muttered.

Ralls wondered what it took to actually impress these kids.

"And ten years have passed," Ralls ended.

Alastair puffed out his cheeks.

"Alastair? Thoughts? Seems like everyone else has some," Ralls said.

"As the energy increases and approaches the speed of light, energy converts to mass infinitely as it gets close to C, which stays constant, so that's why the particles grow in size," explained Alastair. "I get that. But something's not right. It's usually the opposite: the faster you go, the slower time passes, not faster."

"That's correct," said Ralls. "It's called the Twin Paradox. If one twin left earth on a spaceship at the speed of light, time would pass slower for him, dilating to accommodate the speed, and then eventually, when he returned, his brother would be much older, or dead. Here, this is backward. Time passes faster. Ten years for three minutes."

He looked at them like a school teacher.

"And the formula that describes that?"

Alastair didn't say anything.

"The formula?" Ralls repeated.

"Do I really have to?" Alastair said.

"Yes, be proud."

"$E = mc^2$."

"We can thank Albert Einstein for that discovery and our Isaac for figuring out how to goose it, flip it and reverse it. To quote Missy Elliot. I was going to give him credit before he left. Really. Man breaking the bonds of time, bending it to his will. And that's ... that's what this little doohickey is," he said with a flourish of his arm.

He waited for a reaction. None came.

"But?" Alastair asked. "Something doesn't make sense."

"It's so cool, eh? Follow me," Ralls said, ignoring him. "If we are lucky, the drone surveys should still be going on."

Alastair's question was left dangling behind the group as they walked through a set of three airlock doors. Each airlock pumped air in and out like a lung until they were finally exhaled into a humid greenhouse atrium hundreds of yards long. It was bound on one side by open-air access to the inside of Cornerstone's property. However, unlike the riot of jungle outside the dorms, there was a completely different biome here, marked by a lush deep-blue forest. Old growth trees soared above red moss. Soft flowers gave the impression of an ancient biological Eden. Animals flitted about.

Every inch of the forest floor was being studied. The ground was covered in curated plants, tags, and strings. Technology spilled into every plot, sampling the microecosystems thriving up in the canopy. They could see scientists working diligently. Somewhere, the sound of laughter.

"Ho-lee-vache," said Milk, pointing. "What is that?"

SIXTEEN SECONDS

Alastair turned to see robotic drones of every size being prepped for launch. When one disappeared into the forest, it was soon replaced with another, some grabbers and claws carrying biological samples in their clutches. Others held cameras. Large or small, the drones made the place seem as if it was under attack, the air filled with whining and whizzing. Once the drones landed, workers organized the samples of nature their robots had found and returned. There were also land-based robots of all types, quadrupedal drone robots zipping around the jungle on eerily, animal-like legs. There were crawlers, runners, and even swimmers. Alastair saw two women using robotic snakes to fish in a cool pond nestled alongside a slow creek. With a flash of their silver bodies, the snakes disappeared under the water.

Alastair was a fan of drones and robots, and had worked on them after school with Leo for fun, when they weren't in football season. He had never seen anything like this, online or otherwise. The technology far surpassed what was out in the real world. Although they were clearly robots—a mess of zip-tied wires, odd parts, and weird shapes—the drones felt like animals. Their movements were skittish and alert. It was unnerving and exhilarating.

Alastair ran over to a bank of drone operators who were using VR headsets to fly airborne drones. He asked to use one.

"No," said the operator without taking off his headset, blind to the crowd forming around him. He wore rough athletic wear that stretched with microtech. Tools hung off him on looped zip ties; tools, food, and gear emerged from every stuffed pocket. The skin cracked around his knuckles. He appeared to be in his forties, and he looked like had been through a war or possibly all of them. That, or he was the world's most intense Boy Scout leader.

"What are you doing?" Alastair asked.

"I'm looking for someone."

"James, please," said Ralls sternly. "May we have a moment."

The man ignored Ralls. He flicked a switch on the drone controller and slowly articulated its thumbstick. The drone flew up a cliff face into a cave.

"I'd like to. James," Ralls said. "Please, Jimmy."

"Goddamn it. Stop yammering," the man snapped. Exasperated he pulled off his VR headset.

It was the Jimmy Jones, JJ, former underwater welder; however, he was much older now—twenty years older to be precise—and the stress of life surviving inside the Crypt had taken a toll on him. He was as hard and as distant.

Jimmy pointed at a handwritten sign next to him: *Surveys Are Sacred.* *"Comprendes?"* he said and put the VR headset back on.

Alastair pointed out the sign to Leo: also on the sign was the same symbol they had seen earlier—a red circle with two off-center parallel lines and a slash through it. Scrawled in pen underneath the symbol was another handwritten note: *What is this?*

There was a monitor next to Jimmy, allowing the kids to watch the drone's feed as it traveled up a cave river system. Soon it found a campsite. The drone hovered over the spot. A fire smoldered, the smoke making it tough to make out the scene. Jimmy moved the drone forward a bit, and the rotors cleared the air, revealing weapons leaning up against the wall and various cuts of meats hanging in net bags.

"Here we go," Jimmy said to himself.

"Jimmy," Ralls said. "Could you please give us a moment? I am asking politely with a calm voice, as discussed previously. I have some guests."

Jimmy took the headset off, this time registering Alastair and his friends. He relaxed and put his headset down. "So these are the geniuses that are going to save us?"

"We will see," said Ralls with a smile. "I'd like to introduce Albert Einstein."

Jimmy laughed at the absurdity of the line. "Sure," he said. Because of Alastair's embarrassment, he added, "Sorry, didn't mean anything by it, but you ain't Albert Einstein kid."

Alastair suddenly realized he would never escape how he felt right now, or ever, when Albert Einstein's name was mentioned: like a fool or a punchline in a bad joke.

Ralls looked like he was going to explode. "Sorry for the interruption, you are doing important work. Let's move on. We can watch a video of the site from our library."

"No, no, I am sorry. I will give them a tour," said Jimmy. "Why is everyone so sensitive. You okay kid?"

"No," said Alastair. "I mean, I don't know."

"Well, don't be, okay. This place doesn't care and will eat you alive, so toughen up a bit. All right?" He was being nicer now, clearly trying to make up for being a dick.

"Sure," said Alastair, repeating Jimmy's earlier word back at him with the same Texas inflection. They both smiled.

"That's better. Jimmy has been working with us for twenty years," said Ralls, "exploring the cave system here at Cornerstone, creating surveys of the subterranean water systems each time we run a cycle. There is no one on the planet who understands this biosphere better then JJ at this point."

"When it is always trying to kill you and your dad and everyone you love, you get to know the bastard real well," Jimmy said.

"You've been working for Cornerstone for twenty years?" asked Alastair.

"Well, technically it's been less than a week."

Alastair was confused. Jimmy looked at him until he suddenly got it.

"Oh, you were ..." said Alastair.

"Einstein," Jimmy said with a wink. "You want a tour?"

***

Alastair's class sat at a long worktable, each with a drone controller and a set of VR goggles in front of them. Jimmy walked them through how to use the controllers.

"The drones all fly on autopilot, programmed to inspect, hover, and explore on predetermined routes of interest after every time cycle. There are also drones that have been inside for the ten years, patrolling and gathering. The ones that survived are waking up now and returning. We have a loss rate of 85 percent, but the ones we find are invaluable. When ten years passes in a few minutes, we need to figure out quickly what went wrong, what grew, died, and broke. We must decide whether and how to fix it in time for the next cycle. Sometimes I can turn it over in a few days because we have gotten better at building roads, infrastructure, and research facilities that can last a cycle without too many problems. Each of your headsets is capable of taking over the POV of any robot already in the field, allowing you to guide it for collection or sampling, or to further of areas of interest. You basically just hijack it and then hop into another drone. The previous one will go back to autonomous mode and finish its flight plan. Or else, you send that one a command for it to come back home, here."

Alastair glanced at a huge wall behind him. Hundreds of video feeds from the drones spread out across the biosphere. There were views from the skies, through the forests, over desert, along cliffs, in canopies, crawling up trees, swimming in lakes, at the base of raging rivers, and dipping in and out of the open ocean. The views soared, crawled, and climbed, the camera motions following the body type and unique movement of its owner. It was as if every living thing in the biosphere had suddenly come alive and reported back everything they saw, sharing their little lives with humans for the first time.

Jimmy flicked a switch. "Put your VR headsets on. You'll be able to see this whole bank of monitors in your feed. Use the right bumper button to switch feeds. If you find one you like and want to explore, hit your right trigger. Everyone here play Xbox?"

A lot of nods.

"Controls work the same way: right thumbstick is your view; left thumbstick is the direction you want to head. It will all be translated to each drone, so you don't have to worry about what device you are piloting, the POV controls are standard across all of them."

Alastair flicked through the drones, each one's perspective filling his entire field of view. Suddenly, he was a bird, and then a ground squirrel making its way along the forest floor. The perspective changes were dizzying at first, but soon they were intoxicating.

Kat swam through a waterfall. Milk sat mesmerized on a leaf, watching something that looked like a rat gnaw on a hard nut. When she fluttered toward it—as a tiny robotic butterfly—the rat disappeared.

"I am a worm!" Leo said.

Alastair soared in the clouds, mesmerized by the sheer scale and beauty of the biosphere, swooping to get a sense of its scale. Animal life teemed everywhere. However, no matter how close Alastair tried to get to them, the creatures skittered away into water, holes, and jungle cover.

"I feel like I am playing the world's best video game," Alastair said.

"Certainly the most expensive game," said Jimmy, watching his feed. He checked his watch.

Alastair flew toward some gazelles grazing in giant, overgrown fields of tall grasses on a plateau, but he couldn't get there. "It's too windy," he said.

Jimmy started quickly switching Alastair's view. "A lot of times, it's a tail-wind, but if you can learn to tack, you can always get where you want to go."

Suddenly, Alastair was among the gazelles. Their fur had a blue, irides-cent sheen, which camouflaged them in the shadows of the waving green grass. One of them looked at Alastair, only a few feet away.

Alastair felt the animal's magnetic draw, falling into its eyes. He moved forward unconsciously, spooking the gazelle. It ran. The other gazelles fol-lowed and then Alastair. He was able to keep up through the grasses.

"I am a gazelle!" he yelled.

Eventually, the animals got away, blue streaks flashed across a river and into a wall of grass on the other side. Alastair gave up the chase and went upstream until he came to a river cave. It was similar to the one Jimmy had been exploring.

"I wouldn't go in there," Jimmy said.

Alastair didn't hear him; he was mesmerized by the experience. As the darkness in the cave grew, Alastair's drone switched over to night vision. Bats with red wings launched at his arrival, darting around the drone before run-ning out into the sky. Alastair found a large cave pool that had something bioluminescent swimming in it.

Behind the drone, beyond Alastair's field of view, a man sat in the shad-ows, watching the strange beast.

He wore armor made of white bones, hundreds of curved ribs large and small tightly woven together in a macabre kabuki of skeletal remains. Neon bacteria smeared across his uniform gave his presence an otherworldly glow.

His eyes sank back into the darkness, watching the technological threat.

Alastair tried to edge the drone forward to the water, but the robot wouldn't wade in. OVERRIDE flashed up on his screen. Alastair hit random buttons until the screen cleared. He could now wade the drone into the edge of the water to see the glowing animals up close.

Suddenly, the drone was kicked into the water. It sank below the surface. Kaleidoscope colors flitted past its cameras. Red and blue tentacles wrapped around the intruder harmlessly.

"Oh shit," Alastair said. Jimmy walked over.

Eventually, the drone was paralyzed in black murkiness. Alastair tried to maneuver it, but it wouldn't budge.

"Gazelles can't swim," Jimmy said.

"I think something pushed me."

"I told you not to go in there. That is a deep pool. It can't swim."

"I'll pay for it?" he offered sheepishly.

"The research, three million dollars. The drone is about three thousand at this point. But the main cost is time. How much time have you cost me today, for example? To make a new drone, it would probably take me about four weeks, including 3D printing, fabrication, assembling, testing, and software configuration. Four time cycles would pass in four weeks. So, it will take about forty years of cycle time to get that particular drone back into action. Imagine you broke it when the Vietnam War ended—we'd be just getting it back about now. No biggy. We got all the time in the world, right?"

A worker piloted the exact same type of drone up to Jimmy. He waved him away.

Alastair apologized. He went to take off his goggles, but Jimmy pushed them back on.

"If you want to go for a swim, try this one," Jimmy said. He switched Alastair to an amazing view on top of a waterfall. The water seemed to cascade into a hole and never come out. "Follow me."

Jimmy put on a headset. He took Alastair's hand and pushed his thumb forward, diving him off the top of the waterfall down to the depths below. He followed him with his drone. They fell with the water, twirling around each other like a dance. Alastair could see Jimmy's drone as his view sailed past. They were flying fish.

Suddenly, the roiling water below was upon them. Alastair jerked his hands up to his face to block the impact. The illusion of being there was very real. He laughed. Underwater, Alastair's drone was inside a rainbow of electric tropical colors. Thousands of fish darted about, eating tiny jellyfish. Alastair chased them with a flick of his thumb. He had never felt so free.

Milk joined him.

"The jellyfish is a relative of the Irukandji jellyfish," Jimmy told them.

At only one centimeter wide, the Irukandji species was one of the most venomous jellyfish in the world, gram for gram, Jimmy explained. And they had a famously weird side effect other than death. Their sting caused a sense of impending doom. Due to their tiny size, they were often missed as a culprit in emergency rooms. The only giveaway was a patient's insistence that they "were going to die." Some surfers had been known to ask doctors to kill them, so certain were they that their death was imminent.

"I'm glad this is a drone and not me," said Alastair. "I don't like doom."

Milk agreed. She thought it was a nasty little creature.

"If you put it on flock mode—the Y button—it will stay with the fish," said Jimmy. "It uses the same basic logic that they use. Fish always try to keep a fin on their immediate right, touching another fin."

Alastair hit the Y button, and the drone suddenly flowed with the fish, rather than scattering them. It was a simple hereditary behavior that keeps a school of fish, or a flock of birds, tightly together when under attack. The simple rule of how to follow each other—follow that bird!—binds them together unpredictably, pulling and pushing invisibly into one writhing mass. It creates complex dynamics that make it impossible for an attacker to pinpoint one individual among a group.

"It's that simple?"

Ralls watched from behind. "It's amazing, isn't it? What we created," he said.

"I'm a fish," said Alastair.

"What God created," Jimmy said, correcting Ralls.

"Sure, and I put it in a bottle," Ralls retorted.

All the kids were enraptured by their virtual exploration. Milk tried to fly her drone over the barrier wall. She could see the Texas dirt on the other side. She kept turning back and forth. Jungle. Texas dirt. Jungle. Texas dirt.

"You can't fly it out," said Ralls. "There are perimeter sensors that stop the drones in case their autopilot programming is off," he said pointedly. "Or their pilot. And when the effect is on, we don't need a barrier, it is lethal to all life. The barrier wall is just there for when we are *not* running a cycle. To stop things from getting out."

Milk ignored him and flew along the top of the barrier wall, continuing to test the invisible barrier built into the drone's code. "I can't get out," she said.

"As I said, nothing can," said Ralls. "There is a lot of advanced tech DARPA shared with us, and they would be none too happy if it ended up on the internet. Or one of your silly blogs."

"Ha, you would be so lucky," she said.

Next to Milk, Leo let his drone do the flying so he could survey. Underneath the table, he drew in his sketchbook, adding to the schematic map drawings he had started on the airplane. Next to him, Zack had the arms of his hooded sweatshirt pretending to hold a controller on the desk, while his actual arms were underneath the desk, like Leo's now. He blindly dismantled a controller with a pocket tool.

Zack popped out a microchip, handed it to Leo, and then put the controller back together.

Alastair, however, was enraptured still. Caught in the Crypt's gaze, he floated now above a mysterious, white structure that was shaped like a nautilus shell. It was an incredible work of modern architecture nestled in the jungle on a plateau high above the Crypt. Red vines clutched at it, while old growth trees spiraled around it and then outward toward the cliffs. Waterfalls ringed the plateau.

Alastair flew in for a closer look and saw a light turn on in one of the curved windows. And then it quickly turned off. "How do you supply power for ten years if everything is cut off from the real world?" Alastair said.

"We don't supply power from outside," said Ralls.

"I just saw a light turn on. Where does the power come from?"

"A light turned on?" Ralls asked. "Unlikely."

Alastair caught the edge of concern in Ralls's voice.

"This thing is broken," Leo said holding up the controller.

"And this is why we can't have nice things," said Ralls. "And Martin Luther! Can you please stop? The drones can't escape."

"Not if you ever call me that again. Why can't I fly south, over to that canyon?" Milk asked.

"Because you can't."

"Why? What's there?"

Suddenly, the screens all went dark. Ralls had turned them off.

"Enough questions. Very curious crowd, aren't you?"

Alastair took off his headset. He missed the experience immediately, crashing back into his mundane self.

However, something profound had shifted inside Alastair. He had to know.

Everything.

FIFTEEN SECONDS

They walked back to the transportation tunnel. Jimmy chatted with Alastair. Ralls was out front as usual.

"To answer Zack's question about power," Ralls said, "I'm surprised you kids didn't think of it on your flight. The barrier wall turns into a dam when it meets the ocean. It holds the water back. Inside, there is a giant hydroelectric dam. The power from the hydro plants is used to store energy locally on batteries for each ten-year run."

It was not the first time someone had come up with the idea of damming the ocean to produce power, but it was novel for a group to be audacious enough to try it. In the 1920s, a German architect named Herman Sörgel proposed a dam to be built across the Strait of Gibraltar in the Mediterranean. The dam would drain the inland sea by 660 feet, creating new land from the seabed and bringing agriculture to North Africa's arid desert. In the 1930s, Sörgel promoted it as a pacifist counter proposal to Germany's *Lebensraumr Programm*, a nationalist expansion movement that arose after British blockades in WWI.

Ralls became aware of Sörgel's Atlantropa when the idea resurfaced as a way to protect low-lying European coastal areas, including Venice, from rising sea levels. He felt its vision fit his own grand plans, so he appropriated the name in his early funding pitches to the military. When it was discovered that Sörgel had extensively quoted Hitler to demonstrate that the project was not inconsistent with Nazism, Ralls's Atlantropa was renamed the Cornerstone Project.

However, the dam concept survived. Cornerstone needed to be able to generate its own power to stay hidden: they couldn't exactly draw ten years' worth of electricity off the nearest Corpus Christi grid without showing their hand. The ocean dam was one of the rare ideas that came directly from Ralls. It was universally considered genius, making it one of Ralls's favorite topics.

"It takes about a week for the dam's hydroelectric plants to charge the battery systems, okay? That's why we can only run about one cycle a week, typically on Tuesday afternoon. Basically, this entire ecosystem sits on top of batteries. A lot of double-A batteries."

"It does?" asked Zack.

Ralls said, "No, of course not. Lithium batteries. Like electric cars, but thousands of them."

"Why are you always testing us?" Leo retorted, his annoyance flashing up.

"And that's why lithium prices shot up," said Milk. "The Silver Peak mine and Western Case both expanded into federal lands. Raping the land."

Ralls scrunched his nose.

"Yes, Milk. I love your nickname, by the way, I do. You own it," Ralls said, pushing back. "I fought to include you in the list because you need some grit in the gears, okay? Can't go XX to XY, female to male, because you need a Y chromosome from somewhere. But you can go the other way. Male to female, like Eve's rib. A lesser copy."

Milk looked like she was going to hit Ralls.

"Anyway," Ralls continued, "it is easy to hide things with the military," he said, picking up the previous thread, "but not when it comes to Wall Street. And we couldn't control the cost of lithium. Very observant. All of you, very—"

Ralls stopped short when he got to the transportation tunnel. The golf carts were empty. The children were gone.

He jogged back inside the facility and returned with a few workers. They took carts in opposite directions. Kat started down the hall, calling for the kids with Milk. Leo headed the other way, leaving Alastair alone with Jimmy.

Jimmy sat down in the cart. He pulled Ralls's phone out from underneath his leg. It was left on the seat and still on.

"So what was like in there for ten years? I'm afraid to ask," Alastair said. "Was it hard to say goodbye to your family?"

"I brought my family with me, my dad. He was sick, and Cornerstone bribed us with money and a promise of a cure for his lung cancer. We went into a time cycle to help support a bunch of cancer vaccine researchers for the ten year round trip. He was going to be one of their test subjects for trials."

"Was going to be?" Alastair asked.

Jimmy went silent.

"What happened to your father?"

Jimmy flicked through Ralls phone. "He's got some sweet eighties music on here."

"Did he—"

"They cured him," said Jimmy.

"They cured cancer?"

"No, just him—immunotherapy based on the genetics of his tumors, trained his T-cells to kill the cancer. It is not actually a breakthrough; they've been doing it for a while now out in the real world, but since we signed up, he got access to the custom paint job. He is still an asshole, though, so they didn't cure that."

"You said twenty years you worked for Cornerstone. That's two cycles. Why the second one?"

"Second one was an accident," said Jimmy. "I got stuck inside for another cycle when I was on a failed cave dive. They thought I was dead. I wasn't. You'd be surprised how often that happens to me. Wasn't prepared for more than a twelve-hour work day the second cycle. I did bring lunch, so that was nice. There were actually seven of us in my crew, but I was the only one who made it that cycle. Didn't mind the time. My biggest worry really was never seeing my father again if I died."

"I'm sorry."

"It's okay. The Crypt has a habit of swallowing things and killing people you care about. But I made it back to Dad." Jimmy handed Ralls's phone to Alastair. "A present."

"Did you see them?" a voice echoed. Ralls ran toward the cart.

"Looked everywhere," Jimmy said, relaxing his arms back onto the golf cart.

Alastair pocketed Ralls's phone.

FOURTEEN SECONDS

"Zack asked me point-blank if they are going to be put inside," said Paul, much later.

"This is the first sunset my garden has seen in ten years," responded Ralls. He didn't catch what Paul said or chose not to. It was dusk. The sky was the color of red crimson oil paint.

"Last I checked, the sun sets every night," Paul said. He stopped walking, annoyed Ralls wasn't paying attention to him. "And the government owns this now, so you are more like a lessee. I represent the landlord."

Ralls ignored him, strolling with the care of a sergeant surveying his troops. The garden was an ornamental march of flowers, vines, and solid trunks twisted into swirling processions of wood. Whereas elsewhere on the property the jungle was a riot of natural selection, here nature was bent to the will of its master, tortured into impossible poses—animals, portcullises, arches, furniture, woven wood, and flower tapestries grown over centuries by an owner who could only visit once every ten years.

"The kids are smart, but it will seem too big of an act of treachery," said Ralls. "What did Hitler say? 'Make the lie big, make it simple, keep saying it, and eventually, they will believe it.'"

"He didn't actually say that," responded Paul. "And I don't think he should be your inspiration. The US Government doesn't like lying to children."

"The US Government? Is that you?"

"I don't like lying to children," said Paul.

"And what about to grown men? Do they lie to men? To me? I tried telling the truth to Isaac, and look what happened. It's better they don't know yet what's best for them," Ralls said. "The world will chew them up. I am going to protect them and their minds. If they don't realize their gifts, they will forever feel inferior to history. And that's my burden, to help them. I made the mistake of thinking I was raising gods, but really, they are messy, opinionated kids, and I want to fix that. I'm offering them a life in a Garden of Eden, with each other, free from history, to explore their minds and talents."

"So you are acting altruistically?" asked Paul.

"Yes," said Ralls. "It's the only way I know how."

Ralls found a sapling growing at the base of a tree, forced unnaturally into a sculpture of a tormented woman, swept up in the massive arms of an even larger tree whose limbs seemed to be wrestling it to the earth, pinning its soul in a pietà of bark and anger.

"Like all children, they must be trained first," Ralls said, winding the immature tree into its parents. He used iron twists from his pocket to pin it permanently into place.

"I have to be honest. Sometimes I ran the accelerator just to get this posture right," he said, gazing at his work. It cost millions, more than a museum piece. "And if this is all I leave behind, I will be content."

Ralls quietly trimmed errant branches.

"Do you know why we run cycles at three p.m.?" Ralls asked, finally turning to Paul.

Paul stared at Ralls, simultaneously appalled and amazed.

"The sun is right there, at three p.m. standard time, frozen in the sky for ten years." Ralls pointed down the axis of the path. "It really is the secret to the symmetry of this walk. Everything grows toward it, like a magnet forever pulling its branches to me. Occasionally, I'll put the sun somewhere else to sweep some asymmetry into the garden. That's why everything seems to be dancing. I can control the position of the sun."

Paul was unsure how to respond, lost in Ralls's hubris, mesmerized by the dazzling truth of his statement. Ralls did have the power to control the sun.

While all physical phenomena were trapped inside the accelerator's boundaries during the cycle effect, the constant speed of the sun's light flowed into the Crypt in an unending barrage of photons unchanged and unfazed by the parlor trick. It was one of Cornerstone's great mysteries, conjured into existence by the absurdities of general relativity and the machinations of a new Isaac Newton playing with a toy in the role of toddler god, playing with his creation, or a video gamer who got the universe's cheat codes.

Early on, before the eight-month grow cycle, they once ran the accelerator near dusk, and nearly everything died, like in a nuclear winter or the gray aftermath of a volcanic ash sky. Too late in the day, with the sun hovering just over the horizon for ten years, there was not enough light or energy in the system to maintain the life cycle. It wasn't something another twenty-four minutes of bright noon sunshine (and eighty years) couldn't fix the next Tuesday; however, time of day means time for the decade. And Cornerstone eventually chose 3 p.m. for their weekly time cycles for maximum energy absorption. Azimuth 229.16°, elevation 82.48°. And if it was cloudy, they waited, like a film set in search of the perfect light for the perfect shot.

Or so the Pentagon was told.

Paul wondered what other secrets Ralls kept from him. If the man was convinced he could control the sun, believing he had that power and right, how would he be convinced to slow down, to be cautious?

"Once they see the Nautilus Facility tomorrow, they will understand. And it will all be worth it," said Ralls. "And they, like the others before them, will *choose* to work at Nautilus for one cycle of their life, for our greater future. It's just ten years. College plus grad school."

"They didn't choose. They were trapped."

"They would have."

"How many Einsteins are you going to kill to get this right?" Paul asked. "Humans aren't trees."

"I'm not killing anyone, just giving them a different life. To flower. But they must make the choice. I'll give them that."

"Are you finished?" asked an old voice.

The voice stepped out from the shadows, it was Cayce Jones. Jimmy's father. He leaned against a tree, holding on to it as if it was supporting him from being thrown off the earth, and watched the two men grow uncomfortable.

Ralls tried to play it off. "Hello, Cayce."

How much had the old man heard? wondered Paul.

"Life is never finished," responded Ralls. "It just stops in interesting places. Like you. An interesting place."

"Again, misquote," said Cayce.

He had heard.

"It's paintings that are never finished, and your platitudes are empty intellectual bullshit. Pentagon here is right—we need to delay the next cycle until the cleanup happens. People are still missing. We think they may have holed up on the Texercon oil rig for the last cycle to survive, but we haven't been able to get anyone over to them yet. And my son hasn't finished his next dive survey yet. We need to know more about the Black Hole cave site. Two weeks at minimum."

"Two weeks. Two cycles?" asked Ralls, delaying. It was clear to Paul that Ralls's mind, like his own, was racing back to remember what they had said.

"Maybe more," Cayce said, not giving any hints. "Two of the millennial vaults are cracked. Jimmy has to survey more, but they need to be sealed before the next cycle, lest we have another military-grade bioweapon evolving in our ecosystem."

That got Paul's attention.

It was a real problem. One of the reasons the Crypt was so deadly was that when the military arrived, they installed research vaults to test degradation methods for toxic materials. The theory was that part of the accelerator could act as a giant materials disposal facility, a dirty weapon laundry machine. Or a portion of it could. Put radioactive, secret Pentagon material inside, turn on the millennial wash cycle, and it would fully decay. The vaults were designed by the best minds to last "forever," using the same dry-bed technology and inspired ideas on erosion behind the Yucca Mountain Nuclear Waste Repository outside of Las Vegas.

However, time is its own force, its own muscle, and it will eventually open any jar, no matter how tight the lid. The Millennial Tombs, nicknamed in an employee contest, didn't last ten cycles—one hundred years. It would have been mostly harmless, except they didn't just test "a minute amount" of nuclear fissile material. They also tried to evolve bioweapons. Each vault had something deadly and interesting to play with. Pathogens. Exotic materials. The logic was that time would "wash" the vaults' contents, so there was no constraint, so certain were they of the vault's strength.

Designed to last a million years. And like the best-reaching dreams of man, they believed it. They thought of everything, except that the central river, the artery for Cornerstone, could divert itself and an ocean's worth of water, plunging into the hardened facility. The vaults were a road bump before a power that could cut through mountains and carve Grand Canyons.

And the things that the vaults released into the life cycle were still classified, even to Ralls. He had been playing catch-up ever since.

"Also, we found another Russian encampment, a fresh one, hidden by Waterfall Eight," added Cayce. "We think it is the same group we saw last week. They survived the last ten-year cycle. And by the looks of things, they somehow got a fresh supply drop. The Department of Defense was tracking a submarine that went dark south of Cuba, so we know they are in the area. We need to tighten security and do a CSC. And continue to sweep before we take the kids on the tour. I just want to make sure it is safe for them in the morning. I know the tour is only a few hours, but even that is too long in the Crypt." His face was inscrutable.

CSC: clean, sweep, contain, thought Paul, another one of his acronyms that made it out of his white papers into Cornerstone's active procedures. He was amazed at how much his nomenclature—based on pure conjecture and guesswork in a Pentagon basement—seemed to have been adopted but none of his recommendations.

"We can't stop for a day, not for a week, not for a month," said Ralls. "There is an invisible line in time. Currently, we are ahead of the Russians, the Chinese, and whoever the hell else, but at some point, that line will slip by us, and they will be at the front of history, forever accelerating away from us. The class needs to see what they have to play with. The tour will only be a few hours. Jimmy can keep them safe in his Armageddon Trucks. You two survived ten years. What's another couple of hours on the inside? They need to see the Nautilus Facility so they can understand the power of Cornerstone. And then make their choice."

"They won't fix your problem," said Cayce.

"Our problem." Ralls looked at his tree. "You have until tomorrow to fix my garden. Do the tour and get out. Then we fire. Okay?" He gazed down his garden path with pursed lips. "At three p.m."

THIRTEEN SECONDS

"Tomorrow, we are going inside the Crypt for a short tour of the Nautilus Facility. You'll need to know all of the things that can kill you," Cayce said. "I'm the resident zoologist for the Crypt, because everyone else died, and I was all that was left. So don't expect too much. I didn't go to college."

Cayce was actually underselling his role at Cornerstone. After he and Jimmy survived the ten-year cycle, Cayce's meticulous field collecting and species studying in the Crypt—at great risk to life and limb—proved invaluable to the life science's team who stayed safe and sound in the barrier facility.

"We haven't gone to college either," said Zack, being a little too literal.

Cayce took a beat and evaluated them. "Well then, you are as dumb as I am, so probably, you should pay attention."

Alastair plucked at the plastic wrapping on his chair and glanced around the space. Cold with bad lighting and wrapped in empty floor-to-ceiling chalkboards. It felt like someone thought the room would be ideal for brainstorming, but everyone got distracted during the interior design process and moved on.

Almost everyone was there: Jimmy, the Isaac Newtons—both of them—Ralls, Pentagon Paul. The only ones missing were the New Kids, which is what Kat had taken to naming the missing children from the most recent cycle.

"And there are a lot of things that can kill you," Cayce finally continued. His voice was soft; no one talked or breathed too deeply, eager to catch every word. "The Crypt is the most—"

"The Naut," Ralls interrupted politely.

"The Naut"—Cayce paused briefly, waiting to be challenged with another interruption. When it didn't come, he continued—"houses the most dangerous, nasty, villainous, get-in-your-pants-and-kill-you-with-a-bite, suffocate-and-fall-into-some-sticky-kill-your-best-friend, what-the-heck-is-that plant-monster ecosystem in the world." His voice was a metronomic drone that belied the content of his words. He forced a smile. "We didn't design it that way because we didn't design it. Nature did." He limped over to the chalkboard and wrote *1,000,000*. "Over a million years, 55,500 generations, and now everything is just kind of evolved nastiness. Short of starting over, which we can't, we are stuck with it. A big fancy f-you from nature. And. Your. Friendly. Local. Pentagon," he added, pausing for effect after each word. "Good?" he asked, returning his gaze to Ralls.

Jimmy gave his father a golf clap.

Paul whispered into Ralls's ear, and then Ralls walked up to the man and whispered in *his* ear for what felt like a minute.

A lot of ear talk, thought Alastair. The man started over. "Hello, class, my name is Cayce Jones."

"I believe you are *Doctor* Cayce Jones now," corrected Ralls.

While Cayce didn't have his oxygen or any of the low energy that came with it, he had confidence and poise. Despite being ten years older, he somehow seemed younger. Cayce pointed a cane at Ralls for an uncomfortably long time, and then dropped it, defeated internally by some measure of his personality. He was a paid servant of Ralls after all.

"I work on the biosphere research team, one of the world's most *amazing* jungle ecosystems, designed with *every care* to create breathable oxygen, the *right* amount of CO_2, fresh water, and arable land to grow food for ten years of isolation. Is that better, Ralls? Should I say it's got pools and tennis courts? Cause it doesn't anymore. It just has a whole bunch of face-eating, friend-sucking death."

"Just get to it, old man," said Isaac. He perched on a windowsill like a vulture, casting a shadow over the room.

Cayce turned to write on the chalkboard and then whipped around and threw a piece of chalk at Isaac, who fell onto the stairs to avoid it.

Cayce drew a big circle on the chalkboard with a new piece. "Thirty percent of the Crypt is impassable. Death zones," Cayce explained. He went through the region of the Crypt in chalk, describing and diagraming in stark terms all the various threats of the environment. Nitrogen sinks. Histamine death. Unknown species. It was sobering.

Alastair spent as much time looking at Leo as he did the board, trying to see if his reactions matched his.

A chasm so deep that nothing had made it in or out, a category six river that flowed with carnivorous fish the size of water buffalo, a waterfall that fell into a hellhole in the earth and never returned. Ferromagnetic ant colonies that moved the needle on magnetic north, storing metal in their nests, whose saliva dissolved skin and whose emerging swarms covered football fields in seconds. Red things that bite, blue things that poison, big purple things you just avoid at all costs.

"Neat. What's with the color-coding? The red and the blue," asked Milk.

She seems to be the only one who's not afraid, thought Alastair.

"The colors were for us to understand what was ours and what was nature's," said Cayce. "When we first tried to design the biosphere, we hand-picked every plant and animal based on our best science—building an ecosystem from the ground up in what we thought was a balanced, self-supporting system. We grew animals and plants independently, tweaking their genetic code as we saw fit on limited cycle runs to grow new animals that'd be suited, we thought, for life in the Crypt. It was all very cute. Red for carnivores, blue for herbivores. And it was a disaster. Everything died, every time. But the genes survived. They have a tendency to do that. We were running cycles every day. Ten years. Ten years. Ten years. Throwing life at it, trying to get the formula right. We got close to a self-supporting ecosystem on a few cycles, but invariably, on the next one, everything would be dead again. Or else we would have to burn it all down with napalm and flamethrowers for fear of some new pathogen or toxin taking out Texas like something out of *The Andromeda Strain*."

He paused on that last thought. The room started to fidget.

"The entire thing would be overrun with a disease, so we'd burn it," Cayce continued. "Or a fungus. Or insects. Miles of them, like a matt of fungus covering everything. Rough place to be for ten years. Ever tried to kill a nasty spider? Imagine a stadium of them. Then we started building test patches. Different biomes from around the world in limited areas to compete with each other. That seemed to work a bit, letting nature and evolution take their course. And then Ralls came up with the idea of the Scoop Ships."

Jimmy jumped down to the stage. "The problem was that no matter how much he tried to manipulate the ecosystem to help it, he would never be able to stay ahead of it," Jimmy explained. Whereas Cayce was nervous with sarcastic energy, Jimmy was alive, his chest proud. "And Ralls couldn't figure out why the red-and-blue strains didn't stick, with plants pulling the red coloring into the genomes and mixing. They were worried about what we were creating. Animal-plant hybrids started to evolve. So they stopped. And decided to get what they wanted. And what they wanted was a normal ecosystem, a normal life, right, Alastair?"

Alastair's face flushed with confusion over being called out in front of everyone.

"Normal life," continued Jimmy. "That produced oxygen and clean water, smack in the middle of the Texas desert. They should have built the accelerator in Costa Rica, FYI for next time. So Ralls came up with the Scoop Ships to fix Isaac's mess-up."

Now Isaac flushed.

Alastair felt better, then immediately worse. Jimmy was an equal opportunity bully.

Jimmy described the Scoop Ships: retrofitted container ships sent out across the world to collect entire ecosystems. International teams of machines and men, mostly clueless, working under the guise of strip mining, would shear the top fifteen feet of topsoil—all the life they could get from the densest forests, jungles, fields, mountains, rivers, and cave systems—and transport it to the container ships.

"Biomes were isolated to individual ships to preserve the ecological balance. And then they were dumped here." Jimmy was serious now.

"They didn't care if things died. That's normal, but their seeds, the chemistry, biology, and bacteria, they were all scooped up as well. It was like hundreds of life cakes, each the size of an oil tanker, made of the ingredients that work on earth no matter the location were scooped into my ships. They collected life, dirt, dead stuff—everything—until the container ships were full. Like a rusty ark. And planted it here, set the oven to one million years and waited seven months for it to bake."

"Two hundred and eight days, to be precise," Cayce said. "And voila. We got oxygen, clean water, and some really hardy, gnarly animals who were genuinely pissed at us."

"Do you need to swear so much? It doesn't make it any more convincing," Isaac said. "Or smarter."

"Shut up, Mosquito. We can turn the Crypt on and off for a few minutes," Jimmy continued lecturing to the class, "and it doesn't change much in ten years. But like a shitty grandpa, we are stuck with what we got. It's old, it's alive, and its parts still sort of work, but it's cranky, and hanging out with it sucks."

Milk asked how many ships they had used.

Jimmy looked to Ralls.

He told Milk there were over a thousand shiploads and then fought with her over the ethics of slashing and burning whole ecosystems to throw into his "death blender."

"It's all Isaac's fault," said Jimmy, joining in for the first time. "Blame him. He was smart enough to get the physics right but too dumb to think about the people living there."

Isaac suddenly stormed the stage to hit Jimmy, but stopped short and tripped when Jimmy raised a fist. His chest heaving, Isaac looked out at the class in malice.

"Relax," said Cayce, offering a hand to Isaac.

"Get off," Isaac instructed. Standing up, his anger grew with his height. He turned to the students, although his gaze bore into Alastair. "You are here because we have problems. And that small man"—Isaac pointed at Ralls—"and that insignificant man"—he pointed at Paul—"think that I, Isaac Newton, am incapable of fixing them. Despite that Isaac Newton alone made this. This wonder. Me. Isaac Newton."

The class sat stone-faced.

"Bullshit," Alastair said, the words tumbled out of his mouth before his conscious mind could stuff them back inside.

Leo jumped in to help his friend. It was not often that Alastair stepped off the ledge, and Leo wanted to make sure he didn't fall. "Yeah, exactly. So what? I'm Leonardo da Vinci," Leo said. "You'll never actually be Isaac Newton. And that's why you are such a prick. Because you know that."

The room held its breath for the explosion.

The insult had the opposite effect. Isaac calmed down and smiled. His body uncorked, twisting out of its hole.

"I'm going to tell you the problems we need to fix," Isaac said. "I'll explain physics you could never understand. So I can watch you fail, Alastair.

And Zach. And then I can get back to building on God's work. Fair enough, Ralls?"

"Fair enough, Isaac," Ralls responded, unmoved by Isaac's performance. "Get on with it."

Isaac began from the beginning. The history of his first thoughts on time tumbled out in a precise train of thought. His mind was on brilliant display, his hand scratched numbers and symbols in fluid swoops on the chalkboard. With every line of his equations, he seemed to grow larger and larger until he was an ogre at the front of the class, his giant hands gripping the tiny chalk like a sword or a poisoned pen.

Finally, he finished. He turned and sat on the desk, watching the children try to parse the final bits of his inexorable logic. Alastair stared at him. Isaac's imaginary weight seemed to bow the desk, the wood splintering under his achievement.

He terrified Alastair, the performance greater than any insult or comeback. "And that is how you bend time to your will," Isaac said, more to himself than his audience.

"You're still a prick," Leo said.

Isaac ignored him. "Now, you don't understand how I did it. Let's talk about the problems you won't be able to fix. The most immediate issue we are facing is one of quantum wave fluctuations a posteriori time cycle events. The wavelengths of the effects are on the scale of one AU, but we are seeing them on flight landing systems and equipment that uses GPS to perform sensitive operations, including—"

"Isaac," Ralls said, attempting to interrupt him.

"—domestic airliners. And the effect is spreading. What we are looking at is happening, we believe—"

"Isaac," Ralls said again, trying to stop the train wreck from happening.

"—during our downtime cycling. What I am solving for is a way to dampen the quantum wave spread, theta, here, and the oscillations after the T asymptote, here, to contain the time skew."

"Dr. Newton!" Ralls yelled.

"That's better. Yes?" Isaac asked.

"This has been solved already by Kat."

"Do tell," Isaac said, amused.

Kat explained her theory about airline maintenance schedules. Isaac was silent the whole time, a smile frozen on his face.

There were no physics involved. Just lateral thinking.

"And," she finished, "you used 'a posteriori' wrong. It does mean 'derived by,' but only through human observation. Physics cannot be 'a posteriori.' Fancy word, wrong usage."

The whole class burst into laughter.

A pink flush of embarrassment washed across Isaac's cheeks. He paused, the air tense. Then, "You think I didn't think of that? The effect is growing," he said. "We are playing in God's backyard. I'm knocking on his door, and what are you famous for? Fucking a horse? *Catherine. The. Great*?" Isaac spat each word at her and let the attack land.

His voice changed. "It's not just the airliners that are failing, Ralls. Weapons targeting, drone operations, the taking out of the wrong house in Iran. Death, small children dying, these are the effects that I have to fix with the Pentagon while you run around with children. No one cares about another humid flight to Dallas. And these things will never understand what is at stake. I am driving history. There will be books about me. And all of you, you will all be in the footnotes. In seven-point font."

Alastair looked at Kat. She got up and left. Jimmy walked up to Isaac and shoved him off the desk onto the floor.

"All right, class, time for your next lesson," he said cheerily.

TWELVE SECONDS

Isaac ran down the halls, dragging posters off the walls with his fingertips, old staples drawing streams of blood. He slammed the door to his office. The open-air room was cross-sectioned by shafts of light and dust. Glass panel walls running through the middle were covered in formulas, thoughts, and diagrams of Cornerstone. It was like someone had transferred Isaac's brain onto glass to preserve it.

He swayed around the room. His past welled up inside him like a bitter spring forced out of a drought. He started to kick through the glass panels with his heel, thrashing as he went, like a fawn drowning in a sudden flood, sinking deeper and deeper. The last vestige of guilt and regret about what he was going to do sank with him as well until only malice was left to float on the surface.

Amid the shattered glass, he found his bag. Inside, the insect drones Sephora had given him stared up at him as if they were a jury waiting for his final arguments. He turned one on, testing its flight with his phone.

BOOK FOUR

Galileo Galilei

ELEVEN SECONDS

It was 9 a.m. After a long night of arguing about the nature of fate and hubris in their rooms, the class spent breakfast studying the legal documents on treason they were given in anticipation of a trip to the Nautilus Facility at the center of the Crypt.

"Why do we need to go inside?" Leo asked.

"Like really *go in*?" said Milk, for emphasis. "You do realize how dumb that is?"

Alastair was adamant, he had to see it.

***

Jimmy was tired.

He had taken too many one-way trips into the Crypt with Ralls VIP "guests."

But these kids were different. They might be able to fix the mess they were all in. He knew he had failed to understand the Black Hole cave or many of the other impossible mysteries hidden at Cornerstone. But as much as he wanted to protect the kids, he also knew that once they learned what the Nautilus was, it would be their choice ultimately.

So he resigned himself to watch as they argued one last time, curiosity picking them off, one by one, like they did every group tempted into the unknown.

The final standoff between Alastair and his class happened next to two giant off-road trucks in a hangar above the jungle mists. One of the trucks was painted black and white with Blackbeard's pirate skulls and crossbones; the other was covered in huge pink Hello Kitty decals.

Alastair was inside the Hello Kitty truck, hanging out the window. "We have to go if we are going to be anybody. You said it yourself, Leo. It's going to be fun. And necessary."

"I didn't say that," Leo protested.

"Yes, you did, and you were right. It is who we are meant to be. This is way more important than anything we could've imagined. Aren't you curious what it's like in there?"

"And now you are all gung ho. At maximum information. It has only gotten worse every minute," Milk said. "Freaking *now*? As we head into a giant time washing machine of death?"

"Alastair, we shouldn't go in there," said Leo. "This isn't the time to stand up and make a real decision for the first time in your life. Like not now."

"Now," said Alastair. "Right, Jimmy?"

Jimmy was concerned, leaning against a giant wheel. He knew enough about Alastair to know he wasn't a natural leader, but he wasn't going to jump in to help him. "It's their choice," he said. "I wouldn't force them if I were you. Might backfire later."

"Do you forever want to be in Isaac's shadow?" said Alastair.

Zack considered the question. "No," he said.

"Come on, Leo," Alastair said. "Put on your man pants. What else are you going to do, seriously?"

"Live. Be famous. And rich. Even if I do nothing and just get invited to places. And not die. I prefer that destiny. Why can't we just pilot some more drones there?" Leo said to Jimmy. "If you are all so hot to trot to have us see this Nautilus thing."

"I like that idea, too," said Zack.

"No," Jimmy retorted. "The Nautilus is different. Doesn't work that way. No drones. It's what's inside. It's on-site access for a reason. I'll make sure you're safe. It's a quick run out and back. Four hours tops. It's worth it. And I generally think nothing is ever worth it."

Jimmy broke his own promise—he swore to never again promise someone he could keep them safe. Too many had died.

"Four hours," repeated Alastair, happy to have an ally finally. "All the time in the world to visit," he added, checking himself as he saw his friends' looks.

Jimmy didn't add anything. He had to shut up and let them decide for themselves for his own sanity.

The Nautilus was the top secret lockdown facility at the center of the Crypt from which the Naut derived its name. Ninety-eight percent of the Cornerstone staff didn't know what went on in the Nautilus. Ralls liked the mystery of it and the name—"The Naut"—because it could mean different things to different people. When spoken, the name could be interpreted to mean "not," for opposite, "naught," for nothing, or "knot," like a knot of time, impossible to unravel.

In truth, *naut* was the Greek word for "traveler." *Astronaut*, then, was literally "space traveler." *Aquanaut*, "sea traveler." *Nautical*, "sea navigation." In its purest form, "The Naut" could be defined as "The Traveler," Ralls would explain to those who had to listen. And inside the Naut, it was time that traveled, flowing like a river in another valley of reality.

The name "The Naut" also reminded Ralls of the name Odysseus gave to the Cyclops. Odysseus told the one-eyed monster his name was "Nobody." When asked who blinded him, the Cyclops kept saying, "Nobody blinded me," allowing Odysseus to escape in his golden fleece. And like Nobody, Naut was a name that meant everything and nothing.

For a scientist, Ralls had the soul of a philosopher.

Not, Naught, Knot, Naut. The words rolled over his tongue as he said them to himself.

The Naut came to mean the mysterious force necessary to bend time.

Mostly, it was simply short for Nautilus, but for Ralls, it also served his various branding purposes well. He knew the marketing power of mystery.

The adults who did understand the power of the Nautilus facility at the center of the Crypt—among them Ralls, Isaac, Jimmy, and Cayce—were all tight-lipped. They had to be. It was Cornerstone's crown jewel and the one mystery that the Russians still didn't understand.

When the Pentagon moved in and discovered the possibility of creating the Nautilus, they instituted the top secret protocol systems SCI and SAP—Sensitive Compartmented Information with Special Access Programs—a black-ops classification that added a thick layer of secrecy upon the already secret project. In military parlance, SAP trumps top secret clearance. It was like two-factor authentication. It wasn't necessarily higher than top secret clearance itself; you just needed it as well. Those who held SAP approval became shadow kings of their domain. And at Cornerstone, at the top of the dark pyramid of clearance levels, sat the Nautilus Facility. If the president had shown up to Cornerstone without SAP, he wouldn't be granted access. (He was.)

"Guys?" Alastair asked.

No one budged.

"Okay, I'm going alone. Jimmy, will you still take me?"

Jimmy nodded, sensing where Alastair was going.

"And if I die, it's all of your faults," said Alastair.

Leo folded first. "I'm going under protest," he said, "because you are emotionally manipulating me." Leo climbed up into the driver's seat of the pirate-themed truck. "But not in Hello Kitty."

One by one, everyone caved, choosing Hello Kitty or the pirate truck. By the end, it was Alastair, Milk, and Kat in Hello Kitty with Jimmy. Leo and Zack chose the pirate truck piloted by Jimmy's father, mostly as a form of protest.

Jimmy ran through a physical and mental checklist, verifying that his vehicles were prepped.

***

"I'm not afraid of the Crypt," said Kat, squeezing in next to Alastair. She watched Jimmy use a wrench to hammer a lid closed outside. "But this guy is going to get us killed."

"Then leave already. I am sick of this."

"You are becoming less predictable," said Kat, putting on her seatbelt. Milk's seat belt had been cut off for some other purpose.

The Armageddon Trucks were Jimmy's prize creations—the product of ten unplanned years inside the Crypt. They were giant, fast, horse-power sucking, indestructible Swiss Army knives meant to handle any threat the Crypt threw at them. With hermetically sealed cabs, underwater breathing engines, hooks, grapples, winches, gas, liquids, food for days, drone repair and launch stations, weapons (both hand and truck mounted), emergency quarantine suits, liquid nitrogen, explosives, and enough wire to bridge the Grand Canyon wrapped around it in miles-long loops, the Armageddon Trucks were the ultimate survival vehicles. And they were massive, the wheels as tall as Alastair.

"What do you think?" Jimmy asked as he filled deflated bags with gas. They were mounted on the sides of the truck, and as they filled up, they hung off like water balloons or polyps. "Why carry the weight of metal tanks when they are empty?"

"I think you are missing something," Alastair said from the window.

"Yes?"

"A kitchen sink."

"Got one," said Jimmy, flipping up a metal cover to reveal a washbasin. "Chemical washing station for exposure to unknown toxins. Saved my life a couple of times."

Leo took pictures from the other truck.

"What are you doing?" Jimmy asked him.

"TikTok."

"Online?"

"Yeah, it's an app. Oh. I'll erase the photos."

"No, it's okay, I'll do it," Jimmy said nicely, holding out his hand. "Let me see."

He took Leo's phone and dropped it into a firebox. He hit a button.

"Here you go," Jimmy said handing the destroyed phone back to Leo.

Cayce, Jimmy's father, walked up slowly. "I'm coming too."

Jimmy was having none of it.

Leo found the stereo. He blasted music out of huge speakers on all corners of the truck.

"Despite having sworn that I'd never set foot in that godforsaken place again, I'm coming," Cayce yelled over the music. "Not a foot or an inch. I said that. But I'm coming. Not sure how many of your adventures I have left in me. But I coming to keep your ass safe."

"Turn that off! Leo! Yo, Leonardo!" Jimmy pulled a baseball bat out of somewhere on the truck and slammed Leo's door.

Leo got the message. Cayce pulled his son aside. "Ralls is up to something," Cayce said. "This isn't just a trip. You think we can be back by two p.m.?"

"I could. Not sure about your driving skills though."

"We just need to be back safe by three p.m." Cayce climbed onto the step-ladder of the Blackbeard truck. Though he was feeble with age, he had built these trucks with Jimmy and knew them inside out.

The trucks shuddered to life as if they too sensed that death was coming.

TEN SECONDS AND COUNTING

The Armageddon Trucks pushed through thickets of blue-and-red vegetation. They were on an abandoned highway, chunks of asphalt chewed up by roots and the trucks' enormous wheels.

"This was a brand-new road yesterday," Jimmy muttered to himself. "Nothing stays the same. Every week, a new cycle and the same thing. A complete mess. All 'cause Ralls wanted to show off to you idiots."

The highway cut through a section of forest that, to Alastair, felt like blood vessels. He imagined they were blue muscles thickening around deep-red tree trunk arteries, squeezing the life out of them. Red mesh gossamer-like filaments wove through the underbrush while insects serviced crimson-and-blue flowers.

The humidity was close to 100 percent, and the air dripped with color, giving everything a pulsing sense of life. *Like driving inside the guts of an animal or into a fresh wound*, thought Alastair.

He sweated and talked with the animation of someone finally free of self-doubt.

"So if the circumference of Cornerstone is fifty miles, it should only be about"—Alastair did the fast math in his mind—"about twelve miles to the middle of the diameter? Thirty minutes? Though I'm in no rush, this is amazing. I can't wait to talk to Leo about this. So much blue, it's such a rare color in nature, did you know that? And red. What happened to all the chlorophyll? You think the constant sun redshifted the chlorophyll? Is that even a thing?" Alastair couldn't stop talking. "I'll have to talk to Leo about all the blue and—"

"Thirteen miles," interrupted Jimmy, "if it were a straight line to the middle. Should take two to three hours, depending on what we encounter."

Alastair stared out the window.

"Couldn't we take a helicopter?" asked Kat, the idea clearly dawning on her a little too late. "I thought you said this place was dangerous by land."

"Princess, you travel by helicopters now?" Jimmy said.

The truck struggled with an enormous log across a mud-and-river-swollen trail.

"I just think a straight line is better than this mess," Kat said.

"The Crypt eats helicopters too. It's even less safe by air," Jimmy said.

Jimmy explained that gas pockets form over the swamps during every cycle, sitting like trapped poison, acting as kidneys and livers for the ecosystem, drawing out toxins and slowly filtering water to the bedrock deep below it. When the weather comes in after a cycle, the noxious clouds drift. If a helicopter hits one, they lose their lift and flame out. And crashing was the easy part. The Crypt was the hard part.

"We've run through a bunch of them now. I wipe my ass with downed helicopters, and princesses, and know better than to play with either."

The truck pushed through a dense patch of vegetation and emerged on the edge of a black flowing river. It had a mossy look with a thin layer of fog rolling over it. It was almost impossible to get a sense of its depth, but it was clearly powerful and daunting to cross, even for the Armageddon Trucks.

Alastair leaned into the windshield, trying to resolve what he was seeing. There was something weird about the river he couldn't quite put his finger on.

The truck's giant tires edged into the murky blackness. Jimmy leaned out of his truck's window, watching the tires get quickly enveloped.

Alastair stuck his head out. "What the—" he said, his eyes widening. "That's not water. Are those—"

"Ants," said Milk. The word caught in her throat.

"We're not—" started Kat, crawling up her seat.

NINE SECONDS

"We are," said Alastair. He hopped to his knees. "This is insane."

"Who are you? No, we are not," said Milk.

Jimmy stopped the truck. Cayce parked next to them.

"The only way there," said Jimmy, "is Black River. It's been a feature of the Crypt for a few months now. Or a few hundred years, I guess, depending on how you look at it. The ants are marching endlessly in a circle, never eating until they die, but there are always new ones. Vicious little things. Not much larger than our own, but with a few surprises. We think they have become an important feature of the life cycle, a sort of transportation system for bacteria and microorganisms for the Crypt."

Jimmy explained that it wasn't a new idea. While ants have never been great pollinators, there are many ant-plant mutualisms in nature. Nearly a third of herbaceous flowering plants in North America rely on ants foraging and transporting their seeds. The plants' outer shell carries key amino acids, sugars, and lipids the ants need, and in return, the ants bury the seeds safely underground so they can germinate out of harm's way, continuing the cycle.

And one species of ant and plant are so intertwined that they can't live without each other. Acacia plants' internal structure have evolved *domatia*, a Latin-derived word for house, to accommodate ants, which in turn pay rent by being security guards at their housing project, fighting off insect and herbivore threats.

So it was not a first in nature.

"But it is really inconvenient," Jimmy said as he inspected the outside of his truck. The kids watched him with deep concern.

"At first, we hoped they'd just die out," Jimmy continued, ratcheting waterproof bags with straps. "Then we tried to kill them. But they breed as fast as they die, in a perfect balance like everything in the Crypt, and we discovered they were necessary for the whole ecosystem to work. So we gave up. They just march, forever following each other, unconsciously carrying things the Crypt needs, like an immune system." He got back in the cab.

"They are ferromagnetic. Mess with radio traffic too, which is why we can't communicate with the hub while we are inside the perimeter of Black River. Every time we build a bridge, they'd consume it over ten years. So I've reengineered the trucks to make the crossing."

Jimmy hit a switch. All the vents in the vehicle closed and the windows tightened, squeezing into thick rubber membranes at every seam. Some sort of liquid poured down the windows. Another switch and they were on internal oxygen.

"No!" said Kat and Milk together when the obvious dawned on them: Jimmy intended to drive the truck into the swarming, swiftly flowing biomass.

"How deep is it?" Milk asked.

"Not sure. Just kidding. It's really deep," Jimmy said.

"You could've been working at Waterworld," said Kat to Alastair. "Just saying."

Cayce's truck was already disappearing into the blackness ahead. Jimmy inched his truck forward. By the time the ants were at window height, they started to get into the cab somehow.

"This ain't right," Jimmy said.

More ants were getting in. Jimmy ripped open the glove compartment and foam repellent cans spilled out. "Get 'em."

"It's your fault we're here," Milk said to Alastair.

"Over there," Alastair said.

Milk kept ranting. "Kat, over there!"

Ants were flooding in on Kat's side.

The truck went deeper. Blackness descended in the cab and the running lights turned on, making the marauding ants that much more menacing. Kat hyperventilated, her face pressed up against the glass in terror as the Hello Kitty truck completely disappeared under the surface. A moment later, the scene was calm, the roar of the trucks muffled. Both vehicles were gone and the Black River continued to flow like it had for hundreds of years, oblivious to the fact that there were two foreign bodies crawling somewhere below the surface.

Jimmy's truck lurched to a stop. He jammed the gears, reversed, and went forward again, but they weren't moving, stuck in both directions on some unseen boulder.

It was pitch black, save for the soft yellow illumination. The kids fell quiet. Suddenly, there was a crack and another wave of ants poured in. While Jimmy tried every countermeasure to move his truck, the kids fought off the ants with the foam spray. It killed the insects on contact, but it wasn't working fast enough. The inky darkness and flood of ants into the suffocating cabin drove everyone's panicked voices up an octave.

"We're stuck," said Jimmy. The cans of spray started to run out. Kat desperately hammered her cans on a roll bar, but they were empty.

***

On the riverbank, Cayce's truck emerged and released its sheet-white occupants onto land. Leo danced around, trying to dislodge the last ants on his body. Cayce climbed down and turned to look at the river.

Where are they? he wondered to himself.

Leo and Zack slowly realized what concerned Cayce and stood by his side. The other truck wasn't emerging. Cayce tried to radio Jimmy, but it was just static.

***

At the bottom of the river, ants swarmed the interior of Jimmy's impregnable truck. Milk was lecturing everyone and no one. Kat focused on the ants matting into her hair. Jimmy had both hands on the gear shaft, trying to crank it back and forth as he pumped the clutch and gas in an attempt to rhythmically rock the truck out of its abyssal hole. Just when it seemed like the truck was on its way up and out, it suddenly fell deeper, slamming ass-end into a new hole, its front pointing almost straight up in the black swarm of ants.

There was no getting out.

***

Cayce stared at the river, almost willing something to happen. And then it did. Two giant flames, like rocket engines, burned white-hot out of the river in a giant V shape, extending in both directions from below at an angle. After a moment, the flames turned off, and the river ran black again. A second later, flames burst out of the river once more, burning a hole in the carpet of insects.

***

Inside the truck, scalding flames and dead ants melted against the windows. They were ensconced in fire; the cabin's temperature was quickly driving upward.

"Come on, Dad!" Jimmy yelled.

***

The realization burst upon Cayce. "Oh, shit!" Cayce ran to the truck, yanked out a chemical suit, and started to pull it on.

"You're not," Zack exclaimed. "What if you don't come out?"

"Let me go kid," said Cayce.

"I don't want to come out if I can't save my boy. And If I don't, then head that way," Cayce said, zipping shut the hermetically sealed suit. He turned on his oxygen and grabbed the winch on the back of his truck.

Leo stopped him. "If you want your son to live and my friends, which I do, you have to let me go."

***

Down below, Jimmy gave up trying to move the truck. He sat patiently and put on some music, blasting the Offspring at full volume. The kids were a writhing mess behind him, twisted up in each other's bodies and a black mass of ants.

Jimmy absentmindedly took a sip of coffee and spit it out when he realized it too was full of ants. He checked his watch.

Leo slowly waded into the stream of ants, fighting the terror and the tiny insects dragging him down. They tugged on his legs like a powerful river.

But it was alive.

It was tough to keep his footing, and finally, he too disappeared beneath the surface. Leo was immediately lost in black, his breathing ragged with fear, steaming up the glass in front of his face. Ants crawled across his cheek, stinging his eyes.

Then slowly, he heard it.

Music.

He headed toward the sound, determined not to let his friends die.

And not to cry.

***

Up on the riverbank, Zack stared at the winch line. It was slack now, swinging side to side. Up and down. He was confused.

Cayce stared into the ants, as if he were willing them to part with his mind.

The cable snaked again. Suddenly, it hit Zack. The winch. It was Leo's signal to turn it on.

He was alive!

Zack hit the lever. The cable locked into place and groaned. But instead of the line slowly coming out of the river, Cayce's truck was instead being dragged *toward the river*.

Cayce ran back as quick as he could, trying to lean into the truck. The parking brakes weren't holding. Zack took another cable to anchor it somewhere, but when he got to a tree, the truck was already too far away.

"Over here!" Cayce yelled. He had found a rock to lever with a tree limb. He was trying to roll it in front of the truck before the vehicle also disappeared.

It was too heavy. The truck was almost at the river's edge, dragging itself into the ants.

Zack burst into action, running as fast as his twigs could carry him. He ran up the log like a squirrel. When he got to the tip of it, he grabbed the end, flung his legs over his head, and then swung down below it, his body dangling off the end.

The boulder started to move; Zack's weight dangled off the end of the log, slowly winning the contest with gravity.

The leverage worked. Suddenly, the giant rock was free. It tumbled end-over-end toward the truck in an agonizingly slow fashion, each flip of the giant rock seeming like its last.

The truck was up to its wheels in ants by the time the giant rock picked up enough speed down a muddy incline and caught it broadside with a giant *crunch*. It was jammed under the truck's undercarriage, stopping it at the river's edge, against another rock.

It was the winch's turn to protest.

It whined and smoked under the stress until the cable started to move again. Moments later, it dragged Hello Kitty out of the hellscape. On its hood, Leo was draped like a shot deer, spread-eagled and motionless.

Before Hello Kitty was on shore, its occupants fell out of the doors. Ants poured out alongside them. Jimmy dragged Milk to the shore. She was unconscious.

Cayce used a powerful fire hose to cover everyone with a mix of foam and water, while Jimmy went to work trying to get Milk to breathe. Everyone surrounded her.

Leo said it first to Alastair. "This is your fault."

With every pump of her chest, ants poured out of her mouth.

When the truck had shifted with the winch, she got pinned under Kat's feet in the sudden movement, ants swarming over her entire body.

Jimmy took a can of the ant repellent. He slammed a key into the side of it like he was shotgunning a beer. He covered the hole with his thumb and then pressed the open end into Milk's mouth.

Sodium tetraborate decahydrate flooded into her lungs. Jimmy pinched her nose to make sure the harmless, but irritating chemical didn't escape while Cayce pumped her chest again.

"This is all your fault," Leo repeated. There was no anger in his voice. Leo wasn't looking at Milk; he stared straight at Alastair.

In fact, all of Alastair's friends stared at him. The weight of their accusation pushed him away, until he sat, alone, with his back to them.

When Milk finally stopped coughing, Alastair wasn't watching. He heard her gasps and crying, but he was lost in his own thoughts, still suffocating at the bottom of Black River.

EIGHT SECONDS

With every mile from Black River, the tension in Jimmy's truck grew rather than diminished, like a suffocating fog that comes on slowly and thickens into a damp wall.

Alastair leaned his head against the window, gazing outside, while Milk, Kat, and Leo talked about him as if he wasn't there. They furtively glanced at him every time his name was mentioned, checking to make sure they weren't crossing some unexpected boiling point.

Alastair knew they didn't blame him for Cornerstone, in general, or even Milk's near miss, but ever since he had seen that tree mature into an adult in mere minutes, he had been the one pushing them out the door, as if he too wanted to grow and mature just as quick. It wasn't a usual stance for him. He was the measured one, often with Milk at his side, pressing for reason and caution in all things they had encountered across their time together in high school. Now, when he started taking risks, it meant that the natural order of the group was off balance, spinning quickly beyond their control. And he was the one who stepped off the edge first.

It was his fault.

With Alastair silent, Milk defended Alastair, making the argument that he wasn't to blame, that blame can always be traced further back, right to the beginning of time, for all causes and miseries of man. Alastair wasn't to blame any more than the ants were. Or the sun. Or the wash of borax that clung to her lungs and made her cough uncontrollably in between her oratorical flourishes.

Milk had it all wrong, thought Alastair. This wasn't about ants.

"If you beat your kid, you can't blame the kid if they act out," said Leo. "Make bad choices, sure. It's dad's fault," he continued, picking up the thread of Milk's logic and weaving it into his own. "But eventually, that kid grows up, and if he beats his kid, now you gotta blame him. At a certain point, decisions have consequences. You can't just keep traveling blame further and further back."

"And what did you do? You decided to go on this joyride too," said Kat. "And if I seem to remember, you were the one who convinced us to come to Texas."

"I was emotionally manipulated," said Leo. "My ego got in the way. But that was before I knew about Cornerstone. And I had incomplete information. I was just digging on being Leonardo Da Vinci. Is that really that unfair of a reaction, considering?"

"And so now you have complete information, genius?" asked Kat. "Where are we going?"

"I don't know, and that's what scares me," said Leo, softening. "And why won't he tell us?"

They all looked at Jimmy. When he didn't answer, they went silent, looking outside at some new alien vegetation brush leaving blue-and-red foam on the window like a cheap car wash. The conversation didn't pick back up.

They passed by fallen trees the size of buildings, and rivers cut through pink rock, sites no tourist would ever admire. Fields of towering sunflowers and mud mowed down by trucks in giant swaths, like running over paper trees. Finally, the group reached a frayed suspension bridge that disappeared into the mist over a chasm that darkened into verdancy below.

"If your assholes weren't puckered enough," said Jimmy, getting out of his truck, "welcome to the Guitar."

The bridge did not look passable by foot, let alone by truck. Hanging off the bridge, old broken cables were frayed, like flyaway pieces of hair drifting in the updrafts. Somewhere, the echo of water thundered.

Jimmy and Cayce cranked open the doors to a building on the precipice's edge. Inside the structure were miles of cable coiled on great spools. Jimmy dragged out two stainless steel cables and winched them tightly to the two trucks, locking them into place. The terminus of another two cables lay on the bridge's deck, evidently arrived from the other side of the chasm. Jimmy attached them to the front winch as well, tightened them down, and got back in the truck. With two tight cables coming out of the front and back of the truck, it looked like part of a pulley system.

"At some point, it would seem counterproductive to not tell us anything. You get that, right?" said Kat.

The wheels inched onto the bridge, gingerly testing it out like a toe in a scalding bath.

When the truck's full weight finally came to bear, the bridge groaned under the insult.

"Every cycle, we must restring the Guitar," said Jimmy to no one in particular.

Everyone was too preoccupied with death. Another bridge cable snapped, and the two cables bolted to the truck tightened.

"It's wired like one of those bathroom towel machines. To use it, you have to pull a fresh towel out, and the old stuff goes back onto the coil on land. Everyone who crosses has to bring fresh cables with them so the bridge always stays new."

With that, another cable snapped, dropping the truck two feet.

"Ish," added Jimmy.

Although it wasn't as long or strong as the Golden Gate Bridge, Jimmy explained, the Guitar Bridge used the same technique to string cables. Thousands of twisted pencil-thin steel wires were wound into super cables designed to deflect up to twenty-five feet in any direction.

Jimmy couldn't stop talking. While the Guitar Bridge would never see the car traffic of the Golden Gate Bridge, it was designed to be equally as bombproof, to withstand hundreds of years of time without any real maintenance. One of the default failure points built into the bridge was the ability of the main cables to lose individual strands and have new strands twisted on. In each anchorage of the bridge, as with the Golden Gate, there were strand shoes used to anchor the dead weight-bearing wires while the live wires were pulled across the bridge by a spinning wheel on the other side.

Jimmy engineered a way for his trucks to be the spinning wheel, dragging across the new wires. Every vehicle that crossed had to bring its cables with it. They were copper plated and magnetic to repel ants, amongst other things.

"This was all *your* idea?" asked Leo.

"Ralls, despite being a narcissistic, petty, overinflated windbag of a leader, is actually pretty smart sometimes. I'd love to take all the credit."

"Hey!" Kat quickly twisted in her seat, climbing up to the back of the truck and peering down through the back window.

"I think I just saw some people hanging underneath the underside of the bridge," she said. "They were there in the shadows looking at us."

At the last second, before they disappeared, she glimpsed the three black shapes, their faces caulked with white paint.

"I think you guys are right to go easy on Alastair," said Jimmy, ignoring Kat. "The Crypt kills things, people. Everything. It wasn't his fault. Black River is a nightmare we haven't figured out yet."

"Did you hear Kat?" Milk asked.

"Yes, I heard you," Jimmy said. "You're seeing things."

Jimmy counted the arches in his mind as they continued to the bridge's end, only partially paying attention to the ensuing conversation. *They were sixteen spans back.* He had no idea why the Russians were there, if it was them, or the Migrants, but it didn't bode well to see people so far from the boundary wall. They were on the move.

The Migrants, thought Jimmy. Although no one had ever seen them, signs of their existence had been increasingly evident over the last few months at Cornerstone. They were nearly invisible, living in the tiny caves that pock-marked the Crypt like sea urchins under rock ledges in tide pools.

Jimmy thought he knew where they came from, just not how they survived. In the early days of the Crypt, Cornerstone hadn't properly secured the boundaries, and immigrants crossing from the Mexican border through Texas would inadvertently get caught in a cycle on the property. Their decayed remains would be found, or the desperate and futile measures they took to escape their invisible jail. It was not until the million-year grow cycle that Cornerstone finally got the problem under control and secured the facility. But for the Migrants to exist, their descendants would have had to survive a million years. Ralls initially thought Jimmy's theory was bunk, impossible, but when the evidence started piling up, it was the only option that was never ruled out.

"Right, Jimmy?" Milk asked.

"Huh, maybe," he said, not sure of what they had been saying.

They got to the end, leaving the chasm and the miles-long bridge behind them. He tied off the cables to the shoes with a ratcheting system built into the foundation. Jimmy gunned the engine, and the bridge tightened, then he disconnected the cables from the trucks.

"Time to walk. It's not far," said Jimmy, locking the doors to the truck and grabbing a machete. He tucked it into his belt and tossed his keys to Alastair with a wink. He started to walk, but no one followed him. "You never know when there is a boost crew in town. These tires would go for a lot on eBay," said Jimmy before he realized everyone was staring at something.

There was an enormous decapitated animal head hung on the terminus foundation of the bridge, an iron spike driven through its jaw, pinning it in the air. The beast must have been the size of an elephant, and yet it was clearly some sort of rodent. Or boar.

Its blood had been used to paint the image of a circle with two lines and a slash through it. Underneath were the same letters they had seen back at the barrier facility: U+0338.

Leo stepped up and touched the red smear dripping down. "It's not blood," he said. "What is this?"

"Zack, you have to tell us," said Kat. "It is scaring Alastair." She laughed, trying to quell the rising fear in the air.

Zack stared blankly, but then his mind changed after some internal twist.

"U+0338 is Unicode, a hex value for coding the character Combining long solidus overlay Nonspacing Long Slash Overlay, which is the formal Unix 6.0 description of a circle circumscribed by a slash through it. That's how you would code that symbol. Only we would recognize that. It's a message just for us."

"You mean only you would recognize that," said Kat.

"And Alastair," Zack added.

"I think you have more faith in my coding than I do," Alastair said.

"So?" asked Leo. "What does it mean?"

Zack didn't want to say more; the attention embarrassed him.

Kat took his hand, and he relaxed into it.

"It's a map," Zack explained. "This circle represents the Nautilus, I think, and the two vertical lines are the width of one of the barrier sections to establish distance and units." He pointed with a stick: "They want us to go there, where the slash crosses the lines. It's a location."

Everyone considered this, the hum of insects a soft backdrop to their spinning thoughts.

"So it's not a warning?" Kat asked. "That's what you said before, that it was a warning."

"Long slash zeros are also shortcuts to crash a runtime program, a back-door kill switch," said Zack. "You drop one in—U+0338—everything dies, and the program is unrecoverable. Hackers use the symbol to threaten one another, like a sort of death threat."

"Are you sure it's not just a 'No Smoking' sign?" said Jimmy.

"So I don't get it," said Milk. "It's either a death threat and, if you ask me, a sign to stay away from there, or it's an invitation only we would understand to go to some specific location?"

"Yes," said Zack. "Exactly."

"That's not exact; it's the opposite of exact!" said Kat. "Opposites, when taken together as ends on a spectrum of outcomes, describe all possibilities. So it's not exact! It's the opposite."

"Exactly," said Milk. "I agree with Kat."

"You guys are such nerds," muttered Jimmy with a smile.

"So are we going there?" asked Zack.

"No," said Milk and Kat in unison.

"I think we—" Alastair began but stopped suddenly when he heard something.

A rhythmic thumping sound was starting to rise up. Whatever it was, it carried a growing force, thrashing through the jungle toward them.

Something big was coming.

And it was coming fast.

Kat turned to look at the giant severed boar's head dripping behind her. Her eyes grew wide.

SEVEN SECONDS

The Gene-E Corp helicopter barely cleared the jungle fringe, choking and sputtering, struggling to stay aloft. When it finally landed, the true monster emerged.

"Les Kiddiwinkles!" said Ralls with a sweep of his arms. The helicopter spun down, and Paul got out, not looking quite as enthusiastic as Ralls.

"Risky," said Jimmy.

"Big day, our children at the Nautilus, had to be here. And I'd rather crash than be consumed. *N'est pas?* How was your dip in Black River, Dr. Jimmy?"

"Refreshing," said Jimmy. "What do you think, Dad?"

Cayce leaned against his truck, picking his teeth. He didn't say anything.

The short walk to the Nautilus Facility followed a majestic river that fell through mist and old growth forest. Once again, the students' internal scales tipped away from cynicism and toward awe at what Cornerstone had achieved. Even Milk delighted in the nature, picking alien flower stems and twisting them into her hair.

Ralls scrunched his nose at her to indicate that it might not be the best idea, but she ignored him.

"It's so bizarre to think this is all still technically in Texas," said Milk, adding to the garland in her hair. "Every time I want to hate them, I'm struck by the beauty of all this."

Zack had slowed down to think.

"Come on, Zack," Kat said. She took his hand.

"I've never felt more connected. Is that weird?"

"You're weird. Always have been," Kat replied.

Milk took Zack's other hand and swung him like a little brother as he walked, until he pulled his hands away to scratch thoughts in his notebook.

Zack's mind raced. He was on the edge of understanding something, but he couldn't quite put his finger on it, and no amount of half-built equations could get him closer.

Pentagon Paul joined Zack, pestering him with questions he couldn't hear. It was a trick Zack employed often. When there was extrasensory information that distracted him, he would put it in a box and label it. In this case, people's pointless chatter went into the "talking" box for Zack to revisit later, or never. All of Paul's words went into the box where they couldn't distract Zack from his main task: to figure out why he felt so uneasy. He knew an idea was trying to poke through his subconscious. Zack searched for it like a diver in a murky sea cave, following a thin rope of thought into the darkness. His gut felt tight. *Where is it?*

"This is the wettest spot on earth, technically," said Ralls, stopping at a particularly stunning view. "And this plateau is in the dead center of Cornerstone. Precipitation collects at the top of the weather system directly above us like a solar collector, or a terrarium, and it rains down here, falling in spiral patterns, creating this unique growth. And the water eventually eroded the plateau to the shape you see today."

"*Dead* center," emphasized Kat.

"I may be ancient myself compared to you sprites, but I can still understand sarcasm, Katherine," said Ralls.

Zack's eyes traced the curving jungle. It was like all the vegetation was following some invisible line, spiraling out from the center like it was planned. Zack raised his hand. "You planted this all at the same time, didn't you?" he asked.

"The rain differential falls so consistently that it's created this unique growth pattern," Ralls said, his voice playing the grandfather. "It's our little Eden. There are no poisonous species or animals up here. No insects or little bitey things. We planted Eden and it has stayed as Eden."

Milk pulled a garland out of her hair and went to eat it, testing Ralls. His smile held as she finally put it in her mouth and chewed it.

"It's sweet?" she asked.

"Yes," Ralls responded, amused.

Zack put Milk in a different box labeled "courage."

They kept walking. Green vegetation gave way to crimson flowers that ran along the ground like a red carpet, leading to a building in the distance that was buried in vegetation.

"The Nautilus!" Ralls exclaimed.

Zack recognized the building from the drone tour. From the sky, it had seemed like a perfect, tiny seashell nestled into red cloth, but here, it was enormous—easily three stories high—and covered in moss and clutches of vines.

Everything was a spiral, thought Zack. *Spirals*. He pulled on the tenuous thread some more, drawing himself closer to something.

As they approached, Ralls explained to them that the building was made entirely of plastic derivatives so it could survive much longer than the typical shelf life of building materials.

The entrance was made of glass. A keypad separated them from what looked like a sort of airlock. Ralls didn't make much effort to hide the code.

"1234!" Milk stated incredulously. "Are you kidding? This is the secret code to the supersecret no-one-in-the-world-can-know-about-this-place place? 1234?"

In many ways, it was apropos for a large government boondoggle: for a long time, the nuclear launch codes were a bunch of zeroes. John F. Kennedy instituted PAL codes (Permissive Action Links) for what he saw as an important foil to any unauthorized uses of their nuclear arsenal. However, the Strategic Air Command in charge of implementing it was more concerned with speed of use and functionality when the command and control structure was compromised. So the nuclear brats left the codes as 00000000 as a bit of a middle finger to the security brats. The code was even in the checklist for the Minutemen in the tubes so there would be no mistake.

"1234," Ralls repeated, pushing a button. The door opened to the airlock. He went in, and the first glass door closed behind him. "It's a DNA lock," he explained as he put his thumb into another box on the inside, where a microscopic jab sampled his blood. "Better, Martha? It's programmed for only a few people. All of you have authorization, of course, but it's still a little fritzy. One at a time. Everyone's got to go through."

One by one, they went inside until only Zack and Alastair were left.

"Go ahead," said Alastair.

"Can you think about spirals?" asked Zack. "With me."

Zack's request was his odd way of saying he wanted to kick around ideas with Alastair. They often worked hard physics problems together when they were bored during lectures, and Zack would always start with "Can you think about ..."

"Right now?" asked Alastair.

Zack nodded.

"Sure, what about them?" asked Alastair, gesturing to the door.

"I don't know. I thought you might."

Zack knew he was being cryptic, but he also knew Alastair spoke his language—if he was in the mood, that is.

"Go ahead. I'll think about them," said Alastair. "I promise. Spirals."

Zack went through, but when it was Alastair's turn, the DNA lock didn't function. It was broken. He was stuck in the airlock. The air was dry with a whiff of ozone. On one side of the enclosure, the glass seemed to be almost a foot thick with streaks on it. Alastair ran his hand over the glass, suddenly noticing there were claw marks on the outside of the airlock, deep grooves in the bombproof glass, similar to the ones they had seen earlier at the border facility.

There was blood in the grooves. And looking closer, Alastair saw that there were concentric, spiderwebbed cracks in the glass, like something had switched tactics and tried to hammer its way in.

Ralls emerged. "Ignore that," he said, chuckling like it was a funny memory.

Ralls put his own finger in the DNA lock, and then pushed Alastair through the door with him, like they were sharing a MetroCard in Manhattan. "A little fritzy," Ralls repeated.

Inside, Alastair's class milled about in a gorgeous midcentury modern foyer. They were used to waiting for Alastair by now and didn't complain.

"The door was broken," Alastair explained.

Though there were lots of windows curved into the mahogany and white walls, many of them were overgrown on the outside with crimson vines. The ambient light was warm red, or hellish, depending on who was looking.

Zack talked to a woman in her thirties, dressed in white.

"I would like you all to meet Sephora Neiman," said Ralls.

Alastair took a step back, trying to place the face.

"Sephora is our newest director of the Nautilus Facility," Ralls continued, "or should I say soon to be oldest? She recently donated ten years of her life to the next cycle, a very gracious act."

Sephora nodded, not breaking eye contact with Alastair. Alastair finally recognized the tan skin and graceful posture. It was the woman from the bench on the night of the graduation. She seemed even more mysterious now, hidden away in this secret building on the edge of time.

"Like all of the facility directors and staff before her," continued Ralls, oblivious to the look Sephora shared with Alastair, "she has made a great sacrifice. We run through them very quickly, as you may imagine."

"Hello, Albert, very nice to meet you," Sephora said in perfect American English. Her British accent was gone. She offered her hand.

"Um," Alastair started, but paused, when she squeezed his hand.

Sephora raised her eyebrows. The perfect skin on her forehead creased into thin lines.

Alastair lost his train of thought.

"In many ways, for reasons you will soon see," said Ralls, "signing up to the Nautilus is like a one-way trip to Mars, or the elderly that volunteered to clean up the Fukushima reactor meltdown in Japan. It is a one-way trip on behalf of all mankind."

After the devastating nuclear meltdown in 2011, a force of over 250 elderly scientists and emergency workers formed the Skilled Veterans Corps. They argued that the long-term effects of radiation wouldn't affect them, as they'd be dead soon enough. Also, the elderly have less cell reproduction, meaning less chance for dangerous mutations. In a society that respected elders, it was a clever idea that captured the public's imagination. However, it wasn't until after an advisor to the prime minister called them the Suicide Corps that public opinion turned and their offer was politely declined.

"It's a great sacrifice Sephora has made, especially being so new to Cornerstone. My new—well old really—staff has welcomed her," said Ralls, straightening his shirt. "On your behalf, actually."

Now that Alastair's eyes had adjusted to the darkness, he realized they weren't alone in the facility. Old people wandered around the space, working on various tasks, some dressed in lab coats, others simply in soft clothes. The only defining feature they shared was their advanced age. Most of them appeared to be in their eighties or nineties.

"Also, they got paid a lot," added Ralls. "You are looking at a few million dollars in staff salaries right here."

Sephora objected. "Their grandchildren get paid; they die here. Probably. And get to do unfettered research," she explained with a welcoming smile.

"It's like you run a suicide machine," said Milk. "Old people in, dead people out."

"Ideas and research are an output as well. Depends on your perspective," said Sephora. "My mother is here somewhere, so don't judge. I would argue that her output is more valuable than that. She gets ten years of quiet in Eden with me, safe from the world up here, studying. She has access to the greatest libraries on earth, and the most advanced technology labs and equipment. Books for miles. And my family inherits more than she could ever give me. Is it such a bad trade?"

"It's horrifying," Milk responded. "You are literally killing old people. So your mom dies of old age down here, and you get millions of dollars."

"Do you agree, Sephora?" asked Ralls.

"My mother is dying whether it is here or there, Ms. King," she said. "How different is it from getting a condo in Hawaii to retire with a good life insurance policy?" She offered an arm to Alastair. "Shall I show you around? Perhaps you will see through her eyes and mine."

Milk shot a "Don't you dare" look at Alastair, and he kept his arms folded.

Sephora switched tactics and offered an arm to Leo instead. "You are a beautiful creature. May I?"

"Likewise," Leo said with a formal nod, happily taking her offer.

Sephora walked ahead with Leo. She led them down a spiraling staircase at the center of the facility. At the bottom, there was a hallway that curved away from the stairs. Its arc opened as it went, as if it was uncoiling from the center of the seashell-shaped building.

"This is the crowning glory. Everything you have seen pales in comparison to this," said Sephora. "Pales. I want to see if you can figure it out," she said, looking at Alastair.

Alastair blushed, unsure of why he was being singled out again by the beautiful woman.

"Go on," Sephora urged. "Take a look."

The hallway had a sterile blue feel to it. Its end was out of sight, hidden by a curve, giving the place an ominous, vertiginous feel.

"What's down there?" Alastair asked.

"You mean *in* there," Sephora corrected. "Go, all of you."

Ralls watched the proceedings like a proud parent.

Paul seemed less impressed, shifting his weight from foot to foot.

"But please, do not go in the rooms," Sephora continued. "You could die if you do. So just look and think. Consider it a little test."

Alastair wandered away from the group. Every few feet, there were thick doors staggered on either side of the hallway. As they stretched away, the doors were farther and farther apart. They were each labeled with an identification number and had a thick locking handle and a digital panel next to them. The first door said 1. The next door also said 1. The third door said 2, then 3, 5, and 8. The numbers continued to randomly jump up in chunks from then on: 59, 85, 144, then even higher with doors seventeen and eighteen numbered 1597 and 2584. By the time the kids stopped, they counted twenty doors in total. The last door said 6765.

That was it—other than large warning signs and locks that suggested it was very dangerous to enter any of the doors.

***

Watching them from the end of the hall, Ralls asked Sephora and Paul whom they thought would figure it out first.

"Katherine," said Paul.

"Please, I am serious," said Ralls.

"Me too. We need to keep an eye on her. You underestimate her."

"It will be Albert," Sephora offered.

***

Alastair counted the doors again, thinking to himself while his classmates' conjectures ranged from a lockdown zoo to some sort of biological weapons lab. He went back to the three adults.

"Well?" asked Sephora.

"Can I borrow that?" Alastair asked, pointing to the pen in Ralls's front pocket.

Alastair took the pen and strode up to the first door, yanked it open before anyone could stop him, and disappeared inside.

"Alastair!" yelled Milk.

She ran up to the door and tried to get it open, but now it was locked. Leo couldn't get it open either. The digital panel next to it was now lit. A timer counted down.

"Let him out!" yelled Milk.

"What's in there? What's happening?" asked Leo.

"You can't open it," said Sephora, smiling.

The numbers on the screen ran out. The door unlocked. Milk yanked open the door and poked her head into the room, flinching at what she may find.

There was nothing. It was just a large curving room, as if it were shaped like a banana. Other than its odd shape, it seemed more or less innocuous, with a small kitchenette, a lot of computers, workbenches, and various sealed glass enclosures as one would see in a chemistry class or university lab.

Alastair sat at a table on the far side, writing on some papers while drinking a glass of orange juice.

"You okay?" said Leo.

"OJ? I fresh squeezed it," said Alastair, offering them a large glass of juice.

"I'm good. You?" said Leo.

Alastair finished off the juice, drinking it in one long chug while everyone waited for his explanation. "I'm good." Alastair checked his watch and hit a button on it with a beep.

He stepped out, looked at Zack and said, "Spirals."

Zack's face lit up.

"What time is it, Leo?" Alastair asked.

"Four thirty p.m.," Leo answered.

Alastair showed them his watch. It said 5:30.

"That's what the one means on the door, one hour to one minute in the hall. I just spent an hour in here. How long has it been out there?"

"One minute."

"And the next room is one hour as well," continued Alastair. "Then Lab Three is three hours, five hours. Lab Eight is eight hours on the inside to one minute outside. All the way up to—how many doors are there?" asked Alastair.

"Nineteen labs," said Sephora trying to suppress a smile. Alastair did some mental calculations.

"It's Binet's formula," said Zack.

"Spirals," said Alastair, pointing to his temple.

Zack laughed.

Alastair showed them the diagrams and formulas he had worked on inside the room. "Tt transcribes the nth position of the arc of the golden mean. Zack was the one who got me thinking about it. *A Nautilus.* Right?"

As he spoke, Alastair drew the Nautilus over the spiraling golden mean and the rooms with their doors adjacent to the ascending numbers of the famous sequence and its formula.

"The last door, door nineteen, is 2,584 days for every minute. Just over seven years. And the effect spirals out until the entire Crypt sits in the last chamber for just over ten years."

"Did you do that calculation in your mind?" Sephora said, with just enough exaggeration.

"That's 4,181 days," said Ralls. "Really eleven years. But oddly, for marketing purposes, ten years was a cleaner pitch. Didn't want to give our little spiral secret away by sharing the exact time, 4,181 days, if you catch my drift." He laughed.

No one thought the joke was funny, and Alastair's mind was elsewhere, regardless.

"Hope there are more than oranges behind that last door," said Milk.

"There are always enough supplies for two time trips in every time vault," said Ralls. "In case someone gets trapped before we refuel. The room is never empty."

"How did you know it was one hour, and not one day, or one year? The one on the door could have meant anything," asked Sephora. "You could have *died* of starvation," she said playfully.

Alastair blushed at her attention. Sephora fixed her hair. As her arms went up, Alastair followed the curve of her neck.

Milk scratched her ear, like something was irritating it.

"Nineteen doors," said Alastair. "If the spiral ends at ten years–ish, that puts these early doors in hours. Then days down the hall, and finally years.

And when I saw the spiraling growth pattern outside, which Zack pointed out, it started to make sense," said Alastair, his voice swelling alongside Sephora's pride. "It continues outside. It's the whole of Cornerstone. We are at the center, where the time spiral is tight. It wasn't until I saw the sequence on the doors that Zack's comment about spirals added up. It's like time is swirling down a sink, and we are sitting on top of the drain."

Sephora seemed proud of him.

"You love it, Ralls," said Alastair.

"I do. I admit it," he said.

"Luck," said Milk, "is not intelligence. You may impress long legs here but not me."

"I didn't know for sure," Alastair said, walking down the hall, "but I figured if the time skew kept spiraling out from this center to the entire property at this ratio, it had to be right. I didn't know precisely. Could have been one year in lab one, and I would have been screwed."

"Correct again," said Sephora. "The chambers get larger along the sequence. The last chamber essentially encompasses the whole property."

"I wanted to do the conversions on Binet's and figured that an hour was enough time to solve it, which I did."

Alastair liked it when he was surprising. It was a function of always feeling like an imposter. Judging by the looks on his class's faces, they were impressed.

But none more than Sephora, clearly.

"I thought about going in the eight-hour door so I could grow a beard—to be more dramatic, you know—but I would've gotten bored," Alastair said playfully.

"Alastair, you originally asked what was down there. Time is down there," said Ralls. "As you have proven in your very convincing demonstration, we have bottled time. So you can play with it in this building. Like little toddler gods. This is all yours now. And Sephora's. To play with."

Sephora put her arms around Alastair and squeezed, and he felt pride. It glowed inside him like warm honey, intoxicating.

"And count me impressed, as well," said Sephora.

"Now that you have seen it all," said Ralls, "we have a simple question for all of you young patriots."

SIX SECONDS

"This would be your crash pad," Sephora said with a sweep of her arm. "And the Nautilus will be yours to experiment with. I will be here with you as well, to learn from you."

Leo smirked. He caught Kat's eye. She rolled her eyes. She wasn't buying it either.

But Alastair was rapt, held in a trance.

Sephora opened a set of doors to reveal a modern living space with high-end couches and seating areas, semiprivate sleeping areas, working desks tastefully hidden in nooks.

Alastair's eyes didn't follow Sephora's arm into the room; he continued looking at her.

Milk was quiet. She drew a circle on the polished ground with her foot.

Numerous screens had movies or video games playing in a loop. It was like some sort of homey Best Buy, the fancy Magnolia section, where Mom sits on a couch while Dad debates the cost of HDMI cables. The walls were covered in books—even the roof had tiered bookshelves that canted out over the space, like a zero-g library crafted inside the mind by Frank Gehry. Every horizontal surface was covered in pitch-perfect midcentury transitional furniture and soft halogen lights.

"We want you to live here," said Ralls, "for one cycle with Sephora and her staff. Consider it the time to get a master's and a PhD, which we could organize for you, of course. And consider your government. They want it as well." When no one reacted, he added, "For you."

The class stayed silent, processing everything.

Alastair forgot Sephora for a moment, now in awe of the space. It was even more splendid than her. It reminded him of the *Twilight Zone* episode he had watched with his dad, where a bank teller is finally given enough time to read all the books he desires—his dream. Only when a nuclear holocaust leaves him as the last man on earth, with all the time in the world and all the books, does he realize that his glasses are broken, so he can't read. There is a dark side to every utopia. Even now, Alastair could sense it beneath the intellectual splendor and visual power of the dorms. But the possibility was intoxicating. And when they were done, only three minutes would have passed. His mother wouldn't have missed him at all.

One side of the space was bound by curved convex glass three stories high. The view faced into the maw of a primordial jungle. Giant white roots pressed up against the lower sections of the glass, mixing with dirt and living things until they sprung free, soaring upward into impossibly tall trees. Huge vines like twisted muscles struggled to keep the trees from escaping. They pressed against the glass, like knotted fists wanting to get out.

A waterfall seemed to descend from nowhere and everywhere. Water. The verticality of the jungle made no sense. Water coursed through the dirt and channels, cutting through vegetation and then plunging again to some unseen space like a circulatory system pumping green-and-brown blood. Flowers, roots, leaves, trunks, even the dirt felt oversized.

"Well?" asked Ralls. "I can't force you to change history. You have to choose. I get that. So I ask you. Humbly."

"There is nothing humble about you," said Alastair.

"I convinced you?" said Ralls.

"This did," said Alastair, referring to the room. "And the Nautilus."

Ralls's eyes lit up. "It is the safest place in the Crypt. It's getting here that is the tough part. Otherwise—" He held up one finger. "Who's in? We've got one."

Alastair glanced at Sephora again, belying his less conscious motive, wanting the same reaction from her.

Zack sidled up to Alastair. "Me too," he said. "You got me."

Ralls beamed and held up a second finger triumphantly. "Curiosity is a powerful draw, isn't it?" he asked.

"It is."

"Ten years," said Milk to Ralls, "with this bunch?"

Ralls nodded. "Ten years."

Milk looked at Sephora.

"Ten years, it is," she said. She took Alastair's hand in her own.

Sephora's look hardened, inspecting Milk, like she was gauging new prey.

"Leo?" asked Milk. "Someone else here?" Milk was a surprise to everyone.

Alastair couldn't figure out why she would agree, but she was always the most surprising among them, so in that way, it was par for the course. In due time, he knew she would share.

"Hypocrites. Seriously." said Leo. "You two were the ones who criticized everything about this place, its mere existence as an 'affront to God.' A couple of magic tricks later and you're both all bought in? 'Cause it's safe here and they have a few books?"

"People can change their minds. Your ass just hurts that I figured out Ralls's quiz," said Alastair.

"Have fun," said Leo.

"Okay, no Leo," said Ralls. "There is work for you on the outside anyway, especially with rebuilding the infrastructure each cycle.

"Leo," urged Alastair, trying to get him to join. There was a decade of friendship in the plea.

"I can barely get through a bus ride with you, let alone another ten years," said Leo.

The comment stung Alastair. He waited for an apology or a joke to soften the blow, but it didn't come.

Leo walked away. "When are we going back?" he asked.

***

The helicopter's blades spun up. Ralls held the door open for Leo and Kat. Alastair didn't move, his feet planted firmly in his future. Kat stood next to him, looking at the helicopter. Jimmy and Cayce announced they'd be taking the trucks.

"I thought you were going," said Alastair.

"I am," said Kat, not moving. "But I am still calculating which death is worse."

"The next time we see you," Leo said to Alastair from the door over the roar of the helicopter, "if we see you, you will be twenty-eight. And we will still be eighteen. I will be eighteen, Alastair."

Alastair knew what he was saying; their friendship would never be the same. "Then you'll have to listen to me for once," said Alastair. "It will be just three minutes for you. And I'll have a great story. Top ten. Top one. And maybe some great ideas too. Maybe I'll find my inner Einstein."

"I don't get it, Alastair," Leo said. "What about your mom?"

"It'll be three minutes. She won't even notice," he responded. "You're perfect. Everyone loves you. Maybe I'll actually do something for once."

"Have fun with your girlfriend," said Leo, shooting a look at Sephora. "You just don't get it." He disappeared into the dark of the helicopter.

Alastair thought about his mom. No time would be passing, really, for her, just three minutes, so she wouldn't miss him. But he would miss her. It felt like a cheat code. On life. But he was acutely aware his mother also would be missing out on ten years of his growth if he survived. The rotors were at a full spin now. He started to doubt himself again, panic rising in his throat.

"Let's go. It's almost three p.m.," said Ralls. "Sephora and Jimmy will continue the orientation. I'm disappointed you haven't gelled enough as a class to all stay together. But"—he looked up to the rotors and then across the plateau—"if I had to pick who stayed and who went, I got two out of the top three, so that's not bad. Come on, Katherine, we'll find a use for you."

Kat hung back for a moment.

"You knew?" Kat asked Jimmy. "You knew he would ask us this, and still you brought us here. This is your fault."

Jimmy didn't defend himself.

Kat was the last one in. "Enjoy your death popsicle," she added, and then the door thudded shut with finality, leaving Alastair, Milk, and Zack behind.

"I really like her," said Cayce.

"Me too," said Jimmy.

The helicopter left. The rotors thrummed the hard afternoon light, disappearing into the hazy sun.

Alastair felt the growing distance of the helicopter open up a hole in him, like a thread unraveling. It would be ten years before he saw them again. It was on him not to change. For them it would be just three minutes.

But who would he be?

The alien vista before him offered no clues, just the promise of mystery.

Would his friends still like him?

As with all big choices once made, he checked internally to see if he felt relief or regret. He felt regret. And fear. And worry—suddenly second-guessing his decision, as usual. Just as he started to disappear down a new hole, questioning his decision, fate rose up to answer.

A few miles away, in the path of the helicopter, an army of insect drones ascended from the jungle floor. The tiny robots flew in perfect formation, each one tethered to individual strands of nanocarbon filament, which hung down like an invisible curtain across the sky.

The helicopter's intakes sucked the indestructible wires into the rotors, and it was suddenly trapped, like a metal fly in a silk spiderweb, falling, with Alastair's friends in it. The helicopter dove downward toward the Guitar Bridge in the far distance, smoke and fire coming from its engines.

Alastair yelled for Milk to look, pointing at the red smear of smoke—his friends—plummeting toward the great chasm.

No one would be leaving now.

FIVE SECONDS AND COUNTING

Before Alastair could formulate a complete thought about the downed helicopter and the terrible consequences of what it meant, something else happened.

Something terrible.

It had only been seconds since he lost sight of the helicopter when sharp staccato concussive *booms* rocked the plateau behind him—a new, more immediate threat to his quickly unraveling decision. Alastair flinched instinctively with each explosion, searching for the source. Kat and Zack were frozen in place. Then he saw it through some foliage at the fringe of the cliff. The explosions seemed to come from the base of the great barrier dam that held back the ocean in the distance.

It was breaching.

The scale of the disaster—miles of ocean barrier dam giving away all at once in some sort of giant, impossible action movie—was too much to register for Alastair. It was like the entire universe was telling him he was wrong to stay, and now he would have to settle his bill immediately.

The Gulf poured into the Crypt, angry at being held back by something as insignificant as dirt, cement, and hubris for so long.

Its rage exploded into the jungle, but from the distance, it looked like water pouring into a giant's salad bowl. The dam fought back with diminishing reservoirs of strength. Skyscraper-sized chunks of cement loosened, first by tendrils of water and then torrents—all sent by nature to exact revenge, for no dam of this size had ever been built, and never had humans so brazenly broken their implicit contract with the universe.

The terrible beauty of an ocean pouring into the infinite hole of man's greed spoke truth to power.

***

"Breach, breach, breach, breach!" screamed an automated warning.

Isaac fell out of his chair, bug-eyed at the screens.

Three p.m.

Back at the barrier wall facility, the accelerator control room sprang to life. Technicians ran up to their computers.

"Emergency cycle protocol. Set the countdown!" Isaac yelled.

"Dr. Ralls isn't out yet," said Sheila, the cycle manager.

"He'll make it. Thirty seconds! Emergency protocol approval: FM-LISAAC2. Prime the coils," Isaac screamed.

"The helicopter's disappeared," someone said staring at her screen.

"Magnets online," another technician said. The team had practiced this hundreds of times. In case of a dam breach—or any number of other emergency issues, like a nuclear attack—the protocol was to immediately trigger a time cycle to slow it down at the perimeter, giving the people inside enough time to store research and information, head to high ground before the water that did make it in flooded everything, and prepare for long-term survival.

"Come on!" yelled Isaac.

"Twenty seconds," someone yelled.

"Coolant charged. Releasing the particle."

Isaac slapped his hand down on a button. A countdown on the screen came up with a graphic that tracked the speed of the growing infiniton particle as it raced around the property, gaining mass and speed.

He twisted a knob. On a digital panel next to it, the number of years climbed from ten to one hundred.

Isaac ran out of the room into the atrium and then outside onto the overlook, eager to see the barrier dam breach with his own two eyes.

Warnings and alarms shrieked at him to come back inside. Two technicians joined in.

"Isaac!"

"The doors!"

Isaac was mesmerized by the immense spectacle of the dam releasing its hold on the ocean. By the time he turned back, the doors were closing automatically for the accelerator firing. The technicians tried to hold them open.

Isaac ran, sprinting the twenty yards with all his force, but the delay proved too long. He slammed into the doors and pounded on the glass.

"Open it! Open it!" Isaac screamed.

Inside, the pounding couldn't be heard. The countdown hit zero. Then the time dilation began, and the glass went opaque, trapping Isaac on the wrong side of time.

Outside, Isaac pounded until he was sure the technicians couldn't see him anymore and he couldn't he see them. He stopped the hysterics, stroked his hair back into place, and checked his watch. He set a timer for seventeen hours.

He had seventeen hours to get out and restart his life.

His plan was perfect.

IGNITION

The helicopter was upside down. Kat knew this because her screams were below her feet. Odd. She looked up at her shoes, and even though she couldn't see anything particularly odious grabbing them, something pulled at her with the force of a thousand suns. Or she was dead and just imagining that she was being ripped out of a helicopter as it spun downward into a never-ending chasm.

The helicopter's door was jammed open. Wind, yellow smoke, and pollen roared through the cabin, choking out her screams. Hands clutched her yellow-powdered body, trying to keep her in the helicopter. Shouts. And then, suddenly, Kat found her screams were above her feet again.

Kat spotted a river—then the helicopter tilted to reveal it was actually a waterfall. Then it was a river again. Then it didn't matter. They were all going to die.

The centrifugal force finally yanked Kat free and she was flung into the air.

Below, the waterfall was not a straight drop, but more like a steeply cascading river grooved into the side of the canyon walls. Kat headed straight for it.

Without a second's hesitation, Leo leaped out of the helicopter after Kat, dragging his duffle bag on the way out.

Paul tried to open his seatbelt to join, but bent metal pinned him to his seat with blood and pain. Ralls unbuckled, rolled onto the floor, and disappeared out the door like a fat rag doll thrown from a spinning carnival ride.

Below, Leo caught up to Kat midair, only seconds before they hit the waterfall. They landed in a deep pool on a high plateau of the waterfall just before the rush of water pulled them onward to take another fifty-yard plunge down the cliff.

Leo was unconscious, having partially hit rock. His body swept down a small set of rapids toward the next plunge, dragging his bag along for the ride.

Kat was alive. She needed to think fast.

Before the next drop off, Kat clawed, then forced Leo's duffle bag behind a rock to stop his descent, pinning them to the rocks, trying to deal with one crisis at a time. The water fought back, attempting to dislodge them to their deaths.

The anchor held, if only for the moment.

Kat took stock of their situation. The next fall would kill them if Leo wasn't already dead. She attempted mouth-to-mouth until she realized he was breathing.

She considered climbing up, but the cliffs were covered in what looked like flat pulsating worms. They were blue, the color of a deep bruise with hints of red—each the size of a human—and they clung in every nook and cranny.

It was impossible to climb up, especially with Leo's state; however, the drop down was equally as precipitous. Too far to fall. Too violent.

The waterlogged duffel bag gained weight and strength by the second, threatening to drag her and Leo over the edge before she could formulate a plan. But something else was wrong. It was not the bag dragging them down.

Worms dislodged from the rocks and swam toward her. Leo was already covered in them. Kat felt a weird sensation in her legs as she saw one, then many, attach themselves to her. Then it all came together in one, horrifying second.

Leeches. Leeches!

She was surrounded in a bowl of thirsty leeches. Kat tried to push them off her skin, but they were firmly attached now, blood seeping out the side where their mouths met her flesh. Her legs went numb, as the leeches' anesthetic saliva started to course through her veins.

Kat pulled herself closer to the edge and the next drop, now desperate to throw herself off of it. Another proboscis dug into her, its teeth clamping on tightly. The leeches engorged themselves, slowing Kat. She felt her pulse dim with the power of the leeches' blood draw, tugging against her will. With every suck, the cliff's edge looked farther and farther away. She reached a toe for it, then her foot. Her leg hooked a rock. A twist of her hips.

Suddenly, her legs slipped over the precipice, pulling her. This time, the force was welcome. She shoved her arms under Leo's shirt, grabbing her hands on the other side of his shoulders, locking him to her in a lover's embrace while the fight between the rushing water and the leeches carried on.

She spread her legs out into wide scissors, trying to take the full force of the current. The water won. With a sudden drop in her gut, she fell again, pulling Leo with her until they both disappeared.

Kat's and Leo's bodies hit another pool, then dropped again, rotating around each other like wet laundry knotted in a washing machine. The leeches detached on the way down, scraped off by rough rocks, padding her fall.

But Kat never let go of Leo. With one long, last drop, they plunged into the pool at the bottom of the canyon. The water was dark and still, feeding a river cave a few hundred feet away. The jungle was a deep, monochromatic purple. Light barely penetrated from the sky above, making the scene some sort of macabre Grimm's fairy tale, where a witch had turned the forest black like her heart.

Kat's face burst above the surface. She still had Leo in one arm, fighting his dead weight to get oxygen.

Beneath them, another leech swam up to the lunch party. But this one was different. Bigger. The size of a car—a fat, mean, bloodsucking car. Shock raced through Kat. The leeches above on the falls were just the babies. This was their mama. *What place could conjure up such monsters?* thought Kat. If she let go of Leo, she could escape the leech's clutches, but he wouldn't, not Leo. Her grasp tightened even as she grew weaker. Suddenly, it was upon her, clamping down a mouth the size of her back. The pain drove the last air from her lungs.

She sank. Blood streamed around her. She looked down through growing sleepiness, gauging how deep the water was—where she would die—and saw Leo's bag shimmering in the filtered light of her impending death.

Leeches swam up to her like angels.

SEVENTEEN HOURS AND COUNTING

The cacophonous sound of rushing water stopped suddenly, like someone threw a switch on the concept of sound itself. The air quivered, but there was no whisper of the dam's destruction. Even the animals held their breath.

Alastair ran for a better view of what had just happened with Milk huffing at his heels. He bobbed through the willow trees, tracing the cliff's edge, until he found a vantage point to see the carnage.

The full view almost knocked him over. He sat down slowly, trying to regain his sense of the world and its rules. The water, the concrete, the dam structure, everything was frozen—stuck in suspended animation—a wall of rubble and water hanging over the Crypt. Alastair's mind tried to comprehend what he was seeing. However, no matter what he did, the input still didn't make sense. The dam was frozen in midair, its process halted by the force of time. Someone had turned on the accelerator and time had essentially stopped outside.

Milk joined Alastair. She held his hand, the fear pressing into his palm, communicating everything she felt.

The windstorm died down. Insects chittered. The smell of dirt and vegetation wafted over Alastair. He let his hand sink into the softness of Milk's palm until it was warm and sweaty.

Zack arrived. Usually not the first one to speak, he glanced at them and said, "You are holding hands," as if that were the most remarkable aspect of the moment.

Alastair gently tried to pull his hand from Milk's, but she gripped it tighter. He thought she was going to lean her head into his chest, but it was

Milk, so she just stared at him for a moment too long, her strength mixed with warmth.

Alastair would go on to forget events, whole weeks, even his own name, but never, to his dying day, would he fail to remember the smell of lavender in Milk's hair at that moment.

Milk reached for Zack's hand and pulled him down to join them. He leaned his head into Milk. Their bodies formed a solid triangle before the great wall of water.

"Cute," a voice said. "Cuddles."

Sephora appeared, a gorgeous stink suddenly sitting on the rock above. She patted sweat on her forehead. "So, Al, Albert, I renew my employment offer to you."

"Someone blew it up," said Alastair.

"Yes."

"Was it you?"

"Sort of?" said Sephora.

"And you expect us to come with you. To Russia," Alastair said. "For your own accelerator project, now that this one is destroyed."

"Yes, you're correct. And our project is in China, technically, if you re-member."

"I remember," said Alastair, catching his fatal mistake only after Milk pulled her hand from his.

"You know her?" asked Milk, incredulous.

Alastair realized he had never told Milk, or anyone for that matter, about his encounter with Sephora after the Spaghetti Factory dinner with his par-ents. That night, he had decided not to go to the Cornerstone internship, but by the time he changed his mind—and raced to connect with everyone al-ready on the plane—he had forgotten about meeting Sephora and her cryptic job offer to him.

How long ago was that? thought Alastair. Why didn't he mention it? He had no answer and felt trapped by it; every excuse would seem like a lie.

Milk inspected Alastair's face. Her look was like the sun, and right on cue, his cheeks started to burn a guilty red under the scrutiny.

Alastair didn't know what to say: not telling his friends about Sephora's offer would be considered deceptive, and now, anything he revealed would seem like a lie and too late.

"I ..." Alastair said to Milk, faltering, waiting for her to set her anger on the table so he could respond to the charges one by one, but she stayed silent, which was worse.

"It is time to go to Russia, Alastair. The clock is set. Cornerstone is over. And you too, Zack. Or you can die here, quicker than you imagine," Sephora said. "Just to clarify the parameters of your next choice."

None of the kids spoke.

"You can do the calculations on the water, so I don't have to convince you," she said, her leg pressing against a tree. She was backlit by the ever-present sun, outlining her shape. Something bit her and she pulled away from the bark, swatting at it.

"Please. I would say that we're running out of time, but it would really seem like a bad pun. If I was more skilled, we could have left last week, Alastair, and avoided all this. And you would have convinced your friends."

Alastair was only focused on Milk. "I forgot," he said to her.

"Look, Alastair. Look closely at the water," Sephora urged. "Apply your mind and think for once. I know you are saddled with hormones and youth. But think. Use that impressive mind of yours."

Alastair wasn't paying attention to Sephora's rambling speech. He felt Milk's eyes harden, her distance turned into a dam that held back a new, more terrifying ocean—one without her presence. *Speak. Fight with me*, he thought.

"He wants you to say something," Zack said to Milk. At first, it sounded like Zack's typical inability to notice the finer social subtleties around him, pointing out the obvious—as if Milk didn't already know. But his voice sounded older, a little more mature. He was asking her to give Alastair a chance.

"Look," said Sephora. "Pay attention. The water is still moving. Tell me what that means. Do the math."

Trust, once broken, is only ever glued back together. It is never made whole. And now Alastair burned inside like an oven fire. This wasn't his fault.

"Tell me what it means," requested Sephora. "Pay attention."

Suddenly, a switch flipped in Alastair. The fear of losing Milk, the embarrassment at having been played, and worry for his missing friends all redirected into rage at Sephora, his intellect pouring like lava into a dangerous place.

Alastair was suddenly calm. And when he was calm, he was deadly. He would dismantle this obnoxious woman for taking Milk away from him.

"What's wrong?" Sephora prodded again, smoothing her hair. Her voice changed, less sure. "Look. Solve it."

Alastair inspected the dam. There was the faintest movement in the water, like a cloud that appears frozen but through patient observation eventually changes shape from a bunny to a train to an unmoving monster consuming the whole sky. *There is something wrong*, Alastair thought, searching for the answer. The wall of water wasn't frozen, just temporarily slowed down at the barrier.

The water was still coming. That was a very bad thing. When they were below it.

When St. Francis Dam catastrophically failed in 1928, twelve billion gallons of water rushed down a California canyon. It was the largest loss of life in state history other than the Great San Francisco fire. Chunks of cement weighing twenty million pounds were found almost a mile away; bodies were scattered in the mud like dead insects. Dam bursts were violent events. Alastair knew they also made for very difficult fluid dynamics exam questions.

He started to do the math. Alastair wanted to take Sephora's intellectual parry and shove it down her throat, sword and all. More importantly, he was desperate to explain everything to Milk.

Focus, Alastair, he thought.

This barrier dam was about five times higher and one hundred times longer than St. Francis, thought Alastair, with an entire ocean, not a reservoir, behind it. But the more he thought about it, the more Alastair realized that the physics were closer to a tsunami, which can travel up to five hundred miles per hour in deep water (another exam question he once did well on).

He knew enough of the speed, the height, and the weight of the water to solve the problem Sephora dangled before him, but what about time? Now that time was nonlinear, it too would have to play into the equation. Alastair tried to mesh Einstein's physics—the science of Cornerstone at the barrier—with fluid dynamics to figure out how long they had before the water got to them.

The rush of water wouldn't follow a linear progression. As it moved away from the perimeter and time released its grip, the water would speed up, filling Cornerstone like a soup bowl in an increasing rush of violence.

"That's what you want me to solve," said Alastair. "How long will it take for the water to get here? Hours? Days? Or years?"

"Knowing the right question is always the beginning," said Sephora.

How long ago was it that he'd sat on that bench with Sephora? Why didn't he tell Milk or Leo?

Alastair tried to work the numbers, but Milk's anger blocked his sight.

He wanted desperately to prove to Sephora that he could best her in this intellectual battle.

But he couldn't. Not with Milk unhappy. He couldn't focus. Alastair gave up.

"Time's up! Figure it out?" asked Sephora. "Maybe you are not Einstein after all. Why is the water still moving? Because the time effect is not in full force yet. Don't forget, time still passes on the outside. The accelerator takes three seconds, real time, to get to full power. Three seconds for the effect to take hold completely and seventeen hours for that time to stretch out here as the accelerator gets up to the speed of light. Then, at seventeen hours—three seconds on the outside—we can no longer cross the barrier. After seventeen hours, it is impossible to cross the perimeter of the time effect. It is lethal. We can wait here for the rains of God to come flooding down faster and faster with every minute, or you can come with me now while there is still time, literally, to escape. To China. A or B. Albert and Isaac, what shall it be?"

The answer made sense to Alastair, but there was still something that was wrong. A lost bit of physics didn't add up in her explanation, but he couldn't put his finger on it. His mind ran two parallel trains of thought, his subconscious brain searching in the dark for the missing physics puzzle piece. It would stay there until he found the answer, drawing power and attention away from the main task at hand—to survive.

"Miss King, you are, as a group, certainly smart enough to understand?" Sephora asked, taking a new tact when Alastair wouldn't speak. "Convince the boys, won't you? They can continue the work that their DNA and history demand. Or else, you can all pickle slowly on this soon-to-be island refuge until you die from starvation. Or you kill each other for food. It would be such a waste. The first Einstein uncovered special relativity, and his cheap copy, you, didn't even bother, blinded by his hope for a little sexual satisfaction."

Milk pursed her lips but kept quiet.

Alastair hoped the shared hatred of Sephora might bring them closer.

"There is only one way out, a broken section of the wall on the beach we have been hiding for this reason. And we have seventeen hours to get there."

"What do you think, Dad?" a voice said suddenly.

Alastair spun, relieved to see Jimmy and Cayce.

"How far?" asked Jimmy.

Cayce looked back into the center of the Crypt, away from the self-dismantling dam.

"I think the helicopter went down near the Guitar Bridge," Cayce said, inserting himself between the kids and Sephora. "If we take the trucks—and the timing will be tight—we could winch down, find the helicopter, winch up, and then race to the border facility in the northeast."

"And we get over and out," Jimmy said, "or rather, through the wall and out."

"I thought you said nothing gets out?" Alastair asked.

"Things get out." He checked his watch. "For the next sixteen hours and fifty-one—"

"You will be forgotten," said Sephora. "Albert Einstein is—"

"I'm not—" Alastair started.

"I mean Alastair. I'm sorry, but I'm the only one who knows how to escape this right now. I created it, forced their hand, so you can get the respect you deserve in China."

Alastair considered the possibilities. Staying here made no sense. The dream of an idyllic life with Milk in the garden of knowledge and time was gone now. They had to leave.

"What do you think? Should we go?" Alastair asked Milk.

Milk jerked her head back. "What about Leo and Kat," she said. "And Ralls. And the pilot dude. Leave? Without them?"

Alastair's face flushed when he realized she thought he was saying leave with Sephora when he really meant go with Jimmy and Cayce to search for their friends. He had no intention of joining Sephora.

"You are welcome to go with this hag and be Mr. Genius, but I am going to go find my friends."

Alastair froze, like the water beyond them, moving too slowly. "I meant—"

"That way?" Milk said, pointing deep into the Crypt, away from safety. "We have seventeen hours to find them?"

"Sixteenish now," Jimmy replied.

Milk looked at Zack. "Boy wonder? You think it's possible?"

"How would I know?" said Zack.

"You trust these guys?" asked Milk.

Zack looked at Jimmy and Cayce. "Yes."

Alastair couldn't look anyone in the eyes, embarrassed that he had now, for the third time, failed his friends. He had pushed them to go into the Crypt. Milk almost died. He forgot to tell them about Sephora's offer. His friends were missing, and he didn't know what to say.

He was a coward.

"I meant, let's go find them and then leave," Alastair clarified. "Not just leave them. You know me—"

"I thought I did," Milk responded.

"I get to choose what I think," Alastair said. "I do! Not you."

"No, you don't. Not today."

SIXTEEN HOURS

Tendrils of Kat's hair were matted in blood. She sank deeper, weakened, bleeding toward the bag at the bottom of the waterfall's basin.

Leo's bag.

Leo was next to Kat, unconscious. They sank together, attended to only by black saints.

Leo's bag.

Kat fixated on that thought and the slowly approaching NHL logo, dimly aware of her context.

Leo. Leo!

Kat snapped awake and saw Leo at her side, both of them sinking to their deaths. Kat grabbed him one last time and fought to drag them to the surface and onto shore in a tug-of-war battle with the hungry leeches.

She swam with all her might, kicking at the leeches as she went.

Pull.

And then they were out, finally on the shore's solid ground. Kat found a flat rock and viciously scraped all the black vampires off Leo. She flopped to the mud. Leo was alive, but unconscious, unaware of the way Kat looked at him as they lay at the edge of a waterfall in a place that shouldn't exist.

Kat gently brushed hair from his face. He was breathing. She wiped mud and blood from his eyes.

"Leo, wake up! TikTok is waiting for you. Da Vinci's trending," she urged. "Wake up. Wake up!"

Something stirred in the jungle. Kat heard a low moan and a snort. She stopped. Her hand hovered above Leo's face. Again, the moan, but this time, it was closer. Something was with her by the shore. Kat thought back to the curved skeletons at the atrium and shuddered at the memory.

A wheezing sound with a gasping whine. *What was it?* Kat started to kick and pull Leo back through the mud away from the dreadful sound until a black-and-white fleshy mass fell to the ground. Kat stared, unsure of what to make of it until she realized it was a pudgy arm.

Teigen Ralls. He was covered in leeches. Kat grabbed her flat rock, performing a second leech massacre on the surface of Ralls's fat, bloody body.

"You're welcome," said Kat.

"The sky is not moving," said Ralls, pointing up at the sky.

"No, it is not," Kat replied.

"We have to go up," said Ralls. "It's the only way out of the chasm. We have seventeen hours, or else we'll be trapped. Forever."

"He won't make it up," said Kat, eyeing Leo's ankle. It was bad, maybe broken. Kat kneeled next to Leo and listened to his breathing. When her ear got close to his mouth, his eyes opened briefly, and a little smile swept across his face. When she pulled back, he pretended to still be unconscious.

"He's not waking up," said Kat.

"We have to leave him. He will be okay. The others will find him eventually," said Ralls. "And he'll ride out the ten years. I am too old to be here. You know that. We must leave him."

Kat looked at Leo suspiciously. She knew he was conscious.

"Yes, you're right. Let's leave him," said Kat. "He's lame anyway."

"What!" Leo said suddenly.

Kat laughed.

"You can't leave me. You can't abandon Leonardo da Vinci."

"I can make another one of you," Ralls replied, getting up. "But there is only one of me."

"And to think people looked up to you," said Kat.

"I'm kidding," said Ralls. His smile faded. "I could make another of me as well."

"So what next? There is no way we can climb that," Kat said. "Ever."

Ralls stared at her and then up at the frozen clouds above the impossible black, leech-filled cliff.

"Well, we have seventeen hours to get out," Ralls replied. "If we go up the falls, we might be able to make it. Once up top, we can hit the main road and hike back. Down is death," he said, looking at their only other option—the dark cave.

Leo gingerly stood up. His ankle couldn't take the weight. Kat caught him as he started to fall.

"Once we get to the perimeter," Ralls said, "we will have to find a way into the barrier wall facility. It locks down automatically on the trigger. And that's if we even get there in time."

They all looked up at the falls again. It was a monumental cliff of wet rock, overwhelmed with massive gushes of water, moss, and leeches. It went up for almost a mile, disappearing into a green mist. The glint of the Guitar Bridge high above was the only sign that it ever stopped.

Kat shook her head. "There is no way."

"I can do it," said Leo.

One look from Kat withered his confidence.

"What's down there that's so bad?" asked Leo, pointing to where the pool fed into a black cave entrance with cliffs on either side.

"That cave?" Ralls slowly replied. "Unknown depth. Unknown everything. It formed six hundred thousand years ago, and nothing comes out that goes in. We don't know how deep it goes or what grows in it. But some of the water does eventually come out the other side into a lagoon that feeds the Gulf. We have dropped dye in to confirm it. A few people went down once to figure it out."

"And?" asked Kat.

"We found a helmet and—"

"And?" Kat tried to get Ralls to finish the end of his sentence.

"It was melted."

"By what?" Kat asked.

"We don't know."

"That seems to be a theme."

"We couldn't identify the compound. We weren't even sure if it was an acid. Or heat. And we have no idea where the majority of the water goes. It is like a giant drain hole that descends deeper and deeper. At least we think. We've never been able to figure it out."

"But if some water makes it out," said Kat, "we could make it out too."

"*If* we could make it through *and* we stayed with the river on the other side," said Ralls, "we could theoretically make it to the barrier on the Gulf side in time. There are gaps on the far southern beach we haven't repaired yet. We *could* get out."

"In seventeen hours?" asked Kat.

"Yes, if we make it through the caves," said Ralls. "That is possible."

"Or we just accept that we are here for the next ten years," offered Leo. "That's an option. Let's just wait it out with Alastair and the gang. And you and I can have babies."

"I'd rather die in that cave," said Kat, smiling. "Gross."

Leo's eyebrows went up. "Gross? Or awesome?"

"There is no waiting for ten years. Unacceptable," said Ralls. "My life's work would be wasted. And we are just as likely to die."

"But you said down is death," Kat countered.

"Yes."

"And up is not possible?"

"No," said Ralls, "apparently not."

"I feel faint," said Kat. She was still bleeding.

"Sit down. Then we go down, 'cause up is impossible," said Leo. "What's the cave called?"

"Cave 91a," replied Ralls.

"That's not very poetic," said Leo. "Seems like it deserves something better."

"Most people call it the Black Hole," said Ralls.

"Ah. Cave 91a it is," said Leo. "I prefer that."

FIFTEEN HOURS

Alastair fumed. He listened to Sephora, but he could think only of Milk and his anger. Milk was still silent.

"You will not be going deeper into the Crypt right now to find your dead friends. I wanted to give you some choice, to preserve the illusion of free will, but now we move to my next formal offer." A large man appeared next to Sephora. He was dressed in jungle fatigues and was as weathered as the Crypt itself. "To help you in your purchasing decision, I'd like to introduce you to Iosif Vissarionovich Dzhugashvili."

Blank stare. Where was this going?

"No?" Sephora said after a pause. "Okay, joke is on you. He's also known as Joseph Stalin."

Joseph Stalin, Alastair mouthed, not understanding the words. "Stalin? Like Stalin, Stalin?"

"Like Stalin, Stalin," said Sephora, parroting Alastair.

In a world where Isaac Newton, Albert Einstein, and Leonardo da Vinci had returned, the implications of Sephora's introduction was still absurd.

"What the f—" added Milk.

Alastair inspected the man's face. It was tough to see with the sun behind him, but the silhouette was imposing nonetheless.

Joseph Stalin was one of the most brutal dictators in history. Starving millions, the original had tried to create a socialist utopia, throwing bodies at ideas until they stacked up. The macro forces of history tell his brutality in statistics, but it's the personal details that mark his cruelty in harsher relief. When his son was captured in WWII, the Germans offered up a trade, requesting one of their generals back. Stalin's response: "I would never trade a general for a lieutenant." He left his son for dead.

Alastair remembered reading that the story of Stalin and his son was considered propaganda at the time. But after the war—while Stalin was justifying the man-made famine he had created—he confirmed the myth, saying "How could I save my son, when so many others sacrificed theirs for Russia?" No one, including his son, stood in the way of his ideals.

And now he was standing before Alastair, a monster resurrected. *His reappearance is an affront to Nature*, thought Alastair, who was only dimly aware that the same logic could be applied to his own existence.

Another silhouette joined Sephora.

"And this is Genghis. He also thinks we should all leave right now. Bit of an ogre, Mr. Khan. It took us a while to get him right."

Genghis's muscles were cut like granite.

Historically, the great leader of the Mongolian steppes had a softer side than Stalin. He first offered peace to his continental neighbors. It was only after the Assyrians killed his envoy that Genghis decided to invade, killing 1.25 million people in his rampage.

But he had been provoked.

More people arrived, backlit by the sun.

"Pol Pot," said Sephora.

The Cambodian Killing Fields. The bodies piled up before Alastair.

"Ching Shih."

One of the most successful pirates of all time.

Plying her reign of terror in the 1800s off the south coast of China, she commanded an army of over 1,500 ships and 70,000 men. She was so successful in controlling the territorial waters that in her retirement, she was able to negotiate a peace treaty, as if she was a nation unto herself, granting amnesty to her pirates. They kept their gold and lived like kings. She returned to her first love—prostitution—and ran an opulent brothel and casino in her elder years.

With each name, another villain of history joined the group surrounding Sephora. Some were more obscure than others.

"Japan's Shirō Ishii of Unit 731."

WWII medical experiments.

"Elizabeth Báthory."

The Blood Queen.

A sixteenth century Hungarian countess, she was known for over eighty serial killings. Many of them were young girls, innocently brought on to serve her, only to be scalded by hot tongs and ritualistically tortured for minor offenses. At her trial, the staff that survived claimed she killed over five hundred.

Now, she was back.

Alastair contemplated the monsters that had been conjured from the dead. He tried to see their faces to confirm Sephora's outlandish claims. While he couldn't identify all of them, he could see that they held rope, blunt objects, and other ad hoc weapons.

"And Winston Churchill," finished Sephora.

"You may call me Church," the man said. He had early hints of Churchill's trademark jowls, but when combined with a Russian accent, they seemed to lose their English bulldog effect.

"But you're a good guy," said Zack flatly.

"Aren't we all heroes of our own story?" asked Church, now feigning a perfect English accent. "I would argue that you work for the bad guys and that this is a bad place. It threatens the world. And *we* are the heroes, here to stop you."

"You Americans sought intelligence. We seek power," explained Sephora. "And in this last World War, power and the ability to wield it without a regard to sentimental consequence will be the currency of victory. The yoke of history can harness the same horse for different purposes. Churchill is a good guy again. Unsentimental."

It was a different version of an argument Alastair encountered in AP history. Do great men create history, or does history create great men? Here, before Alastair, was a living test of the question. Will Churchill always be a good guy? Or can he be a bad guy too in different circumstances? The Churchill standing before Alastair certainly had more muscles. And from the malevolent look on his face, it seemed the argument in favor of history shaping man would win out in the end.

"Hello," Church said.

There was a polite cough from the shadows.

"Oh, I forgot one," Sephora said. "It's quite a group, really. So *many* of them," she added with a touch of facetiousness.

The trees moved with a gust of wind. Light fell across a final figure. Alastair recognized him immediately—his eyes, the hair, his downturned mouth. The moustache.

It was Adolf Hitler.

FOURTEEN HOURS

Isaac was late.

He had hidden a motorbike in the Crypt's jungle fringe earlier that day, but it had taken him too long to find it again after it spent ten years in the scrub brush. The trail had grown over. Now he was scratched and bitten and swatting at branches like it was their fault instead of Ralls's.

Isaac had planned ahead by wrapping the bike in layers of plastic and tape, hoping to protect it against the elements for the ten years it would have to wait for his return. Ten years was a lot of wear and tear on the Crypt, and it still infuriated Isaac that Ralls treated his accelerator like a toy.

The bike was half-buried in mud like a tree stump, and retrieving it was difficult. Isaac cut the plastic off. There was a beehive in the engine block and the saddle, but otherwise, it looked fine.

The gas containers stored next to the bike concerned Isaac. Gasoline starts to lose octane after a few months without fuel stabilizer and even then, the additive only pushes the shelf life to eighteen months at best. Gas is essentially organic, like fresh vegetables, and once processed it needs to be consumed quickly before it goes bad, like Grandma's vegetable soup on Sunday.

A user online suggested it could survive for up to eight years in a perfectly sealed nonoxidizing container, but Isaac was hesitant to hand his life over to *Oliverclothesoff.* He had looked into diesel, but it tends to grow algae, even when stored perfectly. An electric bike would need charging. It wasn't until someone suggested a fuel stability foam developed by the Department of Defense that he figured he might be able to store the diesel long enough, with a catch. The various additives—metal deactivators, fungicides, biocides, stabilizers, and foam—couldn't be used all at once. As there was overlap in what the different additives accomplished but not their required shelf lives, Isaac had to create a time-release system. This initially involved chucking in plastic bottles of the various additives and hoping they dissolved at different times.

Oliverclothesoff did not approve. The plastics would degrade into a sticky gum when left in gasoline, but he did suggest to *Adventurbikr*—aka the resurrected Isaac Newton—that putting the chemicals in glass bottles with differing amounts of bubblegum in their necks could work. The gum would harmlessly dissolve at a consistent rate, and they would release at different times. It was genius!

Isaac opened the gas canister, his life depending on the bottles being empty and the additives having worked their magic. All of the glass bottles still floated on the surface, the bubblegum intact.

It was not genius.

Isaac hated the internet! He wanted to design a new version that made it impossible to be anonymous so he could hunt down and throttle *Oliverclothesoff*. He inspected the gas closely, trying to divine whether it would let him live or die. When it didn't answer, Isaac poured the gas into the bike, got on carefully, and started it. The engine worked. Sort of.

After a few more hiccups, the engine found a rhythm, but it was angry. The bike sputtered and coughed at Isaac, irritated he'd waited so long. Isaac got on and felt the rubber grips in his hands. He had never actually ridden a bike before, and the thrum of power between his legs felt alien.

He fished a chocolate bar out of his pocket and took a bite, listening to the motorcycle. For a moment, he was lost in his thoughts. He put the chocolate back in his pocket, and with a twist of his wrist, disappeared into the green below.

***

Isaac coaxed the motorcycle over another washed-out gully. He was behind schedule. He had been going for hours but had not gotten very far. The descent into the jungle was slowed by fallen trees that forced him off the trail into darker and darker jungle. The air was heavy, and he traveled through a stand of low trees that were black as ink. With dark, broad leaves and red moss hanging off their limbs, they were like black witches draped in bloody shawls, waiting for Isaac to make a mistake.

Watching.

He slowed. Something in the air stung his eyes, making them weep, like they had grit in them.

He smelled smoke.

While a forest fire was always a worry in the Crypt during a cycle—there was a set amount of oxygen in perfect balance inside the 5,026-mile ecosystem—it was wet enough not to be a problem. *And the world's biggest wave is also bearing down, making it sort of moot*, thought Isaac. There was a more ominous reason for the smoke, but he put that thought aside. He had a motorcycle. He stopped to get his bearings, taking a bite of some chocolate he had brought with him.

Another two hundred yards. Another fallen tree. He stopped to wipe his eyes again. They stung! In his blurry vision, he realized two things. One, he was hopelessly lost, and two, he was directly beneath a *Metopium brownei* tree, the black sap poisonwood tree. The witches sighed in the wind, their leaves rustling like laughter.

Isaac's foot couldn't find the clutch, frantically searching the side of the bike, while he pulled his shirt over his face.

It was too late; the reaction had begun.

Black sap trees had not been introduced purposefully into the Crypt. No one would be that stupid. They were a stowaway on one of the last Scoop Ships. With one of the world's strongest strains of urushiol in its sap—the active compound in poison ivy—the trees flourished across the Crypt during the million-year grow cycle. With a slight mutation in its DNA—picked up somewhere between years 300,000 and 400,000—the trees developed a powdery form of urushiol in its flowering pollen, driving away animals. When its flowers bloomed, the airborne urushiol bathed large swaths of the Crypt, covering people and animals alike in blistering welts, sending the message: *stay away.*

But why the smoke?

The tree was deadly. The pollen triggered a death spiral in people's immune systems. The worse the inflammation, the more the immune system fought and the worse it became. After just a few minutes of exposure, workers would end up in the ICU or dead. It was the black sap tree that gave the Cornerstone's jewel ecosystem its macabre nickname because although it was just one of the many vicious species that rooted during the million years, it was one of the most lethal.

No matter how many cycles Ralls ran after the grow cycle, he couldn't rid the Crypt of it. It was like a bad stain that wouldn't come out in the wash. Eventually, they just made sections of the Crypt off limits.

But Ralls was stubborn. He refused to accept the intruder in his Eden and sent a team to Central America where the worst families of black sap poisonwood lived. Wedged between Panama and Colombia, the Darién Gap was one of the most inhospitable regions on the planet, an impassable wall of jungle swampland, home to some of the deadliest species on earth: guerillas, human traffickers, and cartels.

In probably a first for a botanical field station, the scientists were outnumbered by security forces thirty to one.

It was the largest, unreported US military incursion on foreign soil. All in search of a plant.

It wasn't long before Cornerstone's biologists discovered what they were looking for: a plant species symbiont to the black sap poisonwood designed by Mother Nature herself to keep it in check. *Bursera simaruba*. There was nothing in the scientific literature about it, but the scientists could see it working in plain daylight. The locals called it gumbo-limbo, and they would rub it on their skin to stop rashes, chuckling at the men who "discovered" the salve as if they had discovered the sun.

The black sap poisonwood and the Gumbo-limbo evolved together in nature like brothers. One would cause problems, and the other would smooth things over.

The Cornerstone biologists wanted to accelerate the process in the Crypt by grafting the two trees together. They didn't have the patience to organically grow gumbo-limbo. It was *their nature* to want things faster than nature provided. The hope was that the new gumbo-sap hybrids would outperform the Crypt's native black saps and be self-neutralizing.

It worked but barely. Humans can hack nature only so much. Workers no longer died from exposure; they were just temporarily blinded and in pain for weeks. It was an improvement. Large swaths of the Crypt stayed off-limits.

But the smoke.

Isaac's face welted, as did his hands. It became more and more difficult to see. Blisters began to form on his face. There was more smoke now, thick clouds of it.

Smoke. *Why?*

The question was on the edge of his consciousness. On the list of threats facing Isaac, it wasn't yet at the top, so the smoke mystery wasn't getting the resources he needed to solve it.

Isaac squinted, trying to find the jungle road. It seemed to lead down into the darkness, rather than up to the plains and out of the poisonous groves.

How did this happen?

Isaac thought he had chosen the route carefully. The road was bordered but avoided, not too many remote cameras, had a decent history of surviving a few cycles, away from the major water sources that could erode it and, most importantly, no damn black saps.

It shouldn't have been this hard.

Isaac imagined Sephora waiting for him on the beach in a flowing dress. He knew she was already with a Soviet-class submarine in the Gulf, or maybe a G5 luxury private jet on standby in some secret hanger to escape to Russia.

He knew it. It was so simple.

Once he was able to send the Russians the barrier dam access codes, they would blow the dam, setting the Americans back years. And all he had to do was trigger the emergency time cycle protocol, slowing time so that people trapped in the Crypt could prepare for the coming disaster inside, and so he could erase his tracks as he crossed the Crypt. That was his idea. He was not a monster.

No one would be hurt, he had told himself then. Now, he was not so certain. His eyes hurt, for one. *It's still worth it.*

Once in China, Isaac Newton would be in control of his own accelerator tech, not Teigen Ralls. He would control what experiments to run, what energies to set and probe. It would be Isaac Newton's toy, and with it, he would unlock the universe's secrets. If it weren't for the damn black sap tree.

The bike's front wheel bucked against a root. With a final shove, Isaac was up and on his way again. He gunned it, and the bike answered with a rush of energy, but he couldn't see well enough for the speed. A boulder jumped in his path. The bike jackknifed, smashing into a heap, throwing Isaac ahead.

Isaac landed not far from the bike. He could hear its engine, but his eyes were almost swollen shut. More smoke wafted over him. He followed the sound of the engine, crawling on his hands and knees, bleeding and blind, fighting unconsciousness in the deadliest place on earth. He knew if he passed out, it would not be long before he was consumed. The Crypt was not wasteful.

He got to the bike and found his water, pouring it on his eyes. He rolled over onto his back with a prayer that his eyesight would recover in time to make the rendezvous. He started to hallucinate.

Out of the smoke, a wraith emerged, a disfigured man three feet tall and armored in white bones. The figure stood over Isaac in judgment; a branch smoldered in its hand. As Isaac tried to clear the sand from his eyes to make his case with death, the wraith blew on the branch and the smoke thickened, wafting down onto Isaac's now unrecognizable face like a blessing.

THIRTEEN HOURS

Adolf Hitler, the second one, wanted to be called Kris.

"I call bullshit," Alastair said to Sephora. "I can make up names too. Castro. Bin Laden. Mussolini." He dangled the keys to Hello Kitty behind his back so Milk could see. "And what a stupid thing to make up, and even dumber if it's true," continued Alastair.

Jimmy slid closer to Alastair to hide from Sephora's line of sight.

Alastair quietly jangled the keys again, trying to get Milk's attention. He wanted to get them to Jimmy.

"It's true," Milk chimed in, finally taking the keys and slowly handing them to Jimmy. "The Russians destroyed every inch of Hitler's body, and if your goon squad here is the real deal, then you suck, all of you, for killing so many people."

Milk nudged Zack, and he got the message, shifting his weight to get up until his shoelace caught on a branch. Milk undid his shoe without looking down, trying to be as unassuming as possible.

"This is like a who's who of history's assholes," Milk said, also moving to the right, subtly digging her foot into a solid branch.

Jimmy's hand gripped his machete.

"Hitler killed himself in a bunker, and his body was destroyed," Alastair said. He was distracted. They were all in concert now, invisibly preparing for the inevitable fight or race. "Get it right, and don't insult our intelligence."

"I am not Hitler. I am just a piece of hair, resurrected," argued Kris. "Turns out, I was quite collectible. My clothes too. Like a saint. Though you probably have more mugs and cups than I do. It's not a competition. Relax.

Take it easy. 'American jeans.' 'Bubblegum,'" Kris said, thickening his Russian accent in parody. "Let's be friends, Russia and America?"

"You're not Hitler, then?

"I'm Kris."

Cayce and Jimmy edged closer to the kids.

"Once a Hitler always a Hitler," said Alastair finding his confidence.

"So it's all right for you to be Alastair, but I cannot choose a different life for me?" Kris asked. "We are more alike than you think."

"I think you are Adolf Hitler."

"Yes," said Kris. "So did I."

Something about Kris's tone told Alastair he would have to unpack this exchange someday, but right now, he focused on escaping the tightening noose.

"Enough parrying," said Sephora. She waved a hand at Joseph and Genghis.

Neither Joseph nor Genghis moved on Sephora's command. The two thugs looked to Kris. Kris chuckled. "The boy and Einstein," he said, asserting dominance over Sephora. "This thing is useless," he added, gesturing to Milk.

Genghis and Joseph descended toward the kids, clubs in hand.

TWELVE HOURS

Hands. Being carried. Isaac heard whispers and then more hands touched him. The hands rubbed something on his face. They took off his clothes and rubbed ointment on his chest and legs. He started to feel better, despite the repulsion at being touched.

Relief.

A cooling liquid poured onto his face, fingers traced his eyes, and soon, his sight started to recover enough to see.

He was in a small village, maybe one hundred feet wide and circular, surrounded by black sap trees. The ground was covered with salamanders of all sizes, gazing at him with their indifferent stares. They were white with red gill-like appendages fringing their heads, almost as if their faces were surrounded with tiny red hands.

There were five huts around the central clearing. Each hut was larger and more ornate than the next and made from what looked like whitewashed wood. The wood was carved into odd shapes, forming patterns and mosaics of increasing intricacy on the doors and walls of the huts. Faces peered out from entryways.

The Migrants.

They were the elusive denizens of the Crypt. Every cycle, it was assumed they were dead, but then some small sign they were alive would appear. Officials had no idea how long they had been actually trapped in the Crypt, nor how they stayed hidden. One thing was certain: according to the scientists of Cornerstone, humans couldn't survive the million year grow cycle as a species, no matter how many successful generations were born. To remain in symbiosis with nature on such a small acreage of land without being rendered extinct was deemed impossible.

Apparently not, thought Isaac.

They were a pest, like cockroaches. The Migrants would steal or destroy something of value during a cycle and more effort would be poured into finding them, but they'd disappear again, the proof of their existence washed away by another ten years.

What was more surprising than their sudden appearance was the fact that they helped him. With that thought came guilt. Isaac realized that while everyone at the Nautilus could get out before the water came, including the Russians, this village wouldn't. He hadn't thought of the Migrants as real people, and now they were here, helping him. He resolved to return the favor.

Isaac's eyesight continued to sharpen. An old woman chewed gumbo-limbo and pasted it into his eyes. His stomach turned, but then the relief hit, and he let her continue her work.

She was much shorter than him, but her hands carried great strength and confidence. She worked Isaac to health in a ritual she seemed to have performed hundreds of times.

She was disfigured. In fact, they were all disfigured, some missing limbs. *Living in the Crypt is not an easy life*, thought Isaac.

"You need to leave," he urged, "I can show you the way." As he said so, he realized he would need his bike to make the trek in time, and it was a one-person ride.

Next to him, honey bubbled in a wooden bowl, warming over a fire. They took large handfuls of it and rubbed the substance onto his body and arms. The warmth relaxed Isaac, increasing his guilt in equal portions.

"You have to leave," he repeated, not sure if they spoke English. After hundreds of thousands of years, he wasn't even sure if they were still human.

He saw the wraith again, now just a man, putting out the burning branches in a bucket of water. Smoke filled the village, and when it wafted over Isaac, his eyes stung and he winced again. The women fanned him, clearing the air.

Another woman had no flesh on her forearm, just gleaming white bone attached to a limp hand, the flesh healed at the intersection somehow. Isaac stared at the mystery.

More honey. Why was Isaac so relaxed? He looked at the bowl with the honey and the ladle they were using to stir it. It was not wood. The ladle was made from a femur. Suddenly, he couldn't feel his arms.

The bowl was made from finger bones. He inspected the gleaming wood of the huts and realized they were not made of wood but of bones of all types. Skulls, fingers, hands. Animal bones.

And human ones.

Isaac couldn't feel his face. He laughed. It felt funny.

Why was he laughing?

More honey. Isaac felt relief, and for some reason, continued to giggle. A moment ago, he was dying, blind, and lost, not only in place but also in time, his life soon to be snuffed out by the indifferent universe.

But now he was saved, at least temporarily, by a bunch of disfigured, half humans. It was funny. The women continued to wash the fear out of him with every stroke of honey. It gave him time to think.

What was the rush? This felt so nice. They were so nice.

The Migrants were mythical creatures at Cornerstone. They terrified the Cornerstone workers, which seemed silly to Isaac now. After every cycle, a new warning seemed to be left by the Migrants to stay away. Skulls, blood, and bones left to mark territories, or so they assumed.

If a worker went missing, it was always the Migrants who were blamed. A few times, a worker would be found flayed alive, attacked by some unknown animal. Flesh scraped off their bodies, exposed bones brilliant white, picked clean, but the organs avoided. The worker would be found laughing, completely unaware of impending death, seemingly amused as they bled to death, their muscles stripped like a skinned rabbit. Something picked at Isaac's brain.

The workers were unable to identify an animal that would eat the flesh off of bones but not kill its prey, almost as if that was the plan. The blue-collar workers, born-again conspiracists, blamed the Migrants, the Crypt's bogeyman. They were an easy target.

Waterworks shut off during a cycle? The Migrants. Substations go offline in a cycle? The Migrants. A forest fire destroys a century's worth of growth and work? The Migrants.

The administration had a different take. The Migrants were a pest, certainly, but nothing more—harmless, like an annoying insect problem. Officially, the Migrants didn't exist in any literature. When evidence of them arose, it would be destroyed or buried. Ralls knew that if the public knew that people had been trapped during the million-year grow cycle and generations had survived the eons, it would shut down Cornerstone.

Ralls argued that it would be like suddenly discovering a tiny human lived in your kid's hamster cage. No matter how precious the hamster was or how great the cage, the public outcry to protect that little human would stop everything in its tracks. No more hamsters for regular-sized kids. And no more Cornerstone for Ralls.

There had been an effort to find and potentially relocate the Migrants ethically, but the problem was they could never be found, even with the entire drone survey fleet looking. It was like the world's most dangerous game of hide and seek. Ralls once suggested leaving poison for the Migrants, like they were groundhogs to get rid of. He only laughed once he saw the horrified look on his staff's faces.

"A joke," he had said, returning to his latte. "You guys are sick."

Ralls had a habit of saying outrageous things while drinking his Tuesday latte. A ritual. He would grind and press the beans, cut a new filter, and slow-brew it while listening to the last-minute preparations for the ensuing cycle. He started the coffee when the cycle began and timed the last drop for three minutes later, ruminating in between sips. It was his personal ritual to acknowledge the power of Cornerstone. "In the time it took to drink this coffee ..." Ralls would begin, as a way into a fresh speech. He said the refrain so often that it became a joke, techs mouthing it behind his back.

Ralls would have murdered the Migrants it if were socially acceptable, thought Isaac. He watched the old women paste a new substance on his arms, numbing the pain of the allergic reaction. What a tragedy that would have been. The Migrants were friendly. They were helping Isaac. He giggled again.

Isaac's foot hurt. He looked down and saw one of the women tying knots tightly around his ankle, the rope winding around his leg and up into a cinch around his hips.

He laughed. He couldn't stop laughing. Why was he laughing?

Next, the women tied down his arms down. His wrists and elbows were pinned to flat stones. Another woman wove thin ropes around each of his fingers ritualistically. She pulled them taught to the stone, each one fanning out on the cold rock. The strings were attached to a small wooden wheel, and once she was finished knotting the ropes to his fingers, she tightened them.

It looked like it should hurt; in fact, all of the bindings did, digging into his flesh, but he didn't feel anything. He was numb.

A boy brought out a curved knife made of bone and handed it to the woman to his left. But it wasn't the knife that drove fear into Isaac's heart; it was the fact that he couldn't stop giggling. Something wasn't right.

The woman whispered to the knife. She tested its sharpness on her forearm, blood emerging from the line she drew. Isaac's eyes blurred again, the chemicals in whatever they rubbed onto his skin now showing their toxicity and power.

He laughed a little too loud. And that scared him. Through the haze of intoxication, Isaac took another look around the village, trying to figure out what lurked at the edge of his mind.

The knife sliced into the palm of his hand and circled outward, precisely following the fat of his thumb. He didn't flinch, nor look down, trying to piece together the puzzle. He couldn't yet feel the pain.

The men in the village lit more branches on fire, beating the smoke into the air. Isaac could feel it sting his eyes.

A realization. It was the Migrant's smoke, not the black sap trees, that had blinded him. A man blew more smoke into Isaac's eyes, blinding him as the woman worked. She finished the ornate knots around his toes, fanning them out like his fingers.

More Migrants emerged from the darkness of their huts to watch the proceedings. They were a disfigured bunch, crippled by incest, some of them missing arms, legs, or portions of their faces. *Effects of intergenerational mating*, thought Isaac.

His mind wanted to solve the problem unfolding before him, but it also desired to relax and join the party. Children emerged and took seats at his feet to watch.

One of them said, "Hello! They are going to eat you."

"I know you," said Isaac, smiling and unfazed. "You are—"

"Gally," the boy interjected.

"Galileo! Hello! I am Newton," said Isaac, slurring. "Isn't that crazy?"

Isaac recognized the boy and his friends from earlier in the day. They were Ralls's newest experiment—born, grown to ten years old, and disappeared from the barrier facility all in one day. They were raised by the Migrants, though what had happened to their handlers and guardians was still unclear.

"Why would they eat me?" Isaac asked with the air of a kindergarten teacher.

"But it's okay, you will grow back," Gally replied. The other boys nodded. Isaac's mind searched for something, but he couldn't grasp it. *Where had he been going?*

"You are a very cute Galileo," said Isaac. "We should work together when you get older. Your twin was very famous. Although the Pope did get very angry at him."

"It won't hurt," said Gally.

"What won't hurt?" Isaac asked.

"And when we are old enough," Gally continued, "we will sacrifice our bodies too. When the sun goes out seven times."

"It's a great honor to be you," said a different boy. "Our Elder Worm was a First Sun."

A woman started to delicately carve the flesh off Isaac's fingers. Another woman took the first strip and placed it in a bowl. They were careful to only take the muscles. Isaac watched them. He felt the pain, but it was distant. He couldn't scream. He could only laugh, and that terrified him.

He felt like he was six years old again: no control over his emotions, surrounded by strange people saying impossible things. He tried to clear his mind, but every time he sought an answer to what was wrong, it only grew cloudier.

"My mother and father were unpure," Gally explained. "They didn't grow back. And Mr. Glover too. He was weak. They died. It is a test of purity. But when the Seven Suns go out, we grow. I can tell that you are pure. You are the first. And you will grow back. We will build a house of your bones, for you to live in, as a sign of our respect."

The women made quick work of Isaac's hand, carving around his blood vessels and nerves, removing the bones of his fingers one at a time. She cleaned them, removing muscles like a skilled butcher in search of new cuts of meat. Isaac watched his hand come apart in fascination; a beautiful, red-and-white flower opening up.

The drugs wormed their way into his visual cortex, rendering the world in kaleidoscope. A tug at his foot and Isaac looked down. One of his feet was undergoing a similar process, turning into a red lotus flower, veins like vines winding up his leg.

The woman removed his forearm muscle using a rope as a guideline. His arm was candy-striped, red flesh and white skin. As the women worked, they hummed and rocked.

A man came up with a thick paste and slathered it on the ends of Isaac's flesh. Pain choked Isaac's system, ripping him back into the present moment. He screamed.

His left hand was completely flayed now, a skeleton hand exposed like a classroom prop, although the tendons kept it attached to his wrist. Blood streamed down grooves into a bowl. The woman removed his bones until only his wrist and ulna were left.

Every time they removed muscle or tendon, or cut through another nerve bundle, the man pasted a thick tar-like substance onto the fresh wound.

Isaac's ulna, the bone of his forearm, went into the growing pile in the bowl. It looked delicate removed from his body, and gleamed white from being bathed in pink water.

Isaac could hear himself screaming, but it was distant, like a sound emerging from under a thick blanket in a locked room.

"You will regrow. And we will eat until the next Seven Suns," said the young Galileo. "And then you will regrow again. All things in balance come back. And we will eat of you. And you will eat of us. And we will build a home of your bones," said the boy, reciting his teachings like a mantra.

Isaac tried to remember what he'd been like before this insane, confusing place. Every time the black paste was applied, pain shot through his body, giving him a moment of clarity. He wanted more pain. Black paste went on his leg, rubbed into his exposed, skinned muscle. It helped him think.

"I have to leave," he said.

"It's only until the next Seven Suns," said Gally, "that you will feed us, and then a new darkness will release you. And it will be our turn. We will be grown up then. And your house will be built. And you will be one of the Bone People. And it will be our turn to honor you with our bodies."

"Seven suns," said Isaac, slowly resolving what Galileo meant. Seven sunsets. Every cycle, the sun froze in the sky for ten years for these people, and then for one week, when the cycle was over, the sun would rise and set for seven days until the next cycle froze it for ten years.

The Seven Suns.

Humans had been using nature's rhythms to worship and trade omens since the dawn of time. Ten years of sun and suddenly there would be seven nights. Isaac realized in his haze that the Migrants had built this unnatural phenomenon into their mythology. The sudden nights would make no sense to a primitive group, unaware that they were caught in a giant time washing machine. It would seem the work of God. The Seven Suns meant something significant to them, but it was arbitrary, a quirk. Cornerstone waited a week between cycles. Seven days. Seven suns. They easily could have waited three days. Three suns. Or two weeks. Fourteen suns. Cornerstone played God to these people and didn't even know it.

How many other astral phenomena throughout time had been given mythic significance as a result of a quirk of the universe's machinery? Solar eclipses presaging war. The blood moon warning of danger.

This would go on until the next Seven Suns, Gally had said. That was ten years from now. Isaac wouldn't survive another five minutes, let alone ten years. He would die long before then.

He understood that now. But what did the boy mean about regrowing?

Something tickled Isaac's mind again. More black paste, more pain. Isaac leaned into it, searching for clarity, but the deeper he went, he found only terror. He walked the line between his conscious mind and unconscious panic; somewhere between the two worlds there were questions he needed to answer and quickly. But he couldn't reach them.

Primitive, basic, survival chemicals flooded Isaac's mind, crowding out his consciousness. His amygdala produced fear and panic, his thalamus spiked his adrenaline, and his basal ganglia dropped his blood pressure, sending blood to his organs. Shock swept over Isaac. His brain's race to survive was an automatic emergency protocol no man could fight.

Except for the greatest mind ever born. Isaac's intellect fought back, as if in a trench warfare, one thought at a time, each new stretch of barbed wire laced with chemicals designed for flight or fight. The one-in-a-billion mind would not succumb.

He listed the questions: *Why are they killing me? Where am I going? Why am I laughing? Why is the boy saying I will regrow?*

Why do they think I will regrow?

A white salamander sat on Isaac's lap, having wandered over to watch the proceedings. It was missing a limb. Isaac looked at it. It looked at him.

Nearby, a woman worked a pestle into a mortar bowl, grinding the dried carcass of a dead salamander, mixing it with mud and black weeds into a paste.

Isaac pulled himself out of the pain, over another trench, back into his higher mind, sensing the importance of the white amphibian with red gills. They were everywhere in the village. *Why?*

The salamander went into Isaac's pocket. Its head peaked out, munching on Isaac's chocolate, content to stay in the pocket for the proceeding, safe for now.

"We will honor you, we will," said Gally blankly. "You will be one of the Seven, like my mother, but then she died, and she could not be one of the Seven. She would not regrow."

"I can't regrow," said Isaac.

"If you are pure, you will regrow," said Gally, seeming less sure of himself.

"You can regrow your arms?"

Gally smiled. "Stop being silly."

They could regrow their limbs. At first Isaac thought it was incest that caused the deformities, but now he realized it was not inbreeding. They did this to themselves. It was a ritual. He looked around and saw the Migrants in a new light. Many in the village were deformed, but now, in the place of missing limbs, he could see nubs and half grown hands. Legs that terminated in red healing flesh. Webbed feet waiting to regrow their toes.

The Migrants were ritual cannibals, but rather than eating their enemies, they ate each other in suffering and collected the bones to build their village to acknowledge their sacrifice to the Seven Suns. Then they grew back their limbs, starting the process over again. It was the ultimate form of balance, the Migrants in perfect symbiosis with their flesh and bone.

Isaac could see the wizened elders sitting in the huts built of their bodies. The biggest huts were for the oldest members, who must have had given the most bones. Isaac thought of the body of Christ and the Catholic Church's belief in transubstantiation, bread and wine becoming Christ's blood and flesh.

This religion was much more hardcore.

Even in his haze of confusion, Isaac saw the consequences of this new evolutionary trait. His mind was beating back his fear. For decades, scientists attempted to regrow injured spines, teasing stem cells back into their nascent form, using DNA as a roadmap to grow perfect parts where damage and disease existed before. In fact, a large selection of grants requested for Cornerstone concerned genetic stem cell studies. If the Migrants' genetic traits could be studied and harnessed, it would save millions of lives and prove fantastically lucrative. Cancer, spinal injuries, brain injuries, severe accidents—all could be reversed, people's own bodies and DNA providing a roadmap to complete recovery.

More bones went into the bowl. A tibia, an ankle joint.

Isaac passed out. Another substance was rubbed on his face; pain and shock shot through his system, waking him. He watched a long, carving line go down his quad muscle, and it was lifted off in one piece.

"How many of you are there?" he asked.

Suddenly, the thought that had been eluding him shot to the front of his mind. He remembered! *The barrier dam. They would all drown.*

It didn't matter. Nothing did. He gave in to the shock, his higher mind unable to cross the last trench, where death lay in wait.

A Migrant, more deformed than the others, still bleeding from his own sacrifice, took Isaac's leg muscle and put it over a fire for the coming feast.

***

Galileo Galilei, the second one, was the first to eat Isaac Newton's leg. It tasted different, like his mother's.

Nearby, Isaac hung off the chair like a bone and blood scarecrow, though his bindings were gone now. He still had one leg. It was stripped of skin from the knees down but retained muscle. Natural antibiotics unknown to science and clotting agents worshipped for hundreds of thousands of years kept him alive but on the edge of death.

The Bone People gave thanks to the Seven Suns and to Isaac for his sacrifice, praying for him to regrow his flesh and limbs quickly so the ritual could begin again. He would build a house of his bones, and they would eat of him in honor.

A man ran into the clearing. He was full-fleshed and strong. He spoke in panic to the elders, his words like staccato knocks on wood. Gally wasn't close enough to hear what the man said, and the boy ran after the elders when they suddenly left the village. He followed them up a tall tree used for a lookout. He saw a wall of water, hanging above the entire world.

When Gally returned to the village, Isaac was missing. So were his bones.

ELEVEN HOURS

Milk and Zack got to the Nautilus before Alastair. All three had managed to get past Joseph and Genghis. Jimmy's fists bought them enough time to scramble away.

Jimmy was tough.

They all had escaped the immediate trap, but only with a slight head start. They ran. But for what? Where would they go? Alastair's mind raced alongside his feet. He found a spot to hide behind the wheel of one of the Armageddon Trucks.

Above, Jimmy and Cayce explained their plan to Milk. Alastair could hear them whispering but couldn't make out what they were saying. An idea. And then Jimmy fired up the truck and drove off, leaving Alastair exposed.

Milk made a break for the Nautilus building, changing directions in the swirling dust. "Come on, Alastair!" she screamed.

History's thugs raced toward them.

Alastair was the last one to the DNA airlock. Milk and Zack were already in the building when the inside door swung shut, leaving Alastair stuck in the airlock for the second time that day.

Think.

Once again, Alastair couldn't get the machine to read his blood. The airlock entrance was about five feet wide on three sides with impaneled lighting and thick glass. The door itself was almost a foot thick, made from a glass-plastic composite often used for bombproofing embassies in the Middle East. Despite the nice light filtering in, the small enclosure felt suffocating to Alastair. No matter how many times it pricked him for blood, the door wouldn't open. Alastair slammed against the inside door. Too many things didn't work in Cornerstone. If they couldn't get a simple door to work—and why the overengineering?—how many other things were on the verge of breaking? It only made sense that Cornerstone was crashing.

Alastair didn't want to be there when it finally hit the ground. His fist flattened against the hardened glass door. Joseph and Genghis were on the outside now. There was a lock. Alastair hit it. Joseph looked at Alastair like he was a specimen in a cage.

He walked away. Genghis smiled. He was missing teeth, and despite the foot of glass between them, Alastair felt like he could smell him. Alastair gave him the finger.

Genghis didn't respond. Then he laughed, his reaction very late.

Alastair did a little dance. His moves got bigger until—in a final rush of adrenaline—he pulled down his pants and mooned Genghis Khan, his white butt checks pressed against the door, taunting him.

Genghis laughed again, pointing.

Alastair turned to check the DNA-locked door on his other side. Why weren't they coming to get him?

When Alastair turned back around, Genghis stepped aside with a sweep of his arm—like he was presenting a princess—to make way for Joseph Stalin, who was riding a giant chicken.

The ten-foot-tall chicken ran in a full sprint and was headed straight toward the door, the former dictator of Russia on its back. The creature's wings were featherless, plucked, and bleeding, twisted up behind its back, pulled into place by taught ropes clenched in Joseph's hands. Its head was smooth like bone. And when Joseph jammed a Taser into the soft flesh of the chicken's flank, the beast increased its speed, rearing up its head at the last minute and then lowering it like a battering ram, slamming into the glass door directly in front of Alastair.

The chicken—could you call it that?—was insane with anger. It pounded the door with its thick-boned head, cracks emerging in circles where it hit the glass. The animal canted up on one foot, raising a claw like a dancer pirouetting on point, its hip muscled and thick with power. The end of its claw was almost twenty feet in the air, briefly eclipsing the sun before it came down with the power of a million years of evolution, of scratching, biting, and surviving. Its claw scratched furiously into the door, penetrating the glass by an inch and sticking there, infuriating the avian nightmare even more. It yanked and yanked, and then the claw was free and at it again, until once more it fell, blood splattering into the glass. Alastair stood wide-eyed before it, frantically pounding on the door behind him.

On the other side of the door, there was no sound, the soundproof structure well engineered.

Another Taser hit, another headbutt. The glass gave away just as Alastair was yanked from behind. He fell to the floor at the feet of Milk and Zack.

"Where were you?!" Milk yelled. "We've got a—What the—"

"Ack!" yelled Zack. "Angry chicken!"

The angry chicken broke through the outer door, spattering hot blood on Alastair.

"Gross!" Milk said, grabbing Alastair's shoulders and yanking him through the inner door.

Zack tried to shut the opening, but the tip of the claw swung down along the crack and caught Zack's pants, pulling him through the door into the airlock again.

"Open it!" Alastair instructed.

"What?" said Milk. "Don't open it!"

"Open it, open up the door!" said Alastair again. He tried to yank the door open, fighting Zack who was trying to close the door on the claw dragging him out. "Open, open," Alastair kept repeating.

He pushed Milk back, squeezing between the wall and the door to lever it open with his body. Milk tripped back over a squirming Zack, giving Alastair the chance he wanted.

The door flung open. "Okay, okay, enough. Enough!" Alastair yelled.

His sudden appearance surprised the chicken and it paused. Alastair was exposed under the claw, which hung over him now. Blood dripped onto Alastair's face.

"Stop, okay?" he said.

Joseph removed the Taser from the angry chicken's side and the beast calmed, pulling its claw from the outer door.

"You are smarter than you seem," said Joseph, dismounting.

"Psych," said Alastair. He pulled the inner door shut.

They were safe inside.

"How did you know that would work?" asked Milk, coldly.

Alastair didn't say anything. He took a deep breath and rubbed his shoulder.

"How?" Milk repeated.

"He just did," said Zack, defending Alastair, catching the accusation in her tone. "Thanks, Albert."

"No problem, Isaac," Alastair said.

"You two are a joke!" said Milk. "Albert. Isaac. That thing could have killed us. *Killed us.* Like dead," she said sarcastically. Her face reddened and her eyes started to water. "You think your intelligence can solve everything, but I am here to tell you that your brains are worth shit here. It is just death and sadness. This place should not exist. And now we are trapped in here. With the ocean coming for us. How about you guys show a little respect for the gravity of this place? That could have gone either way. One more swing of the claw, and it could have been your neck and not that door that took the brunt. And *gonzo*!" Milk was yelling, her voice a fiery sermon. "And I am traumatized for the rest of my life because the boy I—" She cut herself off. "Even if I survived, I'd be dead!" Milk exclaimed. She threw a punch into Alastair's chest. "Just get with the damn plot! You don't get to choose how this goes. You are not Albert Einstein."

Alastair's arms stayed pinned to his side. The fear and adrenaline of the moment washed over him in one giant flood, like his own interior barrier dam releasing after holding back an ocean. But before he could explain his fear—and why he always made the wrong choice and never knew what to do—Milk left.

Alastair stood there, drained.

"I just sort of fade into the background," said Zack. "It works for me. And then no one expects anything of you. So you can do what—"

"Please," Alastair interrupted, raising his hand. "How old are you?"

"I am fourteen," Zack answered.

"Exactly," said Alastair. "Not so smart."

"Not so smart," a third, British voice added with a touch of mockery.

Alastair and Zack spun. The inner-door was wide open.

Sephora was framed by the light. She walked through and wiggled her hand at them. "If you forgot, this is my house. Not so smart," she continued. "Or should I say *ne ochen'umnyy*? We have to start working on your Russian. But we have time enough? N'est pas?"

"That's French!" Zack said and kicked Sephora right between the legs. When she hit the floor, Zack grabbed a leg and dragged her out of the inner door. He pulled it shut quickly before she could react.

Alastair was already on the plot, and he smashed the electronics that supported the door's DNA lock with a small side table, buying them some time.

***

Jimmy and Cayce stood on the Guitar Bridge. The pirate Armageddon Truck flexed the suspension wires beneath their feet. Jimmy looked for the occupants of the downed helicopter with binoculars, while Cayce unpacked a drone.

"There they are!" Jimmy shouted over the roar of the waterfall beneath them. He could see three dots trapped at the bottom of the falls, sheer cliff walls extending up on all sides. The dots moved toward the only exit, the dark hole to one side of the pooling water.

"Shit!" said Jimmy, running to the truck. "Stooooop!" he yelled, but his voice was swallowed by the sound of the waterfall. Jimmy ripped a flare out of the truck and quickly wrapped it in duct tape, scribbling on the tag. He lit the flare and threw it over the edge with all of his might.

The flare dropped, arcing down the waterfall, illuminating the leeches and alien life with crimson red light.

When it landed in the mud at the edge of the pool, Ralls, Kat, and Leo's backs were to it.

***

They were at the entrance to the cave. Water plunged into the blackness. The edges of the cave weren't rimmed in rock, but rather a soft, fleshy growth. Kat ran her hand along the surface.

***

The three dots hesitated there, arguing, and then they finally entered.

The mouth of the cave closed behind them like a red, puckered anus or the underside mouth of a bottom-feeding sea creature swallowing its next meal.

Below, the flare finally sputtered out.

On the tag, it said, Cave = Death.

BOOK FIVE

TEN HOURS

The world was dirt. And vines. And insects. Paul was a mite, crawling along the underside of it, lost and scared. He was alone somewhere in the Crypt with an ocean—and all of eternity—bearing down on him, crushing his chest in panic.

The helicopter crash had been violent, but he survived. The pilot counter rotated the blades, feathering the descent just enough for the steep jungle cliffs to catch the helicopter, spilling down the ravine, its innards spilling out grotesquely.

When the pilot died and the search for Kat, Leo, and Ralls proved impossible, Paul headed out on his own, following the sun, southwest he hoped, back toward the Nautilus, which was the closest point of safety. But it was a guess.

He was lost. And itchy. And in pain. The man from the Pentagon—who spent most of his time in drab offices—cleared a rise, hoping to see the Nautilus to confirm his bearings, but he slipped, rolled down another hill, and ended up beneath a large mangrove tree, knee deep in a thick mix of red-streaked mud and an odd noxious mucous.

The red mud is ... blood, thought Paul inspecting it. *The tree is bleeding.*

Paul knew there was a plant somewhere in the Crypt Jimmy had nicknamed the Creatree. The "Crea" part was short for creature. When Paul had asked him what it was, Jimmy blew him off. Now Paul wished he had pressed Jimmy more—on a lot of things during those mandatory survival courses he had to take in case of emergency.

This was an emergency.

The Creatree poisoned animals at its base with a slurry of toxins from symbiotic organisms and then dissolved the animals slowly once unconscious, like an oversized Venus flytrap, but instead of flies, this plant was devouring Pauls. He started feeling woozy.

Panicked, Paul yanked at a root to pull himself out of the bloody mud.

The tree shook. And then it moaned—a dreadful, baleful sound that pierced right through Paul.

Paul swore to himself that he was going to pay attention more next time. In general. His heart wasn't strong enough; he couldn't handle another surprise.

Again, the moan.

Then an important thought hit Paul. *Trees don't have vocal cords.*

Paul pushed himself forward to investigate, pulling back a large branch, flinching, to reveal Isaac.

It was not a carnivorous tree he had stumbled into.

It was Isaac Newton under the tree's foliage bleeding to death. His wounds were extreme, but healing, and his blood fed the water, leaking his life into the mud and the Crypt, both of which were nonetheless perpetually hungry for death.

Before Paul could move closer, Isaac dragged himself a few feet toward him like a zombie—bones akimbo, flesh red from insult. Flies swarmed around Isaac's eyes, which were swollen shut, but he was alive. A sticky black substance covered in maggots was slathered on every open wound and terminus where flesh met bone.

After Paul applied a tourniquet from his shirt, Isaac became human again, but barely, enough to explain the black paste he needed for the pain, begging for Paul to apply it for him. Paul thought it would lead to infection, so he resisted giving Isaac the substance, which was now in his possession.

Whatever had happened to him must have happened nearby, thought Paul. He looked into the jungle and then determined to get moving in case whatever animal had attacked Isaac was still hungry.

He pulled Isaac up onto his feet and tied his upper leg to his own.

They could walk very slowly in this way. Isaac was like a bloody puppet animated by apprentice puppeteers, conscious enough now to beg for the antiseptic black paste again. Paul complied, if only to get Isaac to calm down so he could think. Seeing how it calmed Isaac's pain almost immediately, Paul applied the cream liberally.

At a clearing, Paul and Isaac finally had a view of the barrier dam in its entirety, or at least where it used to be. The wall was completely gone, replaced by a curved hump of ocean caught in slow motion. Below, the Gulf's wave front had finally made it through time's grip at the barrier and had now caught up to the Crypt. Water rushed across the jungle, crushing through its river system with more force every second toward them.

NINE HOURS

Joseph had no idea where the kids were. Time had run out. As much as he had pledged his life to Russia, he didn't want the genius children to die. He had searched the Nautilus for almost forty-five minutes and was desperate. The mission would be deemed a failure. But more importantly, the children didn't deserve to die. He knew about being trapped inside time and wouldn't wish it on his worst enemy. Even America. What had started as a kidnapping had quickly turned into a rescue mission.

The kids clearly didn't understand that their only hope was a hole hidden along a twenty mile stretch of barrier wall. They needed to leave, with him, if they were to have any chance at survival.

He walked down another endless corridor, shouting for them. *They could be hiding anywhere*, he thought, *inside a little cupboard, under a bed, behind a bookcase.*

Joseph ran his hand along the clean white walls. He had never been in the Nautilus before. It was weird to be inside after years of surviving in the wilds of the Crypt. For ten years, the Nautilus had been a jewel beckoning to him on the plateau—tempting and teasing him with its endless supply of food, entertainment, research, and cool air. He'd lived like an insect in the mud, hiding from drones, sensors, and animals. It had been a long ten years.

Joseph and his comrades had been attacked, stalked, eaten, blinded in one eye, flayed, and suffered maggot-infested wounds. Infection and alien bacteria had wrenched his guts for months at a time.

And there were other humans hiding in the Crypt as well. Did the Americans even know that?

At first, Joseph thought it was another nation come to put a stake in the American heart. He hunted them, but when he finally found them, burrowed into a muddy cliff face like larval worms in wet clay, he realized they were primitive and as deep-rooted into the Crypt as the trees or rancid waters.

He couldn't kill them. He tried. They never died from their wounds.

The Worms, as Kris called them, hunted Joseph and his comrades, stalking the woods barefoot with poisons, until they learned about guns and stayed away. A truce formed between the wretched.

All the while, above the alien, terrifying world of the Crypt, lay the Nautilus, perfect in its execution and safety.

If the Americans only knew what they created, they would have burned the place down years ago, thought Joseph.

American hubris once again threatened the world, but this time, they had created a time weapon, which had a million-fold chance of ending civilization. The Americans' failure to check their exceptionalism left civilization in danger. The Russians were forced to perfect the art of mass suffering as a foil to American superpower.

Russia didn't want another Cold War, nor a hot war either, for that matter, and it was up to Joseph to see that neither happened. Russia needed to win before the time war really got going.

It was up to Joseph to find these kids. He was a one-use product, disposable, but it still had to work. Then they would make a new Joseph for the next project.

Like astronauts, he was trained for one mission. He had to succeed if he wanted to get ongoing government support when he left the program. That was the deal. He overturned furniture in the dorms, toppling bookshelves to see behind them.

Patience. Joseph had patience, honed the hard way. He moved to the labs. It was only a matter of time before he found them, wall of water be damned.

The Russians also had access to a working accelerator. It was Joseph's home growing up. While the Americans overcomplicated a simple problem—how to keep humans alive for ten years at a time inside a giant 5,000-square-mile ecosystem—the Russians used brute force (and suffering) to catch up.

The Russians knew they couldn't grow an ecosystem—the Americans had proved what a bad idea that could be—so they built a space station there instead. They had experience keeping men in space for over a year and realized it would be better to build on the technologies they understood. They also had the benefit of seeing the Americans fail with the Crypt, and so they created a new engineering process called "folding" to catch up quickly.

The first group to survive ten years consisted of three engineers who lived like astronauts with enormous stores of food and oxygen built in airless storage around the living quarters. The engineers' only job—other than not dying or killing each other—was to perfect the engineering plans for the next ten-year cycle.

When the ten years were up, the Russians had mountains of materials, expert builders, and cheap Chinese labor waiting for them outside, like an Olympian anticipating grabbing the baton in the 4×100 sprint relay. Entire factories were built on-site, ready to supply the necessary machining and materials to execute the new plans in as short a time as possible. In three minutes, the Russians developed engineering systems that usually took years to perfect.

No managers were ever involved, nor any politicians—only engineers were allowed inside during a cycle—so the station was renamed Purity by the scientists. It was as close to a platonic ideal for the mind. And as they got close to the end of the build cycle, engineers clamored for the opportunity to go back. Reality proved not as idyllic as life in the time cycle.

The time cycles chewed up lives in mere days and weeks, but Purity grew. And while engineers ruled the day in Russia below, politics drove Cornerstone above. The Russians kept adding. Without an ecosystem to tend to, they could fire every few days if necessary, tweaking and solving problems in ten-year chunks over the course of minutes.

The only initial limit on their pursuit was how long it took to execute the plans after every cycle. Soon the engineers created an entire project management system to complete the build in the fastest possible time. And they left plans for future cycles, so parts and materials could be shipped to the site ahead of time.

The Americans knew the Russians were building a facility; they just didn't know where. They even knew its name: Purity. But no matter how many tools they brought to bear to find it and no matter where they looked, they couldn't find the ultrasecret site.

Every time Purity expanded, another cycle was fired with even more engineers working. The second cycle had seven engineers, the third cycle seventeen, and by cycle fifteen, they had a small city of over thirty people living in the earthbound space station, which disappeared in and out of time. Each cycle had a different priority; some cycles were entirely devoted to the most pressing problems, like recycling air. The engineers were richly rewarded with retirement and enough money for their families to live a comfortable life, but they didn't exactly get a choice in the matter, which was also very Russian.

One cycle, the water supply experts—a cross between government scientists and rough-handed plumbers—mutinied. They didn't do the work and were executed when they got out, setting the Russians back three days while they found their next group of "volunteers."

Eventually, the builders could live inside the station as well, creating a 3D-printing infrastructure to speed up new construction.

Over the course of a few months, Purity became a terraforming machine, purifying the air, producing water, recycling elements in perfect balance with the variable consumption and wastes of the humans inside. Able to support over one hundred people by cycle 21, the Russians laughed at Cornerstone with its toxic ecosystem, an emblem of America's corrupt soul and another reason the name spoke to the Russian achievement. The habitat was always a perfect version of its current state and with every iteration, it evolved to a more perfect form, one that was capable of lasting another ten years.

It was like living inside of an idea.

They ran twenty-one cycles in just seven weeks, averaging three runs a week for 210 years. Entire careers were consumed inside Purity, come and gone in the time it takes most people to make a single decision. From the first day, it was a gestalt, a growing symbiosis of engineering, material science, biological needs, and even psychological health (the only thing that was not typically Russian about Purity).

The Russians took care to monitor the mental health of Purity's occupants, mostly using America as a bogeyman to maintain a sense of purpose. The social conditioning program was designed by a bunch of old Stalinists, so everything had the stale flavor of the KGB at Purity. Rules related to health, wellness, and cleanliness were created to fight any chance of disease. They were expected to shave their entire body, every day. It was a draconian existence in a Spartan world.

Joseph stopped in the kitchen and made himself an espresso, enjoying cool air for the first time in ten years. Purity was nothing to the grandeur of the Nautilus. Americans always knew how to do luxury. It was why they were so soft as a nation. He thought of the ocean bearing down on him and his odd life.

Joseph was born and grew up inside Purity until the age of twenty. The last ten years of his life he lived in Cornerstone. In total, if you included the few weeks in between the cycles, he was only two weeks and nine minutes old in real time. Fourteen days old. A baby!

The American cloning program was a last-minute surprise to Russia. When they discovered its existence in the spring, it took six valuable time cycles to engineer their own program and reverse engineer human husbandry. Sourcing the DNA took the most time. They focused on world leaders who left their DNA all over historical records and collectibles, though it took the entire KGB apparatus to source the genetic material. The sudden genetics program slowed their engineering and weapons development by a few weeks, but the sixty years Russia's greatest geneticists spent inside bore fruit. In the last two cycles, Joseph and his friends' lives whisked by in the course of an afternoon.

Growing up in Purity, Joseph's life was wholly devoted to learning the skills necessary to survive Cornerstone and the knowledge to destroy it. If he died before he completed his life's mission, another Stalin would be born, raised, and sent to accomplish what he failed. When he got to Cornerstone, Joseph hungered to be the Stalin that led his country to victory over the deceitful, impure, impulsive Americans.

The Russians believed that because Joseph shared DNA with the great Machiavellian leader, he would represent Mother Russia's greatest ideal and not let sentimentality get in the way. But Joseph knew he was as disposable as a plastic water bottle, and if he died in the ocean's wave, so be it. Another crop would be born and raised in a day, with much grumbling from the engineers, who make for terrible, if not organized, parents.

Stalin—the DNA—knew how to make hard choices, the Russians assumed. But Joseph—the person—wasn't so certain. Was he just DNA? Or was he Joseph, who loved espresso and jai alai? And greyhounds. And horses! Or at least he thought he did. He had never tried any of them. It was all he dreamt about growing up, mostly because the library's section on America was very limited. It highlighted the vices of the upstart country—gambling, moral turpitude, sex, and violence. All the fun stuff. To a kid surrounded by the rigid personality of Purity, America felt thrilling. The attempt to poison him against America had the opposite effect. By fourteen, he secretly wanted to be a gangster, a gambler, and an inveterate slut.

But for right now, he just wanted to drink coffee inside an air-conditioned room. The treachery of taking a break from the frantic search made the drink that much more delicious.

Joseph swirled the drink with a stick. It was all almost over. Once he found the kids, Sephora would lead him to the submarine in the Gulf and on to freedom. He had been trapped outside the flow of real time his entire life, a cork swirling down to its very own Charybdis, disappearing into nonexistence. And now he would escape the beast that waited for him.

For Joseph, time was a life-eating monster. But no more. He was finally going to escape the Crypt's grip. He had served his time in the American gulag.

***

Genghis found Joseph staring at an empty cup of coffee. "Why did they never let us have any?" Genghis asked. "Is it good?"

"I don't know if it's good," Joseph said, "Did you see the library?"

"I did," said Genghis.

They were both silent for a moment.

"What do you think Miami will be like?" Genghis asked.

Joseph shrugged. "Who knows, but if it's anything like this, it'll be great."

"Kris thinks the kids are hiding in the time vaults. It's the only place they could be."

They were hidden inside time, thought Joseph.

Like him.

EIGHT HOURS

Milk cuddled with Alastair on a couch, watching the *Matrix* trilogy for the third time. It was the only entertainment they could find in the cramped room.

Zack was in the kitchen a few feet away making eggs. The time vault was not very large, but it was a marvel of efficient space usage. The room was warm and made almost wholly from handcarved wood and machined stainless steel, like a master carpenter's final exegesis. It had a compact kitchen, a living room that doubled as a gym and an office, an additional office with computers, sleeping bunks for four, and a bath—though it was filled with engineering manuals—all stuffed into the size of an average hotel suite. It seemed to be modeled after those Japanese transforming apartments. Beds slid under tables, desks emerged from walls, and sliding doors served as privacy for a hidden toilet and shower. The kitchen was, in an act of miraculous creativity, cantilevered down from the ceiling. Every wall had a collapsible activity that emerged only when the square footage was needed.

Zack served up egg sandwiches and sat cross-legged at their feet to finish the movie. His parents had never allowed him to watch movies, and he had begged Milk to watch them after they had finished their escape plan on day two. She had never seen them herself on intellectual grounds, but now she was enjoying the films more than anyone.

Alastair, meanwhile, barely watched the movie, feeling the warmth of Milk against him, laughing along with her when there was something overly acted. It was a weird pause in the action—the dam and the missing friends and the violent war criminals of history chasing them—but a welcome one, like someone grew a pocket of time and stuffed all his romantic hopes into it. He couldn't sense the change in the relative flow in time, other than perhaps the pause button on the wall of water, but even that seemed surreal, like a really good VR video game. But now that they were in the vault, he truly felt the power of "time distance." He and Milk had made up on day four.

Jimmy had explained the concept of time distance on the drive to the Nautilus. Alastair had understood it intellectually, but now he felt it emotionally. While time was linear on earth, there was no need to differentiate different flows of time. In fact, the first time the concept of relative time flow was encountered was with Einstein's theory of special relativity, which was mostly reserved for scientific journals and college textbooks.

But it was the discovery of the Crypt that necessitated a new term. Everyone aged at different rates in Cornerstone; things got confusing quickly. Is someone three minutes older? Or ten years older? What about after two cycles and three visits to different time vaults? Since each time vault had a different flow of time, people's relative ages decoupled. One had no idea how old people really were, when they were born, and *where* they aged. Colleagues would have to spend a few minutes explaining their age, calculating on the fly. It got especially weird when people were still inside the Crypt. After a long time vault visit, they would have aged relative to other Crypt inhabitants at one rate but at another rate relative to real time.

Jimmy's concept of time distance cleared up the mess. Time distance (TD) was tied to real time (RT), the normal runtime for all the time-impoverished people on earth who didn't have an accelerator. Jimmy argued that RT was the only variable that remained constant from a practical point of view. The longer you were in an alternate time flow of any speed, the more distant you were from real time. So if you went into the Crypt for one cycle, and ten years passed in three minutes, you were ten years time-distant from real time (minus the three minutes that elapsed while you were gone.)

In some ways, it was similar to how the Greenwich Mean Time is used for time zones on earth—tied to the time in Greenwich, England—except it measured the distance from real time.

For someone who came out of the Crypt, it made no sense to tell people you were fifty years old even though you may have lived for fifty years. For those on the outside, you would certainly look fifty, but fifty years in real time would put your birthday a decade earlier than it really was. Instead of being born in 1980, people would assume you were born a decade earlier, in the seventies. It was a mess. And for those people who used the variable time vaults inside the Nautilus, it was even worse. They were all flowing at a different rate of time. Age no longer made sense. Two colleagues could grow years apart in one cycle. It was all very hard to communicate.

Jimmy promoted and gifted expensive, classic watches that tracked the time and the date, including the year. They became very popular. They were the only way to be certain of your true chronological age without having to do a long TD calculation when you bumped into a colleague in the hall. When new people joined the Nautilus, or if friends hadn't seen each other in a while—asynchronous in their use of the vaults—they would show off their handsome watches. The farther into the future the date and year, the longer they had been in the vaults.

Time distance, like the watches, collected all of the different flow rates of time into one neat number. A sixty-year-old who went into the Crypt would age ten years before they returned to real time, so they were 60 + 10 TD. Their watches would be ten years into the future. If they also went into one of the Nautilus vaults, and found an extra year in there, they would be 60 + 11 TD. It was easy to see they were seventy-one years old—you just added the two numbers up—but now you could also see they were sixty years old before they disappeared into time, and they had spent eleven years at a different flow rate: 60 + 11 TD.

The formulation gave you everything you needed to know so you weren't asking an octogenarian where they were when Kennedy was shot, despite them being born in 1982. Time-distance added it up and provided a simple term to figure out people's ages and experience. It was a quick way to communicate age and experience. The heroes of the program were anyone whose real time age was less than their time distance. One of the earliest Crypt volunteers was young when he went in and stayed for five cycles. He had an age of 23 + 50 TD. He died in a Houston hospital at the age of seventy-three, despite being only twenty-three years old in real time five weeks earlier.

23 + 50 TD was a hero.

A visitor came to the hospital late in the evening, the room bathed in amber dusk, and gently removed the old man's Patek Philippe watch from his wrist, ceremoniously wrapping it in silk.

It read July 14, 2068.

And now Alastair understood time distance in his bones. He had been caught in the most pressing vice of stress and survival he had ever experienced, with a head start of mere seconds on the Russians, and now he had days to hang out with Milk and make up to her.

He had Zack to thank for it.

Zack was the one who made a beeline for the time vaults at the center of the Nautilus to buy some time. They had a few minutes to shop for the right amount. They wanted to make sure they wouldn't starve to death, be stuck for too long, or most importantly, be too information-starved on the inside. Each room was different when they peeked in—some rooms were sparse labs with fridges of MRE—the military's calorically rich, tasteless field food. Others were full of animals for test research or garden rooms full of nasty little plants and poisons. There were rooms that seemed to be solid computers and servers while others had every known scientific device stuffed into them—microscopes, fluoroscopes, 3D printers, chemicals, flasks, beakers, and Bunsen burners—with a simple bed in the middle. Each vault had a different university department jammed into it. Alastair and Zack had initially argued for a room that was floor-to-ceiling stuffed with miniaturized books. Milk convinced them they needed more than books.

They had a lot of options, but finally settled on vault 7, the one-week vault. It was a small room, simple and cozy. Most importantly, they found engineering diagrams of the Crypt on the computer and printed on the walls, and an exhaustive amount of research on the caves and oil sands below. It was just what they needed.

It also had *Matrix* movies.

The movie ended. The lights came on and Alastair's fairy tale also came to an end.

"Well, I stand corrected," Milk said. "It just gets better."

"Ten minutes," said Zack. Alastair looked at the clock on the wall. It counted down the remaining time. When they first arrived at the vault and it said 7, meaning a seven-day vault, Alastair felt that they had all the time they needed. But now he wanted more; the nightmare outside rushed back to his forebrain, like waking up from a good dream on the morning of a terrifying exam. With death on the line.

They only had a few moments left. It was time to set in motion the elaborate plan they had concocted. They had tried to come up with better ideas, but Zack's won out in the end.

Milk hugged Zack, and then she kissed Alastair. He kissed her back, but there was no surprise lingering below anymore, just affection and connection. They had been kissing a lot in the last week.

Alastair felt older. And ready.

Time counted down on the door. Their plan was insane. The moment was upon them. Real time approached the outside of the door, and they were ready to jump into its swiftly flowing river. Alastair grabbed the door handle, his body in the pose of a discus thrower, ready to burst into action. Zack packed clothes into a bag he found in a closet while Milk put the Crypt's plans into tubes and slung them onto her back. Alastair checked the knots, thinking things he couldn't yet say to Milk.

If the plan worked, she would get out alive. But one mistake and she would die. The next five minutes had to go perfectly.

They had the prior denizens of vault 7 to thank for the plan. *If it weren't for them*, Alastair thought, *Zack would have never thought of the idea*. On the wall, there was a framed photo of them with their three watches.

From what Alastair could tell, their predecessors had one of the most intense research schedules ever conceived (when regarded from real time). They worked for one week in vault 7, intensely focused on the science of oil extraction in sandy shale. The older women were from Alberta, and there were little signs of their home country found in odd places around the vault—desktop photos, bacon in the fridge, and a stack of k.d. lang CDs. They would then live in the Nautilus for three weeks, exercising and socializing, engaging in everything except for work. Based on the diaries Milk found, the whole Nautilus worked inside a vault one week a month.

It was a neat magic trick to extend the output of the Crypt. And that was just for the Canadian scientists who ended up in the one-week vault. Others would go in for a month, even a year or more. The only limits on time extension were how long they could live. The scientists in the Nautilus were careful to enter and leave the vaults at the same time so that even though they were aging at different rates, they would emerge in tandem, like friends catching each other at a distant port before shipping out again, swallowed by the sea. But in this case, the endless sea was time itself. People aged at different rates, accelerating toward their demise in front of each other's eyes.

A death in a vault was a serious thing. No one wanted to live with a corpse for a week, let alone a month or a year, so each vault came with hermetically sealable morgue drawers to vacuum pack the body, pumping in inert gas as an extra protection against decay. A friend entered a vault, and a mummified, plastic-wrapped ex-friend could come out. As a result, each time someone went in one of the wretched doors, there was a little ceremony—as simple as tea with a friend—to say goodbye, if only for a minute.

While the schedule of three weeks off and one week on worked for the Canadians, other scientists felt their life slipping away, dislocated from time. When someone chose to go into one of the doors that delivered over one year for a mere minute of Crypt time, the whole Nautilus stopped to recognize the sacrifice.

The longer the time in the vault, the closer the door was to the center of the spiral—the doors were closer and closer together as the hallway curved tightly toward the last door. People couldn't see the moment someone went in because the hall curved away too quickly; however, they would hear the *thunk* of the door and know it had begun. Sometimes people would hold their breath for the full minute, waiting for their peers to come out with a thumbs-up, or simply breathing and not as a limp body.

The diaries Milk read told of all this and more, of loves lost, the pressure to go into progressively deeper time wells, pushing the bounds of what was reasonable, even for the Crypt.

For Milk, Alastair, and Zack, the most they were willing to give up was a week of preparation and research. After they made sure there was enough food and access to the Nautilus's database, maps, and systems, they pulled the trigger, and slammed shut the door just as Genghis, Hitler, and Ching Shih showed up.

Now the two timelines were about to resync. The door would open, and Chronos would be paid. For the Russians, only a few minutes had passed (and a consumed espresso) since they broke through the door of the Nautilus.

Zack removed the three watches from the Canadian scientists' picture frame and handed them out. They put them on their wrists and bumped hands.

"It's 7:52 p.m. on Thursday, July 10," said Alastair.

The timer on the wall ran out. The door unlocked.

"Ready!" Alastair shouted, yanking it open.

SEVEN HOURS

Cayce unspooled the Armageddon Truck's winch, agonizing over whether he was sending his son to his death. He clipped the hook into Jimmy's harness and then watched Jimmy climb over the rail and dangle above the great Leech Falls.

Jimmy bounced up and down in the harness, testing its strength. He rotated and put his feet on the bridge to say goodbye. Neither spoke now.

"Wrench," Jimmy said eventually. Cayce handed him one. And a radio. Jimmy hit the wrench three times on the taught cable, saying, "Got it?"

"Don't unclip. One promise."

"Nothing's ever come out, Dad."

"Just don't unclip, promise me that," said Cayce.

"I won't."

Cave 91a was the most mysterious place in the Crypt, a black hole in the ground that consumed everything that went into it. Now it would devour his son. Water. Dye. People. Animals. No matter how much science was applied to it, no matter how many simulations were run, nothing could explain its insatiable appetite for life. It was a gaping hole and a gaping question carved by water over a million artificial years stolen from mother nature and wedged into a Texas afternoon. Cayce feared the cave unlike he feared anything in the Crypt; it was a mystery that bordered on magic, mocking him to solve the impossible problem. There was no solution for it in physics or otherwise. No formulas. No models. No theories that could predict, explain, or even conjecture at what it was.

They spent ten years trying to solve it on behalf of Cornerstone and failed.

Rather than press into its darkness, Jimmy and Cayce chose to avoid it intellectually, physically, and spiritually. But despite their best efforts, Cave 91a still had a grip on them, a perpetual itch.

On the Guitar Bridge, watching the kids and Ralls disappear into the mouth of the cave, Cayce had flushed with anger when he realized he was too old to go in. Jimmy volunteered before he could put a voice to the emotion.

"Where did all the water go?" It was a single bullet-point question buried in a long list of unanswered questions in a TXT file on Cayce's desktop that they were assigned to solve in the ten years on the inside.

Ultimately, it was how the cave got its name. There were also problems with Caves 91a through 91j, all related to the enormous, unexplored cave system they were hired to explore, but the first question—Where did the water go?—was the biggest. The Crypt needed water, and it was draining. Would it drain the world?

Cornerstone needed a solution. They had ignored the larger question of *why* the water was disappearing and chose to focus on *how* to replenish it at the same rate, watering the Crypt like a thirsty garden during each week's cycle.

Vast sluices would open from the Gulf, flooding the land. Originally designed for emergency pressure relief on the barrier dam, the sluices served well in their secondary role as the world's most expensive irrigation system. While the water was always brackish, the death caused by it at first would slowly replenish and renew the life cycle, bringing new life.

But now that his son was going into the maw of the mystery, Cayce had to face the gnawing question once more: What was Cave 91a?

There had been conjecture that the cave was not a natural phenomenon born of water erosion and that instead, it could have something to do with time. This idea gave rise to its nickname, the Black Hole. But the guess was more rooted in rumor and fear than science. Time was always an easy bogeyman at Cornerstone. It was often magically conjured when there was a question the engineers couldn't answer. The truth was that time was rarely the culprit. Cayce knew this. The Crypt was a unique mess of life, hydrology, geology, engineering, and evolution. Claiming that some quirk of time was the issue was a form of giving up.

The engineers had models of how much water Cave 91a consumed and at what rate, but other than that, no one knew where it all went. There was a theory about an underground lake, and another about an old, uncharted mine. Jimmy guessed that something was filling up like a bathtub beneath the Crypt over the ten-year cycle, and then after it ended, the water spread out from Cornerstone into Texas. Reports of increased well water and water table changes across the region fed this idea, but those changes could have been due to the rain from the storms that Cornerstone spawned.

All this ran through Cayce's mind as he finished prepping Jimmy. He had only one piece of advice for his son. "Don't unclip." He hit the winch. The metallic whine protested the effort.

Jimmy lowered into the mist. Cayce had watched other scientists make the same descent, fed into a meat grinder, never to return. Cayce knew the routine. He winced. As the spool of cable unwound, it carried something precious away from Cayce.

Jimmy made it to the ground, waved to his father, and then disappeared into the cave, the mouth slowly closing behind him.

The cable continued feeding into it.

***

Something was following them. Kat could feel it. Or hear it?

Did she hear something?

They had been traveling downward into the cave—the only way out—for what seemed like an eternity. The river was far behind them. Even more than the darkness, the silence and heat were suffocating. Kat tried to strike up conversation with Leo and Ralls, but Ralls kept repeating that they were going to die, so in exasperation, she asked him to shut up. Now it was silent again, save for their steps in the mud, their breathing, and ... something else.

What was it?

Kat told everyone to hold their breath. Something softly scratched along behind them, creating the kind of noise that wakes a light sleeper on a quiet night but quickly recedes and invites slumber.

Kat's mind played tricks on her in the blackness of the cave's depths. She tried to pick the sound out of the shadows, but the glow of Leo's flashlight went only so far.

When they first entered the cave, Kat quickly realized they were inside some sort of mouth. "It's a harmless feeder animal, a relative of the sea pickle," Ralls said, trying to calm her down. The Cave Pickle, as it was known, grew like a plug in the cave's mouth during the initial grow cycle. Like a sieve, it strained the river for decayed, dying biomasses; there were an abundance of them in the Crypt.

The animal was almost fifty feet long and twenty feet high at its highest, and ribbed on the inside, diverting the flow of the entire river through its guts. The water was torrential inside the beast. Kat saw small animals, fish, and plant matter caught in its filter fibers, thrown up in the turbulence. They pushed through the spongy material and out of its anus. When the roar died down, Ralls repeated that many of the cave rivers were plugged by the species.

It was like the Crypt itself had evolved a mouth and a digestive track, now used to shit Kat out into this current nightmare.

Ralls outlined the cave's complicated history. He was unguarded, talking to them as if they were biographers, and he was unloading decades of professional guilt. Kat knew it was an expression of *his* fear, a rush to explain his life and decisions in advance of a coming judgment.

In the early days, the Pentagon requested Cave 91a as a site for research. The military planned to evolve biological weapons that could target specific DNA strands, and they wanted to do so deep underground—far away from people—Ralls explained. The goal was an "ethical" weapon that could selectively kill, using specific DNA strands as its key. Cave 91a was first in line for the location for the biovaults due to its uncharted depths. The higher-ups figured that if the water never came out, neither would a rogue virus if they made a mistake.

Kat chose not to speak, pulling at Leo's sleeve when he started to protest the stupidity of the idea.

The Cave 91a DNA virus experiment was based on CRISPR technology. The plan was to evolve a virus that could spread easily and mostly harmlessly but be trained to kill a single person. For most, it would seem like the common flu. For the one unlucky person it was designed for, a runaway cytokine storm would brew in their lungs, the inflammation impossible to treat, until they drowned in lethal mucous.

Ralls's voice went up an octave at the end of every sentence, turning his pronouncements into questions.

Kat pointed out that giving the entire world the flu to kill just one person was not very nice—and quite a health care burden!

"Well, it could target a group of people," Ralls said, "who share a unique DNA marker. Not just individuals." As if that made it better. Ralls explained that the Pentagon made the weapon development contingent for the vast flows of money to continue—a different, necessary form of watering the Crypt. It was his Faustian bargain.

He used that word—"Faustian." It rolled around in Kat's mind. Goethe's Faust made a deal with the devil in return for ultimate power.

Faustian.

The Pentagon agreed that it would be wise to bury the DNA vaults deep within the earth as a concession. If there was an outbreak, time would be the kill switch. They would leave Cornerstone on and cycling for thirty-six minutes—120 years. It was enough time to kill off any surviving "hosts."

"Scientists," Leo had corrected him.

Less death. More strategic accuracy. At least, that was the argument. Radiation is so nasty. Bombs kill everyone, including babies. This was a more moral weapon. How could they not build it?

Ralls claimed he pushed back and won. The military promised they wouldn't develop bioweapons, but they also decided that some of Cornerstone security clearances were too lax. They requisitioned underground portions of the Crypt, upped informational access to the highest security level—excluding even Ralls—and went dark. He didn't know if they built them or where. The military told him not to worry.

That was all before Kat started to hear the gentle scraping following them. Or did she? Was she losing her mind?

The ground under their feet grew steeper. The walls, which had been heating up the deeper they went, now started to cool and slicken. Small crystals poked out, shining like little rainbows when the flashlight swept over them.

"Anywhere else, they would be precious," said Ralls, "but not here. Not diamonds. Items whose worth is based on how long it takes them to be created are now valueless. Mere trinkets."

Leo chipped off some giant diamonds, nonetheless, pocketing them. "Souvenirs," he muttered.

They kept on walking.

The world collapsed in on Kat. She was forced into an impossible eddy of life's probabilities, where no human should ever find themselves: deep inside a cave of unknown origin, life, length, and most importantly, means of escape.

There it was again. The scraping.

"Stop," she instructed.

"I can't keep stopping," Leo responded.

"You stopped for diamonds," said Kat. "Shhh. It's there again. The sound."

"Then why are we stopping?" Ralls asked.

"Stop. Shhhh."

Kat pointed up. Her eyes grew wide. She gripped Leo's hand and swung his light above their heads, toward the distant cave ceiling.

High above them, hundreds of beasts hung. Their bodies were each the length of a toddler. They had wings and long talons, which they used to wedge into the rocks and hang like bats. Their skin was translucent, giving the flesh a pink, bloody tinge, like uncooked sausages, or a finger held over a flashlight.

Kat recognized the talons. It was the small species from the atrium at Cornerstone.

Ursus arctos horribilis.

"What is *that*?" whispered Leo.

"It is a grizzly bear," Kat replied. "Little one."

"Was," said Ralls.

The "horrible bear of bears." How long ago was that?

"I think you need to add *nocturnis*," Leo said.

A tiny, translucent Ursus opened its jaws. It hissed, spreading out its wings, spitting anger and fear at them. The show of aggression kicked off a chain reaction. All of the bears shook their wings, shrieking. Then all of them started to pulse in an undulated wave of motion, like a hovering moving carpet.

Then the roof looked at them.

A giant bear face, ten times the size of a smaller Ursus, gazed at them languidly, at first. Paper-thin skin stretched over its skull, exposing the blue and red vessels beneath. It had the look of a fresh shrimp spring roll wrapped in rice paper. The giant beast took slow breaths. Leo swung the light over its body. It too clung to the roof, gripping giant, exposed pipes. The pipes were the source of the cold, Kat could see, the buried liquid helium feeds Ralls described that cooled the magnets in the accelerator loop. The big bear was wedged between the exposed pipes in the dark cavern with hundreds of small bears clinging to its back like bats. *Maybe once it had been a polar bear,* she thought, her logical mind momentarily able to disconnect from the intense fear she felt.

This bear had giant, fragile wings, which wrapped around the smaller bears, protecting them.

Kat, Leo, and Ralls all exhaled.

And then the Ursa spread its wings wide to encompass all sides of the cavern in an awesome display of aggression. Its claws gripped the liquid helium pipe, crushing it slightly. It roared, fangs bared.

Ralls jumped back with a choke.

A thousand shrieks and barks joined the chorus, filling the blackness.

The Ursus took flight.

***

Cayce checked his watch and glanced at the sky, looking for an indication that time had passed, despite knowing that the clouds were frozen. The world was on pause.

He was done waiting for Jimmy. He knew his son wouldn't return without the group, and the chances he would find them were low.

Time was up, plus some. He couldn't bear to lose him. He turned the winch on, hoping to drag his son back to the land of the living.

Then, he heard a groan and a whine. The cable dragged the truck to the edge of the bridge. The force on it was tremendous, like something was purposefully dragging it down. Whatever it was, it was much stronger than the truck, and even the bridge.

The bridge started to give. The wires broke like guitar strings, twanging with giant electric pings, snapping past Cayce with violent force.

Cayce tried to disconnect the cable from the winch, but it was too late. The truck flipped on its front and the winch jammed into the bridge's deck, pinning the cable release beneath its great weight.

The truck hung in the mess of cables like an insect caught in a giant spiderweb. And still the cable kept pulling like there was something on the other side of it determined to kill.

SIX HOURS

What were they going to do?

Paul couldn't leave Isaac Newton to die. He couldn't leave anyone to die, but especially not the greatest genius to ever live—or relive.

Isaac was in and out of consciousness and of little help. However, if Paul didn't run for safety from the dam's wrath, there was no way he'd make it to the perimeter in time.

"There's a surgery center at the Nautilus," Paul said, ignoring Isaac's grunts with every move. "We could stabilize you there on high ground and plot a way out with a vehicle."

Magical thinking, thought Paul. Waves of pain washed over Isaac. His wails increased with every step.

A noise in the jungle. Paul shushed Isaac, frozen in fear now. He shushed Isaac again with a finger and pointed to the edge of the jungle. The foliage moved ever so slightly.

Paul took a tree branch. He was about to swing it when a large four-wheeled autonomous drone emerged.

Paul bent in front of the camera. "We're here, hello!" he yelled. "Can you see us? We are here, somewhere!"

Now it was time for Isaac to hush Paul. "There are others," he said hoarsely. "Who did this to me. Flip it over."

The four-wheeler was packed with sensors the size of a lunchbox. Paul tried to flip the drone over. Its lights turned red and it started emitting human-sounding shrieks to deter animals. The wheels spun furiously, and it released an electric shock, causing Paul to jump back. "Nasty bugger."

"Nasty ecosystem," said Isaac quickly, clearly panicked by the increasing shrieks coming from the drone. "It's programmed to protect itself and return to the Nautilus for repair if it is attacked by an animal."

"I'm an animal, right?" asked Paul. He kicked the drone. And kicked it again, trying to turn it over. "Where's home, little fella?"

FIVE HOURS

The hallway of the Nautilus's time vaults curved away into a vanishing point. Joseph stood at one end finishing his coffee. Genghis waited at the far end out of sight.

Close to Joseph, the doors in the hallway were spread out. As the hallway curved, the doors got closer and closer to each other. He waited, enjoying the coffee, dimly aware that it might be the last sips of his life.

A pair of eyes poked out of a door about thirty feet away and then disappeared. Joseph put down his drink. Suddenly, Alastair, Zack, and Milk exploded into the hall. They each split up, heading for three different doors.

Alastair sprinted toward Joseph and then slid under his legs, flying into a vault. He yanked the door shut before Joseph could stop him.

Down the hall, Genghis emerged at a run. He tried to get Zack and Milk, but they disappeared through separate doors, pulling them shut just in time.

"Which one?" asked Genghis, joining Joseph. There were only two of them and three doors.

"You wait for Newton! Forget the girl," said Joseph pointing to the door Zack went in. He positioned himself outside Alastair's door, waiting for one minute to count down and the door to unlock again. "Baby Einstein is in here."

Kris walked up casually. It stressed Joseph out. Kris looked at him curiously with a slight smile on his face, as if he was a child playing with a lighter whose mother had stumbled upon him.

Joseph explained what was going on, which room the kids came from, which rooms they went into, and what their plan seemed to be.

Kris nodded slowly. "Intriguing," said Kris. "They will expect you to *not* focus on her. Shift your mind to their time frame. What would you do if you had weeks to prepare for this moment?"

"Couldn't they have predicted we would think that too?"

"Don't get ahead of yourself. They will still be dumb kids in one month's time. They are not that smart," Kris responded. "Yet."

Kris had everyone position themselves outside of Milk's room. It was a three-month time vault.

"Most likely, she is dead if there is no food," said Genghis.

"There is food," said Kris.

"Good, good," Genghis replied. "That would be a horrible way to die. Much better if I finished her off, yes?"

Genghis stood in front of the door, while Joseph stationed himself on either side, prepared to spring into action. Kris leaned his back against the wall, talking.

The timer was at thirty seconds.

"You have to think not about the chess move but about the chess game itself," Kris explained. "If you play the game, you are trapped in a maze. But if you flip the table over and burn the pieces, you also win, no?"

***

The timers on all three doors ran out. Alastair and Zack exploded into the hallway and ran for other doors.

Zack disappeared into another time vault down the distant hallway, the door slamming behind him. Alastair hadn't gone as far, searching for a specific door. When he found it, he suddenly stopped before going in.

He wasn't being chased, and it clearly threw him off. He looked toward Milk's door, his hand frozen on his own door handle. His eyes widened.

Kris smiled and waved his fingers at Alastair. He pulled open the door to Milk's room, but didn't go in, staying clear of the door. He nodded at Genghis to explore.

"It's me you want!" Alastair shouted.

Kris laughed. Genghis cautiously went into Milk's room. The vault wasn't very big, and there didn't seem to be anywhere to hide, but Milk was nowhere to be found. It was empty. Kris held out a hand to stop Joseph from joining Genghis, pushing him back to the wall on the side of the door.

The space was well lived in and messy—appropriate considering Milk had lived alone in the room for three months. There were food wrappers piled up. The shape of a body was covered by a dirty blanket.

On the wall, there was a beautiful drawing—a mural of Martin Luther King with a quote about saying goodbye. The words *No Food* were scrawled on the wall in blood.

Genghis bent down to inspect the lifeless form. When he lifted the blanket, he discovered doctors' scrubs stuffed with paper.

All the books on the shelves were just outer hardcovers, stripped on the inside.

Behind Genghis, Milk crouched above the door on a makeshift perch. Her back pressed against the ceiling. She had tilted the bunk bed frame up against the wall on one side of the door, and a wood table top stretched from it to a set of shelves on the other. A rope was tied to the inside of the door handle, and a second sturdier one was tied securely to a water sprinkler on the ceiling.

A clockwork trap.

Before Genghis realized where she was, Milk leapt off her perch and swung down on the rope, arcing out of the door into the hallway in one fell swoop, dragging with her a large stuffed duffle bag. She crashed onto the floor, and before Genghis even had time to turn, she pulled the door shut with the other rope.

It locked. For another three months. The timer, inexorable in its power, counted down.

Milk sprang to her feet and right into the arms of Joseph.

Kris leaned against the wall. Alastair watched the whole thing go down, horror on his face. His hand remained frozen on his door handle.

Kris opened Milk's duffle bag. Inside were all the spare food rations.

"Is there any food in the vault?" he asked.

Milk shook her head. Joseph dropped Milk and ran to the door, pounding on it.

"He's already dead," said Kris, emotion creeping into his face. It first appeared in his tightening mouth, and then it moved up his cheeks like a summer squall announcing its arrival across a lake. And then it shimmered across his eyes, transforming his face from smug to malicious. He rubbed his eyebrows and then took Milk's wrist.

"Stand up. I want you to see what you did." Milk tried to yank away, but Kris's grip was strong. "Stand up."

The one-minute timer ran out. Joseph opened the door.

Genghis was dead, now a corpse rotting on the floor. His flesh caved in on itself, putrefying into a liquid that pooled in the grout between the tiles. He was curled up in a fetal position—like a child—or someone hiding from fire.

"This stain will live with you forever," said Kris quietly to Milk. "Look at me." His eyes were ferocious, his voice an intonation. "You, Martha King, have chosen to murder. You have killed, consciously, by choice. You will be a captive of this decision and will think of it when you take your last breath. This is my prayer for you. You killed him, starving him in a room. Alone. You are no less ruthless than a common murderer, and whatever high ground you claimed, it is gone now. Your decision. And while you may think you are Martin Luther King Jr., it is your choices that define you. *Your choices.* I want you to remember this. I want it to haunt you. This is my prayer for you. You are a murderer, Martha King. For all time."

The words were like hammer blows on Milk's soul. Though she had been struggling with the decision for weeks, she clearly hadn't come to peace with it yet.

"I'm sorry," said Milk. "I'm sorry."

Kris let go of Milk's hand.

"Milk! Run!" yelled Alastair.

But she couldn't. She sat on the floor, gutted by Kris's words.

Joseph sprinted toward Alastair.

"Milk! Run!" Alastair yelled again, trying to get her to move, but Kris's spell was complete.

She was frozen in remorse. "I can't Alastair," she said, emotion throttling her voice.

Joseph chased after him, but just before he got to the door, Alastair entered the vault and pulled it shut.

"One year!" he shouted to Kris.

"Bold," Kris responded. He yanked Milk to her feet and dragged her by her hair down the hallway to Alastair's vault. "I want you to lift her up and strangle her," he instructed Joseph. "Crush her throat. Squeeze it. I want him to see it when the door opens."

Joseph obliged, picking up Milk by the neck. He pinned her against the wall opposite Alastair's door. His thick hand pressed into her soft neck, closing her airway with the violence of a man bred for harm.

Joseph's touch, powered by anger, squeezed a message into her: *You killed my friend.* He could feel each finger communicating this to her trachea, unforgiving.

"When the timer is up, keep her there," said Kris, "as bait. He will come out. If she dies, so be it. But do not move."

Milk hadn't taken a breath in forty seconds. Her feet kicked against Joseph's knotted quad muscles, scratching at them, searching for purchase. Her shoe fell off.

The minute was up and the door to the time vault opened. Milk still fought, holding on despite her increasing weakness.

Alastair was at the far end of the room, standing behind glass in a small lab, the type used to isolate dangerous chemicals. He had turned the vault into a makeshift workout gym.

Alastair was shirtless with a thick beard. He looked different. Harder. Alastair posed like a bodybuilder, showing off his incredible physique.

He's clearly been waiting for this moment for a whole year, thought Joseph.

Alastair saw Milk's predicament but didn't break form.

"You ready?" Alastair shouted. He swept his arms in a jujitsu move, posing like Neo from the *Matrix*. "Red pill, mothertrucker!" He motioned with his fingers for Joseph to come forward.

Joseph immediately understood the reference. He had watched the film a hundred times growing up in Purity. Neo had downloaded martial arts into his mind, and he'd learned to fight in an instant, just like Alastair. A whole year of training in a minute. But Joseph smiled inwardly, he had a true lifetime of training. *For a kid who is meant to be Einstein, he is not very bright*, Joseph thought.

He dropped Milk and headed into the vault on Kris's command, relishing a fight with the new and improved *Ultimate Fighter*, Albert Einstein edition.

Once inside the room, he froze. He heard a hissing sound. His head jerked right. On a table behind the door, a Bunsen burner burned through the last strand of a thin wire. The wire was attached to a glass beaker with a clear liquid in it. Alastair puffed out his cheeks at Kris, indicating for him to hold his breath, a last-minute taunt. The wire burned through. With a plop, the beaker of liquid dropped into a larger container, pulling with it a third glass cup that had been perched above it. The three chemicals released a hissing, noxious gas.

Kris and Joseph fainted.

Milk was already out.

An emergency alarm sounded in the hallway, and the lights started to flash red, giving the once bright hall a dark, eerie feeling. Powerful vacuums sucked air from the hallway.

Alastair waited behind the glass, looking at his watch. He pulled on a gas mask and emerged.

He stepped over Joseph.

"Psych," Alastair said.

Alastair pulled Milk's unconscious body to the vault marked 1, for one day, and closed it just as Kris and Joseph started to wake up.

Kris saw the door shut. He dragged himself up, woozy, and ran haphazardly, as if he was on a ship in choppy seas, to Genghis's corpse. He grabbed the machine gun from the dead figure, but the strap was tied around his body. He yanked it violently, and the once great Chinese leader's flesh gave way, sloughing off like pulled pork. There were two grenades on Genghis' belt.

In the hall outside Alastair and Milk's door, Kris handed the automatic weapon to Joseph. "Do not stop firing until every inch of the room has a bullet in it. Let's obliterate that little shit brain."

Kris pulled the pins from both grenades. The timer hit zero, turning green. The door unlocked. Just before Kris ripped the door open and dropped in the grenades, there was a new voice.

"Stop!"

Joseph saw a stick figure walking toward them, backlit by one of the red emergency lights.

It was Isaac. Joseph looked at his watch. Right on time. They were getting back on track. Isaac had been the mastermind of the entire timeline, but Joseph didn't expect to see him at the Nautilus. Something must have gone wrong. Their rendezvous was a few miles south of the building.

"Don't be so predictable. Haven't you figured it out yet?" the red figure asked when he reached them.

Joseph thought Isaac looked haggard. Thinner than he remembered.

"They are playing chess with you," the stick man said to Joseph and Kris, "and you keep taking their pawn sacrifice."

"I just used that metaphor," Kris replied. The time counter sat at zero. Kris's hand stayed on the door, the grenade ready, but he didn't open it. "You can't outsmart a grenade. Why aren't you at the rendezvous?" Kris asked.

"Because you are not at the rendezvous."

"Genghis is dead."

"Well, considering you blew up their friends in a helicopter, I think he was probably fair game."

"What's fair?" Kris replied. He turned the door handle.

"Even you can understand their value," he replied, commanding Kris to stop with his voice. Isaac bent down and slowly picked up the pins as if they were explosive themselves and put them back into the grenades. "We need them to bargain with the Americans if we get caught outside the barrier. On the beach."

"How could the Americans react that quickly? It will only have been a few seconds for them in Texas."

Isaac took the grenades from Kris.

"Everyone calm down. Let us use our considerable minds." He put out his hand for Joseph's machine gun. "You think the Americans have no idea what Russia was up to? Think."

Something was off, but Joseph couldn't put his finger on it.

Kris relented, his anger dissipating. He nodded and Joseph handed over the weapon. "So, genius, what's next in our game of chess?"

"I'll talk to them. They are intelligent enough to realize that we are the only ones who know where the exit through the barrier wall is. With an ocean of water bearing down on us, that is a *material* fact. If we apply their minds to the bigger problem of survival, they will see this. They just need to realize our immediate interests are aligned." Isaac put the machine gun strap over his shoulder, his nose crinkling as he smelled it. "Back up. And open the door."

Kris smoothed his hair and stretched his shoulders. "What does 'red pill' mean?"

"It means you are in over your head."

Joseph opened the door. Alastair and Milk sat cross-legged in the middle of the room with their hands in the air.

"We surrender," said Alastair.

"Will you show us the way out if we stop fighting?" Milk asked.

"Yes, of course," said Kris, smiling in victory. "Yes."

"Nice muscles!" Isaac said to Alastair. "That's insane."

Joseph looked at Isaac again, sensing something was off about him. The enthusiasm in his voice was unlike the sour physicist he had secretly been coordinating with for the last month.

Kris took Alastair and Milk roughly by the shoulders. "Stand!"

Isaac coughed. He was ten steps behind them. He hadn't moved. Kris glanced back. The gun was pointed at him.

"Isaac?" said Kris.

"Blue pill," said Alastair.

"What is it with these pills?!" yelled Kris.

"My name is not Isaac, asshole." He shot the weapon at Joseph's feet. "It's Zack."

Kris's eyes darted back and forth. In one horrible moment, Joseph put it all together. Zack had gone into a four-year room and used the time to trick them into thinking he was Isaac.

"Alastair!" A new voice emerged.

It was Paul. Behind him, was Isaac, the real one. This Isaac was still missing his leg. He could barely walk and was smeared with blood and black paste, but he seemed a bit stronger now.

"Hey," said Zack to Paul, clutching the weapon.

"You're—"

"Older. Four years older to be exact."

Paul turned to Alastair. "And you're—"

"Ripped Albert Einstein," said Alastair, flexing.

"Did you know that there is a giant, chicken stuck in the outer door?" Paul said.

"Where's Leo? And Kat?" asked Alastair.

Paul shook his head. "I'm sorry." He explained that their friends were thrown out of the helicopter long before his crash landing. "I have no idea if they survived. I tried to find everyone, I was scared shitless, but found Isaac instead."

"What happened to you? Why are you here?" said Alastair, suspicious.

"I came to find you when the barrier dam blew."

Alastair tried to get a read on Isaac, but he didn't offer anymore.

"Who are they?" Paul asked, to fill the silence.

Kris and Joseph still had their hands in the air.

"This is Adolf Hitler," said Milk, referring to Kris. "He's the one who blew up the helicopter."

"The Russians are doing the same thing with genetics," said Alastair. "He's literally Hitler's clone."

"Hitler," said Paul. "That makes zero sense."

"Ask him," said Alastair.

"He's the one who attacked up our helicopter?" asked Paul.

"Yes," said Milk. "Most likely."

"No, he did," said Alastair.

"And he is *Hitler*?" Paul asked.

Kris shrugged, a smirk on his lips. "Adolf, at your service. But you can call me—"

Paul shoved Kris, born Adolf, into the time vault behind him and slammed shut the door. It was labeled 8. Eight years.

"So what happened, exactly?" Paul asked, keeping his hand on the door handle. Zack kept his gun trained on Joseph.

Alastair explained how they were cornered by Sephora and history's goons and chased by a giant chicken. He outlined what went down in the time vaults. When they first went into the one-week vault, they had time to create a masterplan. Most of their ideas involved making various weapons, but they soon realized that time was their best weapon, and they could use it psychologically. Milk and Alastair would distract the goons with various tactics while Zack went into the four-year vault. Even Milk's emotional reaction to the dead Genghis was planned.

While Alastair explained their plans and antics, Joseph couldn't take his eyes off the vault's countdown timer.

"Four years, Zack?" said Paul. "You agreed to that?"

"It was my idea. Remember, I'm not built like you," said Zack. "I enjoyed the time alone to think. Do you know anything about the Millennium Prize Problems?"

The Millennium Prize Problems were seven problems that were identified by the Clay Mathematics Institute as nearly impossible to solve. With names like P versus NP problem, the Hodge conjecture, the Riemann hypothesis, and Poincaré conjecture, they were like a who's who of physics bad boys. No one could beat them, so the institute offered a million-dollar prize for any one solution.

"Let me guess. You solved one?" asked Paul, smiling. He glanced at the timer on the door. Six years had already passed.

"No," Zack shook his head.

The timer was up. The door unlocked. Paul opened it.

"I solved all of them," Zack said, with characteristic flatness.

Kris ran at them, wild with eight years of pent-up rage, but Paul nonchalantly closed the door once more before Kris could get there. It locked and the timer started again, trapping Kris for another eight years.

"And I also now know every Johnny Cash song by heart, so that's cool," Zack continued. "And I can play the guitar. And I know how to—"

"Hold on," said Alastair, motioning to the vault.

They followed Alastair's cue to wait quietly while the one minute passed, now aware that something profound was happening on the other side of the door.

Time's up. Paul opened the door.

Hitler, the second one, was dead, hanging from the ceiling. He was shirtless and his upper body gaunt, dried out. His hair was almost as long as his body; his pants were in tatters. Terrible slashes scarred his stomach, like he had been counting the months by carving them into his skin.

"Good riddance," said Alastair with false bravado. "The world had—"

Milk shook her head. Alastair fell quiet. Paul closed the door, hiding the sight. The timer started again, but this time, the door was shut for good.

Isaac glanced at Joseph. They made a silent pact with their eyes.

***

The hallway was empty. Inside Kris's vault, time accelerated without an audience, aging the objects, his body, and the air itself.

Hitler, the second one, was dead, but his DNA lived on, vowing a third, a fourth, and a fifth copy. The base pairs aged, desiccating inside follicles of hair, bones, and skin; however, they did not disappear, saving themselves for future generations. Centuries passed in the room and the DNA waited for its next resurrection, from beneath the vast ocean that would soon engulf the tomb.

FOUR HOURS

"Everything's going to be okay," said Alastair, turning his palms up to feel the sun. Birds unknown to science chirped. Pollen was in the air, its burnt-toast smell made him sneeze.

They were outside the Nautilus. The sky seemed brighter than Alastair remembered and less ominous. It had been over a year since he was chased into the building, a distant memory. Nature's warmth was welcome, albeit alien. He took a deep breath.

Zack winced at the glare and pulled Isaac into the shade just out of reach of the angry chicken, which was tied up and calm. He wrapped his brother's arms with supplies they had taken from the surgical infirmary.

Isaac was healing. In places that should still be oozing blood and pus, or at the very least, scabbing over, there was fresh skin. Wounds once fresh and jagged now blushed pink, the hue of regeneration. Zack moved to throw away Isaac's black paste, which was tied in a satchel under his neck, explaining they now had real medical supplies. Isaac pawed at the sack, stopping Zack, demanding he continue to use it, like a junkie. He shoved his pant legs down, hiding his wounds.

Paul had the gun trained on Joseph, though the Russian didn't seem like a threat anymore. Things seemed to normalize or, at the very least, depressurize. It was the first time in a long while that Alastair didn't feel like his life was in immediate danger with death on the other side of the door.

He knew what he had to do.

The pirate Armageddon Truck was fueled for the trip to the barrier. They had enough time. Joseph had already mapped out a hidden shortcut. It was an easy drive cleared of debris and fallen logs. It would take a mere thirty minutes, he said. They had four hours to get out before the seventeen-hour deadline locked them in for a decade. It was more than enough time to reach the beach escape.

"Check this out. Chicken," said Paul. The angry chicken was tied up, roosting near the entrance to the Nautilus. "I bet this thing lays massive eggs. Wonder if—"

"I wouldn't," Milk advised.

Alastair watched Zack's newfound maturity as he worked with Isaac. He chatted with Isaac about his discoveries during his four years in the vault.

"I hope this place burns to the ground," said Alastair to himself.

"Or floods more likely," said Milk, pointing to the massive wall of water. It was closer. "We should get going."

"I am not going," said Alastair.

"Not this again," said Milk.

"I am going to go find Leo and Kat."

Silence.

"How, exactly? We are taking the truck," said Milk.

When they had first exited the Nautilus, they had tried to contact Cayce and Jimmy. There was only static. There had been no word from them, or any of their friends, since the helicopter crashed.

"They are gone," said Paul. "I saw it happen. They were thrown into the air. We were high. If they are alive, they could be anywhere."

Alastair dug in, stubborn.

"Hey!" Milk yelled, stopping him in his tracks midsentence. "I've had enough death. There is nothing special about us. There are no rules that keep us alive. Everyone dies. But because we are the center of our own story, we feel special, like we will buck the odds, but we're not and won't. People die when they fall from large heights. Or small heights. On Sunday afternoon with the family. People die from catching the flu at the grocery store. Kids catch it from their mom or a classmate, and they die. There are no free passes. And it is cruel. Leo and Kat do not have superpowers just because they are our friends," she said. Her tone was flat and full of sadness, but her words themselves were weaponized. "You are no one to the universe Alastair Albert Mayes. Nor am I." She took a breath, her mind seeming to go elsewhere for a moment. "People die. And we make what we can with it."

Alastair waited for her to finish, as she continued to argue that they had to leave. It was their duty to Zack and even to the injured Isaac.

As he listened, everything came into focus for Alastair. This wasn't about Kat or Leo. It was about Milk and her guilt for what happened in the time vaults. She had been the one to argue it was okay to trap Genghis, to kill him. But it had been an intellectual argument. Emotionally, she had not won herself over. This wasn't about Alastair either.

"I'm sorry," he said. He shifted under her glare.

Milk got in the truck, slamming the door shut. Alastair followed, hoping to resolve the argument, but she didn't relent. He pounded on the window. She lowered it and tossed a backpack at Alastair. He made a show of going through the truck's outer storage compartments, pulling ropes, bags, and tools, trying to find anything that could help him, but Milk didn't take the bait.

"Alastair," said Joseph. He had been trying to interrupt for a while.

"Be quiet," said Paul.

"Take that ATV," said Joseph. "It has a beacon that can track other vehicles, helicopter included." He pointed at the truck. "It's how we found you."

"Go ahead," said Paul.

There was an ATV and a motorcycle strapped tightly onto the back of the truck. Joseph released the straps, and they crashed down.

The small, four-wheeled, off-road menace was a marvel of engineering, a mini Armageddon Truck. It was as if the big truck had a baby with just as many tools strapped to it: extendable fishing rods, nets, climbing gear, extra lights, additional canisters, scientific sampling jars, cages, and more. Alastair half expected to see missile launchers. He spotted two shotguns strapped to either side. In any other situation, it would be the coolest thing ever.

Now, he just wanted his friends to come and get him. He sat on the ATV watching everyone load into the truck, leaving him outside.

Finally, Milk poked her head out of the window. "I've had crushes on you at various points over the last few years. You might think this is the moment where I get upset. Or cry. Or tell you that I will wait for you at the barrier dam. But this is not that story. And I am not that girl. You are an idiot for chasing this. And worse than being angry, I am disappointed that you are being so selfish. Just 'cause you need to prove something to yourself, doesn't mean you have to prove it to us. You can be average and miserable, and that's better than being dead to those who love you. Goodbye."

The truck rumbled to life, and then Alastair was alone. But he felt a quiet resolve checking out his ATV. He turned the key, ready for a new adventure, but it didn't start. It was out of gas.

There was no gas.

Einstein?

Alastair considered his options, fear swelling. The truck was too far gone to chase it. It was a terrible start to his rescue mission. He turned on the tracker, a little dirty screen on the side of the steering column. He could see two trucks nearby: one was Milk's driving directly away from him. Jimmy and Cayce's truck was in the opposite direction: at the Guitar Bridge. But how would he get there?

He swore loudly. A loud *squawk* answered back.

Roped to the wall, the angry chicken was growing restless, like a rough horse in need of taming. A terrible idea struck Alastair.

Alastair slowly approached the beast. He removed the electric shock strap around the animal's chest. He ran his hand along its feathers soothingly.

We could be friends, thought Alastair, trying to project warmth at the animal. The primordial chicken struck out its claw. It ripped Alastair's shirt, almost disemboweling him as he tripped backward. He approached the beast again, hands outstretched, trying to coax millions of years of flight response out of the first chicken able to fight back. This time, the chicken punched him in the stomach with a closed, fist-like claw. Alastair got up, determined.

"Chicken shit," he said, kicking dirt at the bird.

Again, he was rebuked, falling to the ground.

And again.

***

Alastair jogged further and further from safety; the heat and his allergies squeezed his lungs, slowing him down. Despite his new and improved body, he struggled to keep a steady pace. Riding the chicken was his second failed idea after the ATV. Now, intense loneliness chased him as he headed toward the Guitar Bridge. He was more afraid of never seeing another human again than he was of the idea of dying in the Crypt.

He had a thought on repeat in his mind. *What if there wasn't a sign of what to do when he got to the bridge? What if he couldn't find the truck?* Hopefully, Jimmy and Cayce would be there with his friends, packing up Hello Kitty to leave, and he wouldn't have to make any hard choices.

When Alastair arrived, heaving for breath, he found the truck, but not where he expected it to be. The bridge was gone. Destroyed. Far below, metal cables were strewn across the chasm like a bowl of old spaghetti tossed out of a kitchen window. Beneath it all, the Hello Kitty truck was a smoking wreck at the base of the waterfall.

Jimmy and Cayce were likely not alive, thought Alastair darkly; however, Hello Kitty might have extra gasoline for the ATV. He had to get down there somehow. There was no feasible route. The cliffs were too steep. He could climb the cables running down the sides of the jungle ravine, but it would take too long and be too perilous. One unlucky slip and he'd be dead, and maybe Leo and Kat as well.

Alastair rifled through the gear in his backpack, searching for a solution. He had rope. He counted off the yards as he wound it around his arm. It was too short. He wouldn't make it to the bottom.

Inside a custom pouch zippered to the outside of the backpack, he found a lightweight parachute. It was for base jumping, the kind of device one wears to leap off cliffs. Alastair put it on and readied himself without hesitation.

He jumped without much thought or fanfare. Having seen enough You-Tube videos, he knew to hold the chute's drogue in one hand and to toss it as soon as he cleared the cliff's edge.

The main chute opened after a sickening plunge, momentarily revealing the Gene-E Corp logo, but it immediately caught the first tree below and ripped. Alastair fell down the cliff, the chute grabbing at every tree, shrub, and rock on his behalf, like it was trying to save Alastair. The device slowed his violent descent just enough to knock some sense into him about how stupid his idea was. He finally stopped midway, momentarily convinced that he was not going to die, until his chute quietly filled with water from an eddy in the waterfall and yanked him backward over the edge again. He fell for another one hundred feet into the maw of the churning water below.

The leeches came for him. The chute pulled him down, but he still had his strength. Soon he was safe on the water's edge, pulling metal and cable off of the truck. It was jammed near the entrance to the cave, partially blocking the water flow.

Alastair found Cayce trapped on his back, staring upward through the wreckage. Water roared through the truck, washing away Cayce's blood as soon as it seeped out of him.

"Nice jump," said Cayce. "Do me a favor. There is some morphine in the glove compartment."

Alastair fought downward into the truck's wreckage, opened the glove compartment with some punches, and located the first aid kit. It was then that he noticed that Cayce's legs were almost severed. Cables had cut through the truck and Cayce's upper quads. His legs were pinched down to the width of a few inches. There would be no way to get him out without the rest of his blood escaping with them. As Alastair processed the scene, Cayce injected a long vial of morphine into his arm.

"So you don't have to make any more stupid decisions," said Cayce.

"How much did you take?" Alastair asked.

"I've never understood why it isn't standard protocol to give dying patients in pain, at the very end, a whack of heroin to flood and release all their last serotonin," said Cayce. "It's not like it can ruin your life at that point." He smiled, the morphine calming his face. "Go out in a blaze of ... ? So I am going to ..."

Alastair pulled on the cable trapping Cayce. It wouldn't move, pinned down by the weight of the truck.

"... to sleep. Jimmy is in there, my boy," said Cayce, motioning to the cave entrance. He started to slur, the powerful drug taking hold. His eyes swung back and forth, in and out of focus. He fought to stay awake. "And so are your friends."

Alastair found a knife in his bag and sawed at a seatbelt, not willing to give in to Cayce's fate yet.

"If the winch still works in twenty minutes, turn it on," said Cayce, "for Jimmy. Hopefully, he has the others with him. Wait for them here. Don't go in. Someone needs to operate the winch. That was going to be me, but now it is you."

He gripped Alastair's hand, stopping him from cutting the seat belt. "The winch is the only way out. Don't go in."

Alastair lowered the knife.

"You can't go in," said Cayce. "Even if my boy doesn't come out. Don't go inside. You will die. This cave marks the boundary between your life and death." He was on the verge of consciousness. His words rolled on top of each other. "If you go in there, you will be in a shadow world. No amount of science or logic works. Nothing has ever come out. There is only madness down there. Okay, kid? You can't go in. You are too important. For the world. It needs your goodness." Cayce's breathing was labored. His eyes closed.

Alastair was self-conscious about what to do, how to be in the moment of Cayce's death. He took the old man's hand and whispered the only thing he could think to say into his ear.

Then Cayce Jones was gone.

Alastair folded Cayce's arms over his chest. He noticed there was a giant leech attached to Cayce's back, greedily drawing what little blood the man had left, and started to cry.

***

Alastair waited twenty minutes for Jimmy. Nothing happened. There was no metallic twang of the winch cable being struck somewhere deep inside the cave, no signal to pull the group out of the dark mystery. The Crypt had swallowed them.

He waited another ten minutes. The mouth to the cave grew larger with every second, beckoning Alastair. The cables of the bridge were strewn over the entrance, and as millions of gallons of water poured through them, they created a deep vibration. The powerful hum seemed to come from the depths of the earth itself, calling for Alastair to go downward to his death, like an incantation.

There had been many forks in the road to arrive here. Many choices, conscious and unconscious, through action and inaction. Alastair had chosen to chase the plane to Cornerstone. He decided to stay and risk ten years in the Crypt for a chance at glory when his friends wanted to leave. And then, when everything went to hell, he chose to head out against the odds to find Leo and Kat, who were probably dead. But now, with Hello Kitty destroyed, no clear way back up the Falls, and the words of Cayce warning him against going into the cave, he faced the true unknown.

Alastair looked up. Even if he managed to find everyone in the cave—*maybe they got lost and just needed to find the winch cable*—they would still have to climb up and out of the ravine. With less than four hours, it was un-likely they would have time.

But at least they would be alive, thought Alastair. Maybe they could get back to higher ground in the east and survive the flood with enough supplies for ten years. He knew the odds were close to zero.

Everything about Alastair had changed. It was not his muscles, nor the strength they gave him, nor the conviction he had found in the year he spent alone in the time vault that made him feel different. It was the melancholy with which he now faced the one inexorable truth about life. The only truth. There are doors, once passed through, that lock forever. His youth, that long hallway of endless open doors, was behind him, apparent only in hindsight. Alastair couldn't even see thirty feet into his future.

In this moment, all these thoughts rushed through Alastair's mind. The mist and the wind of the falls toyed with his hair.

He had to choose.

Alastair tightened the strap on his backpack, turned on every flashlight he had, and faced the cave and the one true monster—the unknown.

***

Over a mile below, in a tiny, dark crevice, Kat kicked her feet at something trying to eat her. Behind it, hundreds more pressed forward, scratching for their turn to seek food. Leo faced the other way, his back to hers, thrashing wildly.

Somewhere, Ralls screamed.

THREE HOURS

Milk felt a knot in her stomach she couldn't undo. They approached the wall of water. It hung like the sword of Damocles over Milk, judging her harsh final words to Alastair.

Martha, the rationalist, told herself that Alastair was eighteen, an adult. She couldn't physically force him to join them. He had made his own choice, and no matter how dumb it was, it was his to make.

Martha, the hopeful, imagined that Alastair had already found everyone and was right behind them, racing along the same dusty road in Hello Kitty, just barely out of sight. Sometimes things in life work out perfectly.

Martha, the orator, spun lies in her mind, trying to ignore every fiber in her body screaming at her to turn around. She knew it would mean risking not only her life but also the lives of everyone in the truck.

Martha, the fatalist, thought Alastair was already dead. They all would be soon enough. It was slow going. The road wasn't fully cleared, and they would have to wait for Joseph to use a chainsaw, under the threat of a gun held by Zack, to remove fallen tree limbs from giant trees when they couldn't drive around.

There were only three hours until it would be too late to escape the Crypt. They would be stuck for ten years, or more likely, they would drown when the wall of water was finally released from time's grip.

Milk adjusted the rearview mirror for the tenth time, trying to see if she could spot Hello Kitty following them in the distance. In the back seat, Paul tried to inspect Isaac's wounds, but Isaac refused help. He seemed to be hiding something.

Milk suddenly jammed on the breaks. A woman waved frantically at them in the dust. It was Sephora. She was covered in blood and looked desperate. Milk slowed the truck.

Zack argued against picking her up. "How do we know it's not an act?" He told Paul what happened back at the Nautilus, about Sephora's turn, and elaborated on the appearance of history's violent goons at her side. Hitler, Genghis, serial killers, and even an evil Winston Churchill. It was like a special edition alternate universe comic book, and she was the ringleader.

Milk didn't care. She had already executed someone that day. She didn't want to add more evidence to the argument that maybe she was a murderer at heart.

When they pulled up alongside Sephora, she was hysterical, missing a hand, and bleeding profusely. She stumbled forward, clutching the bloody stump to her chest. Despite Sephora's sorry state, Milk didn't open the door. She sensed something was off.

When Zack moved to get out and help Sephora, Milk pushed him back. Her intuition told her to get more information.

"What happened to you?" Milk asked.

Sephora ignored her, spotting Joseph. "Let me in, Isaac. Isaac!" she screamed. "They are all dead, the others. Churchill, everyone. We were attacked. Let me in!"

Milk spun, looking back at Isaac, suddenly suspicious of him.

How did Isaac know Churchill?

Paul tried to look at Isaac's leg again. "I just want to see it for a second," he urged.

Isaac swatted away his hand.

Something wasn't adding up.

"Isaac," Sephora repeated.

"Let her in," Isaac said. "Please."

Distracted by Sephora, Isaac relented to Paul's inspections. Paul unwrapped his leg bandage and was shocked to discover that Isaac's foot had almost grown back. Where before there had been ankle bones, now there was a fleshy foot nub with the beginnings of five toes. It was red and angry, but it was new growth.

Something dawned on Paul. "His foot grew back." He looked at Sephora and her missing hand.

"How do you know Sephora? And about Churchill?" Milk asked Isaac. "You weren't at the Nautilus when we met her. And Churchill …"

"I … Well, she is a part of our program, of course," said Isaac.

"Sephora referred to 'the others,'" said Milk. "Who is she talking about?"

On the roof of the truck, four shadows crouched. Winston Churchill, Shirō Ishii, and Elizabeth Báthory hung near the front cab, careful not to make a noise while Sephora talked. Ching Shih was with them as well, quietly uncoiling a large accordion tube attached to two tanks on the top of the truck. One was labeled A-SIDE ISO. The other was labeled B-SIDE POLY—industrial hardening foam.

Inside the truck, Paul looked at Isaac's foot again and then at Sephora and her bleeding hand.

Her hand was cleanly severed. They were not attacked.

"It'll grow back!" said Paul. "It's a trap!"

Suddenly, an upside-down face appeared at the top of the windshield. It was Elizabeth Báthory, the Blood Queen. She held Sephora's severed hand and waved it at them.

Everyone was too horrified to react.

"They are monsters!" screamed Sephora.

Up to this point, Zack still had the gun trained on Joseph, but with the distraction, the gun drifted, and now Joseph seized it from him.

"I knew you were still an asshole!" Milk said.

Milk jammed on the accelerator and then, just as quickly, hit the brakes hard. This threw Joseph forward, knocking the gun loose. On the roof, Elizabeth held on, though Sephora's severed hand went flying, followed by Ching Shih, who rolled off the hood of the car.

Milk hit the gas again and ran Ching over, squeezing her guts into the dirt. Another death.

The Blood Queen shrieked.

The truck's back wheel ran over Sephora's bloody hand. Sephora scrambled for it in tears, digging it out of the dirt while the truck took off down the road without her.

The vehicle picked up speed. General Ishii and the Blood Queen reached into the windows. Milk drove into trees and vegetation to try to knock them off. A cliff appeared on one side. Below there was a raging, boiling river, its anger fed by the front wave of the approaching Gulf-sized tsunami. Time was releasing its grip; water rushed with the force of a thousand planets into the Crypt, raging and smashing through the river canyons.

The truck's outer wheel went an inch from the edge of the cliff. Milk fishtailed back onto the road, and the momentum swung Elizabeth out over the steep drop into the chasm, flinging her to the river far below.

Winston Churchill tried to retrieve the industrial polyurethane tube. It was flying all over the place. The truck swerved and hit a dirt berm, catching air for a moment, almost kicking Churchill off. He held on and finally took control of the nozzle at the end of the tube.

Inside the truck's cab, the impact triggered the emergency oxygen masks, which dropped down as if they were in an airplane. The masks bounced up and down, adding chaos to the already out-of-control situation.

"What *didn't* he put in here!" Milk yelled, trying to move them out from in front of her face. "Jesus Christ."

In the back seat of the truck, there was a scramble for the gun on the ground. Joseph got a hold of it for a moment, but Zack managed to get the clip out, which fell on the floor. When Zack went for it, Joseph grabbed him by the pants to pull him up, but only succeeded in pulling down his pants. Upside down, his butt sticking in the air, Zack unloaded the clip, dropping the bullets blindly out the window. Joseph grabbed his hand to stop him, so Zack started putting the remaining ones in his mouth.

"I will dig the bullets out of your stomach," said Joseph, reaching down to squeeze Zack's face, like a dog owner trying to retrieve a chicken bone.

"Stop the car! Milk, please," Isaac pleaded.

Sephora disappeared into the distance.

Churchill was at Milk's window. He jammed the end of the industrial foam hose into the window. Milk tried to close the window, but all it did was jam the hose in place, pointing directly at her. Churchill pulled the lever, and high capacity polyurethane poured into the cab.

Science was on the attack. The isocyanate and the polyol combined in the tube and solidified quickly, forming a lightweight, cement-hard substance which began to cover the inside of the truck.

"Holy sh—"

The cab quickly filled up. Milk was out of ideas. If she stopped the truck, they would be screwed. If she didn't, they would be entombed.

It was getting harder and harder to steer.

Zack scrambled onto his seat to escape the flood of foam. His window wouldn't go down. They looked like they were trapped in a foam rave party with no emergency escape route.

"Turn off the child locks!" Zack screamed.

The dirt road kicked ever upward. They were high above the raging, impromptu river now, the edge of the road a steep, unforgiving cliff.

"Cliffs!" shouted Paul.

"I know!" Milk yelled.

Her body was almost encased in foam. She could barely see out of the window, making it hard to drive. Her arms felt like they were moving through taffy.

"What is this stuff!?" said Milk.

"Shock foam!" said Isaac. "It will ki—"

"Good enough," said Milk, and she yanked as hard as she could to the right, rolling the truck off the cliff—on purpose.

The truck cartwheeled sideways into the chasm, smashing through the first line of trees, picking up speed, and then disgorging everything Jimmy had stuffed into it. Churchill flew out into the space above the raging river. General Shirō Ishii was stuck on the side of the truck, along for a wild ride as the vehicle careened down the jungle ravine.

The truck's roof ripped off. Milk and everyone inside were launched from it. The hardening foam cocoon that enveloped them now acted like armor, protecting the group as they fell down the ravine alongside the truck. The cube-like, rock-solid object—with a bunch of humans lodged in it—went end over end, losing both foam and people with every tree it hit.

There was a final free fall, and the block hit the river, breaking into a few pieces. The largest chunk floated like a cork—with Milk embedded in it—rotating in and out of the water as it tumbled down the raging river.

In another block of foam, Joseph was stuck with Zack, but there was no open space that allowed both to breathe. They would take turns rolling their body weight, allowing for one person to breathe before being plunged back under the water, and the other came sputtering up to the surface desperate for air.

Paul had his own block and a fairly comfortable ride, all things considered. The foam locked his legs together up to his hips, giving him the appearance of a giant pin cushion, but he was lucky to be bottom heavy. He started trying to paddle backward in the violent water.

They were headed for a waterfall.

Church and the Blood Queen were already out of the water and safe on a fallen tree. They reached for General Ishii, dragging him out of the rushing river.

The three floating foam corks weren't so lucky; they swept past the last tree and flew over the falls. Their screams were swallowed by the roar of the Crypt.

***

Sephora walked, not sure what to do. She had created a makeshift tourniquet from wire for her severed wrist, but it wasn't enough. She was woozy from losing so much blood. The flood from the Gulf was increasing on all sides.

She heard something chitter and halted. After a pause, she continued walking but then stopped again, certain she wasn't alone.

The giant rooibaadjie insect stood behind her, having hopped onto the road to see what was going on. It stepped forward, casting a black shadow over her.

Sephora spun to see the giant insect impartially watching her.

The rooibaadjie took its needle-like foot and pushed her down with a flick, like it was toying with an idea. And then it stood on her. Its foot punctured her stomach, pinning her to the ground.

Sephora didn't die immediately. Somehow she stayed conscious, her back pressed against the dirt road. The rooibaadjie stood there, content to wait. A skittering sound drew her eyes upward. A mass of smaller, infant rooibaadjie crawled out from under their mother's belly and then down her legs. Sephora suddenly understood that Mom was feeding her babies, and she was breakfast. The first one zeroed in on Sephora. She screamed at it, swearing in Russian. Undeterred, its mandibles sunk into her flesh, crushing her hip and the last of her spirit in one swift motion. Sephora lifted her head, hoping the next bite would be the last.

TWO HOURS

Alastair waited twenty minutes. Nothing happened. Despite the terrible timeline he was under, he was bored. He hoped to hear a *twang* in the first few minutes, signaling that it was time to pull Jimmy—and his friends—out of the cave. But there was no such sign, and now time was running out. He knew, and he dreaded, what he needed to do.

He gathered more fresh supplies: flares, batteries, water, rope, food, gasoline, and an axe.

Alastair faced the cave, standing at the threshold. The hum of the cables rushing through water thrummed through his core, warning him to stop. He fought to put one foot in front of the other. It felt like he was forcing his body into a fire when it knew better, but he pressed forward. He passed the ribs of the Cave Pickle, keeping one hand on Jimmy's metal winch cable. He followed it downward into the darkness.

Before entering the cave, he had also scavenged pencil-thin guide rope from Hello Kitty. It was the kind used by scuba divers—strong enough to wind through caves without breaking but not so thick that it caught on every rock and crevice.

The rope was not just to find his way out, however.

He had tied the end of the yellow rope to the truck's winch lever handle. If they had to go up a vertical drop, he could trigger the mechanism and drag everyone out to safety. All he had to do was yank on the rope hard enough. The winch handle would pull down, and the metal cable would wind back to its home on Hello Kitty, pulling them all out of the cave.

Or at least that was the plan.

He knew it wasn't foolproof. If the guide rope got caught on anything, he wouldn't be able to pull the winch handle, and he would also be stuck in the cave.

Of course, he also had a cowardly option.

He could leave immediately, head back to the ATV with the newfound gas, and drive to catch up to everyone else.

In the darkness, Alastair climbed down another section of the cave waterfall. Neon mushrooms lining the walls stained his hands, making him look like a raver who had gotten lost at the acid factory. In any other context, Alastair would have remarked on their beauty. By the time he made it through the mushroom patch, he had traveled another few hundred yards and looked like a Saturday morning cartoon. He wasn't sure if the colors would ever come off. He tested his rope as it unspooled, trying to keep it taut so he could pull the winch handle at a moment's notice.

After a relatively scary series of near falls, he made it to the bottom of the first waterfall and started to travel horizontally, alongside the cave river.

The temperature dropped, and he soon encountered the source: buried liquid helium pipes. The sight of the industrial engineering calmed him. *Someone has been here before.* He was not in the depths of hell.

The river was close to freezing due to its proximity to the pipes. A cold fog flowed over the water. In some areas, Alastair had to traverse sections of river ice, praying he wouldn't fall through. The cold fog, blue ice, and ever-present darkness kept him on edge.

He clipped a carabiner onto Jimmy's cable for safety, surprised he hadn't thought of that already. The cable was the only thing to which his hope clung; it could lead him to Jimmy and his friends. It was his breadcrumb trail. As long as Jimmy was somewhere, Alastair was safe. Jimmy was the most practical, capable man Alastair had ever met.

His foot went through the ice. Glow-in-the-dark neon liquid swirled under the surface. He watched it in fascination, when suddenly, he heard a distant scream.

Despite the quick flash of terror that rushed through him, Alastair was buoyed. *He wasn't alone!* He raced ahead, chasing the pipes and Jimmy's cable. After a few more turns and slips into the ice water, he reached the edge of a cliff. The neon water poured into the blackness below. The liquid helium pipe stretched out in front of him over the chasm and then disappeared into a sheer rock wall.

It was a dead end.

Jimmy's winch cable was also at its end, clipped to the liquid helium pipe over the void. Where it was attached, the pipe was bent forcefully and there was a small leak, which explained why it was so cold.

Alastair thought he heard more yelling, but over the rush of the water, it was hard to tell. Now he wasn't even sure if he had heard the first scream. It might have been conjured by his mind, luring him deeper to his death.

He yelled into the blackness below. Alastair had an extra halogen lamp. He was planning on saving it for when his first batteries ran out, but this was a sufficient emergency. He dropped it, hoping it would cast a light on his friends. The lamp landed in the water one hundred feet below, illuminating the subterranean space.

Alastair didn't like what he saw.

The lamp cast a spotlight across a section of the waterfall. There was some sort of giant animal on it. It stood on its haunches, scratching at the rocks and flapping its paper-thin wings. He could see the beast's veins backlit by the flashlight, creating a terrifying shadow puppet on the wall.

The wings flapped in great swoops. The animal's talons pulled at boulders, slowly moving the rocks out of place to get at something hidden inside. It looked like a skeletal, sickly polar bear left to die by retreating glaciers.

Alastair's eyes continued to adjust to the light. Then he saw more gorgons of the deep—these ones smaller—flying around the larger one. Some clung to the giant beast, egging it on with their screams. The beast roared when a large boulder caught its foot. Suddenly, Alastair realized it was the beast's screams he had heard, not his friends. There was no way he could have heard a human's noises over the sound of the waterfall.

His heart sank.

Under the boulders, beneath the beast, a small flashlight beam fought back. Someone *was* down there.

"Jimmy! Kat! Leo!" Alastair yelled. There was no answer. He yelled again, this time hoping to divert the beast's attention, but all it did was attract some of the smaller animals circling nearby. They swarmed toward Alastair, making popping and clicking sounds, and then suddenly stopped, hovering opposite him like bats. Their wings stretched skin over claws to create lift.

All wings were once arms and hands—finger bones and wrists elongated over millions of years to create flight. The bears were the result of life challenged, over time, to develop nocturnal solutions to surviving in an extreme cave environment. It was an example of convergent evolution—different species finding the same solutions to the same environmental challenges.

During the grow cycle, bears must have been introduced to the Crypt to provide diversity of life, thought Alastair. And what had started as hibernation soon became isolation. With so few resources to fight for on the surface of the Crypt, the bears found a niche they could exploit inside the caves. They slept during the winters, evolving ways to hunt over hundreds of thousands of years.

It didn't make sense why the mother was so much bigger, but often in constrained, isolated environments, speciation leads to gigantism, like the Komodo dragons of Indonesia.

Alastair guessed that the smaller, more mobile bears were not children; these were the males sent to hunt for food for their enormous matriarch. Like a hive.

And she was hungry.

The bears dove for Alastair, forcing him onto the liquid helium pipe. He held on to the struts as he fought them away with his flashlight. He was scratched by a bear and dropped it. The flashlight landed on the giant beast below and went out. He heard a great *whoosh* and popping—pops more like blowing speakers—and the smaller bears scattered. He couldn't see anything.

Surrounded by darkness, Alastair lit a flare.

The giant bear was at his eye level, although it didn't have eyes. Skin membranes were in their place, like stretched speakers used to create sonar popping sounds—like a bat. The beasts' winged claws grasped the helium pipe also in the same way a bat holds on to a branch, hanging beneath it. It bellowed at Alastair. The rush of the roar and popping eye membranes were so great it blew his hair back.

Alastair threw the flare at the beast. It bounced off the animal's nose.

***

Leo, Kat, and Ralls had managed to fight to a stalemate in the tiny crevice in which they hid. A large boulder had been protecting them, but a group of determined bears had been working on it, and they were about to get in.

Leo kicked at them. Their claws sliced into his calf muscles and ankles.

A flare landed in the rocks outside their hiding spot, distracting the animals.

Someone had shot a flare!

ONE HOUR

Milk had to get out of the water. The violence of the rapids had further dismantled her foam block. She tumbled alongside trees and debris. Dark shapes swam past her.

Prehistoric piranhas attacked the foam, eating it in a frenzy. The fish were red and blue and enormous. The mix of flashing colors and white water gave the river the feel of a large, undulating American flag.

The block disintegrated with every furious bite. Milk grabbed a tree branch and hauled herself out of the water just as the last of the foam block disappeared.

Paul's block was undamaged. It carried him into a safe eddy and wedged into the mud like a boat coming ashore. The block was off center from Paul's weight and he face-planted into the mud. Milk rushed over to save him from suffocating.

It took them a while to get Paul out of the foam, eating into precious time. They knew the situation was dire. Already they could see that the river had risen. They needed to move, but they didn't know if seventeen hours had passed or not. The sun never moved, so it was no help in establishing time. If the seventeen hours had not passed, they should try to make it back to the road and then to the beach exit.

The question was: In what direction? If they couldn't get to the beach by the seventeen-hour deadline, then they should head back inland to the Nautilus. It was also above sea level. There would be food for ten years. Paul pointed out that each time vault had enough food for a decade, as well. There would be no issues surviving there.

Milk wanted to head to the barrier. Paul wanted to head to the relative safety of the Nautilus's high ground. They could survive and wait there for the end of the cycle. He didn't trust that they could make it to the barrier in time, especially in a world that was slowly flooding from all sides.

Milk disagreed. She reminded them that food is not the only element necessary for survival. Where would the fresh water come from? Would the Nautilus still have electricity to store perishable food? It was a crapshoot. Paul agreed, so he voted for just giving up.

By the time they stopped yelling at each other, five more minutes had passed. They were no closer to a solution. Unable to decide a next course of action, the decision was made for them.

"Run!" yelled Paul.

"Not falling for that again," said Milk. When Paul took off down the river trail at full speed, Milk sensed that she'd misjudged him. She turned to see Elizabeth Báthory, Churchill, and Shirō Ishii walking toward them. Milk jumped up and ran.

General Ishii split off and went after Milk. And by the time Paul kicked the last piece of foam off his leg, he was at a full sprint, only a few steps ahead of Churchill.

***

Milk followed the river trail. She soon found a fire road. There were truck tracks. Milk accelerated. Maybe it was Jimmy. She rounded a bend, breathing hard, hoping to see Hello Kitty but only finding a large cement bunker buried in a hill. It was a dead end.

Mangrove tree roots framed the mysterious building. Giant doors were embedded in the dirt below a natural earth berm. It was an impressive use of the landscape to camouflage the location. She had run right into it, but there was no way anyone could know it was there, otherwise.

She turned to look back. General Ishii was still on her trail. But he walked, clearly not in a rush, and it was obvious why. There was nowhere for Milk to go. An impenetrable wall of vegetation hemmed her in on either side of the road. Milk's only options were to turn back and face General Ishii or to somehow get into the bunker.

There could be a vehicle inside.

She opted for the bunker, but she had to get in first. Next to the door, there was a keypad and an old plaque. It read, PROPERTY OF THE DEPARTMENT OF DEFENSE.

Next to it, there was another engraving:

YOU CAN'T GET IN WITHOUT DECIPHERING THE CODE: ASK THE PENTAGON

—isaac newton

Beneath there was some extra text: 10.811 u ± 0.007 u.

"Decipher the code," Milk repeated aloud.

She needed to make a move. There was nowhere to go but inside. She typed in 00000 into the alphanumeric keypad and hit enter. The screen flashed INCORRECT. It didn't work. She had about one minute to figure it out, the general was still walking leisurely toward her.

She tried ABCDE and hit enter. No luck.

Decipher the code. Maybe it wasn't referring to the pin code. Maybe there was a code in the warning itself.

A riddle. Isaac liked to play mind games. Maybe this was a game?

Milk looked at the weird number beneath the warning.

10.811 u ± 0.007 u

To Milk, it looked like a molecular weight. She had aced organic chemistry early on in high school and was well on her way to finishing college-level courses on the subject. Molecular weight is the mass of an element multiplied by the number of constituent atoms: 10.811 u ± 0.007 u was the molecular weight of boron. Or was it freon?

She typed FREON into the password field. It didn't work. She typed in BORON.

The screen flashed up a big block of text now:

nice guess. count me impressed. that is the molecular weight for boron. so you are not an idiot at least. but that is not the answer.

***

What was she missing? She hated Isaac. She looked again at the last line of the warning.

YOU can't get in without deciphering the code: ask the pentagon.

Isaac had a terrible sense of humor. That was a clue too. Maybe "the code" referred to "ask the Pentagon."

DECIPHERING THE CODE: ASK THE PENTAGON.

She typed in THE PENTAGON and hit enter. No dice. Had she been right, it wouldn't have been the oldest (dumbest) riddle in the world. It was no different than "This is the code," the trick answer being "This."

Milk also tried PENTAGON. It didn't work either. She returned back to the molecular weight. It had to be the key to cracking the code. There was no reason for it to be there. It was an IQ test for someone wanting to get in. A filter for those not worthy. She had to remember Isaac's extreme ego.

She was certain it was the chemical notation for Boron. What did it mean, though? She thought about the element.

By this point, General Ishii had arrived. He leaned against a fence and watched, amused.

Boron is not a very complicated chemical element, thought Milk. It was not that dangerous. Industrial boron was used to make things like fiberglass and boric acid, which was a good antibacterial. She listed off all the things she had memorized about boron to impress her dad in sixth grade. It had a melting point of 2,076 degrees. Its largest known deposit was in Turkey. Its molar heat capacity was 11.087 joules.

More basic, thought Milk. Boron was the fifth element on the periodic table. Milk paused on that thought. It was the fifth element.

Five.

She looked at the riddle again: ASK THE PENTAGON.

Pentagons have five sides. Boron is the fifth element.

She clicked the number 5 on the pad and hit enter. The door didn't open.

"Try again," said General Ishii.

His voice shocked Milk. She had been so preoccupied with the riddle that she forgot she was being hunted.

General Ishii waved his gun at her. "Try again."

Milk typed in F-I-V-E.

It worked. The screen went green and flashed, YOU ARE WORTHY.

Milk entered and slammed the door shut behind her. Automatic lights flickered on. Milk deflated. There were no vehicles. No weapons. The bunker was mostly empty. Its walls were pure white. There was a lab enclosed in glass in the center of the sterile space.

Outside, General Shiri Ishii walked up to the door. He also typed FIVE and entered.

When Milk heard the door unlock, she realized she was trapped. There were no other exits. It was all for naught. Milk went to the lab to see what she could scrounge as a weapon.

The lab stood in the center of the cavernous room, like a fancy museum exhibit that had been abandoned decades ago. A thick layer of white dust coated the floor, though it was probably only one cycle old—ten years since it had been visited. She left footprints as she headed to the glass lab, as if she were walking on fresh snow. General Ishii's feet kicked up dust as well, making it feel like an early winter flurry.

When she opened the glass enclosure, air whooshed in with her. It was a negative pressure room, designed to keep pathogens from escaping. The system still worked, despite having clearly been designed to be left for decades to run on its own.

General Ishii walked casually toward Milk, whistling a traditional Japanese tune. He dragged his foot in the dust like a tap dancer.

Inside the lab, there were experiments behind the glass: clear liquids, molds, plants, caustic acids, chemicals, and gasses. There were some odd-looking groups of insect colonies as well. Everything was clean and organized, as if it were a museum display.

The list of chemicals, elements, and organisms were a who's who of deadly things. Some of them were listed on a chart.

2,3,7,8-TETRACLORODIBENZO

DIGOXIN

SODIUM CYANIDE

DIMETHYLMECURY

VX

BATRACHOTOXIN

RICIN

THALLIUM

IRUKANDJI

HEXAVALENT CHROMIUM

SARIN

ATROPA BELLADONNA

CHONDRONDENRON TOMENTOSUM

ACONITE

Milk knew that they were some of the deadliest compounds on earth, all in one spot, an exhibit curated by a chemist with a death wish. On the glass next to each sample, there was red wax writing noting interesting aspects of the poison, venom, or chemical weapon.

General Ishii joined Milk. He read the labels. "You are Martin Luther King?" he finally said. "The orator. I didn't like him, you know. He was a pacifist. I met him once."

Though only thirty years old, General Ishii talked as if he himself was the infamous World War II surgeon who experimented on live prisoners at Unit 731.

Milk had the unfortunate pleasure of knowing all about the war criminal.

The original Shirō Ishii was a madman, a sociopathic serial killer who was given license and great resources by his government. Under the cover of war, he conducted some of the cruelest series of experiments ever conceived, a level of depravity only matched by Mengele at Auschwitz. Under his command, his staff infected women and children with venereal diseases and then vivisected them alive, without anesthetic. He froze limbs, shattered them with hammers, and then "studied" the gangrene that set in. Or he would just watch his victims die in puddles of vomit and pain. Flamethrowers and grenades were tested on people at various distances, and some survived long enough to suffer flaying. People were spun to death in centrifuges, injected with sea water and animal blood, poisoned with X-rays, buried alive. Burned. Stabbed. He removed stomachs. General Ishii was untethered from humanity, a golem formed out of cruelty. For the thousands that were unlucky enough to have ended up in General Ishii's backwater of history, they were test subjects of man's potential for barbarism.

And Milk was stuck in a room with him. He had a gun, and they were surrounded by the world's worst toxins. It did not bode well.

"It's impressive," said General Ishii, appreciating the compounds in the lab. "What I could have done with these." When he talked, he had an odd habit of waving his hands around his hips. His gun pointed in every direction at the floor. It was a very un-Japanese quality about the man. "The Pentagon is very lucky to have weapons like this."

"This is for research, not weapons. This is America."

General Ishii took a breath and smiled. It was unnervingly warm. "Why would the United States government try to evolve biological and chemical weapons?" he said. "Because they can. And should. Science always comes before sentimentality. Isaac knows that. And so should you. So to that end, I propose a game. An unsentimental battle of the minds. The great orator versus the great doctor."

He put the gun down on the table and then sat on a clear glass stool opposite Milk. He rotated the gun to point at Milk.

In between them was a hermetically sealed glass box with a single test tube. It held a white powder suspended in oil. On the glass, it said RICIN.

"I think we both agree that there is no escaping now. The flood is coming. Time is almost up. And they can certainly create another one of me. I'm not even the second Shirō Ishii. I'm the fourth, technically. I am disposable. So why not have a little fun at the end of the world? A game to the death?"

"And if I win the game?" Milk asked.

"I give you the gun. You can trigger the emergency kill switch, right there on the wall. And then you can leave."

Milk hadn't noticed the emergency switch. It was a sealant system designed to encase the experiments in a liquid alloy, rendering the facility harmless. She had seen something similar on a university lab tour once.

"And if I lose?"

"Well, first let me tell you the rules. We each take turns consuming the substances in these various vials and enclosures. They have been here for decades, and some will be harmless by now. Failed experiments. Others could be wildly virulent or poisonous. Some are antidotes if you know your organic chemistry. And we will see who lives and who dies first. The great orator versus the great doctor."

"You said that already. You're repeating yourself. We are neither of those things."

"Ha. True. I'm worse because I have no sense of self-preservation. I am a photocopy of a photocopy. Blurry between the lines."

Milk jumped for the gun, but General Ishii quickly pulled it away.

"Don't be so selfish. Or boring. I'm not finished. If you lose, I will release the plague and the infections as my last act, ensuring they survive the cycle. So we play for your life, which is very short in either case. And for Texas."

"Okay. What are the rules?" said Milk, stalling for time.

"There are no rules," said General Ishii. "We just take turns. Until someone is dead. But I chose the game, so I will go first. Usually an advantage."

General Ishii wandered through the glass lab, peering at the various compounds. He left the gun on the table but out of reach. "The main thing you need to figure out is, what is the shelf life or half-life of these compounds and elements?" he said nonchalantly. "Do they need oxygen? Are there catalysts involved in their processes? Maybe some are controls in the Americans' experiments, not deadly at all, designed to compare to the others? Were they alive once? Or basic elements? I think there's a bit of scientific process in this game too. We need to figure out what exactly the Americans were testing at this site. Right?"

He's having fun, thought Milk. It truly was a game to him. As General Ishii wandered back, Milk edged toward the gun. General Ishii plucked it off the table at the last second and pointed it at Milk, like he was handling a foil.

His smile disappeared. "You know what I am capable of. I will dissect you, like my twin dissected the others. You will be alive as I open your stomach and swap your organs. Liver to kidney. A lung to your colon. Or ..." General Ishii opened the glass container in front of him. There was a gentle hiss of air upon its release. He took the vial inside. It was marked with its scientific name, RICINUS COMMUNIS.

He drank it. "... we play my game." General Ishii waited for an effect. "Tastes like tin. Your turn."

Milk hoped he would die, but she knew the effects of ricin happen over days, not seconds. "That wasn't going to kill you now, and you knew it," said Milk. "Ricin inhibits protein formation. It takes days."

"But it will kill me. And hence, we have a game, no?"

Ricin was a naturally occurring byproduct of the seeds of the castor oil plant. Easy to produce, tough to detect. It was famously used to assassinate a Bulgarian dissident on a busy London street. The assassin used an umbrella outfitted with an air canister to fire a pellet of ricin into the man's leg. He died a few days later in the hospital, bleeding from every pore. It took a special division of the British Ministry to spot the pellet during the autopsy. They were impressed.

"I know!" said General Ishii. "It does take days. That's why I started with it. It's a mulligan. Your turn, Martin Luther."

"You are still going to die," Milk said. "There is no antidote to ricin."

"Aren't we all going to die? Isn't it just a matter of timing?" He tapped the gun on the desk. "Pay attention. You are still alive. Your turn."

"Is everything in here fair game?" Milk asked.

"Yes. Any substance."

"You are a man of your word?"

"Of course."

Silence.

A pen holder sat on a desk. Milk dumped it out. Bic pens scattered onto the table. She squeezed the ink out of the pens, one at a time, into a glass beaker, then she added a bit of water. It was almost a third full by the time she got to the last pen.

"Are you done?" asked General Ishii, amused.

"Cheers," Milk added a little water and drank the blue ink.

"That hardly counts as a turn. Ink is nontoxic. Always a joke with you. Go again."

"I know," said Milk. "That wasn't my turn." Milk opened the glass enclosure next to General Ishii. It said, THALLIUM. She closed her eyes, plugged her nose and drank the poison.

General Ishii waited for Milk to finish and then burst into a wide smile, like a proud father watching his daughter score a winning goal. "Brilliant," he said, slapping the desk.

"It was."

"You drank an antidote first. You sequestered the heavy metals in advance with the ink."

"Queen takes pawn. I did. Your turn."

Prussian blue, a common industrial dye, is used in everything from paint to plastic to ink and, importantly, is the only antidote for thallium poisoning. Hospitals have access to a medical-grade version, but the official antidote is basically no different than common ink. Just packaged differently. And less blue.

Milk knew this. Her prodigious memory—the genius used to memorize long, stirring speeches and facts—was coming in handy.

"The question is, of course," said General Ishii. "Did you drink enough ink?"

Milk hadn't thought of this. She smiled. "Tasty." Her mouth and lips were completely blue. She feigned confidence, suddenly scared that she hadn't thought enough about dosage. She started to second-guess her perfect memory. Usually the only time she relied on it was for exams and parlor tricks to impress Alastair. Now her life depended on it.

"My turn," said General Ishii. I could look for something that might be inert. Rendered safe by time. Or ..." He walked past VX, digoxin, and 2,3,7,8-Tetrachlorodibenzo. He considered each one as if he was shopping for flavors at an ice cream shop, the only difference being every option had a major international treaty banning its use.

"Or ..." He stopped at a case. "Now, this is interesting. And very unexpected. The label said, PARAPONERA CLAVATA. Do you know what this is?"

"I don't," said Milk, truthfully.

General Ishii laughed. "This is my next choice. It is venom from the bullet ant, *Paraponera clavata*."

"And?"

"It has the most painful sting on the planet. If bitten, the only medical advice is to lay down on the ground and scream. It is a terrible weapon in this form. Very popular in my family history. Completely incapacitating but not deadly. And as we are running out of healthy options, I choose this."

It was the first time Milk saw a break in General Ishii's demeanor. It was one thing to be suicidal, but pain isn't death. He paused before he drank the liquid. He took only a small sip.

"Uh," said Milk, motioning with the palm of her hand for him to finish up.

"Your turn," said General Ishii. His gaze was steel. He slowly blinked his eyes, like they were in molasses, preparing for the oncoming onslaught. "Go, please. If you take too long, this game can still end." One of his hands gripped the table, the other held the gun, which was still pointed at Milk.

Milk went from enclosure to enclosure but couldn't find anything that wouldn't kill her painfully and quickly. She was rushing and she knew it; she was likely to make a mistake. She couldn't identify all of the substances. She went back and forth.

Pain started to stretch General Ishii's face into a false smile, but he leaned into it, like he enjoyed it. "You can't find one, can you?"

Milk paused. She backed up and looked at one of the cases she had decided against: DEADLY NIGHTSHADE. And then she crossed the room to another: SARIN. And then back. Something struck her. She tried to figure it out in her mind, fighting defeat.

The gun was still leveled at her.

She made her pick: a vial of sarin. Milk joined General Ishii for the deadly cocktail.

"Sarin will kill you," said the general.

"I know."

Milk crossed herself and drank the colorless, odorless nerve agent.

"So I have won," said General Ishii. "It will be only minutes before you die."

Milk knew he was right. Sarin disrupts the neurotransmitter "acetylcholine," which leads to a violent death. Vomiting, defecation, and drooling are followed quickly by spasmodic convulsions, coma, and finally, asphyxiation.

General Ishii grimaced. "An honorable death," he said. The pain of the bullet ant's venom had started in earnest.

"Your turn," said Milk. She was calm, using every ounce of her willpower to sit without emotion.

General Ishii grunted though the pain. "My turn? Have you not lost?"

"Your turn," Milk repeated. She could feel the first tendrils of the sarin affecting her. She had to hurry. "Can I make a suggestion?" she said.

"Interesting. Yes, go ahead," said General Ishii. "There is nothing left that acts as quickly as sarin. You will—" he had to pause. The pain washed over him in a wave and crashed down. "You will die before I do."

"The Irukandji."

"The jellyfish venom? That's not a quick death. I will still win."

"It's not fast, but it's my pick for you. A delicacy. In honor of the game."

"In the spirit of a game well played, I agree."

Milk handed General Ishii a small vial with liquid that held a tiny jellyfish. The general's hand shook, but he was able to drink it.

The second he finished it, Milk mustered all her energy to sprint across the room, looking for something. She found it: deadly nightshade.

A small glass box held a cluster of dried, black, cherry-like fruits, but there was no clasp. She smashed the box and wolfed them down, chewing on them to speed up their effect.

"Explain," General Ishii said, gasping from the pain now.

"Nightshade is the only poison in the world that is also an antidote. It was labeled here by its nickname 'deadly nightshade' and not by its real name, *Atropa belladona*. 'Atropa' stands for atropine."

General Ishii's eyes went wide, realizing he had been bested. He tried to lift his gun, but pain wracked his body.

"Atropine and its alkaloids turn off the nerve receptors targeted by sarin," said Milk. "You must know that. The two cancel each other out. It is common knowledge. But the only way you'd know that nightshade was a rare source of atropine was if you read anecdotal stories about World War II test subjects surviving cruel tests by eating the plant on the edge of your camp."

General Ishii's head started to droop from pain.

"It was not my—"

"But to know this you would have to see prisoners as humans," Milk continued. "To have read their stories and studied human rights and atrocities and genocides and injustice across the world.

"And the jelly—"

"The jellyfish? I learned that here in Cornerstone from a welder. The Irukandji venomous jellyfish has two side effects, one being death."

"What is the other?" he managed.

"A feeling of impending doom."

As soon as Milk said it, despair crept across General Ishii's face. The pain of the bullet ant venom combined with the bottomless sadness from the Irukandji pushed him over the edge. He dropped the gun, weeping in pain.

Milk picked up the gun.

It was over.

General Ishii sobbed in great wracks, his chest heavy, alternating between pain and despair. He moaned and rocked, tears streaming down his face. The combination of the bullet ants attack on his pain receptors combined with a dread that knew no end was unbearable. It was the ultimate torture for a man who practically created it.

Milk had turned General Ishii's cruelty against him.

The general swept his hand across the table, looking for the sarin, knocking it over. There was still some left. He used all of his power to grip the vial. His hand shook as he brought it to his lips.

Before he drank, he said a prayer. The general drank the sarin. Eventually, he started sweating, then he vomited, heaving over, and started to convulse, much like the desperate prisoners of Unit 731 decades ago. But unlike them, he chose this fate, defeated by the great Martha Lexie Klein.

FIFTY MINUTES

Alastair would be trapped in the Crypt for a decade if he didn't get moving. He was still stuck on the pipe, pinned down by the bear, unable to move. The stench was worse than a Manhattan heat wave.

Alastair had an idea. It was a desperate plan, but he was out of options. He couldn't stay on the strut, hiding from the bear. If he did, there would be worse things to deal with in the future; the fear of that unknown forced Alastair out of hiding. He unclipped and wrapped Jimmy's metal cable around the pipe's circumference twice, throwing it up and over. The carabiner clanged against the pipe, drawing the Ursus's attention. Alastair caught the end and reclipped the cable to itself. When the Ursus drooped, curious to hear what he was doing, Alastair took the opportunity to climb back on top of the pipe. The Ursus made popping sounds at him, but they were different now. Each eye membrane made a slightly different sound, at a different interval, as if it were watching Alastair in stereo, using each as a different perspective, like two eyes, to see a three-dimensional shape.

Alastair ran to the end of the pipe and turned around. He checked that his guide rope was securely attached to his harness. It trailed back into the cave, but there was no tension. Somewhere, far above, the rope was tied to Hello Kitty's winch. *How much slack was there?* He hoped that it was less than a hundred feet. His life depended on it. He ran along the top of the pipe at full speed and then leapt directly toward the Ursus.

Albert Einstein, the second one, flew over the giant animal, barely clearing its jaws. It was the second leap of faith that day for Alastair, but this time he had had no choice.

The beast stopped to watch, as if even it was shocked at the audacity of Alastair's decision.

Alastair gambled that, as he fell, his weight would draw the slack in the guide rope, and it would pull the winch's handle, triggering it. He guessed that the hundred-foot jump would give him enough kinetic energy, but he didn't know for sure. He calculated on the fly that he would be going almost fifty-four miles an hour before he hit the ground, a kinetic energy of over 105,814 joules. This translated into a force of ... a lot. He didn't know exactly. He had run out of time and pipe—his feet beating his mind—before he had to leap.

Alastair fell toward the rocks below. His flare cut an arc in the darkness; his rope trailed behind him. Everything felt like slow motion: enough time to pray that his rope would catch before he hit the rocks below, that his leap of faith was answered with grace and not death, and that, above all, Jimmy's winch would work. As Alastair fell, the guide rope slithered through the caves above in a desperate search for tension.

The slack finally reached all the way back to Hello Kitty and then, finally, the winch handle. The handle yanked downward. And held. Alastair stopped only feet from his death. The rope had caught him with enough give. The winch turned on, and Hello Kitty's metal cable started to wind back home. The cable quickly snapped into tension.

"Come on, Kitty!" Alastair screamed. He hung on the rope, still a bit too far from the ground to touch. The Ursus turned and came for him. Alastair desperately tried to untie, but the tension made it difficult for him to release the rope. He was only two feet from the ground, dangling like tantalizing bait on a fishing line. Alastair screamed at Hello Kitty again.

The metal cable continued to pull on the liquid helium pipe, but it wouldn't budge. Its engineering was as stubborn as Jimmy's truck.

Then the pipe started to deform, imperceptibly at first, groaning under the force. The Ursus popped at it loudly, pausing, surprised by the sudden denting pops of the pipe under pressure answering back.

It was working.

The cable's force bent the pipe.

Far above, Hello Kitty dislodged and dragged toward the entrance to the cave. It caught there. The winch and the helium pipe were in a battle for supremacy.

"Come on!" Alastair yelled.

The Ursus went for Alastair just as the liquid helium pipe burst. In a flash, the giant bear's face took the brunt of the cold. Its eye membranes froze in place. It could no longer use the popping sound to echolocate.

The smaller Ursuses in flight were also caught in the blast. They fell out of the air, shattering around Alastair with the force of little bombs. The violence scared off the rest of them.

The Ursus went insane with anger, blindly sweeping its wings and claws.

The liquid helium continued to pour into the cave, flash-freezing the river torrent into an incredible ice waterfall, forming a plug. The Ursus smashed at the newly formed ice, searching for its tormentor. The temperature plummeted; water turned to ice. Alastair was safe, but only for a few moments. Liquid helium continued to pour into the cave above, transforming the space into a dazzling, deadly ice cavern. He finally found his knife and cut the rope, falling the last few feet.

Next problem.

Hello Kitty had saved his life, true. Alastair had guessed correctly that she was strong enough to break the pipe, but now there was no way back to the surface. The winch was destroyed. Ice blocked the exit. And even if he found his friends and they got past it, soon there would be an ocean's worth of water filling in above the cave. Impassable. Impossible.

Alastair pushed the thought out of his mind. He had to find his friends. *And then what?* He looked up, unsure of what to do. Above him, the bear was like an ice god frozen in a terrifying, menacing pose. The reflecting light of the flare made the ice look as if it was on fire.

The flare sputtered. How long would his light sources last? His flashlight batteries? He needed to go deeper, continue searching for his friends and fighting for his life. He tightened his belt and straps, ready to turn once again into the unknown.

Someone tapped on his shoulder.

"What the—" a voice said.

Alastair spun. It was Leo. Kat was next to him. Behind them, Ralls. No longer pinned down by the smaller Ursus, they had been able to escape their hiding place.

"You're jacked!" said Leo. "What happened?"

In a flood of relief, Alastair bear-hugged Leo.

"Where is everyone else?" Ralls asked.

"It's just me. We have to go," Alastair replied. "Or we will freeze."

Liquid helium continued to pour death and fog into the space.

"Go where?" Kat asked. "How long do we have?"

Alastair pointed at a growing hole in the floor of the cave. The ice above had stopped the flow of water into the cave, causing the lake at the bottom of it to drain, revealing a possible passageway.

"Down," Alastair responded, uncertain of himself. "This water has to go somewhere. We have less than an hour to escape."

"Just because water can go down," said Ralls, "doesn't mean we can."

In an explosion of fog, more liquid helium blew into the cave. The super-cooled liquid reached what was left of the lake, flash-freezing it. They needed to move.

"Maybe it will run out," Kat said. "And then we can somehow climb up the ice."

"It won't run out," Ralls replied. "This is our core supply pipe."

Liquid helium was a valuable substance, and Cornerstone had cornered the market, Ralls told them, directly tapping the United States' strategic supply. In the 1920s, the US created a billion-gallon reserve of helium in anticipation of the rise of the Zeppelins, the helium dirigibles they believed would soon crisscross the country and world. It wasn't until 1996 that the government decided that the coming age of blimps may never arrive. They wrote legislation to sell off the reserve with the Helium Privatization Act, but the anticompetitive flooding of helium onto the market drove manufacturers away, increasing the price of liquid helium and making it affordable to only the richest industries and universities.

The Cornerstone project made it worse. The project lapped up liquid helium like a thirsty dog; ten years of liquid helium were consumed every week. With a single stroke of a pen, a secret amendment to the act was included. It authorized the building of a direct, underground pipeline from Amarillo, Texas—where the Bush Dome Reservoir is located—to Cornerstone. The pipeline cut secretly under the city of San Antonio before hitting the coast and heading south past Corpus Christi to the mysterious facility. With Cornerstone's long straw sucking up the US reserves on the sly, liquid helium prices spiked worldwide. The official reason given for the limited supply was the desire to create a real, fungible market for the rare liquid. It was one of the first signs to the Russians that something weird was going on in Texas. A popular episode of *Planet Money* brought the issue into public consciousness, but nothing came of it. Liquid helium was complicated. It was dangerous. And it was flooding into the cave.

Everything was freezing around them. The temperature was already thirty degrees below zero and dropping quickly.

"We have to go," Alastair urged, shoving flares into everyone's hands. His voice was three octaves too high. The helium in the air affected his vocal cords. "Come on!"

They ran for the hole before it too froze over. Each of them lit a flare as they jumped through the opening. Alastair paused at the entrance. His friends slid away from him, disappearing into the hole like it was the entrance to a waterslide. Above, ice continued to encase the bear. The towering ice sculpture tipped and then crumbled under its own weight.

"Sorry!" Alastair exclaimed. He jumped onto the luge just as the frozen bear crashed on top of it in an explosion of ice. Liquid helium poured into the hole, chasing after Alastair. He accelerated. He felt like he was sliding through the center of the earth, plunging toward his oblivion.

After a long slide in pitch black, rushing water replaced ice. He was in a river again, tumbling down rapids in the darkness of the cave. The water flash-froze around him, almost sealing off the cave until he broke through with a rush. He barely kept ahead of the wave of freezing liquid helium that chased him. He fell. And fell. And fell. Deeper and deeper. Finally, the river dumped Alastair over another waterfall into blackness. It was the longest fall yet, and the force launched him deep into a lake.

The swim up to the surface seemed to take forever, longer than it should have. Alastair struggled to hold his breath, finally breaking through the surface with great gasps. Before Alastair could catch his breath, he realized there wasn't a waterfall cascading down near him. It was gone. They were in the middle of a giant lake with no shore. He could sense that this new lake was massive; there were no echoes when he called for everyone else.

He was surrounded by blackness, his flare illuminating fragments of rocks and mist. Finally, Alastair found the others in the dark. He still struggled to breathe, coughing instructions at Leo, Kat, and Ralls. They needed to get to shore.

There was something wrong with the air.

Leo splashed toward some rocks and dragged Alastair onto them. He pulled Ralls out until they were all on their backs, struggling for breath. But there was no relief. Each gasp provided less oxygen than the last.

"The air! What's wrong with it?" Alastair asked, panicked.

"What is this place?" Kat exclaimed. "I can barely breathe."

A light flickered through the fog. Alastair extinguished his flare to see better.

At first, Alastair couldn't make out what was approaching them. Soon, a figure on a skiff resolved from the mist. It looked like a man using a pole to move the boat along, like the mythic River Styx of the underworld coming for the dead.

Behind the mysterious skiff in the clearing fog, Alastair could see a white building. The structure was enormous, undulating, and curved around itself. It was on an island and glowed a soft, otherworldly white, lit from within.

The mysterious man arrived at their rocks. His face was a mirror. He had a white cloak tied around his neck. Under it, to everyone's surprise, he wore an astronaut suit. It was bulky and looked a lot like a modification of the suits used at the International Space Station. The hooded cape covered the helmet, revealing only the gold-mirrored faceplate.

An astronaut? thought Alastair. *Why is there an astronaut hidden inside a hole beneath a river inside a cave below the center of the Crypt?*

Kat flopped into the astronaut's boat first, but instead of coins for her eyes—for the customary crossing to the land of the dead—the man gave her a portable face mask with bottled oxygen. Convinced, Alastair and Leo jumped in with her, taking deep heaves of clean oxygen.

As the skiff headed to the facility, Alastair realized he had saved his friends. Someone else was now in charge. He lay on his back. He could breathe.

Above him, Alastair saw tiny pinpricks of light on the ceiling of the cave. Were they glowing, distant insects? Or crystals catching the light? Then, Alastair's eyes resolved. He realized what they were: stars. *How is that possible?* thought Alastair. They were miles beneath the surface of the earth. They had only gone downward, deeper into the earth, like desperate, burrowing worms. Never up toward the sky.

The others were also lost in their own thoughts. The only noise was the drips from the pole as it went in and out of the water. The skiff slid toward the island, guided by the mysterious astronaut. Alastair identified constellations to assure himself that they were actually stars. The Big Dipper. Orion. The Seven Sisters. The constellations were all there, but they were in the wrong places, which was just as concerning. He checked the lesser-known constellations: Cepheus, Volans, Pavo, and Ophiuchus (the serpent bearer). They were there too, twisted on their axis like the world was tilted into craziness.

Why was the air so bad? Why couldn't he breathe without the mask if he was outdoors? And if they were outside somewhere, why was it suddenly dark? Nothing about the physics of Cornerstone explained the sudden appearance of a starry night. It was afternoon in the Crypt for the next ten years.

A new thought crept up on him. Had the bad air played tricks on his mind? Was he actually still miles below the surface of the earth, hallucinating that he was being rowed across a noxious lake by an astronaut in a cape? Alastair felt his mind loosen with each new question. When a fundamental constant of the universe breaks, all assumptions are off. Even the insane ones. Other crazed ideas raced through his mind. Was he somewhere else in the universe? Had they gone through a wormhole? Was he in space? Was there an alien in the astronaut suit? Was he in an alternate universe?

A tide of self-doubt washed over him. Like most of the problems in his life, he thought, he should just give up and let someone else figure out what to do. This was clearly above his pay grade.

They finally made it to the shore, no closer to any answers. The facility loomed over them. The building was a perfect soft white. While the Nautilus building inside the Crypt echoed the shape of a nautilus, this building looked like an actual shell. There were no doors and no windows—just one elegant curving piece, like a giant seashell forgotten and buried on a muddy beach.

On the outside of the curved building, there were instructions hand-stenciled in Russian Cyrillic. They were the only markings. The astronaut waved his hand over a red X and backed up.

A few seconds later, the wall stretched out like a square fist pushing through a deflated balloon. It had no hinges or bolts. Thousands of layers of rubber expanded, opening like a flower, revealing an entrance between two soft bulges. It was the most ingenious airtight door Alastair had ever seen. They entered an airlock, and the process reversed behind them.

Alastair took off his emergency oxygen mask. Inside, the airlock smelled like a mix of cat food, decay, and ozone. He brought the mask back up to his face, sucking clean oxygen in greedy gulps.

The man who saved them took of his helmet. It was Joseph Stalin, another one, or at least it looked like him. Though this one was much older than the last one, thought Alastair.

He was in his fifties and looked exactly like the infamous dictator. His hair was styled exactly as he had worn it, and this one also had the trademark thick mustache.

Stalin silently stared at the kids, carefully inspecting them.

Eventually, Ralls's patience ran out. "Can we hurry up?" he demanded, as if he was still in charge.

Stalin wordlessly scrutinized Ralls. He put on a pair of glasses, his brow went up and down. His eyes closed for a second, and then they opened again to inspect Ralls. He did this with all four of them. Each time, a different thought seemed to flit across his face, a different surprise. He seemed about to speak, but then his face would flit to the next thought. Brow up. Brow down. This went on for longer than expected. Stalin returned to inspect Alastair. This time, he brought his face much closer.

Stalin pursed his lips. "And I know you," he finally said to Ralls, turning, wagging his finger with a wry smile.

The cryptic encounter was too much for Ralls. "How—" he started, forcefully. Suddenly, another wall opened, and a blast of fresh, beautiful air whooshed in. Alastair realized that the putrid smell was the cave air still lingering inside the airlock. On the other side of the hole, a face appeared, a very familiar face. It was—

"Kat?" said Leo.

"Catherine," said the new face, correcting him.

It was another Catherine the Great.

What was going on?

Alastair felt like he was losing his mind.

Kat recoiled, clearly—understandably—shocked to suddenly find a twin of herself.

This one was slightly older, maybe twenty, and a touch prettier, thought Alastair. Her eyes were brighter, her smile wider. Or maybe she just appeared less cynical and suspicious than Kat, which had the same effect.

"Hello. Hey, it's great to see someone new," said Catherine, her voice exuding openness. "Come in." She had a slight Russian accent.

The real Kat stood next to Alastair. She didn't move. "I'm done," she said, crossing her arms.

"How is this possible?" Catherine ran her hands over Alastair's biceps. "How did you get in here? Well, come along."

She took Kat's arm. "Onward, sister." Her voice was markedly less friendly.

Stalin stopped Ralls before he passed through the door. He pressed hard into Ralls's sternum with a rough finger. "Welcome to Purity," he said.

***

Isaac, Zack, and Joseph had been sprinting toward the barrier for almost thirty minutes when they were suddenly stymied by a huge river. It smashed through the jungle in front of them, carving a new path. The world was being consumed by water, intent on locking them inside the Crypt forever.

"We have to keep going," Isaac said, panic rising in his voice.

Zack clasped his hands behind his head, fighting a cramp. He didn't have much left in him.

"We need to start thinking about how to survive for the next decade," said Joseph above the roar of the water. Trees snapped like explosions around them. "We are too far to make it to the barrier by foot."

"You don't get it, do you?" said Isaac. "It wouldn't be just for a decade. If we don't make it out of here, we will be stuck for one hundred years."

"One hundred years?" Zack repeated. "That's—"

"Yes. We have less than an hour to get out," said Isaac.

"And five miles," said Joseph. "We won't make it. We never could. We need to get to higher ground."

"Where, exactly?" asked Isaac. His voice was almost a scream, hoarse with fear and anger. They were in a flat area close to the sandy coast.

"There," said Joseph, pointing through the trees.

Zack side-stepped to get a better angle, and then saw it.

The oil rig.

It towered over the jungle, hundreds of feet in the air. Its steel legs were covered in jungle and vines. High above, birds circled the platform. It seemed to be covered in life, fruit, and flowers.

"The oil rig!" Isaac exclaimed. "Why are we here? This is not the right place at all! We're farther from the barrier!"

"It was our only chance," Joseph responded. "It will sustain us."

"You led us here?" Isaac screamed in disbelief.

***

Milk sat in front of the military bunker, consumed in a haze of insects, wondering what to do next.

There was a growing whine of a motorcycle, and then on cue, Paul flew through the air into the enclosure on a motorbike. He landed and spun donuts. It was either an expert move, or he was totally out of control. Milk couldn't tell. His tongue hung out; his foot dragged in the dirt.

"What up, genius?" He came to a stop in a cloud of dust. On the back of the bike, Winston Churchill was hog-tied, unconscious, and covered in terrible red welts. His eyes were swollen shut, crusting over.

"What the—"

"Apparently, Winston Churchill doesn't know much about the histamine reactions of the hogweed *Heracleum mantegazzianum*."

Milk wanted to know where Paul got the bike and why Churchill was unconscious.

"It's Isaac's. Found it. And it's got a map to the exit," Paul explained. "Churchill was being a jerk. Long story on that one. And I have no idea how to ride a bike. But considering that there is a forest full of scary cannibals chasing me, it felt like a good idea to try. What's with the blue?"

"Huh?" said Milk.

"Your mouth. It's blue?"

"I ate something weird. Wait—"

"Why's your mouth blue?"

"I drank ink. Wait, focus, what did you just say?" said Milk, wanting to rewind.

"Like, they're after me right now."

"Cannibals?" Milk repeated.

An arrow sizzled through the air and stuck into Paul's leg. He didn't react—at all.

"Yes, people that scare me," said Paul.

"Your leg!" said Milk.

He glanced down at the arrow in his leg and then yanked it out. "Like I said, long story." He took a fistful of black paste from his pocket and smeared it onto the wound.

Bone People poured into the enclosure, adorned now in battle armor made from their own bones. Projectiles made of twine and rocks flew through the air. Milk climbed onto the bike behind Paul, sitting on Churchill.

"What about Zack?" said Paul.

"Did you see them?" said Milk.

"No. They're on their own," said Paul. He consulted Isaac's map, which was pinned to the handlebars. "The exit's that way." He gunned the throttle. The arrow was still stuck in his leg. The back wheel spun. They punched through the dense foliage into no-man's-land, the world opening up to them again, with the Bone People in close pursuit.

Nearby, an old shaman sat alone, fanning a low ember fire. White noxious smoke rose in great clouds, announcing a coming feast.

BOOK SIX

Albert Einstein

FORTY MINUTES

Catherine led Alastair through the halls of Purity, chatting with him as they walked. Ralls, Leo, and Kat followed behind them, pestering Stalin with questions that he refused to answer. The undulating rubber continued stretching, forming pillars and supports. The lines between tension and structure were fluid. In some areas, the rubber stretched like a balloon to reveal light, giving a glow to the space. They passed laboratories, engineering rooms, a prep room with more astronaut suits, and finally, a nursery.

On the other side of the nursery's glass, in a softly lit room, there were almost a dozen babies. Alastair could see that their cribs were labeled with various dictators from history, more copies of Hitler, Stalin, Mao, Pol Pot. However, there were also intellectuals: Niels Bohr, Turing, Oppenheimer, two more Isaacs, and even one Einstein.

They were all infants, sleeping peacefully in the luxurious space. Alastair wanted to see them, so Catherine let the group inside. Ralls rushed past, going from crib to crib.

Alastair went to the Einstein crib. The baby stared up at Alastair, looking at him. Alastair glanced at the name tag again.

Einstein.

Is this baby really Einstein? Am I Einstein?

"He doesn't look like you," said Kat.

"In time," said Catherine. "All babies look different at birth—temporarily more like their birth father to show paternity. Little skinless rats if you ask me."

"Was I asking you?" snapped Kat, dropping the temperature in the room.

"No Leonardo?" Leo asked.

"Please," said Ralls to Stalin. "Enough mystery. You have to tell me what is going on here. How did you do this here under our noses?"

Stalin motioned for them to leave the nursery, but Ralls wouldn't budge. He wanted answers. Stalin relented and motioned for them to sit in the lounge adjacent to the nursery. The couches were covered with inviting blankets and pillows for nursing. Stalin shooed away a wet nurse, taking the baby from her and cradling him.

Catherine slid next to Alastair on a love seat. Kat was bolt upright across from them. Alastair felt the tension in the air: a fight could break out any minute. The baby fussed in Stalin's arms.

"Seriously," said Leo. "Stop with the mystery."

"You are the mystery, Leonardo," said Stalin.

"How did you know my name?" said Leo.

"We had a few copies of you as well. But they were annoying, so we phased them out."

Every color of emotion swept across Leo's face, until the former astronaut broke into wide laughter.

"Just kidding!" Stalin said. "We wouldn't want you. Albert, on the other hand," he said, wagging a finger at Alastair. "You could be useful. Saves us some time, no?"

"How did you build this under our noses?" exploded Ralls. He had hit the end of his fuse.

"'Under our noses'? What does this mean?" said Stalin to Catherine. But before she could answer, Ralls continued.

"We are in China," Stalin replied. There was no humor on his lips, no hint of a smile. "At the Three Gorges Dam."

"China?" said Kat.

"And I'd like to know how you got in here," Stalin continued. "I was under the impression that during a time cycle, this was an impossibility."

"You let us in," said Leo.

"Not what I meant. How did you get past the perimeter? It is impossible during a cycle."

"You are safe now; that's all that matters," said Catherine, trying to defuse the situation.

Kat laughed.

Something dawned on Ralls. "China?" Realization spread across his face like first light, imperceptible at first, but soon his mouth stretched wide into a grimace. He bit his lips, thinking.

"We were in Texas," said Ralls. "Only moments ago."

"Texas," Stalin said.

"Yes, Texas. Cornerstone. Like the other side of the earth. We just waltzed through the center of the earth?"

"And we're going back," said Alastair. "We'll find another way back up to the surface."

"Where are you going?" Stalin asked.

"You can't leave," said Catherine, as if they had just arrived at a dinner party. She pulled Alastair toward her.

"There is no surface," said Stalin. "You are not understanding where you are."

Kat was already standing.

"Now you can stay with us as our guests," said Catherine. "We have more than enough supplies for the ten years. It is very comfortable. And we can get to know each other," she said to Alastair, pressing into him softly. "We *never* get visitors."

"Ten years?" said Kat. "No thanks. Let's go, Leo."

Leo got up. Alastair tried to, but Catherine pulled him back down.

"We don't care where we are. We are going back to Texas," said Alastair. "To catch up with our friends and to get out before the seventeen-hour deadline."

Alastair felt Catherine's body against his and noticed how her cashmere sweater accentuated her curves. He tried to push away, but she wouldn't give him up.

"What do you think, Albert?" prompted Catherine. "Don't you want to stay?"

"Even if you could somehow get back to Cornerstone and you weren't lying like American pigs," said Stalin, "there is no secret exit for your friends. It was a lie."

"There is a way out," said Leo. "A hole in the barrier wall, at the southern reach. Isaac told us."

"No, there is not. I made sure of that. No one's getting out. We needed Isaac's buy-in to get access to the dam codes. He has no idea."

"Isaac gave you the codes to get into the dam?" said Ralls.

Stalin laughed and lit a cigar, indifferent to the baby wailing in his arms.

"We told him and Sephora that an exit exists, and they had more than enough time to reach it. And that no one would be hurt because they are both sentimentalists. But there is no exit."

"There's no exit?" Alastair repeated in disbelief. He looked to Leo, whose gaze turned to Kat.

"My team in the Crypt knew it was a suicide mission. But I have more copies. Don't I, Joseph?" he said to the baby. The baby in his arm had calmed down.

"We are starting clean," said Stalin. "Like the biblical flood. And only the pure will survive."

"That's you, Albert," said Catherine. "Because you are here. God chose you to survive. In our ark."

***

Paul and Milk stared up at the great wall before them. The barrier dam was intact. There was no exit. A half mile away, water curled over the top of the disintegrating dam, heading toward them with increasing speed.

"It should be here," said Paul. "The exit point."

Milk scanned Isaac's map for the hundredth time. It marked where the exit was—section 72. And they were beneath a giant red 72 painted on the dam's face, but the wall was unbroken and hundreds of feet tall.

There was no way out.

And the water was coming for them.

THIRTY MINUTES

"If you are going to live in Purity, you need to understand the rules," said Stalin. "There are many."

They were in a large control room filled with screens. A small staff tended to the operations. In one area, a group of architects and engineers worked on new versions of Purity. Incredibly vivid three-dimensional projections rotated on their screens, some zoomed into the smallest of details. Alastair wandered through the room, looking for something.

Unlike the rest of Purity, the space was messy and alive with business, similar to the inside of the International Space Station after a long mission. Ad hoc instruments filled every corner; monitors were bolted on top of panels and storage bins. It looked as if each new set of guests brought their own equipment and had to find a place to stuff it. The staff moved fluidly through the cramped space. It was a familiar, well-run operation.

On one of the screens, there was a satellite view of the Cornerstone property. Alastair could see the water moving across the Crypt, consuming it. His friends were somewhere on those screens, *tiny pixels*, he thought. He would save them, despite the immense odds. He had no idea how a rescue was possible. He was locked inside a Chinese facility on the other side of the planet. Even if he could make it out, find a way back, get past the maybe-still-alive Ursus, and through the now frozen-solid cave, there was still an ocean's worth of water pouring into the Crypt. And even then, if they made it past all those obstacles, Cornerstone itself was trapped in time, locked for ten years by the circling infiniton particle.

Despite all this, Alastair was determined to save his friends. One option, he thought, was to find them and bring them to Purity. The better option was to escape Purity, find them, and then escape Cornerstone. The ultimate barrier was time itself, and that door was closing fast.

On the wall, there was a countdown labeled TIME CYCLE LOCK. It read, 48 MINUTES.

Next to the digital numbers was a satellite video of Cornerstone being swallowed by the Gulf, seemingly in real time.

"Is that a live image?" asked Alastair.

"It is. We have been watching the Americans for decades," said Stalin.

"You mean days," said Catherine, correcting him.

"Do not correct me!" said Stalin in a flash of anger.

"For those of us in Purity, it's decades," he continued. "When Cornerstone fires, we know almost instantaneously, and our accelerator automatically starts. This allows us to, one, stay hidden from the Americans and, two, to watch you. When both Purity and Cornerstone are inside a time cycle, time passes at the same speed in both locations."

Stalin explained that Purity's accelerator was exactly the same as Cornerstone's. It was a copy down to the bolt, producing the same flow of time, allowing them to peer inside Cornerstone when it was running at the same speed.

"Elsewhere in the world, the light coming out of the Crypt is a blur," he said, "ten years accelerated into a few minutes. For us, because we are in the same time flow rate as Cornerstone, it is possible for us to unpack the light. And watch."

Alastair jotted calculations in his notebook. "You said that you start your accelerator a fraction of a second after ours?" he asked.

Stalin looked at Alastair, seeing the pencil in his hands and the calculations on the paper. He paused, weighing whether to answer, but then said, "It starts automatically the second Cornerstone is triggered, only a fraction of a second after yours. And it is the only way we were able to keep Purity hidden—by running it during the same three minutes, every week, while the Americans run theirs. This hides any side effects of the cycles. So it would appear to be Cornerstone causing them."

"Like the plane crashes?" Kat asked.

"That was all Cornerstone," said Stalin. "And a pox on your country for not stopping flights once it was clear the accelerator was the cause of civilian airline disasters."

Ralls stood up. He had been quiet in a seat, taking in the nightmare, but Stalin's accusation seemed to push him over the edge.

"Sit down," said Stalin. "We would have done the same thing."

"We were working on grounding planes, scheduling them around our cycles," Ralls said. "But the airlines were very difficult to work with, even with Pentagon authorizations. They were too slow."

"All of time is too slow," said Stalin.

"You knew planes were crashing? And you kept running cycles?" said Kat.

"No planes crashed once we found out it was our fault," Ralls responded.

"But you didn't stop the cycles?" said Kat.

Ralls sat back down. "No," he admitted.

"None of this explains why we are in China if what you say is true," said Leo.

"It does not matter," said Stalin. "Thanks to Isaac, Cornerstone is dead, and we have Albert Einstein."

"Thanks to Isaac?" Ralls repeated in confusion.

"How else do you think we got the plans? For a man with autism spectrum disorder, he was not hard to trick into loyalty. All it took was a few Pokémon cards and some love. Which he never got from you."

"Isaac would never do that," said Ralls. "He built Cornerstone."

"And now, he has destroyed it," said Stalin.

"I don't feel well," said Alastair. He stuffed his notebook into his pocket, but no one wanted to leave.

Alastair secretly mouthed to Kat and Leo, *We have to go ... now.*

"I'm tired and have reached my grossed-out limit," said Kat. "Can we take a break and continue this fascinating shit show after dinner?"

Stalin turned back to the monitors and watched the ocean flood across the alien ecosystem. Swaths of blue and red swirled in the great waters. In another context, it would have been beautiful.

***

Catherine led them to their dorm room. She was quiet and left without a word, carrying herself like a beaten dog since Stalin yelled at her. As soon as the door was shut, Alastair ripped his notes out of his pocket. Ralls looked out the window into the dark gloom.

"Guys, this is serious," said Alastair. "Look. I think I know how we got here."

He drew two spirals stacked on top of each other. One was Purity, the other Cornerstone. He then joined them together with vertical lines. The two spirals were slightly displaced from one another, creating a twist in the lines connecting them, like a funnel. It looked like—

"A wormhole," said Alastair. "At least I think it is."

"I can't believe Isaac would do this to me," Ralls groaned, lost in his own thoughts.

Alastair ignored Ralls and continued. "These equations show that the two particle accelerators are entangled when they are on at the same time, like quantum particles entangled with the same spin."

He pointed at the relevant formulas. "See here?" he asked.

"No," said Kat, "all I see is chicken scratch." It was true. Alastair's diagrams were a mess of numbers, figures, and variables.

"Because Purity's accelerator starts a fraction later," he continued, "the two infiniton particles are displaced in time from one another on either side of the earth, staggered in the acceleration, and that's why ..." As he talked, he erased and rewrote different sections of the formula.

"That's why we could go through the earth?" Leo asked, finishing his friend's thought.

"According to physics ..." Alastair erased another section and then added more numbers. "I think ..." He erased something. "But that's not the real issue. The real issue is that the wormhole might be temporary. Once the accelerators get up to full speed in real time—"

"At seventeen hours?" said Leo.

"Yeah, once it gets to full speed, I think they'll disconnect. See." He pointed at an indecipherable jumble of numbers. "Only when there is an acceleration difference between the two accelerators is there a stable wormhole. Once they are both at the exact same speed—full speed—there is no difference in energy. No time frame dragging. And no wormhole."

"And no way to get back to Cornerstone to get them?" Leo asked.

"That's right. They will be trapped there," said Alastair.

"And us here," said Kat.

"That's right. I think."

"How long do we have?" Kat asked.

Alastair looked at his watch. "Forty-two minutes. We gotta get going. How do you think we get out of here?"

Ralls shook his head. "Ha. You are not going anywhere. You didn't pay attention in physics for years, and now you are telling us you solved the quantum dynamics of two independent systems entangled on either side of the earth. Even Isaac needs a computer for that. We aren't in art class anymore, and despite your pretty drawings, this would be a suicide mission. You are not going back. They will have to figure it out on their own. They are smart enough. You have always been a pain in my ass. From day one, you couldn't just shut up and listen. You never understood what I did for you. None of you did. Ungrateful brats."

Alastair knew Ralls's ire was directed at Isaac.

"I don't think you understand," said Alastair. "This isn't Cornerstone. You are not in charge anymore. You don't own us. We're going."

Leo nodded. "I trust Alastair. If he says we have to go, I'm with him."

Kat nodded as well, though she seemed less confident. "Are you sure you're right?" she asked Alastair, looking over his formulas. "Because if there isn't a deadline on getting back there, we could do a proper rescue mission, take our time, get the right equipment from Purity."

"There's no time," said Alastair. "The math is accurate."

Ralls didn't say anything. His shoulders dropped, as if he'd just made some sort of internal decision and a weight had been lifted. He looked outside and then back at Leo, Kat, and then Alastair, locking eyes with him.

"You are not Albert Einstein," he said.

"I know. Goddamn it. Everyone's been telling me that. I don't care who I am. I am me, okay. I know I'm right. The math is correct. This is why we are in China," he said, pointing to his drawing. "And it's also why planes were crashing and the time effect was spreading each cycle. The Russians were pouring energy into our system, copying it, and running it at the same time. And we had no idea. Now our friends are about to die. We are going to go get them, whether you like it or not."

"Let me be a bit clearer," Ralls said, steeling himself. "You are not Albert Einstein. You never were." His eyes were made of glass, staring at Alastair, tracking his reaction. "There is not a lick of Einstein's DNA in you. You were the control in the grand experiment. You are no more Albert Einstein than I am."

Alastair's face flushed red. He didn't say anything.

"Those figures are gibberish, and you aren't even smart enough to know that," said Ralls.

"Bullshit," said Kat. "I don't buy it. You just don't want your prize possession walking out of here."

"Am I bullshitting?" said Ralls. "I knew we would have some of nature's greatest minds in your class, especially Zack. But I also wanted to see if we could nurture one as well. Create it and curate it, like my bonsai garden. Could we create genius, socially engineer it using an average kid? Provide the final answer to the 'Nature versus Nurture' question? You were the control, Alastair, to test my hypothesis. And then, I kind of fell for your useless laziness. So I kept you in the program. You're a nice kid."

Alastair sat down, dumbstruck. He looked at his math and figures. All of a sudden, they looked suspect, like the scribblings of a child. Were the numbers right? Was he willing to risk their lives on it? Fear and indecision flooded back into him. Even if Ralls were lying, who was Alastair to figure out what was going on?

What did he know?

It would not have been the first time such an unethical experiment was attempted on a child. In the 1970s, Hungarian educational psychologist László Polgár infamously experimented on his children from birth to prove geniuses were made, not born. After debating what discipline to teach his daughters—physics, business, languages, or mathematics—he decided to turn them into chess prodigies. A decade later, his eldest daughter, Zsuzsa, was the best female chess player in the world. Her sister, Zsófia, was the second. And Judit, the youngest, is now considered the greatest female chess player of all time.

"Am I—" started Leo.

Ralls nodded. "Yes, you are still a famous artist."

"Thank god."

"And you are a pathological liar," Kat spat at Ralls. "Don't listen to him, Alastair. Nothing he has ever told us, from day one, has been honest. He just doesn't want you to go."

"Be quiet, Katherine!" said Ralls, cutting her off. There was fury in his voice.

"Is that why I couldn't get into the Nautilus, at the door with the DNA lock?" asked Alastair.

"Yes, they had programmed the door with Einstein's actual DNA," said Ralls. "I have the real Einstein's DNA now, of course, for a coming cycle. As do the Russians, clearly. But twenty years ago, I didn't. I didn't think to make sure the DNA lock also had your actual DNA. I missed that one with you, I admit."

"You okay?" said Leo, concern edging his voice.

Alastair took a deep breath and opened his papers once more, folding them down onto the desk. He took his pencil and ran it through the calculations, making notes on the side.

"I'm okay, but I want to know more," said Alastair. He didn't lift his eyes from the page, continuing to recheck his work. "Who else knew? My parents? Do they know I am not really Einstein?"

"They thought you were Einstein too. It is not hard to convince a parent that their child is, uh, special. To be fair, your parents were above average in every way. That's why they passed all the early testing to get into the surrogacy program. And there were some reasonable physical similarities that we looked for in choosing them. But most importantly, they were malleable. Pleasers. Like you."

"The numbers hold up," said Alastair.

"Did you hear what I said?" asked Ralls. "You are not Albert Einstein! You have no special ability. None of your physics make any sense. It's garbage."

"But it's *my* garbage," Alastair shot back.

"Are you willing to bet your life on that?"

"I ... I'm not sure," Alastair stammered, oscillating like a metronome between confidence and self-doubt.

"Alastair, you're—" said Leo. "Are you correct?"

"I ..."

Before Alastair could answer, there was a knock on the window. They all spun around.

It was Jimmy.

He was outside Purity, peering in. He had a makeshift plastic hood over his head, duct-taped together, and an inflated homemade balloon. He pressed a note against the window. It read, *We need to leave. Now.*

TWENTY MINUTES

Isaac, Joseph, and Zack climbed a ladder on the oil rig. It was one of many that had dotted the inland shores of the Gulf of Mexico, this one now abandoned just on the inside of the great barrier dam, which was still crumbling, fighting time's grip on the ocean.

They were tiny figures on the great structure, pushing through vines and vegetation all the way to the top, desperate to stay ahead of the coming flood.

The platform towered over the jungle. Although it was over 180 feet above the ground, it once sat just above sea level and was certainly almost the oldest rig in the world, having survived twelve cycles—over 120 years. It was almost completely consumed by nature, like an ancient ruin—or Detroit—but somehow it still stood tall. It was originally engineered to survive even the worst hurricanes in the Gulf of Mexico.

There were no hurricanes inside the Crypt, but time could be just as violent. The rig was probably on its last legs and cycle.

At the top, Isaac reached out a hand to Zack and pulled him up. Joseph strode across the platform. Isaac's arm was perfectly healed. In fact, Zack noticed Isaac's legs were not only healed but had grown back. He'd gone from being completely disfigured and crippled to fully recovered. In hours. Not days, weeks, or years.

"You're healed," said Zack. "Your body is—"

"What difference will it make?" said Isaac, sitting on the ground. From his vantage point, it was obvious that the flood would soon reach the rig, wiping out the world below. They were out of time and options. While the barrier opposite the rig held, it was clearly losing its grip on the ocean. The wall was coming down in slow motion, like a wave traversing a beach, a perfect rip curl approaching the southeast. It was only a matter of time before the section of the barrier dam opposite them would give.

And then, assuming the legs of the oil rig could withstand the force of the water, they would be stuck on the rig for a lifetime. It was the only thing above sea level. Even the Nautilus would be destroyed. There would be nothing but the rig.

We're going to die, thought Zack. His happiness at making it to the oil rig in time was fading. It was a prison in the sky. *It is also an Eden*, Zack thought, looking around.

Now that he had caught his breath, he saw that the oil rig was not an overgrown wilderness; it was well tended. Fruit-filled trees and bushes wrapped around the entire structure. Flat surfaces were covered in boxes overflowing with rich earth, growing food in the unending light of the sun. There were even solar panels that fed electricity into little pumps, misting and watering plants with a constant flow of irrigation. Some trees were twisted into place to form structural supports where old metal was finally rusting away, giving the once modern structure the feel of a jungle paradise grown on the back of a lost civilization. It wasn't so far from the truth. The beauty and symbiosis of nature and technology were remarkable.

Someone had lived here and created a garden in the sky, completely self-sufficient and isolated from the vicious ecosystem that was now in its final death throes.

There was fresh produce everywhere. Zack took a bite of an oversized mango. It was delicious. Fruit dripped from trees and was collected in baskets and jars. There was every type of vegetable, including many Zach had never seen before. Someone had been living here a long time, tending the garden, safe from the terrors below.

He wandered through a nearby door in search of the owner. Isaac silently followed him, clearly going through a similar thought process. Inside the room was a library. Thousands of books were stacked floor to ceiling in well-built wood shelves. There were cozy nooks to read, write, and think.

It wouldn't be the worst place in the world to live, thought Zack, *all things considered*. There were books, food, and sunlight. A true Garden of Eden, a paradise for the mind. At the very least, he'd be able to continue his work in solitude.

There was a play of light in the corner, and he was drawn to a bed, which had a light mosquito net in front of it. Zack pulled it aside and found a dead body—a woman on her back with one arm folded across her chest. She looked like she was sleeping. Her cheeks were only now losing their pink. Next to her was a skeleton in the same repose.

She was holding its hand clutched in her other hand.

Zack read it aloud. "I can't live for another ten years alone. Teigen Ralls, I am now alone in an infinite hell of your creation. You are the great Satan. I come to haunt your soul."

Zack looked around, contemplating what it would be like to live on the rig for a decade. What it would be like for them. Would he and Isaac kill themselves? Kill each other?

He went outside and looked over the edge at the coming flood waters. Isaac joined him at the rails.

"We will be able to survive here ten years I think," said Zack. "We can grow enough food if we stay in a sustained balance with this garden and with constant sunlight. Water and rain will be the question, but it must have existed here in ample amounts. There is no plumbing or irrigation, only cisterns."

"We won't survive."

"I think we will. At this point, I think you'd give me enough credit to consider my opinions," said Zack, his confidence flashing.

"No, you don't understand what I meant," said Isaac. "Look!" Far below, a tiny speck raced across the mud plains toward the oil rig, chased by giant, tidal waves that came from all directions. The water swamped the ground, creating new gullies and channels.

It was Paul—on a motorcycle. They were alive!

Paul was barely ahead of the water despite traveling at the highest speed possible. The tires ripped through the mud. Milk held on to the giant bike, gripping tightly to survive every bump and swerve. They shot over a dune and caught air, almost throwing everyone off, including the still unconscious Churchill.

Water flooded in from either side, washing over the muddy plain. Right when it seemed like they would make it safely, an enormous wave of water swept over the last remaining dry land route to the oil rig. It was only a wave—not the ocean itself—and it soon passed, revealing one last muddy route to the rig's legs.

"Come on!" Zack screamed. "You can do it, Paul!"

Zack leaned over the edge. The wave had deposited something at the base of the rig. Giant lobsters with bisecting blue-and-red bodies littered the mud field beneath the oil platform. There were other ocean animals as well—sharks, blue octopuses, and red fish the size of cars—gasping for water. It looked like someone had drained a bathtub and left all the toys at the bottom, except these toys had claws and sharp teeth—and they were pissed.

***

Paul raced past the first lobster, throttling his motorcycle to a full tilt. A giant blue claw almost took off his head. He swerved through the minefield, dodging animals and deep puddles, until he was finally under the looming legs of the platform. They had made it. Almost.

Milk got off the bike first and started untying Churchill, slapping him to wake him up. He was groggy, blind, and slow to gain consciousness.

"How are we going to get him up there?" Paul asked.

"Hey, it's Zack!" said Milk.

Zack waved wildly down at them.

Milk waved back. "What is he doing?"

Zack yelled at them again, but Milk couldn't hear him over the rush of the impending water. It was too late to help Churchill. They had to start climbing. The water was returning, this time backed by the entire ocean. The rising water released the fish from the ground. They flapped and swam, searching for deeper water.

"What's that?" Paul asked.

There was a speck of black quickly approaching them. Milk was already climbing, briefly chased onto the leg of the oil rig by a passing shark. Paul was dragged away by a lobster and lost most of his pants by the time he escaped its grip. Separated from Milk, he too climbed up the first rungs of the oil rig.

A rope fell past Milk, she contemplated using it to get up, but she was making better time on the ladder. However, Zack was gesturing wildly, and then she realized what he wanted her to do.

***

Up top, Zack tied the rope to his waist. He looped it around his shoulders in a figure eight butterfly and backed up, ready to start running.

"You are not heavy enough to get him up," said Joseph.

"Isaac," said Zack. "Please. I need more weight."

***

Below, it was dire. Milk was back at the waterline again, along with Churchill, working the rope around his unconscious body as the water rose. She had to dive down to continue as the waves grew. Sharks and eels swam around her, readying themselves for a snack.

Paul dove off the ladder to help her, wrapping his arm around the rope a number of times, binding his fate to hers.

***

Up top, Isaac shook his head. "No way."

Joseph strode past him, taking up the rope Zack worked with. He wrapped the rope around his arm and shoulder and stood on the edge of the platform next to Zack, ready to be the counterweight to drag Churchill and Milk up.

Isaac ran at them full speed, hitting Joseph just as he turned around. He grabbed him by the waist, forcing the three of them over the edge with enough weight to pull Churchill and Milk out of the water and up toward the sky.

They met halfway up the oil rig, all dangling at eye level.

"Hey, Zack," said Milk.

"Why's your mouth blue?" Zack responded.

Water had completely flooded the ground below, but they were dry for now.

In the distance, Paul saw the Bone People. They were on a small navy of boats, paddling hard for the oil rig, the only safe spot in the growing ocean.

TEN MINUTES

"I am not Albert Einstein," said Alastair. He leaned against the wall, talking to Catherine in a hallway.

"We all feel that way at some point or another," Catherine said, her Russian accent and the soft light adding to her allure. She took his hand. "It is hard to get used to—that you are exactly the same as one of the greatest minds ever born. But you have a right to your mind, just as much as the original Einstein did. He didn't pick it either."

Behind Catherine, Leo and Kat were sneaking astronaut suits into their dorm room. They were bulky and tough to manage.

"I know that, intellectually," Alastair said. "But I don't feel it. In my heart. It is sort of this absurd statement. Like if someone told you that you were Albert Einstein. It doesn't make any sense." Alastair's performance was flawless.

Overloaded with a suit, Kat dropped a helmet. It slowly rolled down the hallway toward Catherine. Catherine began to turn to see what the noise was, but Alastair pulled her closer to him.

"Just imagine," said Catherine, "he is only a twin brother. You can love him and still be the same person here." Catherine put her hand on Alastair's heart.

Kat caught up to the helmet just before it reached Catherine.

"I have had my whole life to come to terms with being Catherine the Great," said Catherine. "You've only had a few days knowing that you are Einstein. It takes time. I can help you."

Kat silently backed up and then disappeared with the last suit back into the dorm rooms. A second later, Kat popped out. Her hair was wet. She was putting it into a towel on top of her head as if she had just gotten out of the shower. "Alastair, will you stop hanging out with that photocopy?"

"It takes time," Catherine said. She thought they were having a moment.

Alastair nodded, unsure how to extend the moment any longer. He said, "Your hands are cold," rubbing his hand on hers.

***

"You didn't need to lean into her so hard," Kat responded.

"Seriously," said Leo.

"What did I say?" asked Alastair.

"Your hands are so cold? Cliché. But it worked," said Leo, his smile broadening.

He was right. The plan did work. There were five complete astronaut suits in the dorm room. They could dress in secrecy. Leo peaked outside the window. Jimmy sat on the ground, releasing more bottled air into the makeshift oxygen tent he had taped around his head. He looked up and made a slashing sign across his throat.

"We gotta go," said Leo.

Suiting up for a spacewalk took hours. They only had minutes. Ralls sat on a bed, his arms crossed.

"All I have to do is walk out of this room and tell them what you are doing," said Ralls. Clearly, he wasn't doing that.

"You won't do anything," said Alastair. "You are a coward." The weight of knowing he wasn't Albert Einstein freed him from a burden. He was Alastair again.

"Your actual choice is whether you are going to stay here and be Russia's captive for a decade," Leo said to Ralls. "Or are you going to take a risk with us and return to America so you can resurrect your project."

Alastair knew what Leo was doing, appealing to Ralls's ego and precarious masculinity.

"Do they make ones for fat people?" said Ralls, eying the suits.

They didn't and Ralls's didn't fit in the end. He was too overweight. He couldn't get the hard ring at the waist past his hips, and the top wouldn't join with the bottom. Everyone else was suited up like a ragtag street gang from NASA.

"What are you going to do?" Alastair asked.

"We can find more bottled air," said Kat.

"There is not enough time," said Ralls. He took off the top of the suit and looked at the kids, thinking.

Alastair watched him, not sure what to do or say. Ralls would be stuck for ten years no matter what he chose to do.

"You know, I do love each of you," said Ralls, taking off the rest of the suit. "Since you were babies. I realize the burden of what I did is heavy on you. But I waited eighteen years to tell you. And you have all grown into such strong people. Kat, you are a fierce woman. Your confidence has always intimidated me. And Leo, your intense curiosity and inability to finish a single thing has been a joy to watch. I know you may hate me, but ..." He lost his train of thought. "But I am proud of you." He took off the last boot. "And Alastair."

"I don't want to hear it."

Jimmy pounded on the window. He was running out of air.

"We gotta go," said Leo. He was already opening the door and looking down the hall.

"Good luck," said Ralls. "I'll see you in ten years."

"We really gotta go!" said Leo.

***

Ralls stood in the control room talking with Stalin. On the wall, there were less than ten minutes on the countdown to the time cycle lock.

Ralls swept a ton of papers off a desk. "I don't care what you think!" Everyone in the room turned to face Ralls's showdown with Stalin. "This is not just another nuclear submarine or weapon in the Cold War—you are messing with time!"

"And what were you doing?" Stalin retorted. "Typical American hypocrisy."

On one of the monitors in the background, four white shapes crept along the perimeter of Purity. Ralls spotted them and his eyes widened.

Stalin turned to follow his gaze, and Ralls ran at him. "Don't you besmirch my country!" He hit Stalin in the midsection and wrestled him to the ground.

People jumped up to help Stalin, but Ralls was so big—his considerable weight now an advantage—that the scrum on the ground grew. As Ralls fought, swung, and squeezed, the white shapes finally crept out of the monitor's view, disappearing into the night.

THE BONE PEOPLE

The Bone People were almost at the base of the oil rig. They paddled for their lives, fighting for survival against great, cascading waves that crisscrossed from every direction. For millennia, the world had been a static place of nature and symbiosis. Now, the deluge had come—the end of their world—driving them forward, terrified and angry. They had no mental model for what was happening and only blamed themselves for not sacrificing enough bones during the Seven Suns. But even that didn't explain the chaos that surrounded them.

The sea was wild with turbulence, and despite their great skill from navigating the wild rivers of the Crypt, the struggle was real. Forty-foot waves slammed against the legs of the platform and ripped through the soaked jungle that still clung to it. Huge heaving sweeps revealed and then buried the only ladders up to salvation. The Bone People were in the same figurative boat that everyone else was in. There was almost no more land left in the Crypt. They were forced out of their holes and onto the open water, and now their only salvation was the oil rig rising in the sky above them.

Milk and Churchill were still tethered on one end of a rope, dangling halfway up the oil rig's towering height, suspended over the water. Churchill was unconscious; he hung like a piece of meat next to them. On the other end of the rope, above them, was their counterweight. Zack, Isaac, and Joseph hung in the air as well, stuck. Neither group could reach one of the ladders on the oil rig legs, but they were safe, for now, above the frothing ocean below.

The first Bone People reached the ladders. They attempted to time their leaps, but with the sea heaving up and down as it was, the first few people ended up in the ocean. Women and children drowned. Eventually, the stronger amongst the Bone People started to stream up the ladders, carrying sharpened daggers made of their own bones. Gally was among them.

The first native reached eye level with Joseph's group and came toward them across the open air, knife in hand. Joseph grabbed the man's forearm, keeping the blade away from the rope that held him and everyone else up. They fought and struggled, but Joseph's immense power soon threw the man off, right before another leapt toward them. The bundle of bodies started swinging.

Bone People were now starting to come up the ladder closest to Paul's group. Paul could see murder and desperation in their eyes. He also observed that if Joseph's group fell, they would fall too. Their fates were tied to the same rope.

"Swing!" said Paul.

"How?" Milk asked.

"Hey, asshole, come and get us!" yelled Paul to the nearest Bone Person, knowing that the man's leap would cause them to swing.

The Bone Person jumped and grabbed onto them, swinging his knife in every direction. He jammed the knife into Churchill's chest, using the deep plunge cut to hold on. He pulled the knife out and put it between his teeth so he could climb the writhing mass. Milk jammed her foot into his face and kicked down hard. He almost reached her when she managed to grab the knife out of the man's mouth and stab him in his shoulder. He fell downward, careening toward the ocean.

"Swing! Lean in to it," Paul instructed. They gained momentum with each swing.

Joseph was in a full-blown fistfight with the Bone People now. Zack fought as best he could to keep their knives away from the rope holding them above the raging sea below. Isaac was useless. He was immobilized with fear at the return of the Bone People. Joseph knocked another Bone Person off the ladder, and the man fell toward the waters below. The group watched a shark leap out of the water—its rainbow skin iridescent in the sunlight—and snap the man in half. His blood was a crimson flower in the water, attracting sea life, and the water soon thrashed with sharks and fish sharing a meal.

Paul's group had a good swing going, and they were able to push off a leg to get more acceleration and arc. They swung wide out over the space between the legs and then came careening back violently, heading toward the ladder crowded with Bone People.

Paul straightened out his legs and slammed a Bone Person square on the chest with his feet, knocking the man off of the ladder into the sea below. They kept swinging back out, and with every return trip, were able to knock off another attacker. They were like a Cirque du Soleil act, twisting wide arcs over open space.

Bone People fell into the water. The sharks below were not coming for them, however. The bloodstain in the ocean had migrated in the current, and they were distracted, drifting away from the oil rig. The fallen Bone People waited for their turns in the water, trying to time the swells so they could climb the ladder once again. Paul's plan wasn't working. They could knock them off the ladders, but still they kept coming, and one of these times, the knives would land. They would conquer the rig as their own—an iron island lost outside time.

"How's Church doing?" Milk shouted to Paul.

"Dead."

"Good."

Joseph's group started to swing and use pendulum physics to flick the Bone People off the rig's ladders. But still, the primitive people kept coming, wave after wave, like the ocean itself, forever renewing. Hundreds of them waited in the sea below, eager to climb out of the water.

Milk cut Churchill loose. His corpse tumbled downward into the ocean. When he hit the water, his blood quickly attracted the sharks, turning the sea into a melee of feeding around the Bone People's boats, tossing them into the water. Red-and-blue claws started reaching out of the water as well in the thrash of sea life, cutting the lingering Bone People in half, inviting even more sharks to come and feed. Soon, the ocean went red with the blood of an entire people: the ancient civilization had arisen from a small band of migrant workers, survived thousands of years outside the flow of time, created their own religion, but now they were quickly disappearing back into history.

There were survivors.

More Bone People—one with a child on her back—managed to get out of the water and climbed upward toward the platform above, knives in mouths.

Joseph grabbed the ladder. But he was the only one hanging right side up. Isaac and Zack were suspended upside down, tangled in the ropes from all the fighting. They were unable to climb. Zack's leg was wrapped up tightly in knots.

Paul and Milk finally got to another ladder on a different leg.

Paul looked up and saw the three Bone People above them. They were climbing upward toward the platform. "I need the knife," he said to Milk. "Now." He took Milk's knife and cut himself free before she could realize what he was doing. He started climbing.

"Stop, Paul! There are three of them!" said Milk.

"And one of me," said Paul, pausing on the ladder to look back down at her. He hung by one arm, the ocean below an epic backdrop.

"Those are bad odds, Paul," said Milk. "Like a million-parts-in-an-airplane-lowest-bidder odds."

"Since when do I care about the odds?" he said with a smile.

Paul climbed the oil rig, chasing after the last members of an ancient civilization, intent on killing them. Or at least prepared to die trying.

More Bone People swarmed up the ladders. They kept coming like insects fleeing a flooded colony.

***

The four unlikely astronauts stood at the edge of a lake looking into the blackness below. It was the very same lake and direction that they had come from earlier, and now the idea of descending back into the water seemed insane. Wild beasts, ice, death, getting lost inside a cave, and a wormhole on the verge of closing were all on Alastair's growing list of why this was a bad idea.

"I don't know," said Alastair.

"None of this makes any sense," Kat agreed.

"Does everything need to make sense?" said Leo. "Sometimes you just need a little faith that we are special, and things will turn out okay."

Kat said, "Do you really believe—"

"No," said Leo. "Not at all. We're going to die."

In the distance, lights swept across the land. Vehicles were coming for them.

Jimmy picked up heavy rocks, handing them out. "Walk. It's down there somewhere. We go down and then up. Just like we went down and then up."

"You think there will be a sign, 'Wormhole This Way'?" asked Alastair facetiously.

"Luck counts for something," said Jimmy. "By the way, did you see my dad on the way in. Did he head back? To high ground? I'm concerned he is still waiting."

It was just Alastair and Jimmy now above the lake. Alastair didn't say anything, dropping his eyes.

Jimmy froze. It was a passing question. Not *the* question.

"I'm sorry," said Alastair. "He wasn't—"

Jimmy held up a hand and then composed himself long enough to ask some questions.

The Russians were getting close, but Jimmy needed to know more about his father's last moments. Alastair stood his ground, telling him everything, despite the growing threat in the background.

He would die before he abandoned Jimmy's painful questions.

By the time the last helmet disappeared under the surface of the lake, the first car had pulled up. They fired guns into the water. Bullets zipped past Alastair and Jimmy, but none of them hit.

The group descended into the murky depths—a one-way trip to nowhere. It was gut-wrenchingly steep. Alastair was terrified. He felt the world closing in on him, pressing on the suit until he could only hear his breathing. The lights on the other suits faded from sight as each of them walked deeper and deeper, searching for the way down.

A beeping started to sound louder and louder.

"What is that?" Alastair asked. The sound seemed to emerge from some-one's suit.

It was Leo's.

"Your oxygen is on the low side," said Jimmy, looking at the reading on Leo's back. His voice didn't have the same bravado.

"I took Stalin's suit," said Leo. "He must have used a bunch of it already."

"We have to hurry," said Jimmy.

Leo cracked jokes, but Alastair hit him on the arm to shut him up. Alastair forced his own fear out of his mind and focused on putting one foot in front of another. He was acting on faith alone, and Leo's unfounded confidence that they would find their way out in time. Or back to the caves, at the very least, where there would be oxygen. The beeping started to intensify. Even Leo's voice began to crack.

"I'm just going to stop talking for a bit and slow down my breaths, okay?" Leo asked.

"Sure," said Alastair.

Leo stumbled. Alastair took Leo's hand and started to lead him.

The water began to clear. Leo tripped again, fighting unconsciousness. He dropped his rock, but didn't float up without the weight holding him down. Instead, something very odd happened. The rock floated upward, like a balloon. Alastair watched it rise, suddenly confused about his perspective.

Alastair looked down. He was walking on ice. He could see bubbles of oxygen on the other side—and light.

He dropped his rock to see if he could smash through, but instead of falling to his feet, the rock moved upward past his head.

Alastair's mind's eye suddenly shifted, and he realized they were walking on the underside of the ice upside down. His suit was buoyant. He looked back, and everyone was right behind him. They too dropped their rocks, which sank past their heads, disappearing into the darkness, which he now realized was below. Only a moment ago, it had been upward. His mind felt like a bent spoon.

It seemed that they were underneath a frozen lake walking upside down on the underside of the ice. Their buoyancy kept them from sinking, pinning them to the ice. Alastair could feel a light current, and he swam toward it, convinced that it represented salvation. He dragged Leo alongside him; Leo was too weak to swim.

The ice ended in rocks. Leo was on the edge of consciousness—the beeps on his suit reaching a continuous scream.

Alastair found a hole in the ice. It was less than a foot wide. He put his hand through it, reaching all the way up to his shoulder. On the other side of the ice, Alastair's gloved hand waved just above the surface. There was air, but there was almost a yard of ice in between the two worlds.

Leo was out of oxygen.

Time was up.

Everyone's suits started beeping.

ONE HUNDRED YEARS

A Bone Person headed right for Joseph, who met him with the force of a Russian bear, catching and flinging him to the side with a powerful push. He turned for the next, but soon there were too many of them. It took five Bone People, each to a limb and head, to restrain the great man.

Milk was the next over the railing. Zack and Isaac followed. Paul was still arguing with a Bone Person below, but he too moved up the ladder: a blue-and-red spear was pointed at his ass.

They were captured. Milk hoped to see Joseph and Paul large and in charge up top. But no dice. They were tied up. A fire had been set in an ash box, and the Bone People prepared for some sort of ritual, making signs to the sky, ceremonially applying white ash to their faces and bodies.

Isaac started screaming. He fell to the floor, kicking his legs back, desperate to escape. The Bone People picked him up and started tying him up. The others were tied up as well, tightly. There was no escaping the bonds.

The ceremony of the Seven Suns began. Milk asked Isaac what they were doing and why he was freaking out. He told her what they had done to him. He explained the hundred-year cycle in a mess of words and tears. "Karmic payback," he said. To be eternally tortured like Prometheus for trying to steal fire from the gods—a bird pecking at his liver for eternity until it grew back and the process began again.

Black paste was mixed in a wooden bowl and bone daggers inlaid with jewels were produced.

Three Bone People approached. They had a ceremonial walk. With each step, they made entreaties to the sun and sky, their arms moving in a choreographed dance practiced over decades. One of the Bone People was trying hard to keep up, but he obviously didn't know the ritual moves very well. When they finally got close and started to raise the daggers, miming stabbing them in the heart, Milk saw that the awkward Bone Person was not a Bone Person at all.

It was Paul. He was covered in ash. And mostly naked. His eyes were wide, and he was trying desperately to match the dance that was happening in front of the newest sacrifices for the Seven Suns.

The Bone People watched the ceremony, confused as to why one of them was struggling to remember the dance they'd been taught since childhood.

Paul suddenly gave up trying, knowing the jig was up. He started break-dancing. He did the wave with his arms, and with a final awkward move, he cut the ropes holding Milk to the pipe.

Before the Bone People could figure out what was happening, he moon-walked to Joseph and cut his ropes too. Joseph grabbed the nearest Bone Person and ripped the knife out of their hands.

A nearby warrior, who had been watching the ceremony, was quick to react and ran at them with a spear. At the last second, Joseph pulled a Bone Person in front of him as a human shield. The warrior drove the spear through the stomach of the Bone Person, who screamed in anguish. He tried to push the spear further through his body to reach the spear point to Joseph, who was standing behind him. Joseph only barely managed to wiggle away.

By the time he turned to face the next threat, he realized they were all surrounded by Bone People carrying spears. Paul's plan had failed.

Isaac wept with fear. "I can't. I can't. I can't," he said over and over again, as they smeared black paste on his face and shoulder.

Milk held his hand, readying herself for one hundred years of torture.

***

Alastair was desperate to save Leo. He spun around underwater looking for another option. He spotted something in the hazy distance—an object stuck in the ice.

Was it a mirage? An effect of the reflection of the underside of the ice? Or was there something frozen into the ice?

He swam hard for it, dragging Leo with him. It wasn't until he got closer that he realized it was Hello Kitty. The Armageddon Truck was frozen halfway into the ice, nose downward. A big Hello Kitty cartoon smiled at Alastair. The cab and front half of the truck poked through the ice into the water below. The windows were still open; the cab was flooded.

Jimmy caught up to Alastair and swam inside the cab. "Hellooo, Kittty!" he said.

Suddenly, the world erupted into orange light. It took a second for Alastair to realize that the surreal glow was coming from the topside of the ice, where giant flames roared out of Hello Kitty's tail end. Jimmy was melting the ice. Alastair could see real flames now. There was air on the other side of the truck!

"Leo's out of time," said Kat. "We can't wait for it to melt!"

She's right, thought Alastair. They only had seconds. Not minutes.

"Everyone get in!" said Jimmy.

Alastair floated Leo through the window first, handing him to Jimmy. He had not regained consciousness. Kat followed. Alastair was the last one in, struggling to swim through the window. With their bulky suits, it was difficult. They jammed up against each other inside the cab.

Jimmy tried to roll the windows up. Alastair's foot was stuck, hanging outside. It took him a while to loosen it and drag himself in, finally falling on top of Kat. The beeping in their helmets shrieked at them.

The window closed. Jimmy flicked another switch, and oxygen forced its way into the truck, pushing out the water. A few seconds later, they all opened the fronts of their helmets, taking huge, deep breaths.

"Told you this thing was waterproof!" Jimmy exclaimed.

Leo wasn't responding.

Jimmy elbowed him in the chest hard.

Leo gasped. His eyes fluttered open. "Being Leonardo da Vinci sucks," he said.

Kat put her arms around him, thankful he was alive. Leo went in for a kiss. Kat flat-handed his face, pushing him away.

"I swear to God I am going to get my shit together," Leo said. "I promise."

"We'll see," said Kat.

The ice melted quickly, allowing Jimmy to kick out the back window. He turned off the flames, and one by one, they squirmed out the back of the truck, disgorging onto the ice floor of a cave.

The truck had ended up lodged at the bottom of a cavern. There was air, but there didn't seem to be an exit. Alastair stood up and looked around, hoping to find a way out. The cave was almost solid ice.

"Oh my god!" screamed Kat.

Alastair spun around, expecting to get eaten by something.

A huge metal pipe bisected the cave, vertically. It had a diameter of five feet. On its side, in faded letters, it said, TEXERCON PETROLEUM. It was one of the legs of the oil rig plunging into the sea floor.

Oil rig legs are hollow, enabling them to float into place.

Jimmy was already pulling a welding torch from Hello Kitty. "How much time?" he asked.

"We are in Texas," Kat muttered, half to herself, incredulous.

Alastair looked at his watch. "Five minutes."

THE FINAL COUNTDOWN

They started with Joseph, carving a slice along the inside of his quad muscle. No amount of black paste masked the intense pain, both physical and emotional, that he was suffering.

The Bone People started at one end of the line. Despite the small crowd, only two people did the blood work. Milk was going to be next. Then Zack. The ritual workers each held a slice of Joseph's flesh to the sky and then handed it out.

At first, Milk thought they were going to eat it raw, but then she realized they were wrapping the meat in long, palm leaves, and then placing them above the fires they had set. They were smoking the meat.

Gally Galileo, the child cannibal, sat and watched. "Don't worry, you will grow back. And then we can feed again."

Isaac was swearing up a storm at them.

Paul was trying to knock over bowls at his feet.

But Milk was quiet. She pressed her sorrow and her fear down into the pit of her stomach until they turned into stone. And she could look at it or save it for later so she could contemplate her life now.

Only days ago, she was a typical teenager growing up in Ohio, obsessed with conspiracy theories, blogging, and boys. And Alastair secretly. Though she would never openly admit it. Ever. Now he was dead, drowned somewhere beneath the ocean of water that stretched in every direction. The finality was impossible to comprehend. She had spent a lot of time thinking about her eventual death but had never factored in the pain and suffering. Mortality, in her mind, was always about the existential angst of meaning. She had always imagined she would have some profound insight on the eve of her death. Or a profound realization that no profound insight existed. Both options seemed to cover the gamut of what she imagined she would feel. However, in this moment, there she was experiencing a completely different emotion. She felt like a little girl again—as if she was five-years-old, calling for her mother for help. The fear was bottomless. She cried out.

Joseph managed to get a leg free and kicked a Bone Person onto his back. There was still fight left in him.

When the blade hit Isaac for the first time, his scream of terror echoed over the oil rig. The Bone People stopped, as did the blood workers. Silence fell on the deck.

Milk didn't understand what was happening. Something had changed. The ceremony paused, the workers dripping in blood.

Two astronauts stood on the top of the deck. The gold-mirrored face-plates shone brilliantly in the intense sunlight, making them look like gods of technology.

And to Milk, they were gods. She had no idea what NASA was doing on the oil rig or how they got there. But she didn't care. Someone had come to save them.

Suddenly, a voice boomed out. "Behold, the final stages of evolution! For too long man has mired in the dirt! A mere animal fighting on the edge of existence! And from the primordial fires came—"

Milk smiled. It was Leo's voice.

Paul looked at her, shocked.

What the hell were they doing? thought Milk.

One of the astronauts looked back, waiting on something. Then the voice on the speakers repeated itself, "And from the primordial fires came life!"

With the last word, a giant plume of fire exploded into the sky. Music kicked in. It was "The Final Countdown" by Europe. The two astronauts stood in front of the flames like some sort of 1980s rock concert, their fists in the air—or Leo's dream career, the *Waterworld* stunt performance show at Universal Studios Hollywood.

Zack's face was priceless. "Waterworld!" He pumped his fist.

The Bone People cowered as the raging fire reached higher and higher. Inside a control room, Leo removed his helmet, holding the PA for the oil rig, talking into the microphone. He turned up the volume on Ralls's phone, which was the source of the eighties rock ballad. Leo had a walkie-talkie in his other hand and was communicating with Jimmy, who had made it into the oil rig and was a few decks below in a control room.

Jimmy released gas into a burn-off valve a few floors below. It was a controlled burn but an impressive sight up above nonetheless.

With the raging fire as their backdrop, the two astronauts walked down to the lower platform where everyone was tied up. They passed through the Bone People, who were still immobile, watching in shock and fear. One of the astronauts walked up to Milk and then flipped up his gold visor, revealing his face.

It was Alastair. "Hey Milk, what's up?" he said under his breath.

She was going to respond, but first he said, "Shh, watch," and flipped his visor back down. Milk was dying to know who else had survived, but for now, she had to pray that Alastair had a real plan.

Kat flipped up her visor for a second, winking at Milk.

Kat is alive too! thought Milk.

Alastair turned around, grabbed one of the big black paste bowls at the centerpiece of the ritual, and ran.

Kat grabbed the other bowl and headed the other way.

"That's your plan?" yelled Milk.

The Bone People chased them in both directions. Alastair rounded a corner and ran almost immediately into a dead end on the drill deck. It was a wide space, and there was nothing to hide behind. The ocean raged below. Kat circled round into the same area from the other side. There was nowhere to go except up, but the Bone People had cut off access to the stairs.

They were trapped. The plan had failed. The Bone People circled Kat and Alastair, slowly moving in. Alastair held his bowl over the grate, threatening to tip their precious paste into the ocean. Kat copied him.

Alastair watched their bare feet shuffling forward. Once the last pair were on top of the metal grate, they threw their bowls up in the air, shouting, "Now!" The Bone People rushed forward to save the paste. A volcanic sound rumbled from below. The Bone People froze and looked around, uncertain of what was happening. The sound was coming from below the grate.

Far below, liquid helium flowed into the leg of the oil rig, tapped by Jimmy. The Bone People looked down just as a volcanic eruption of liquid helium engulfed them, shooting upward in a massive cloud of hypercooled gas.

Alastair and Kat were caught in the torrent as well, but their spacesuits were designed for deep space and could easily repel the intense cold.

The Bone People were instantly frozen solid. Alastair kept his fist up the entire time for dramatic effect, the rush of steam and ice making him look like an MTV rock god.

It was over. Jimmy closed the valve.

***

Alastair looked at Gally, the ten-year-old Galileo frozen in a running position, fear on his face. Alastair felt a flash of guilt sweep over him. The kid was just as much a victim as anyone else, caught in Ralls's nightmare time sink. And the same went for the Bone People. Fear and agony were etched on their faces. All of a sudden, Alastair wondered why it was okay for him to be triumphant and for them to die.

Leo ran up to Alastair and dragged him away. Kat emerged from the other astronaut suit and was joined by Jimmy, who sprinted for them.

"We gotta go. We only have a few minutes to make it past the perimeter," said Jimmy.

They frantically untied everyone. Below, the water appeared calm, though sharks could be seen swimming in lazy patterns beneath the oil rig legs.

"How?" asked Paul. "We're not swimming."

"No, but they did," said Alastair, pointing down over the other edge of the platform. The Bone People's flotilla of canoes floated at the base of the oil rig.

The last rope was cut.

"It's not that far," said Leo. "We have to jump. There's no time to climb."

"It's too far," said Milk. "It will kill us."

"We can do it," Paul countered, climbing up onto the edge of the railing, getting ready to jump with Leo. Below, dark shadows circled the boats.

"Wait!" Alastair yelled.

The urgent tone of his voice stopped everyone in their tracks.

He was looking at his watch. The timer said: 17:03:31. Seventeen hours and three minutes.

"It is too late," Alastair said. "The seventeen hours are up."

"Is it precise?" Kat asked Jimmy.

Jimmy nodded and slumped down to the ground. "Seventeen hours."

"One hundred years?" said Kat.

"We won't last even one," said Jimmy. "It's too late."

The oil rig sat in the middle of a calm ocean under an azure sky and a sun that wouldn't set for a century.

THE IRON EDEN

Jimmy's doubt hadn't lasted a minute. And soon, he was already at work trying to come up with a survival solution. Although they had all the time in the world, literally, he was already at work on surviving for the decades ahead. With Kat, Leo, and Milk, he started to catalog the arable plots of soil on the oil platform. Joseph was struggling, but he would survive and be of great use. He was tough and understood how to survive.

Jimmy knew they could fish for food. Maybe they could even figure out how to dive and salvage soil and plants from the flooded land beneath the new ocean. The same went for tools, medicines, gas. It was all down there if they could figure out how to hose-feed oxygen long enough to get them.

They had oil for energy, so it was possible to figure out with enough geniuses lurking around. Solar power. And the Crypt drained every cycle. Now that the waters below were cut off from the Gulf of Mexico, they too would recede, and eventually, the higher grounds could emerge. And in a few years, there could be some livable land. He saw it as a giant problem to solve. As usual, Jimmy was infinitely optimistic about finding solutions to intractable problems. He had survived before; he would survive again.

But there was one problem that he knew would gnaw at him for the rest of his life: his father was gone. And now with time stretching out before him, Jimmy knew he would forever feel his absence. Surviving on the oil rig would have been the type of adventure his father would have loved, but now Jimmy was left to go it alone.

***

Isaac was infinitely pessimistic, bordering on suicidal. He knew he would never be as great as, or greater than, the original Isaac Newton. Rather, he would be stuck on a rusty oil rig in the middle of a sterile sea, a failed twin trapped in time for the rest of his short, brutish life. He blamed everyone else in the world for his tragedy, even though he had created this prison. Only thirty minutes would pass in the real world, but by the time the effect ended, the second Isaac Newton would be dead.

**

Zack talked with Leo quietly about the future. There were only two women: Milk and Kat. He would most likely never have children of his own, nor be married. Or find love. It hadn't been on the top of his list prior to the moment they were caught inside a hundred-year time hole, but now that the future presented itself, it felt important to talk about, and Leo accommodated him.

**

Alastair stared at the formulas.

He had his notebook out, open to the papers he'd scribbled on inside Purity. Had the Bone People not slowed them down, they may have had time to escape the dismantling barrier dam and the time effect. But fate did not have that in store for them.

Alastair wasn't sure why he felt drawn to continue to work the numbers and formulas of the two intertwined accelerators, but he couldn't escape the math. It was like its own gravity well, pulling him deeper into a new mystery. The numbers and formulas rearranged themselves inside his mind, becoming less like symbols and more like thought objects. Each had many multidimensional sides that could be rotated and examined, as if they were colors, combining and mixing.

He scratched down more ideas, working the wormhole problem. Something was on the edge of his awareness, calling to him. Milk came up to talk to Alastair, but he didn't seem to hear anything she said, so she left, frustrated.

The formulas kept swirling in his mind. He wasn't writing now, just thinking.

And then it struck him. All they had to do was slow down the infini-ton particle. That was actually what was trapping them—the particle racing around inside the accelerator, buried in a giant circle somewhere beneath the sea. As long as the infiniton wasn't traveling at the speed of light, it was possible to cross the barrier.

The Russian accelerator had been dragging on the infiniton from the other side of the Earth, creating the wormhole, proof that it could be manipulated by outside forces. But Alastair's idea was only correct if his theories on the formation of the wormhole made sense.

***

"Alastair has an idea," Zack yelled, getting everyone's attention.

Plans to survive were well underway; Zack had been counting vegetables.

Alastair stood up, aware that everyone was watching him, hope in their eyes.

He glanced at his notes. They looked like chicken scratch again. He explained his ideas and discoveries. The logic was convoluted and confusing. "As long as the infiniton is not traveling at light speed—when it is speeding up or being slowed down by the drag of the Russian accelerator also getting up to speed—we can cross the barrier. So all we need to do is slow down the infiniton particle. Somehow."

"That's gibberish," said Isaac. "It is impossible to slow down the infiniton particle once it is at speed, you idiot. If it wasn't, we would have designed an off switch into Cornerstone and had variable speed and time control. Light has mass at relativistic speeds, if you didn't already know that, you fool. It takes three minutes to bleed off the energy, or else the accelerator blows up."

"I am aware of what $E = mc^2$ is," said Alastair, pointedly. He explained his theory on how the wormhole formed and why it proved he was right. Again, he tripped over his words.

Zack wanted to help, though it was obvious that he was concerned with Alastair's theories as well.

"Wormhole?" asked Isaac. "What wormhole?"

Alastair, Leo, and Kat explained what happened to them inside the caves. The Purity station, the stars, everything.

"Are you stupid?" Isaac asked, gaining energy. "You think a wormhole opened up in the middle of the earth and you waltzed all the way to the other side of the planet in a few minutes? That you were actually in Russia? Did you ever think that maybe they were lying to you? That they built Purity under our noses to piggy back on our time? So they could keep up?"

All of a sudden, Alastair felt like an idiot. His theories really didn't make any sense. How could a wormhole open up in the middle of the planet, and not swallow it?

"There were stars, though," said Kat. "It was night. We saw constellations. We were in China."

"Physics aren't magic, Katherine. You were deep inside a hypoxic cave running out of air. You were suffering from oxygen depletion and were delusional." The attack seemed to buoy Isaac's spirits. He always thrived on belittling others.

"Zack?" said Alastair, looking for support. Zack shook his head, looking down. He didn't think it made any sense.

"You don't think there was a wormhole?" asked Alastair.

"I ... I'm not sure, Alastair," said Zack.

Alastair looked at his numbers. He knew in his bones he was right, but now, he was back in middle school, feeling overwhelmed by the distance between expectation and truth. He took a breath.

"I am not Albert Einstein," said Alastair, quietly.

"No, you are not," said Isaac, laughing.

"I am Alastair Albert Mayes, and I am damn right."

***

"How are we going to slow down the infiniton particle without blowing up the electromagnets?" Jimmy asked. "One wrong tweak, and it could create a cascade, then *boom*."

They were inside an office, looking at the map Leo had drawn on the flight into Cornerstone so long ago. He claimed it was a faithful rendition of what he had seen. Perfectly to scale. It included the oil rig's location and the barrier dam—where the accelerator loop was still buried beneath the earth and sea, spinning away.

"I don't see a way around it," said Jimmy. "Even if we could get to the accelerator somehow, how would we slow it down? We don't exactly have another particle accelerator lying around."

"And what if you are wrong, genius," said Isaac, perched in the back of the room. "The accelerator will blow up—with the force of a nuclear warhead, killing us all. E = mc screwed."

"Aren't we dead already?" Kat protested.

"Well, you are inside," said Isaac. "But personally, I prefer to live, even if it is with you idiots."

"If you say 'idiot' one more time," said Jimmy, pounding his fist into the table, "I will feed you to a lobster."

"The numbers are right," said Alastair. "It is possible to put drag on the infiniton from the outside—like the Russian accelerator did—otherwise, the wormhole would not have been possible."

"And how do we do that?" said Jimmy.

"Magnets," said Leo.

Jimmy looked at Leo for a long second. "You're an idiot."

THE MAGNET

"He's right," said Alastair. "Magnets bend the particle into a circle as it gets up to light speed—so theoretically, they could slow them down too. Right?"

Zack wasn't sure.

Isaac plucked a magnet off the wall and tossed it at their heads. "And how are you going to do that?" he asked.

"We are going to turn the oil rig into a magnet," said Leo. "The ocean will be our battery."

"That's genius!" said Alastair, not catching himself before realizing who he'd said it to.

Kat groaned. The last thing Leo needed was his ego stroked.

Leo said, "Well, you know—"

"Shut it," said Kat. "Save it for *People* magazine."

But it was true—it was a genius idea—the kind of outside-the-box thinking Leonardo da Vinci was famous for.

"A giant electromagnet in the middle of a saltwater sea? Sounds real safe," said Alastair.

"And like your kind of science project," said Leo.

"Yes, it does," said Alastair, smiling.

***

Zack flattened out Alastair's formulas on the desk in front of him, evaluating them for the first time. He started scratching things out and writing new numbers, or possibly just writing Alastair's formulas again in clearer handwriting. Alastair wasn't sure. He felt like he was being graded on a test.

"We have to get exactly the right amount of energy," said Zack. "If this is right, you will need to manage it in real time."

"Can you solve for it on the fly?" Alastair asked, deferring to Zack. Alastair sat down behind him.

"The power is going to fluctuate, so yeah, I'll need to figure it out as it goes, I guess," said Zack. "If I can?"

Alastair was happy to defer. Zack had always been the true prodigy. They were falling back into their regular intellectual relationship, Zack doing Alastair's homework for him. Zack worked furiously on the numbers. He was struggling—it was complex to figure out the exact right amount of power.

Jimmy and Leo went down the oil rig leg to retrieve Hello Kitty's miles of metal cabling. It took a while because they had to cut the cables into shorter pieces to untangle and then reassemble them topside. The cable was now looped on a spool, winding around the oil rig's legs.

Leo joined Alastair in the control room. There were a switch and dial on the table and a makeshift readout.

It was not an outlandish idea to make a battery out of sea water—salt and electrolytes were the basis for all batteries, essentially. But no one had exactly ever made one this big.

"So either we flip that switch and get out of here, or else we all get electrocuted by a million joules. Does that sound about right?" Leo asked.

"Yeah, that's about right," Alastair answered. "And we need to get everything metal out of here. When this magnetizes, things are going to go flying."

Milk went around the room, moving every metal object into a pile outside. Paul was already throwing metal overboard—pens, steel boxes, screws, tools—anything that wasn't bolted down was discarded.

A sharp letter opener sat on a window ledge right behind Alastair's head. Milk had missed it.

Kat plucked it off and threw into the ocean.

They were ready.

Zack wrote more numbers down, still working the equations. "Einstein was famous for trying to use electromagnetic forces in his grand unified theory, you know."

"Shame I am not him," said Alastair. "You got this?"

"I think so," said Zack. He had added a lot of different numbers to the page. "The energy is going to fluctuate, so I'll have to solve for it as we go."

"Can you do that? In your head?" said Alastair.

"Don't expect me to help," said Isaac. "You are going to kill us all."

Alastair flipped the switch. Zack started to dial up the power. Everyone's hair stood on end.

Outside, Paul watched dead fish, sharks, and lobsters float up from the sea. They were killing everything. Not only would the species never return, but there would be nothing to eat if they survived. That is, if Alastair didn't kill them in the process.

The oil rig hummed and glowed as electricity flowed through it. The metal table Alastair and Zack were at suddenly shifted, slamming into the wall. Alastair scrambled for the power dial. He needed to control the precise amount of energy pouring into the system.

"How many teslas now?" Alastair asked Zack.

Zack didn't answer. He was holding his stomach. Blood was pouring through his hands.

Four bullets pressed against the wall—dripping blood. They were the ones Zack had swallowed during the fight in the Armageddon Truck.

Zack slumped over in pain, unable to move. Milk and Leo helped him to the ground. Leo looked up at Alastair.

"You got this?" said Leo.

Alastair examined the numbers. "No," said Alastair. Alastair didn't know what the right amount was. That was Zack's job.

Isaac came over to push Alastair aside, berating him.

"I believe in you," said Jimmy. "Get us out of here."

Alastair looked at the dial and the numbers in front of him. He picked up the pencil. He tried to imagine the great accelerator coil underground and the tiny infiniton particle racing around them, trapping them.

If Alastair got the force correct, it would bend, dragging time with it. If he got it wrong—

He closed his eyes and guessed.

THE NOTE

Everyone sat in the Bone People's boats, floating in the middle of the ocean. They were at the perimeter of the time effect—at least they thought so. The barrier dam was completely gone. They had to trust that Leo's map was correct. He had a string attached to his boat that counted off yards from the oil rig.

"I think this is it," said Leo.

With the giant oil rig magnet still under power, they rushed down into the boats and paddled hard out to sea. The ad hoc battery Leo created using the sea water and steel rig was not going to last forever. Dead animals floated everywhere—red, blue, and every other color of the rainbow. Many of them were enormous, including species they had never seen before. Alastair was alone in his boat, trying to paddle past a giant, dead octopus. Kat went to touch a huge red-and-blue turtle that floated next to her boat. Milk pulled her hand away before she accidentally touched the electrified ocean.

Zack was conscious, but suffering. The four holes in his stomach bled out into makeshift rags on his belly.

Paul checked on his wounds. "We don't have much time," he said.

Isaac took a secret store of black paste out of his pocket. "Use this."

"You kept some," said Paul. "You were hiding it."

"If you use that," said Zack, "you will never recover Isaac."

It was true. Isaac had not healed fully. He still had some grievous injuries and would remain that way if he used up the last of the paste.

"Genius is worth saving," he said, "even if itsn't my own."

Isaac took the paste, scooping it out of the bag, and wiped it into Zack's wounds. Zack screamed, trying to get away from the pain. Writhing. Isaac stuck his fingers into the holes, pressing the black paste down.

"Save some!" said Paul.

Isaac swatted him away. The bag was empty. He used every last ounce.

Zack gripped Isaac's hand, to handle the pain.

"We have to move," said Isaac. "Who's going to test the barrier? Not me."

"I'll go," said Alastair. "It was my idea."

"I'll go," said Leo.

"He'll go," said Paul.

"I'll go," said Jimmy.

No one went.

"Are you sure, Alastair?" asked Milk. "Because if..."

Alastair knew full well that he had guessed. But for the first time in his life, he was okay with the unknown. He dug into his pocket to pull out the formulas one last time, hoping to quickly figure out if his guess—his best guess—was close enough. But the papers were in the other pocket. Instead, he pulled out the note his coach had given to him days earlier. He remembered what Coach Schoeffel had said to him: "Never read what is on this piece of paper, no matter how much you doubt yourself."

Alastair opened it, realizing now that he was meant to read it when he doubted himself the most. It said, *Einstein didn't know he was Einstein either. He was just a kid named Albert.*

Alastair Albert Mayes, the first one, started paddling.

THE CHOICE

As Alastair paddled, he noticed a growing sound—a chorus of voices or screams or the sound of the universe itself tearing in great wracking heaves—terrifying him. And with every stroke, it was worse.

But he kept paddling.

There was no visual indication of where the barrier was, but the sound was almost a force in itself, working into his muscles, trying to stop him with fear, lest he suffer a terrible death as a result of his great ignorance.

And he kept paddling.

His belief that he was right—in absence of all evidence—was the only thing powering his strokes. Soon, he was screaming himself. The bass notes of the effect rippled across his cheeks. Tears formed in his eyes. His hair stood on end.

The sound reached a crescendo, like the gates of hell closing, in one anguished roar at the hubris of God.

And then suddenly, the sound stopped. Nothing happened.

Alastair waited. Still. Evaluating himself. He was alive.

He waved at everyone. They paddled up. Then they just sat in the ocean.

"Are we safe?" Milk asked.

"No idea," said Alastair.

Leo consulted his map. "Oh, maybe the perimeter is there," he said, pointing further ahead.

"You have no idea where we are!" said Isaac. "I am in a sea of idiots!"

"I warned you," said Jimmy.

He punched Isaac, flipping him backward out of the boat. Isaac screamed in the water, expecting to die from electrocution. But he didn't. He floated there, confused. Suddenly, a helicopter roared over their heads.

It was the Coast Guard.

EPILOGUE

The press conference came out of nowhere.

Alastair and his friends sat in a lounge at the airport in Corpus Christi, waiting for their flights home to Ohio. Someone turned on the TV. Teigen Ralls was announcing a major discovery. It had only been a few hours since Alastair saw Ralls at Purity, but now the man was ten years older. He had lost all of his excess weight and had a slight Russian accent. A scroll along the bottom of the newsfeed said, LEONARDO DA VINCI CLONED.

Leo ran up to the screen. "Did you see that?"

Pictures of all the kids—even the ones who went to the other Cornerstone internship in North Dakota—scrolled by. Leo turned up the volume.

Ralls's voice boomed through the airport lounge with its characteristic enthusiasm. "And finally, my proudest achievement—Albert Einstein."

Alastair watched the throng of reporters press forward to see an image projected behind Ralls. It was a photo from Alastair's high school yearbook. Beneath, it said, ALBERT EINSTEIN.

"This is going to be so fun!" said Leo.

"For you," Milk muttered.

"For all of us—wealth, fame. We are going to be able to do whatever we want! Any projects. Who would not hire or fund or support Leonardo da Vinci? Or MLK? Or Albert Einstein? Don't you realize? Now that everyone knows, this opens up the entire world to us!"

"Did you learn literally nothing?" Milk asked.

"Do you know me?" said Leo. "You'll never get me down."

Milk broke into a smile. "No, nor would I want to."

Nearly everyone talked over each other. Paul lamented that they hadn't managed to save any of the black paste. The salamander it was based on could have changed medicine forever, curing cancer, regenerating limbs. Zack bragged to Leo about his stint in the time vaults like he'd been in juvie.

Alastair was the only one who was quiet.

Kat went over to him. "How do you feel?" she asked, checking in.

"Hungry."

"Do you think he was lying before?" asked Kat. "Or is he lying now?"

"Can I ask you something?" said Alastair.

"Sure."

"Right before graduation, you said to me and Leo, 'You'll get a kick out of this.' Did you know the truth? About all of us?"

"Yeah. My mom told me during a huge fight in tenth grade," said Kat. "But I knew if I told anyone, it would ruin everything—all of our friendships and families. So I kept my mouth shut. I'm sorry. I was scared of getting too close."

"I would've let you get close to me," said Alastair.

"Not anymore?" Kat replied.

Alastair glanced at Milk. "You think she will forgive me?"

"Honestly, I'm not sure."

Milk caught Alastair's eye. She smiled at him.

"I never thought you were aloof, for the record," said Alastair, laughing. "Just complicated."

"You didn't answer my question," said Kat.

"I don't care if Ralls was lying or not."

"You don't want to know the truth, for real?"

"Right now, I like being me."

The press conference was wrapping up. Ralls said he wanted to highlight one more thing. A wall opened up dramatically behind him.

In the ground, there was a lone oak tree sapling.

***

A C130 military plane waited for them on the tarmac. "I thought we were going home to Ohio!" Alastair yelled at the man at the bottom of the stairs over the engine noise.

"No. Change of plans!" the man said. "We have a pit stop! In North Dakota!"

After takeoff, Alastair watched the world scroll by below, lost in thought. Nearly everyone was asleep. Even Milk. In the front seat, Isaac was awake, clearly stewing. He hadn't said a word since the rescue. Zack went to sit next to him. Something emerged from Isaac's pocket and then looked at Alastair from the armrest between the chairs.

A salamander.

Alastair lured it over to him with a piece of bread.

It was still Tuesday.

- END -

Thank you for reading the first book in The Twin Paradox series! if you want to know what happens next, below there is a sneak peek of the upcoming sequel, Divine Paradox!

Also, if you have a moment, please consider sharing *The Twin Paradox* with your friends on your social sites. I really do appreciate it! It helps indie authors grow our community so much. Here is the link to share The Twin Paradox with your friends. Copy and paste it to whatever your favorite site or app is. Or you can scan the QR code to grab the link.

SHARE THE TWIN PARADOX
https://geni.us/uThQ1

And if you could, it would be great if you could leave a review.
I love reading them!

REVIEW THE TWIN PARADOX

US: https://geni.us/i9Hr
UK: https://geni.us/7gfpF0
CA: https://geni.us/1LDOX
AU: https://geni.us/4vV3Al
IN: https://geni.us/WAYo

If you want to stay in touch,
I love responding to fan email: charleswachter.com

CHARLES
WACHTER
DIVINE
PARADOX

THE STUNNING SEQUEL TO THE TWIN PARADOX

THE DEVIL'S CHAPLAIN

To J. D. Hooker, 11 January 1844

At last, gleams of light have come & I am almost convinced (quite contrary to opinion I started with) that species are not (it is like confessing a murder) immutable.

To J. D. Hooker, 13 July 1856

What a book a Devil's Chaplain might write on the clumsy, wasteful, blundering low & horridly cruel works of nature!

—My dear Hooker | Ever yours,

Charles Darwin

WHAT ROUGH BEAST?

Tierra del Fuego
January 1833

A Cherokee class 10-gun brig-sloop broke upon the waves, nails bent and groaning, driven by a gale. The storm rose in the night like an incantation as the boat attempted to round the land of fire, Tierra del Fuego, at the southern tip of South America.

Vice Admiral Robert Fitzroy sailed over a graveyard of sailors far better and more experienced. Given the command of the HMS Beagle at twenty-six years old, he was still afire with notions of adventure, despite the risk of the tempest bending the ship. The previous commander had committed suicide from loneliness, and as Fitzroy screamed commands to keep eyes leeward for rocks, he knew his decision to run the cape ahead of a storm was just as much the Devil's game.

His square shoulders, once proud, hunched over the wheel now like he protected it from an attacker; the boat rising above and then crashing beneath waves that broke forty feet. Foam blew across him, turning him white, whipped into a frenzy by the possibility of another sacrifice on the rock altars beckoning him.

And the wind.

Fitzroy didn't consider himself a brave man. Surviving the storm would not be a story they told about him: his intensity of focus, the clarity, and the order of his commands. The decision to axe the whale boat acting as a water anchor on each roll. The timely dropping of the main sail, leaving the storm trysails and foresails up. And finally taking her right abeam, just as the Devil tried to grab them with his watery fingers.

No. No one would remember the vice admiral for that.

He knew it.

They would remember the white feather below deck, seasick and afraid, clutching at his glass-bottled specimens lest they break. Even then, Fitzroy understood this, months before their fabled landing on the Galápagos Islands.

Charles Darwin would not die in this storm. Robert Fitzroy swore this to Nature, as if she herself was his adversary, trying to protect her secrets from being known worldwide and forever.

Fitzroy wasn't a courageous man, but he was a technical, intellectual man, and step-by-step, he went toe to toe with the wind and the rocks and the salted water in a fight on behalf of man's ascent to conquer all creation.

It was the final test, and Fitzroy fought, alone, for all mankind.

***

A thousand miles from Pacific surety, the ocean heaved with typhoon, its surface: the back of a golden Leviathan rising and falling with breath under a red setting sun, waiting to consume another story before it could be wrought.

A boat was under sail ahead of the growing menace and fathoms below, in the depths, other follies of man and warfare littered the seafloor.—

Charles Darwin, about to die

Charles knew he was overly poetic about nature, but so was Thomas Hobbes, and old Tom's Leviathan was nothing compared to this one. He felt rightly justified, considering the circumstances. Darwin's Leviathan was a typhoon, and if Hobbes could get all worked up over man's short brutish life, so could Charles about his own personal monster.

His salt-and-tear-stained ink pages would conjure up a Christlike resolve. Thirty thousand–foot black clouds would dissipate. The sun, that golden sword, would cut through that beast and illuminate his writing like a medieval holy text; his battered boat, a raft for all humanity, saving his soul from the eternal depths below.

Or not. He scratched that out and then put a notation number next to it, because he really couldn't be editing his letters when he had only moments to live and water poured into the collection room, full of rum barrels and puke.

It was the stuff of faith, Charles knew, out here alone on the ocean, relying on the dark-spirited man above, but in the absence of any agency in his increasingly surreal situation beneath South America, his writing worked for the moment. Where most naturalists with his experience would be racing around the boat getting in the way, tightening hatches that were already tight, lashing unlashable masts, Charles chose to write.

Fitzroy would forgive him.

It was simple: he was either going to die at twenty-two years old, sometime after midnight at the peak of the storm, or he would live. If he were to die, he'd prefer to leave a last epitaph for God. He'd wrap his diaries, journals, letters, and samples in oiled canvas and pack them in a rum for the Creator. Charles knew the barrel wouldn't come ashore well in a watery region known only for death and the Fuegians, cannibals who ate their women on lonely islands in the winter; however, if another ship spotted it and thought it was rum, it had a shot.

Despite his proclivity for the romantic, Charles Darwin had a practical side. This far out into the middle of the ocean, you only have what Fitzroy gives you. When he asked the vice admiral for a barrel to "preserve history in case they went down," the vote of nonconfidence in front of the men angered the commander, who then kicked the barrel overboard, almost knocking Charles over as well, and told the young naturalist to chase it.

However if I don't die tonight, thought Charles, *that was more interesting*. First off, he'd have another diary entry. Secondly, he might get a featured lecture at the Royal Society again—after his disastrous worm presentation— which would lead to more engagements, which would then pay for another expedition that would lead to more observations.

So it was decided.

Charles Darwin, the first one, would die writing observations to the last. He knocked the cork out of a barrel and started emptying the rum out, taking swig after swig for confidence, more afraid of Robert Fitzroy than the wine-dark sea for the moment.

Charles Darwin burst onto the deck, drunk, as the ship rolled sideways again, waves crashing across the wood. His fear manifested into a desire to fight with Fitzroy finally. Darwin lurched up to him, left and right, and took a swing that landed, bloodying Fitzroy's lip in the crazy tilt of the ship and the wind.

Fitzroy didn't let go of the wheel, taking the punch square. His unwillingness to resolve their longstanding dispute gave Charles enough pause in the wilderness of the moment to consider that Fitzroy, and the seven others brave enough to be above deck with him, were all tied into the deck like cannons, leather straps holding them firmly in place.

Charles was not.

A wave swept at him hard—harder than any punch Fitzroy could muster in return—knocking him sideways. Charles took a swing at the next wave before being tackled into the gunwale by Fitzroy, who was laughing now.

"I fear you and I will be tied together for all eternity," Fitzroy said. He lashed himself to Darwin and then to the gunwale as the sloop crashed down once again.

Blood poured from Charles's mouth where he hit the oaks. From his coat, he pulled a specimen bottle with an eel sloshing about in rum. He took a swig and offered it Fitzroy as a truce.

The vice admiral's smile disappeared, his lip swollen and split. They had been fighting over the rum for weeks. Darwin needed it to keep his collection safe. Fitzroy needed it to keep his men safe.

Darwin took another swig, laughing harder. "Even so, they shall see it was a bloody affair!" He spat blood into the bottle and then held it open for Fitzroy, who sucked blood off his lip and did the same.

"For courage!" Darwin took another draft, then corked the bottle, vowing to write of the moment and their blood bond at the bottom of the world, should they survive.

An eel floated in a bottle. Held up to the light of a cold winter's window in the attic of Copenhagen's Natural History museum, sun sparkled through its translucent skin, though the infamous pinkish hue of the bloodied water was no longer apparent.

Teigen Ralls, a young graduate student, had sought the eel for two years, first as a hobby, then as an obsession.

And now he had it.

The only clue to the eel's significance was a single rare label wound with twine about its cork stopper with a leather tag that noted its number: 7561.

Thirty-two years old, Ralls stooped over the bottle, like a clockmaker considering a delicate gear. His eyes flitted about the details of the eel and the bottle. He was motionless for minutes, staring, as if there was some clue to his future behind the glass.

Poised there, his thin frame buzzed with potential energy, like a spring wound tight, ready to let loose. He didn't move.

Ralls was rapt, feeling himself falling into a story that finally had a beginning, seeing his path spread out before him in a way that only the paintbrush of youth and limitless ambition could conjure.

He wondered at the actual value hidden in the clear liquid, in real dollars, calculating all the things that he would have to do, step by step, year by year, to realize its full potential.

His hair swept across his forehead neatly, not in his usual style. His clothes were tailored to fit, though the young graduate student could barely afford the three-piece suit, to convey the authority of a professor who had the time, and success, to look after himself, though Ralls had neither.

The camouflage was crucial. It allowed him to slip by curators, charm librarians, fool janitors, and to gain access to rare archives with almost no notice.

Now he was free to become himself. His true self. He had found the Blood Eel. The lies could end. And he could emerge from beneath the thumb of academia and chase his own ideas on the value of the twisted helix DNA.

Ralls turned the leather tag in his fingers, his first movement in minutes. He recognized Darwin's handwriting, having studied his journals for months, trying to establish where the lost specimen might have ended up.

The scientific insignificance of the hagfish meant no one had ever attempted to find it—a mere biographical footnote among thousands of pages of personal observations penned over decades of scholarship.

It was a single line in Darwin's diary that led Teigen Ralls to the idea *Myxine australis* was worth finding.

Darwin's DNA in the blood, mixed with alcohol and sea water, would be perfectly preserved. He knew that from his work as a graduate student studying the human genome. It was a chance observation that quickly metastasized into an obsession that threatened his graduate studies.

In writing on his relationship with Robert Fitzroy, Darwin mentioned they resolved their feud over the rum when the ship almost went down. Their blood mixed, as their bond, in a jar that held an eel specimen from Argentina.

Ralls knew that salt (NaCl) and ethyl alcohol (C_2H_5OH) were useful in precipitating DNA out of a solution. It's all he did all day long at the university lab in a terrifyingly boring job only academia and factory work can serve up. He called his work station "the salt mines" to any undergraduate women who would listen, implying his work was anything but physical labor.

He would explain that salt water neutralizes DNA's charge, making it hydrophilic, and less soluble in water. And alcohol helps the nucleic acids precipitate out of the solution. While water destroys DNA over time, salt water and alcohol preserved it perfectly and indefinitely. It was not only the perfect way to store DNA, when combined with the purchase of an expensive drink in a graduate school grotto, it was also the perfect faux intellectualism he needed to get laid. DNA was a hot academic pursuit in the late nineties, and any hint of expertise was attractive in the bruising dating world of academia.

A graduate student with enough knowledge about DNA storage encountering a single line in an obscure diary of Darwin would someday twist the world into something unrecognizable. Ralls didn't know it then, but he could feel it as he shook the blood eel and then started to dance with it.

Ralls knew the story of how he found Darwin's DNA would sell; his talent for theatrics were already well developed, even if his idea for what he would do to commercialize the DNA was not, but his instinct for combining the modern world of genetics with Charles Darwin's early brush with death would prove valuable was correct.

Teigen Ralls was going to clone Charles Darwin. It was the decision that drove him across Europe in search of the Blood Eel. It was necessarily a purely academic exercise at first, involving historical research into Darwin's methods, and one that took him from museum to museum in search of obscure records, and then finally to the Cambridge University Library, which held Charles Darwin's infamous "C" journal from his HMS Beagle journey.

The faded notebook held a lexicon of Darwin's notations, observations, and most importantly to Ralls, it cataloged his arcane field numbering system he used on the trip.

The journal was not on display, however, as it was being photographed for the first time for publication. Ralls couldn't wait to see Darwin's scribbles in the margins on a museum's intractable publishing timeline, so he traveled to Cambridge to see the journal for himself.

The number he needed existed in only two places: on the original leather tag Darwin would have added to the bottle, often discarded, and the inked specimen numbers in the margins of Journal C. It was, to be fair, the most famous field journal in history. The notebook held the world's first drawing of the tree of life, as well as Darwin's first observations on the finches of the Galápagos islands; however, what Ralls needed from the journal was truly mundane. A number and a date. He had to cross-reference the date the specimen was collected with Darwin's field collection number and then trace that new specimen to a specific shipment to Europe in order to know where the eel went first, and where it would have received its reclassification number.

When Darwin's specimens flooded back into Europe during his five-year voyage of the Beagle, nearly every museum and collector routinely stripped off Darwin's tags and entered the object into their own system for classification by an expert, noting all the scientific observations from the field, but not Darwin's own notational system for classification. Had the curators known then that Darwin would upend all of human natural history, they may have taken more care; however, at the time, Charles was just another naturalist aboard a navy ship, working the unknown coasts of the world. Interesting but not historic.

If a specimen went to the British Museum, it would have been catalogued in a wholly different way than if it had been gifted to his friend J. D. Hooker or his mentor Charles Waterton or any other of a number of colleagues and international institutions that the young naturalist hoped to impress.

At Cambridge, Ralls could have taken the time to write down every number and assigned it to a page number and then cross-reference that with further historical research he had done; however, it would have taken hours. And, he realized, he had not told anyone his name or his interest. He had just asked for the university photography studio, where he knew it was being held, having asked formal permission to see it month's earlier and being denied. While the photos must have been taken by now, he hoped the journal was still there.

And it was, on a shelf with other items from the university's vast collection.

He could sit there for hours. So Ralls stole the journal instead, his first in a lifetime of academic thefts. Its disappearance made international news in 1999, but only after months of quiet, then panicked searching. The museum assumed it had been returned to the permanent collection erroneously, placed in the wrong stacks, after it was photographed.

To this day, it is missing.

The thrill of owning the book that had the very first drawing of the tree of life, the branching nature of evolution, spurred Ralls's plans and drove him across the continent, until eventually, he found the blood eel in Copenhagen.

As he marveled at the treasure, twisting the bottle in his hands, Ralls knew something that no one else in the world did.

The bottle, with Darwin's sample of blood, was the most valuable thing Darwin ever collected, because in it, *he himself was stored* for all of history.

As Ralls left the collection stacks and headed to the front of the library, he held the hagfish up again to see if there was any of the pink hue in the changing light. He imagined he could see the DNA, feeling the wash of excitement again that comes with any great mystery solved and adventure ahead.

The specimen had been untouched and uncorked since the days it first arrived at the museum. The original gift had come from Darwin, along with a collection of barnacles he had borrowed and then had returned. The eel was an added gift, as a thank-you, Ralls had discovered.

Specimens from Darwin's voyage on the HMS Beagle had taken on increasingly significant value after he published *On the Origin of Species*, and though the eel was not part of the taxonomy he used to untangle the mysteries of natural selection and evolution, it was nonetheless prized when it arrived in the 1840s, simply because it came from Charles. Darwin's renown had already circled the globe many times among naturalists, and to have some of his specimens at the museum, no matter the scientific value, were of great import. When they arrived unannounced, the barnacles were divided up among scientists eager to ply their expertise and to make observations the great Darwin might have missed. The eel, however, lived on the desk of Darwin's friend James D. Hooker. It was never relabeled. And after 150 years, it was among the thousands of samples gathering dust on the shelves, forgotten and mislabeled, time spinning through the museum's storied cloisters.

Ralls sauntered up to the library counter to check the specimen out. He flirted with the older man to avoid any pressing questions about what he hoped to learn from the eel.

"Funny you should check that out," said the man, enjoying the conversation, writing down the collection number.

"Why's that," Ralls said as nonchalantly as possible.

"Well, according to this, it sat on that shelf for almost eighty years."

"And?"

"Well, you're the second person to want it this week. Just funny to me. Here you go." The man finished writing and handed Ralls the loan receipt.

Ralls kept his hand out, holding the receipt for an extra beat.

"Really," he said.

"I've seen fads come and go. A research article is published, and then suddenly, a ton of grads run in here, chasing the same bit of feather."

"Yes," said Ralls. "Must be that. Mind if I ask who it was?"

"You know, it is really funny. I remember him. A month ago, can you imagine that? But he had a funny name, all considering."

Ralls waited for the name, but it didn't come.

"Would love to know if it's one of our other research graduates from my lab to save me some time," Ralls said, lying.

"Huh? Oh yeah. He said his name was Charles Darwin. Funny that."

PRE-ORDER NOW

https://geni.us/VHUx0w

OR COPY AND PASTE TO SHARE
THE TWIN PARADOX TO YOUR FRIENDS

https://geni.us/uThQ1

Seriously, thank-you.

Made in the USA
Columbia, SC
18 August 2021